LUCAS TRENT 4

THE POWER OF POWER

A FANTASY STORY WRITTEN BY

RICHARD BLUNT

LUCAS TRENT 4, The Power of Power

Typesetting by Magdalena Rogier

ISBN 978-0-9858011-3-7 (sc)
ISBN 978-0-9858011-4-4 (hc)
ISBN 978-0-9858011-5-1 (ebk)
LCCN 2017932220

CONTENTS

PREQUEL

"OK people, listen up!" The man sitting in the passenger's seat of a large black van had turned around to face the team in the back. "A group of unidentified hostiles is attacking Wandsworth prison as we speak. Current intel suggests that we are dealing with six intruders, but information is vague. They are armed and extremely dangerous; we already have three officers down."

In the back of the van a team of eight people was listening closely. They were all wearing black uniforms, complete with body armor and helmets. Their truck was heading at high speed toward the prison from downtown London, lights blazing, sirens active.

"Any hint as to what they want, Inspector?" one of the officers asked.

"It's fair to assume that they are trying to break somebody out, but as of now there is no clue who their target might be," the man in the front seat answered.

"How will we proceed?" another one asked.

"We will assess the situation once we arrive. We are talking about a high security prison here, so if the attackers already had a chance to free some inmates the situation could get messy. If not, our primary objective is to prevent that from happening," the Inspector answered. "We will most likely arrive on site first. Additional units will follow behind us."

"Approaching the prison perimeter, Inspector," the driver interrupted him.

"Thank you, Sergeant." The Inspector nodded. "Stay safe and watch your backs, gentlemen," he then said to the others.

Seconds later the van had stopped inside the prison yard.

"Let's move!" the Inspector shouted and jumped out, his rifle in hands.

"Oh my God, am I glad to see you." A guard came running toward them from inside the main building. Blood was dripping from his hand; his uniform was torn in multiple places.

"Inspector Corben, SO-19," the Inspector introduced himself. "Give me a quick status, please."

"Warden Phillips, sir," the guard said. "I have never seen anything like that before."

"Calm down, Warden. What happened?" Corben asked.

"They just blasted through the doors and walls, like they were not even there," the warden replied.

"So they have heavy weapons on them?" Corben sounded a little edgy.

"That's the thing... I couldn't make out what weapons they were hiding under their capes. But they can't be very large, whatever they are."

"Where are they now?"

"When I last saw them they were heading for cellblock B. That's at the end of the corridor and then left. Our response team is there and trying to fight them off."

"All right. Are you feeling well enough that we can leave you here?" Corben was looking at the bloody arm.

"Don't worry about me, sir. It's just scratches from the shrapnel."

"Very well." Corben nodded. "SO-19, let's hurry up," he then addressed his people. "Full tactical with shields."

The officers quickly grabbed man-sized shields and started moving forward into the prison block.

"Look at that door, Inspector," a man up front said, pointing at a steel gate that had been blasted open. "That's not looking like explosives."

Corben took a quick look. "No, that looks like acid to me. Be careful what you touch."

They continued through the corridors toward cellblock B. It was apparent that they were approaching a fight. They could hear gunfire as well as sounds of things crashing into each other. When they finally got close enough to actually see the fight, they were stunned. On the far end of the corridor, guards had taken cover behind projections of the wall and within various rooms. Between the guards and the approaching officers was a group of five, dressed in black robes with hoods, more or less standing openly in the corridor.

"Armed Police! Freeze," Corben shouted as his men took position.

"Armed Police, Armed Police, look how nice their presence is," one of the men chanted before starting to laugh despicably. "You are always so stiff, officers. You freeze too much." He turned around and looked at them. "Why don't you try to melt for a change?"

Without further warning he threw a flask at them. The officer up front reacted immediately, blocking the throw with his shield. The flask shattered on impact. What Corben witnessed next sent cold shivers down his back. The shield started to dissolve, just like the door they had come through earlier.

"What the hell is that?" The officer with the shield seemed stunned.

"Some sort of very powerful acid," Corben shouted back. "Drop the shield and take cover."

"You are pathetic, Mad Man." A second man in robes had turned around. "I told you before that there is only one way to properly melt something."

"INCENDIO," he suddenly shouted and stretched his hand in the direction of the SO-19 squad, as a jet of flames emerged from his fingertips.

Corben was shocked again for a moment. He just couldn't believe his eyes. Unfortunately, reality caught up quickly when he saw one of his men ablaze.

"Open fire! Open fire!" Corben commanded and immediately the other officers started shooting.

To Corben's horror it seemed that the bullets were ineffective, as if they were bouncing off some kind of force field. And the other side was not getting short of new tricks anytime soon. The Inspector could only just duck when a brick suddenly came flying his way, followed by another bolt of fire.

"What now, Inspector?" an SO-19 officer yelled.

"Let's try to distract them," Corben yelled back. "Throw a flashbang."

The other officer nodded and grabbed the grenade. He popped out the pin and threw it directly at the feet of the attackers.

"Take cover!" Corben yelled and ducked down himself, waiting for the bang. Even though he had turned away and closed his eyes, he could still see the bright flash. Without losing a second he raised his rifle again and took two quick shots at the robed guy in the center. Two thuds were followed by the sound of a dropping body. When his men saw the result they acted almost instantly. Bullets started filling the air, paired with the roaring sound of automatic weapons fire. At the same time the other side was still not short of reaction, throwing fireballs, lightning bolts and more flasks with acid toward them as well as the prison guards on the other end of the corridor. The fighting was furious and somewhat chaotic. For Inspector Corben, it seemed as if this continued for minutes, although in reality everything was over in less than 30 seconds.

Silence followed, accompanied by near-paralysis. And only when Corben heard the moaning from behind he did finally snap back into reality. He quickly turned around and saw his colleague lying there, charred from top to bottom, moaning in agony.

"Medic!" he shouted and ran over to the man.

A second officer had also come over and pulled a first aid kit from his backpack.

"I'll take care of him, sir," he said to Corben.

The Inspector nodded and walked down the hallway to examine the scene. Two more of his men had been injured, which for him was hard to take, as he almost never had injuries in his team. Reality quickly put his mind back down to earth, though, when he approached the area where the prison's response team had made their stand. Four of them were dead, three more badly wounded.

"Your timing couldn't have been better." A man in his early thirties looked up at Corben.

"From what I see we were almost too late." Corben was still assessing the situation.

"Almost, yes. But lucky for us, only almost," the other man said. "I am Ted Acker, prison response team." He shook Corben's hand.

"William Corben, SO-19," the Inspector introduced himself. "Are you in charge here?"

"Seems that I am now, yes." Acker nodded. "The Sergeant is dead."

"Do you have any idea who or what they were after?" Corben had walked back to the attackers and was examining them more closely now. They were all dead, and except for one who was carrying a lot of small flasks in his pockets, they had no weapons on them whatsoever.

"No, not the slightest. But they must have had inside knowledge, or at least a very good plan. They were moving straight toward B-block."

"Please let the investigators know this as well. Maybe they can shed some more light." Corben took one of the flasks and put it into a bag. "Did any prisoners escape during the fight?"

"I don't think so, but I don't know what happened in the rest of the facility. If you don't need me here, I will head back to the monitoring room and make sure."

Corben nodded and walked back to his wounded men.

"What the hell was that, Inspector?" his medic asked him.

"I have no idea, Constable, I have no idea." Corben sighed. "But I might know somebody who does..."

CHAPTER 1

TIME

A few weeks earlier...

It was a sunny Monday afternoon in mid-August 2009. Six teenagers were roasting marshmallows over a campfire near a small shack in the countryside. The scene might have looked just like any other picnic, if it weren't for the fact that all of them were wearing robes. With the hoods pulled over their faces they resembled an occult sect, more than normal teenagers, and in fact, that's almost what they were. With them it just was not about religion at all. And while the world around them still believed that they were regular kids, this was far from the truth. Over the past two years they had discovered that magic was not actually a thing of legends and fantasy books, but in fact a part of the world they lived in. And they were amongst those who had kept with it long enough to actually learn the art, which for them also meant learning the art of deception. After all, you can't just walk the streets of Luton and tell everyone that you are a mage, right?

Leading the pack was Lucas Trent, known to his friends as "Guardian", by now 18 years old, hidden underneath a blank gray robe. In his normal life he was an IT geek, one of the best in Luton IT College. He was the head of the group, and he had learned to accept that role, even though he had never wanted it.

Sitting to his left, in his thick white cotton robe was the only one able to challenge his geek status, Lucas' best friend and school buddy, 19-year-old Darien Stance, also known as "The Professor". While Lucas was the practical guy, Darien was more of the thinker, a man of theory. He was the pure intellect in the team--logical, almost cold, but nearly always right.

Next in the pack was the oldest of the group, and the only one who had left school behind quite a while ago, 22-year-old Jasmin "Psycho" Kramer. Her red robes and her fiery red hair made her stick out quite a lot next to the two guys in their plain, almost dull capes. And that was not by accident... After all, "Psycho" was the group's emotions, ranging from hot-tempered to childishly sweet.

Flanking Psycho's left was Cedric Mason, who was quite a contrast to her. Wearing black robes with gold lace, he looked as dark as Psycho looked bright. He was 18 at the time, son of a nobleman, and by far less righteous than anyone else in the group. He was sort of the black sheep of the lot, but nonetheless a valued member and true friend to all of them. Known as "Whirlwind", he was the one who seldom asked questions and always preferred action, making him sort of the group's sword.

Right next to him was Marcus Gracer, aka "Cougar". Also 18 years old, he wore dark green robes that almost mimicked the color of the trees in the background. A master of different sports, ranging from football to cricket to martial arts, he was the group's muscle.

Last in the circle, sitting between Marcus and Lucas, was Stephanie O'Brien. Just having turned 17, she was the youngest of them and with her shiny, white silk robes, her dark blonde hair and her lovely smile, she almost looked like an angel. Nicknamed "Airmid", after the goddess of healing, her passion lay in exactly that, the high arts of medicine and healing. She had become sort of the group's soul by now.

Together they formed a magic circle. "The mages of the round fireplace" they used to call themselves, in reference to the "Knights of the round table". They all were quite different, even quite incompatible on some points, but together those differences just made them whole. But even more importantly, those differences in the end made them stronger, which over the past few years had saved their lives numerous times. And not only theirs...

"You are aware that things are about to change now, aren't you?" Darien was looking up at the others.

"Why's that?" Marcus asked. "It's not the first start of a new school year that we've had to handle."

"But for many of you it's the last one," Darien replied. "That might not sound so different, but believe me, it is. There is a lot more riding on that; after all, the last certificate is the one that you will be showing to all future employers, so this time it does count."

"But I guess it's even more different for you now, Professor; after all, for you school is already over. You are moving into a steady job now." Lucas smiled at him.

Darien just nodded. He had already had the chance to look into this chapter of his life. A local environmental research company, Harlington Research Corporation, had given him the opportunity of an internship after he had seriously impressed their CEO, a man named Colin Dexter, with his knowledge during a career orientation day in school. Darien furthered that good impression during his internship, so it therefore came as no surprise to the others that a job offer soon followed, which Darien hadn't even hesitated for a moment after graduation to accept.

"So what will that mean for us?" Stephanie, as most of the time when she was uncertain of something, looked almost scared as she asked.

"It won't mean anything for us." Lucas grabbed her hand and firmly pressed it. "We have managed both lives so far; we will for sure continue to do so."

"Yeah," Marcus grinned, "and with those idiot Satanists finally gone we have a lot less pressure on us now anyway."

A cold shiver ran down Lucas' back when he thought about those past encounters. Almost from the beginning of their circle, they'd had to face those people time and again. From the relatively easy first encounter with Wolfman up to the latest battle that had taken them against Cleric and his circle, this group had left quite a trail of collateral damage, ranging from major ecological disaster to a lot of serious injuries to one man who had died. It had taken the combined forces of the Mages of the Round Fireplace, the circle of their mentor Angel and London police's special unit SO-19 to finally stop those people and put them behind bars. And although it made Lucas proud to know that they had played a key role in taking them down, it had also made him aware of the dangers they had faced to get there, which in the end made him even gladder that it was finally over.

"Let's hope it stays that way," he said with a sigh.

The others silently nodded and continued roasting their marshmallows.

A few hours later, the group was in the middle of a training session, with Jasmin trying to sharpen her skills, when Darien suddenly looked up and pointed at the nearby forest.

"We've got company," he said.

"Where?" Lucas turned around and looked, although by now he knew all too well that there was no way for him to spot anything. After all, Darien's special skills included his "magic eyes", an ability that allowed him to make out arcane energy at quite a long distance.

They stopped their session and waited eagerly for a few minutes until they could finally see the approaching person. Lucas recognized the bright red robes instantly. It was Angel, a woman in her late twenties that they had met in the very beginning, who had become their mentor in their magical lives.

"Good evening, my friends." She bowed as she came close.

"Nice to see you again, Angel. It has been quite a while." Lucas smiled and together with the others followed her to the campfire where she sat down on a tree stump.

"Indeed." Angel smiled back at him. "A good indication that you are making progress."

"Why's that?" Marcus asked.

"If you weren't, I would have had to be here more often, don't you think?" Angel still smiled.

"That would imply that we have always been making progress, and I highly doubt that." Lucas laughed, thinking back on the fact that Angel had always been known to appear only very rarely.

"And why would you doubt that?" she asked.

Lucas knew that there was no point discussing this with her, so he didn't answer.

"Well, as a matter of fact, you have made so much progress that I came here today to say goodbye," she finally continued.

"What?" Stephanie asked with an expression of disbelief on her face.

"By now you all call yourselves 'Magus Minor', which means that there is no need for a mentor anymore." Angel smiled. "I am proud of you."

"So does this mean we won't see you ever again then?" Stephanie looked sad now.

"That, Airmid, is up to you now. I am obliged by the rules of the council to respect your privacy from now on. So I will for sure not pay you any more surprise visits in the future. Everything else is for you to decide."

"Well, then let the goodbye of our mentor be the hello of a friend." Lucas stretched out his hand toward her. "You will always be welcome in our midst, Angel."

"I'm honored." Angel took his hand and the others lay theirs on top.

"So are we," Jasmin said.

"So... Angel..." Darien started after they had all sat back again. "What are those rules you just mentioned? Where can we find those? And why hasn't anybody told us before?"

"Interesting questions, all of them," Angel answered. "You can't find those rules anywhere and if nobody has told you yet, then chances are that there was no need for it so far. And in the end it's up to you, anyway, if you follow them or not. Remember what I told you on the first evening? You are only bound by your own conscience."

"Now you have me confused," Darien said.

"You all know that the privacy of other magic users is something you should respect," Angel said. "There is no need for me to explain that to you, nor is there a need for a council rule, although that is a rule, after all."

She paused for a moment before continuing.

"As a mentor you sometimes have to watch a little more closely than you normally would, so this is an exception to that rule, and what I was referring to before. This exception is now no longer valid for me."

"OK, I got that point." Darien nodded. "What other rules are there?"

"Well, it's not that simple." Angel sighed. "There is of course the obligation of a mentor to protect his students."

"Simple enough." Marcus smiled.

"Not exactly." Angel shook her head. "Because there is also the rule that you should respect the hierarchy."

"Like what? Follow the orders of a higher-ranking mage?" Jasmin asked. "That's somewhat contrary to what you have told us so far."

"No, not like that. The rule is not about obedience, it's about protection. It basically means that a Magus should never use his skills against an Adeptus, not even to defend his students."

Suddenly Lucas had a revelation. When they had first challenged Wolfman about a year back, Angel had come to their rescue, but only at the very last moment. He had thought that she was just late, or maybe wanted to let them do their best before jumping in, but he now realized that she had only appeared when Wolfman's mentor Plague had started taking sides in the fight.

"That's a stupid rule," Stephanie threw in. "Why should I not help my friends when they are in need?"

"And how come that nobody ever told us this, if we are supposed to live by that rule?" Marcus threw in.

"Maybe because you are not supposed to live by it? At least not yet?" Angel said. "And as for your question, Airmid... I unfortunately don't have an answer for it. I am quite certain that there is a good reason for it, though."

"OK. What else?" Darien asked.

"A lot else, Professor," Angel replied. "But I am definitely not the right person to tell you all of it. Nor is this the right time."

"So what now? Shall we live by that part of the codex you have just told us or not?" Marcus was confused.

"As with most things in magic you have to decide that for yourself, Cougar," she said. "I have decided to follow the guidance of the council, as I am convinced by now that they know by far more than I do. But again, it's up to you."

Angel stood up and took a step back from the fire.

"And now it's time for me to leave you to your training. Godspeed, my friends, until we meet again." She bowed and started walking toward the forest.

"Godspeed?" Jasmin was puzzled.

"Never say goodbye to a friend. Instead always wish him a good journey," she said without even looking back.

"Godspeed then, my friend," Lucas replied and bowed a little, noticing from the corners of his eyes that the others were doing the same.

"Why would you wish a friend a good journey? We are not going anywhere." Marcus still looked confused.

"Because a journey is something you normally come back from," Darien said. "It is only a temporary parting of ways."

"And our life definitely does count as a journey, so I think it was an appropriate wish in every sense," Lucas said and patted Marcus' shoulder when he walked by him, back to the fireplace.

It took a few days before Lucas realized how right Darien had been. His last year at school had barely even started and the teachers were already picking up the pace tremendously. As a straight A-student, he found it easier to cope with than most of his classmates, but even he felt the pressure and had to focus a lot more to stay on top of the game. It was Professor Tatarski who brought the reason right to the point: With the final exams, and the preparations for them, filling up almost the entire summer semester, they had to learn the entire year's subject matter in half the time now or they would be in trouble later on. Looking through the classroom, Lucas quickly realized how much of a challenge this seemed to be for the others. Even the class bullies, James Tait and Stan High, who normally didn't miss any opportunity to leave a bad impression, were totally silent and had their heads buried in their books. Most of the class was still trying to get their feet back on the ground when the Professor brought yet another topic up to add to the workload: Career orientation day was coming up again and while last year this was more of a relaxing opportunity for Lucas to have a chat with some companies, this year it was far more serious. After all, there wouldn't be another chance for him. But the thing that really made the thought stressful for him was the fact that he hadn't even thought about his future so far. Surely for a student of his level it would not be too great a challenge to find a fitting place in the business world. And then of course he still had the scholarship offer from a major university in his pocket that he had earned last year through a contest. All that did little to improve his comfort, though. Especially after seeing Darien's ascent at Harlington Research, he definitely felt the pressure. In the end he was just happy once again that he and his friends had finished off Cleric and the Satanist circle before, so at least on that front there would not be any more responsibility for him.

After pondering the future for a few minutes, Lucas sighed and brought his attention back to the blackboard, where the professor had scribbled down the dates for the upcoming tests as well as the career orientation day. He quickly popped his beloved golden watch out from under his shirtsleeve and started putting the reminders into it. He was a highly organized person and hardly ever forgot about anything of importance, but by now he had grown very fond of his wrist-bound calendar. The watch had been a gift from a mage by the name of Gremlin, given to him when he had reached the level of Magus Major a few months back. Lucas had always suspected that Gremlin didn't know the first thing about computers, as a lot of this device was for sure based on magic, not technology, but the longer he worked with the little thing, the more amazed he was at the ingenuity of the old mage. This device almost seemed to have a brain of its own, with all the functions being intuitively placed, at least for him. Sometimes Lucas wondered if he had misjudged Gremlin, or if maybe there was another person behind this computer, some kind of an IT geek who had helped him out.

"... and everyone whose last name is not 'Trent' better wear a necktie." Professor Tatarski's mention of his name brought Lucas out of his thoughts. "You might think that everyone out there wants you, but that's not quite what reality looks like. You better impress those people if you want to have a reasonable chance to get the job that you want."

"Hey Trent, you hear that?" Tait shouted from behind. "We need to get jobs so you can go off to university."

"You truly house less intelligence in that big bone-block on top of your shoulders than a mediocre lab rat." Tatarski shook his head. "Don't listen too closely to him, Lucas. If he didn't get it so far, he for sure won't this year."

"Sure..." Lucas responded slowly, not really sure what to make of the discussion. He had known his classmate for far too long now to take him seriously in any matter, but that comment was low even by his standards. After a few moments he decided to just let it go and get back to other matters at hand.

On his way out Lucas heard some other students discussing the career day in the corridor. He could only make out bits and pieces of what they were saying, but it was apparent that there were a lot of different opinions, ranging from total enthusiasm down to somebody who felt it was a complete waste of time. But what was more pressing for him than the actual discussion was that he for the first time became aware that he was alone now in here. With Darien gone into a steady job, there was nobody left close to him who he could discuss things with. The longer he thought about this, the sadder he became. It had only been a little over two years since he had first met with his now-best friend and all the time before he had walked alone, but over the past two years he had really grown fond of the company and the occasional second opinion.

When Lucas arrived at home later that day he had still not recovered from that thought. Remembering how easy Darien had taken the last year and seeing the daunting tasks ahead of him now, he just couldn't help but feel overwhelmed. In the end he decided to give Darien a call later on. After all, not having him around in school didn't mean that he couldn't have a chat with him. And even from his new perspective, Darien would surely be willing to give him some advice on how to deal with the workload.

Up in his room Lucas fired up his computer and then started unpacking his bag while waiting for the PC to be ready. He quickly looked through his emails before he took off his watch to synchronize the new calendar entries. Just when he was about to press the sync button an unusual, green-lettered message on the display caught his attention. Not only had he been unaware that the display actually displayed colors other than the typical black LCD marks, but he also had never seen the behavior at all so far. He hit the Acknowledge button and watched the display eagerly. The text that followed finally reminded him why he had gotten the watch in the first place. "A Magus Major meeting has been scheduled, requested by JJ," the message said. Lucas scrolled through the rest of the content. The watch had converted the message into an appointment and added it to his calendar. It was scheduled for tomorrow, Friday evening. When he saw the address he could vaguely remember that Gremlin had told him before, it was a pub called the Duke of Summerset, somewhere in downtown London. Lucas was not exactly happy to see this meeting come up. He had always been eager to participate in one, both out of curiosity and for the off chance that Gaia, the local member of the Council of Magic Users, would be there to answer some of his questions. But now the appointment seemed to come at the worst possible moment, right when he had no time to spare and his head was everywhere but with magic. He was just about to delete the entry from his calendar when a detail made him stop: The message said that the meeting was requested by JJ. Lucas knew JJ by now; he was the leader of Angel's circle. And if that by itself wasn't already enough for him to reconsider, he only knew too well that it was this circle's intervention that had saved their skin a while back, when they were facing Cleric and his group. So even though he knew that this sidestep would most likely hurt him in his schoolwork, he decided to join the meeting anyway. After all, if JJ was in need of assistance, no matter why, he owed it to him to be there. He quickly looked up the fastest way to the pub, which was fairly simple given the dense public transportation network the city of London had, before getting back to his schoolwork.

CHAPTER 2

MEETING

Friday was an uneasy time for Lucas in school. An exam that had been planned for Saturday was rescheduled because of the career orientation day and was now due today. The entire class was in a state of outrage about this, as nobody had told them before, leaving them only two hours to prepare--two hours that were packed with other topics as well, reducing prep-time more or less to the short breaks in between. Lucas had already prepared for the exam the days before, so he took it better than most others, but even for him this caused tension. After all, the topic was accounting, not an area he was especially skilled in. Additionally, it was very hard to focus at all that day, as company representatives were already arriving and redecorating some classrooms for the next day's presentations, which caused an unusually high noise level in the corridors as well as pretty much all adjacent rooms. He was not really sure what exactly was going on, but feeling the vibrations of the wall and hearing noises that made him expect a drill to pop out of it just next to his head at any moment made him picture pretty major reconstruction work next door. Thinking back to last year, where he had been one of the helpers during the buildup, he now wondered if they had caused similar levels of distraction to the others, or if this year was even bigger than the one before.

When the exam was finally over the relief in the class was noticeable. Even Lucas, who had done relatively well during the test, was more than glad that it was behind him now, and relaxed considerably. With only three more hours to go, and the upcoming classes all his stronger subjects, he almost felt cheerful and was looking forward to the rest of the day.

When classes, and an afternoon of studying, had come to a close later, Lucas began feeling uneasy once again. He was looking forward to the meeting in London, but at the same time he felt insecure. He had no idea what to expect from that invitation, and even less idea what others would expect from him during the meeting. So far their magic had always been theirs alone and all the encounters and fights they had had in the past had been their choice to take on, which was even true with the Buxton encounter, where they had to face a ghost. With this meeting now it all felt different. Suddenly there were others involved, bigger pictures to think about, and certainly challenges that were way out of his league. Gremlin had told him that there were no obligations attached to being a Magus Major, but for Lucas the obligation somewhat came naturally. For him it just didn't feel right to play the ostrich tactic of burying his head in the sand and pretend nothing was happening.

When he got off the subway at Aldgate East and started walking toward the pub he could feel his hand starting to shake. He tried as hard as he could to regain his calm, but it only got worse the closer he came. Seeing the Duke of Summerset sign getting closer and closer, Lucas had to fight his nervousness hard to avoid turning around and walking away again. He knew that there was nothing to be worried about, but it was still a fight to the last step. He took a deep breath before opening the door and tried to look as calm as possible. The pub was just one large room, capable of holding approximately 100 people, but currently occupied by about 20 or so, including the barkeeper.

"I am sorry, but there is a closed party tonight," a woman standing next to the door said to Lucas as he walked in.

"I am sorry, what?" Lucas hadn't noticed her at first. She was in her late thirties, maybe early forties, with long blonde hair and a wide smile.

"I said we have a closed party tonight--sorry, sir," she repeated politely.

"I know, that's why I am here." Lucas was a little unsure what else to say.

"Well, I am sorry, sir, but I do not recognize you. Are you sure that you are in the right place?" The woman seemed to become a little impatient, playing around with her necklace while talking.

Lucas didn't know how to reply. Looking through the room, he couldn't recognize anyone that could maybe have vouched for him, and even if somebody was there, they would hardly recognize him without his usual robes. His thoughts circled around his options and quickly ended in a state of desperation. He was about to just cast a spell to show that he was serious when something caught his attention: The necklace the woman was playing around with had a nacre surface on the back that was changing color, from white to purple and back to white again, whenever she touched it.

"I'm so sorry." Lucas just had to laugh loudly. "You know, this is my first time here. I am a little confused."

He pulled up his watch from under his sleeve and pushed the hidden middle button on it. The upper part immediately sprang open, revealing a locket below it that had a nacre surface, just like the one on the woman's necklace. Lucas briefly pressed his thumb on it and turned his hand so she could see the purple glow the nacre had adapted instantly.

"Happens to all of us from time to time." The woman grinned and stowed her necklace under her blouse again. "Welcome to the Duke of Summerset, brother. My name is Sunshine. I am the gatekeeper of the group."

Lucas had to grin. 'Sunshine' was a really fitting name for her, given her shining light hair and her smile.

"Thank you. I am Guardian. It's a pleasure to meet you," Lucas replied.

"Ah, Guardian." She smiled and pulled out a list, striking his name out on it. "That means we are almost complete now. The meeting will start in a few minutes; make yourself at home until then."

"Will do." Lucas nodded and walked to the bar.

After ordering something to drink he started looking around. Most of the people in the room were easily past 40 years old, and some seemed a lot older than that. The youngest one in the room, besides himself, seemed to be a woman sitting at the very end of the room, who was engaged in a vigorous discussion with three older men. And even she had to be way past 30 already. The longer he looked around, the more he started to feel alone in here. There was no familiar face, which was hardly surprising given that the only two people he might have known, Gremlin and JJ, had both worn hoods whenever they had met so far, and there was nobody close to his age to relate to. Additionally, all the others seemed to know the people in here well and were standing or sitting together in small groups already. In the minutes that followed Lucas tried to listen to some of the discussions that were ongoing in the room. The results were not at all exciting for him, though, as the discussions were all of mundane natures, ranging from holidays to problems with children. At some point he just picked up a newspaper and started reading. Time seemed to pass slowly, a feeling enhanced even more by both his still present nervousness and the very boring topics in the paper. In fact only five minutes had passed since he had entered the room, but for Lucas it felt like an hour at least. When he finally saw Sunshine lock the door and step into the middle of the room, he was relieved and quickly put the paper aside.

"Sisters, brothers, welcome to today's meeting." She addressed the group, turning while she spoke so she was looking at each of them at least for a little while.

Lucas noticed everyone else sitting down at tables somewhere, so he followed the lead and took a spot that was still empty.

"The meeting was called by JJ, so let's get right to it. JJ, if you please." She bowed toward one of the people at the far end, who had earlier been in the discussion with the younger woman, before she took a step back and sat down as well.

"Thank you, Sunshine." JJ stood up, returned the bow and walked into the center of the room. Now that he was talking openly Lucas immediately recognized his voice.

"Thank you all for answering my call," he started. "I do not call upon this group lightly, but a situation has me worried and I would appreciate help going forward with it."

"Don't talk in riddles, JJ, get to the point," a man sitting on the table next to Lucas said. Lucas estimated him in his forties, well-trimmed brown hair, clean-shaven, dressed in high-quality clothes that made him look like a businessman.

"I am trying to, Ranger, I am trying to," JJ replied a little uneasily. "One of the circles that we mentor has encountered some strange things in the woods around their hometown. Entire patches of herbs and even sometimes useless plants have been removed repeatedly over the past weeks. Their investigation led them to a dark circle which is collecting those herbs in large quantities all over the area. Having very strong-minded environmentalists in the circle, they are now about to go to war with this group, which is why I called upon you."

"And why would it concern us that your kids are playing eco-warriors against another stupid bunch of rowdies?" Ranger obviously was not impressed at all.

"Are these Mages we are talking about? Or Adepts?" Sunshine asked.

"Adepts, by what JJ said," Ranger answered before JJ could. "Why else would they clear entire patches and not just take the best plants?"

"It looks like it, yes." JJ nodded toward Ranger.

"So why should we interfere then? You should be more than capable of dealing with a group of Adepts." Sunshine leaned back.

"I totally agree with you, Sunshine. But they are not what has me concerned," JJ said. "They are hardly capable of doing alchemy at all; otherwise they too would know better than to strip-mine the area. Which begs the question: For whom are they collecting the herbs?"

"So?" Ranger asked, annoyed.

"Given the amount they are collecting, I am thinking that there is somebody major behind this. And that has me worried." JJ sighed. "Yes, we can deal with the Adepts, but I am not sure what awaits us when we do. And I don't want to get there without backup if I can help it."

"If you ask me, they are just collecting so much because they can't distinguish right from wrong," Ranger said. "Sorry JJ, but I am not backing up your paranoia."

"Train your adepts to regrow the herbs and ignore those guys," another man, one of the oldest in the room, most likely already past 70, with gray hair and a long white beard, said. "There is no point in fighting just because of some plants."

"Easy for you to say." JJ seemed very unhappy about the reactions of the others.

"This is a minor occurrence, no need for us to get in their ether, sorry JJ," the old man said and pointedly crossed his feet in disinterest.

"Excuse me." Lucas had raised his hand slightly

"This is not school, boy. If you have something to say, spit it out," the old man shouted in his direction in a very unfriendly tone.

"If you value your life you should be very careful now, Merlin," another man said calmly.

"Why? Do you want to pick a fight, Thor?" Merlin snarled back at him.

"I don't. But you apparently do. And I am quite certain that our young friend here is not shy at taking you up on it." Thor almost smiled, but was still totally calm.

"Then bring it on," Merlin shouted at Lucas. "I am not afraid of you, greenhorn."

Lucas was totally unprepared for that kind of hostility. The nervousness he had felt before was quickly replaced by annoyance and anger and he was already about to jump up and challenge the old mage, but Thor responded again, before he could.

"If you really call an 18-year-old Magus Major a greenhorn, Merlin, then you are getting senile. I have seen him in action, and believe me, you don't stand a chance." Thor gazed at Merlin with an ice-cold look.

"He doesn't behave like a Magus Major." Merlin snarled back, his voice level decreasing significantly. Lucas almost had the feeling that there was a little fear in it now.

"You wanted to add something to the discussion, Guardian?" Thor addressed Lucas after a moment of total silence.

"Yes, thank you, Thor." Lucas bowed a little. "Maybe the question is a little farfetched, but do you think this is related to the circle we took down a few months back?"

"You are talking about Cleric?" JJ asked.

"I was thinking more about Eagle, but yes, that group. Do you think we missed one of them?" Lucas nodded.

"I don't think you missed one of them; your blow was quite impressive there. What I am afraid of is that whoever Cleric answered to is now searching for an alternative," JJ said

"Whoever Cleric answered to?" Lucas repeated the words with unease in his voice.

"You didn't really think that Cleric was at the top of the food chain, did you?" The woman in the corner jumped into the discussion.

"I actually did," Lucas had to admit.

"Well, then you'd better think again," she said coolly.

"I am sorry, JJ," she continued after another moment of silence. "But even if this is coming from that corner, it is hardly concerning and I also have to decline to assist."

"How can those guys be 'hardly concerning'?" Lucas was getting agitated. "Especially if there is someone even stronger than Cleric involved?"

"Do you really think that the little disaster that Cleric caused by accident, and not even by his own hand, is the only concern we have? There are even bigger problems all over the planet, and besides that, if there really is someone in England who already is able to replace Eagle, he will surely take a long while to master Eagle's craft," she said.

"So what are you saying? That we should just hang JJ out to dry, just because you have other things to do that seem more important?" Lucas asked aggressively.

"This is not a democracy in here, let alone a dictatorship," Thor addressed Lucas in his still very calm voice. "If you want to support JJ then this is your choice to make. Nobody here would ever stop you from it, regardless of the fact that nobody could, even if they wanted to. But as much as nobody will stop you from doing what you deem right, you are also not in the position to force anybody to join you, if they don't want to."

"I understand that, but I still don't get why you are all so lackadaisical. Aren't you worried about this group too?" Lucas had calmed down again.

"It is nice to have young blood in here for a change." Ranger laughed. "It is very refreshing, in fact." He then turned towards Lucas. "Unfortunately, things are not that easy, and we all have our own problems as well. You will understand that in time."

"Yes, he still has much to learn." The lady in the corner nodded.

"Be that as it may," Lucas said, "I will not abandon you, JJ. I will stand with you, and I am sure my circle will also."

"Thank you, Guardian." JJ bowed a little. "Your help is highly appreciated."

Lucas leaned back after that statement, listening to the rest of the discussion. It went on for another half hour or so but didn't reveal anything new. In the end Lucas still was the only one to side with JJ. Everyone else either explicitly refused or just didn't participate in the discussion at all. Lucas still did not fully understand why they all wouldn't want to help, but the longer he thought about it, the more it became apparent what a commitment he had just made. And given the fact that he almost wouldn't have come here in the first place because of his time constraints, it at least started making a little more sense than it had done before.

"Thank you for backing me up." JJ approached Lucas after the discussion was finally over and everyone had gone back to chatting in smaller groups.

"Anytime, JJ." Lucas smiled. "I still owe you one for Cleric."

"I hope that was not your primary motivation?" JJ asked.

"No," he replied with a laugh. "I will always back you up if I can. That's just in my nature, it seems."

"Admirable trait."

"Might be, but not always desirable, I would say." Lucas grinned. "After all, we only stumbled into this mess in the first place because we wanted to help someone."

"It's also not always desirable to be a Mage," JJ said and sat down next to him. "But I would still not want to have it any other way."

"Agreed." Lucas nodded. "So tell me a little about these bad guys. How much do you know about them?"

"We know very little so far. It's a group of seven. They seem to be on a very basic level mostly, but seem to have a quite strong leader. I would suspect that most of them are Adeptus Minors, except for their leader, who is either Adeptus Superior or already a Magus Minor."

"How about your people? Can they deal with that group?"

"They are only five and all of them Adepts of different levels. But in the end they have to. We can't help them in their struggle with their direct adversaries."

"That's a rule I still don't understand." Lucas sighed.

"That's actually an easy one," JJ said. "If we go in against an inferior circle we would provoke the mentors of that circle to come in as well. All it would bring us is escalation, and there is no point in provoking that if we can help it."

"So you would rather let your mentees draw the short straw in a fight than risk escalation?" Lucas didn't like that thought.

"Yes. If we always go in to rescue them they would rely too much on that help and become reckless. That's what we see a lot with the dark circles. Besides, there are a lot of other things on our minds as well. We can't be around all the time, especially not the ones higher up in the chain, so if we escalate too much, we risk thinning out our support even more than we already have."

"What do you mean?"

"You saw the others too. Not one of them was willing to step in--hell, most of them didn't even bother to join the discussion," JJ said with a laugh. "I have only so many chances to convince them to help. I'd rather use those when it really matters."

"Got your point..." Lucas nodded.

"The one thing we have noticed about the group is that they are collecting a lot of the same herbs that Eagle was using to brew his potion. That could be a coincidence--those herbs are used widely after all--but I doubt it. And I wouldn't want to risk another ghost jumping into our midst just because we were sluggish."

"Hold on a sec." Lucas was caught off guard by JJ mentioning the ghost. "Was that your motivation for stopping Eagle? And how the hell do you even know about that?"

"I had no motivation to stop Eagle. That was you, remember?" JJ said. "But I did realize the threat of this enhancement potion as well. And since you apparently forgot, I was in Buxton too."

"If you were aware of the ghost incident, why didn't you help us deal with it?"

"Because I couldn't. I was there at the first incident, which you mastered before anybody else had a chance to react, and at the second incident everything was already under control when we finally got word."

"Well, anyway." Lucas was a little annoyed. "The ghost was not the real problem. We found out a while later that the magic enhancement capabilities of the potion were just a smokescreen. The real thing this potion does is harm the environment."

"That's interesting to know." JJ seemed to think about something while talking. "But it doesn't change the situation. If anything, it makes it worse."

"I did think that this was public knowledge, sorry. Shall we tell the others as well?" Lucas looked around.

"No. They made their decision, let them stick with it. We handled Cleric by ourselves; we can handle his successor. And Gaia is right, if he really is his successor he definitely does not yet possess the strength that Eagle had."

"Hold on. That woman over there is the famous Lady Gaia?"

"I don't know how famous she is, but yes, that's Lady Gaia." JJ nodded.

"You are telling me that the youngest person in the room is actually a member of the mysterious Council?" Lucas was amazed.

"Well, first of all, the youngest person in the room is you." JJ laughed. "And second, don't let appearances fool you. She is way older than she looks."

"I need to speak with her at some point this evening then. But let's finish our topic first."

JJ nodded in reply.

"What's your plan?" Lucas asked.

"Right now we don't have one. We are trying to find out more about the people in the background and see where to go from there. We are, after all, still hoping that we are wrong and that those kids are just there by coincidence."

"I don't believe in coincidence anymore. So let's assume you find their master and he really is some kind of Eagle replacement. What then?"

"Then we let our kids take their shot at his kids and hope he doesn't interfere. And if he does we go in and take him out."

"Take him out like what?" Lucas asked. "You are aware that we could only get rid of Cleric and his pack because they actually killed a man, aren't you?"

"I have to admit that we haven't figured that part out yet." JJ sighed. "But we will by the time this goes down, I promise."

"Fair enough." Lucas nodded. "So where do we come in?"

"When this confrontation goes down, I would appreciate if you could just be there with us and stay in the background. I would only want you to back us up if something unforeseen happens."

"Fine by me." Lucas nodded again. "I'll give you my phone number so you can reach me directly. Seems better than taking the round trip through Angel."

"Thanks a lot," JJ said when Lucas handed him the number. "Let's hope that we don't need your help after all."

"I hope so too, but better to be safe than sorry." Lucas smiled.

"Couldn't agree more." JJ laughed. "Oh, by the way, I almost forgot..." he paused for a second before continuing, "and I am certain I will regret having done this in just a second... Kung Fu says hi."

"That's nice of her." Lucas had to grin. "Did you tell her that we would meet today?"

"No. She just told everyone in the circle to say hi to you whenever we saw you." JJ winkled.

"I'm flattered," Lucas had to admit. "Why would you regret then telling me?"

"Jesus, Guardian..." JJ shook his head. "The girl is over ten years older than you are. And right now she is acting as if she were five years younger. I don't know what you did to her, but it left a very clear mark."

"Well, I guess the feeling is somewhat mutual then." Lucas laughed.

"If that's so, why don't you go on a date with her then, for crying out loud?"

"Honestly?" Lucas looked a little unsure of what exactly to answer. "For one, because until just a minute ago I wouldn't have dared to ask her and further, even if I had, I didn't have a way to reach her in the first place."

"You two are pathetic, you know that, right?" JJ laughed now too.

"Why?" Lucas tried to look offended although he clearly wasn't. "I can hardly open the phone book and search for 'Kung Fu', somewhere in the London area."

"Point taken." JJ nodded.

"But you can help me out and pass her my phone number when you meet her again. That still wouldn't help me reach her, but at least it would help the other way round."

"Coward." JJ laughed loudly. "All right, I will do as you asked. Let's hope it brings a little peace to our circle again."

"Thanks."

"You're welcome," JJ replied with a sigh. "And now you better get going, before I actually do regret bringing the topic up."

"Yes sir," Lucas said with a salute and jumped up.

He quickly took a look around. Many others had already left; only a few were still sitting in small groups, talking. Lucas recognized Merlin and Ranger sitting together gesticulating wildly about something, as well as Thor sitting alone at a table, watching the others closely. When scanning through the room he almost missed Gaia, who was still sitting in the corner, playing with a cat. He decided to take his chance and talk to her.

"Excuse me, Lady Gaia." Lucas bowed before her. "Might I ask you to spare a moment of your precious time for me?"

"Are you sure you are feeling well, young friend?" Gaia looked up at him with a blank face. Looking at her closely, Lucas could now see that she was much older, most likely already far past 50.

"Actually yes, milady." Lucas nodded. "Why would you ask that?"

"Because you talk to me like I was some kind of goddess. Relax, take a seat and please talk to me normally."

"Thank you." Lucas bowed again and sat down.

"What's wrong with you?" Gaia seemed to be laughing, although her facial expressions were still unchanged.

"Nothing is wrong with me." Lucas smiled. "You are a member of the Council, which means for me that you do deserve some respect."

"Do you even know what the Council is?"

"No, but that's actually one of the things I wanted to ask you about."

"So you pay me tribute for being a member of an organization that you don't even know anything about. Interesting approach."

"Everyone I have talked to so far has told me that the Council knows infinitely more than any of us. That's enough for me to show you some respect," Lucas said.

"Very well, it seems I can't get you to treat me like a normal person, so let's get to the point, shall we? What can I do for you?"

"Well..." Lucas thought for a moment. "First, you could maybe tell me a little bit more about this Council. About its purpose and its people."

"As you wish." Gaia nodded. "The Council of Magic Users was founded way before my time as a communications platform for the most advanced of us. Its purpose was to coordinate efforts that occur on a global scale and find peaceful solutions to conflicts. It is pretty much like this meeting was today, just with fewer people and with bigger issues on the table. For now we still keep the original number of eight members, but I highly doubt that we have the most advanced people there."

"And why is that, if you don't mind me asking?"

"Being a member of the Council is like being in any form of volunteer organization. It takes quite some time and effort and there is not much to gain in return. Therefore some people prefer to not participate in the first place."

"I can understand that." Lucas nodded. "Is this Council located in England?"

"Only an Englishman would think that." Now Gaia really was laughing. It was the first emotion Lucas had seen on her face so far. "I can't tell you where our meeting place is, sorry. What I can tell you is that the members are located all over the globe, so England would most likely not be the strategically best spot to meet."

"Is the Council as hard to convince of something as those people in here are? I mean, do you ever get everyone on the same page?"

"The Council is even harder, believe me. Some members hardly ever say anything and when they do it makes little sense to anyone else. If it weren't for our High Lord, I doubt that we would ever get anything done there."

"I have another question if you don't mind." Lucas suddenly got curious.

"By all means, please." Gaia nodded.

"So far everyone I have talked to was very secretive and always only gave me answers that made no sense. Why are you sharing the information so freely with me?"

"Well, first of all, everything I have told you so far is more or less common knowledge, even though it might have gotten lost somewhere. There have been no secrets involved yet. But more importantly, you are a Magus Major now. This might not be much of a difference for you, but for everyone in here it makes it a whole different ballgame. There are tens of thousands of Magus Minors in the world, maybe even millions. But there are only a very few who rise above this crowd, who have the dedication to be more than that. In the entire UK we have maybe 50 who are at your level. Those few have earned the right to ask questions. And they have earned the right to know the truth."

"If there are so few Magus Majors around, then how many Magus Superiors are there?" Lucas was still curious.

"Look around. What would you think?" Gaia asked.

"Out of the twenty-something today, my guess would be about a quarter or so?" Lucas had no clue; he was just guessing.

"In this entire group tonight, there were only two," Gaia said. "I will not tell you who those were, and it really makes little difference anyway, but there were only two."

"Wow..." Lucas was stunned. He had anticipated that the group was small, but not that small. "What does it take to become a Magus Superior?"

"Unity," Gaia answered. "And belief."

"Belief in what?"

"That, I'm afraid, is one thing I cannot answer."

"All right, thank you anyway." Lucas nodded, his brain still trying to make sense of Gaia's short answer.

"Is there anything else I can do for you then, Guardian?" Gaia asked, as Lucas seemed to have lost his voice.

"Only one more thing: You said that Cleric was not the top man in the organization. Who is, then?"

"That is hard to answer, unfortunately." Gaia was a little evasive. "Cleric mostly worked under the orders of a civilian named Jackson."

"Marcel Jackson?" Lucas couldn't believe it. "I knew that guy wasn't kosher."

"Yes, exactly that one." Gaia nodded. "Jackson is just a puppet, though, for another civilian that I myself don't know."

"Mr. Guthridge." Lucas nodded. He had heard the name more than a year ago in a discussion he listened to between Jackson and Mr. Donovan from JDC.

"Well, it seems you know more than I do. Anyway, somewhere in the chain there is of course another Mage involved, and maybe someone above him as well. It is pretty hard to see who really is in charge when you get to that level."

"So what do we need to do, then, to get these people shut down for good?"

"A lot I'm afraid." Gaia sighed. "There are many people involved, many things you need to consider, and in the end, even if you manage to shut them down, someone else will just appear to fill the void you leave. That's how those things work. Nothing is as easy as it appears to be at first."

"I already got that point, unfortunately." Lucas nodded slowly. "Is it even worth fighting, then?"

"That is a decision you need to make for yourself. Think about it like paddling upstream in a river. You might need a lot of effort to ever reach the spring, but if you stop paddling because of that you will just drift farther downstream, which makes it even harder to get there."

"That's not exactly an inspiring metaphor, I have to say..."

"But a true one nonetheless."

"Fair enough." Lucas nodded and stood up. "Thank you for your time, Lady Gaia."

"You are very welcome. One question for you, if I may, though..."

"Sure, anything." Lucas nodded and sat back down.

"You are by far the youngest Magus Major I have ever seen. What did it take for you to make that step?"

"Desperation, I would say." Lucas laughed. "And actually when it started it wasn't even about magic, it was about my life threatening to fall apart. And thinking about it now, I don't think anything short of that could have ever brought me over that hurdle. It seems that magic always emerges best in times of great need. I don't know if that answers your question, but I don't think there is anything more I could possibly say."

"It was all the answer I could have wanted. Thank you for sharing," Gaia answered with her face again very cool.

"I am glad to hear that. Then again, thank you for your time." Lucas bowed and stood up. "Godspeed milady, until we meet again."

"Godspeed Guardian; may you find peace on your journey." Gaia bowed a little too as Lucas walked away.

CHAPTER 3

PRISON

With schoolwork still piling up due to the lost time on Friday, compounded by career orientation, Lucas spent the entire weekend just to stay on top of things. The time was so busy, in fact, that he didn't even realize that he hadn't talked to Darien as he had planned. Only on Monday morning, when he saw others discussing school topics in the corridors once again, did he remember. For a moment he thought about calling him during a break, but then decided against it. He would see him later today anyway for their training session and he would for sure have an opportunity to talk there.

When the time had finally arrived and he was on his way to the shack, for the first time in a week, he felt relaxed. Somehow the circle meeting had become a refuge for his mind, a time when everyday problems were just not allowed to enter. It was a great feeling, and he really enjoyed it.

As he approached the shack he saw Marcus and Cedric working the fireplace and a big cooler standing next to it, suggesting that one of them had planned a barbecue once again.

"What's the occasion?" Lucas asked, pointing at the box after having greeted them.

"My parents are having snails for dinner, so I had to come up with an evasive plan," Cedric grinned.

"And we are the victims." Marcus laughed and put the roast over the fire.

"And what's on the menu now?" Lucas peeked into the box.

"Hamburgers and hot dogs," Cedric answered. "REAL food."

"Man... No lobsters? What a pity." Lucas winkled with a hint of irony in his voice.

"Shut up, mate, unless you want me to bring one next time," Cedric laughed.

"Please don't." Lucas laughed too.

They continued joking around until the meeting was supposed to begin, by which time the others had arrived, with the exception of Stephanie.

"Has anyone heard from Airmid?" Jasmin looked at her watch and was now scanning the horizon.

"No. And it's not like her to be late," Lucas said.

"Let's give her another ten minutes or so before we start worrying," Darien suggested.

They continued gossiping, but the emerging worry was all too apparent on all their faces.

"Let's give her a call," Lucas suggested after a short while.

"Don't." Darien suddenly smiled and pointed at the horizon. "There she comes."

The others sighed in relief, even though they couldn't see anything so far. When Stephanie finally arrived a few minutes later, they all immediately saw that something had her excited. She jumped off her horse and came running toward them without even tying it down and even before she exchanged any greetings, she started waving a flask around and yelling, "I figured it out! I figured it out!" With that, she jumped into the arms of the first person in her path, which happened to be Marcus.

"Jesus, Airmid," he laughed. "That must be a hell of a discovery if you didn't even take the time to run three more steps to Guardian."

The others started laughing too, except for Stephanie, who still was overly excited.

"Look at that, Professor." She almost pushed the flask into his face.

"Slow down, Airmid, please," Lucas said. "Whatever you found, I am sure it will not vanish in the next two minutes."

"What am I looking at here?" Darien had taken the flask and was examining it carefully.

"What do you see?" Stephanie inquired.

"Intuere Magica," he cast his small analysis spell and looked at the flask once more. "It looks like your healing potion. Freshly brewed, just to perfection. It is nice work, especially if you did this without the help of Cougar."

Lucas smiled at Darien's compliment. He remembered all too well how much trouble that one step in the middle of the brewing had always caused. The timing needed to be so extremely perfect that only Marcus' magic had so far been able to provide them with good quality potion. Stephanie's ability to do this by herself now was quite an accomplishment.

"Yes, I did this by myself." Stephanie nodded. "But that's not the real thing." She still was excited.

"Please don't torture us any longer," Lucas said, waiting eagerly for what else she could have hidden in that flask.

"The real thing is that this potion is almost a week old." Stephanie grinned from ear to ear.

Silence followed that statement. So far the biggest problem they had had with Alchemy was that the potions quickly lost their magical energy. Stephanie's healing fluid had normally become useless within two days at best.

"Wow..." Marcus was the first to regain his voice.

"Double-wow." Jasmin nodded. "This is a major breakthrough. Congratulations, Airmid."

"How did you do it?" Darien was curious.

"It's about the fire," Stephanie said, excitement still dominating her voice. "A non-magical fire will not preserve the energy correctly. If you improve the flames a little, it seems to do the trick."

"Nice." Darien nodded. "Did you create a fire spell in order to test that theory?"

"No." Stephanie laughed. "I accidentally spilled some potion on the firewood. Interestingly, my potion is also able to heal wood."

"In what way?" Darien asked.

"The pieces seemed to regenerate while they were burning. Unfortunately, that effect didn't last too long; the potion exhausted quite quickly."

"So are you sure that it is about the magic in the fire then?" Lucas asked. "Maybe what you see is your potion now regenerating your new potion from within."

"Cool theory," Stephanie said. "I hadn't thought about that."

"Let's test it out," Marcus suggested. "After all, we do have magical fire available."

"Sounds like a plan." Lucas nodded. "If you are up to it, of course, Airmid."

"Of course I am." She smiled. "But before we start, I have a gift for you."

She opened her backpack and pulled out six golden chains with small, beautifully decorated glass vials hanging on them. With a big grin on her face again, she handed one to each of the others and put the last one around her neck.

"If this is what I think it is, you have made us quite a gift here, Airmid." Lucas held the vial in his hand.

"It is exactly that." Darien nodded. "And I am not even talking about the containers yet." He was nearly speechless with excitement.

"I wanted to put it in something that is worthy of you as well as the content." She smiled. "It cost me almost all the money I had put aside. But it was definitely worth it now that I see your faces."

"I feel deeply honored by that gift, I really do." Cedric looked straight at her. "But I cannot allow you to drain your savings for me. So I respectfully request that you let me compensate you for the flasks, or unfortunately, I will have to decline the gift."

"Flasks?" Marcus said to Cedric. "You meant to say one flask, right? Because..."

"Don't even think about going there." Cedric didn't give him a chance to finish the sentence.

Lucas looked at Stephanie, who seemed unsure what to say.

"I have to agree with Whirlwind," he said to her. "No, I will not go there," he quickly added in Cedric's direction before turning back to Stephanie. "The content of this vial is priceless; it is the most valuable gift I have ever received from anyone. Please don't let this gift be diminished by the thought that it might cause you grief later on because of your drained account. So please accept the fact that we will only take your precious work, not your money as well."

When he saw Stephanie smile again, he was relieved.

"Now the only thing we have to get straight is Whirlwind's stubbornness." Lucas laughed.

"Forget it," Cedric said in his very cool voice. "Not now, not ever. Airmid, you let me know what those chains and flasks cost you, and I will reimburse you." He then turned toward Lucas and Marcus and added, "ALONE."

"Don't go there, mate." Lucas put his hand on Marcus' shoulder when he saw him opening his mouth. "He has made up his mind; nothing short of Psycho's magic can change it now."

"Don't you dare..." Cedric immediately addressed Jasmin.

"I would never!" Jasmin ducked down into a defensive position. It looked very convincing, but clearly was for show only. "Especially not with you."

"Settled then," Lucas said with a firm voice. "And thanks again, Airmid."

After giving the others some time to say their thanks, as well, and letting Stephanie finally tie down her horse, he brought up the other topic that had been on his mind.

"Guys, I need to confess something to you," he started. "I have been asked for assistance in a magical matter, and I kind of agreed without asking you first."

"That sounds like Guardian." Marcus laughed. "Was there a beautiful girl involved somewhere?"

"Not really." Lucas had to laugh too. "It's JJ and the rest of Angel's circle. And it could be about those black mages again."

"Cleric and his pack? I thought that chapter was over." Jasmin sounded unhappy.

"Unfortunately, it doesn't seem so. But it's still too early to tell. Maybe it's just some leftover splinter groups."

"So what's on the table?" Cedric asked.

Lucas quickly filled them in on what JJ had told him before. A lengthy discussion followed, bringing up more theories and even more far-fetched speculations, but in the end they all made it very clear that Lucas had made the right choice.

"Thank you for backing me up on this," Lucas said.

"I hope you never doubted that we would?" Marcus asked. "Please don't answer that; the question was rhetorical," he quickly added when he realized that Lucas was about to respond.

"We are all in," Jasmin said. "Can we shelve the topic now, please? I would love to finally get to some Alchemy."

The others nodded and quickly started removing the leftover food from the fireplace to clear it for Stephanie's work. It took them the remainder of the evening and three different approaches, but in the end they confirmed her theory, proving that magic in the fire was in fact the key to a sustainable potion.

On his way home Lucas thought a lot about the implications that this had. It had opened many new doors for them, and it finally made Alchemy as potent as spell magic--and even more so, as they finally could store their power for later use. It was an exciting new turn, one that he was really looking forward to exploring further in the future.

With career orientation finally over and the school returning to normal, Lucas now had time to focus on the upcoming exams over the next few days. He had just finished a written one when a text message arrived on his cellphone. He had never seen the sender's number before and normally would just have deleted the message without even bothering, but something told him not to. When he read it, he had to laugh.

"Hi Sweetheart!" the text started, and Lucas didn't need more than that to know who the sender was. Only one girl had ever called him Sweetheart before, and that was Kung Fu, during the fight they had had with Cleric. "I heard that you are yearning for me."

He thought for a moment before texting back his reply: "Interesting how different some things look from different angles. I heard the same thing about you." He added a winking smilie at the end and hit the send button. Then he immediately added the number to his address book.

The response came only seconds later, and it made Lucas laugh once again.

"You heard right; I always yearn for myself." the text said, followed by the same winking smilie.

Lucas normally wasn't the type for this kind of cat and mouse game, but ever since he had had his first run-in with Kung Fu, he had loved playing it with her.

"When that is what you are yearning for, I would suggest you talk to Airmid. She resembles yourself more closely than I do," he replied.

"Being with another girl is only fun when there is a man in the middle," was her reply, followed by yet another smilie.

Lucas had already typed a provocative answer when he decided to take one step back and try to make something of this conversation.

"Right now, to be honest, I would prefer one girl and a pizza. You wouldn't happen to know your way around that combination by any chance?" he finally sent.

"One guy + one girl makes two pizzas. That I could handle." The short reply came back almost instantly.

"Fair enough. Name a time and place then," Lucas texted just as the bell sounded, starting the next lesson.

He still didn't get what it was that fascinated him so much about this woman. He knew that she was easily ten years older than him, sometimes arrogant as hell, a trait that he couldn't stand at all normally, and he knew nothing whatsoever about her, other than that she was a mage as well. From a logical point of view, she was pretty much the kind of girl he normally would avoid at all cost, but then, what was normal when it came to him and girls? His friends had more than once pointed out this weak spot in his personality.

The lesson took his mind off her for a little while, bringing his focus back to complex programming algorithms, a topic that fascinated him like few others could. But still, when the hour was over and Professor Simmons had left the classroom, he was more than eager to grab his cellphone and continue the texting with Kung Fu. To his disappointment he saw that there was no reply from her to his last text. Had he said something wrong? Maybe scared her off? He was unsure what to do. A lot of ideas raced through his mind, a lot of things that he would have liked to text her now, but those messages would all have been based on assumptions as to why she had not answered him in the first place. He was just typing his fifth draft when her reply came in.

"Saturday afternoon would be great. You pick a place; I am the faster one," she wrote.

At that point Lucas was glad that he hadn't sent another message yet. It once again showed him that interpreting no answer was just a bad idea, regardless of the situation. But then, patience had never exactly been his strong suit.

He thought for a moment before texting her back with a location and the confirmation of Saturday. He chose the pizza place in the mall just outside Luton, where he had been with the others a few times already. It was easy to find, close enough and it was more or less quiet. And, of course, it had good pizza. He wondered for a moment if he should include some provocative reference to her statement about being faster, but all the things he could possibly think of would either have sounded lame or would have had the potential to come back later to haunt him, so he decided against it. There would be enough time for that on Saturday. Kung Fu confirmed the text almost instantly again, and so all that was left for him to do was to write the date down in his calendar, so he wouldn't under any circumstances forget about it.

Over the next days, Lucas' mood was rising noticeably. He wasn't sure what to expect from his upcoming date, but he was nevertheless looking forward to it. He also wasn't sure what impression it left for his parents, but he more than once noticed a strange look on his mother's face when she saw him. For a while he thought about telling them about the reason, but always decided against it. And as they never asked, he tried his best to stay in his room, so he could avoid the all-too-awkward encounters until Saturday.

It was late afternoon on Thursday and Lucas was in his room studying, when there was a knock on his room door.

"Yes?" he said without looking up from his book.

"You've got a visitor." His father had opened the door just enough to stick his head through.

"Thanks Dad." Lucas turned around and stood up. He wasn't expecting anyone, and the strange look on his father's face told him that whoever had asked for him was not someone that could even be expected in the first place. When he walked down the stairs he could see his mother standing in the living room, out of sight from the entrance, but definitely within listening range.

"Hello Inspector." Lucas smiled when he saw Corben standing in the door, but his smile quickly faded when he noticed the grim look on the Inspector's face.

"Good evening, Mr. Trent," Corben replied. "I am deeply sorry to intrude on you like this. Could you spare a few minutes of your time for me?"

"Sure..." Lucas was alarmed by the tone in his voice. "Please come in. We can talk in my room."

"Thank you." The Inspector stepped in and took off his shoes and jacket. When Lucas closed the door, he could see that Corben had pulled an envelope from an inside pocket of his coat before hanging it on the cloth hook.

"Follow me please," he said and walked up the stairs. He noticed his parents had uneasy looks on their faces, and he almost bit his tongue when he realized that he had most certainly caused it with his thoughtless "Hello Inspector" greeting. He was certain at that point that there would be a chat upcoming with them. And he was even more certain that he wouldn't have good answers for their questions. But at that point he also realized that matters at hand would have to be very bad for Corben to risk coming here in the first place. Lucas showed the Inspector to his room and closed the door behind them.

"Please take a seat." He offered him his desk chair and sat down on the bed. "And sorry for the mess--I was not expecting visitors."

"Sorry again for intruding on you," Corben said and sat down. "We had an incident earlier today. I am in desperate need of answers, and I honestly have nowhere else to go."

"I will do my best to help." Lucas was beginning to feel uneasy. If the commander of the renowned SO-19 armed response unit had nowhere else to go but an 18-year-old school boy, then something had to be off quite a bit.

"There was an attempted prison break this morning in Wandsworth," Corben said.

"Cleric..." Lucas' face turned white. "What did he do?"

"We are not sure who the target really was," Corben replied. "A group of five intruders penetrated the prison's security. We were able to stop them before they reached any cells, but the situation was bad."

"Define 'bad'."

"See for yourself." Corben pulled a picture out of the envelope. It showed the demolished front gate of the complex.

"How did they do that? With a rocket?" Lucas was stunned when he saw it.

"Apparently with acid." The Inspector handed him another picture, showing a close-up of the door.

"That must have been some acid." Lucas was quickly going from stunned to shocked.

"You can say that again." Corben nodded and handed him a third picture, showing a mostly dissolved man-shield.

"I am still not sure what I can do to help, though. That looks like military grade technology."

"But that doesn't." The next photo showed a man in black robes, lying dead on the floor. Lucas gasped when he saw it.

"And that doesn't either." Corben handed him one more sheet, showing the badly burned SO-19 officer.

"Was that the acid as well?" Lucas' hands were beginning to shake so badly that he had to put the pictures down.

"No, that was a flame thrower." Corben shook his head. "Our only advantage was that none of the attackers had one."

"Jesus…" Lucas still was beside himself.

"You can say that again," Corben repeated. "The final result of the breakout attempt was four dead officers and five more injured, two of them critically, plus five dead intruders. It is one of the most violent crime scenes I have seen in my career, and believe me, I have seen a lot."

"I still don't understand what you expect from me."

"Some answers would be helpful for starters." The Inspector sighed. "Those people were shooting acid, fireballs and lightning. In addition, they were able to protect themselves with some kind of force field that deflected our bullets. And all of this without a single piece of equipment other than a few of these flasks." He pulled out a vial with a green liquid in it. "Do you want to know what that is?"

Lucas nodded silently, looking at the little bottle.

"According to the chemical analysis this is pure water with food coloring. Except, of course, for the fact that it dissolves everything except glass."

Lucas was still stunned by what he had seen and heard. He couldn't think clearly.

"Those five guys killed four police officers with their bare hands and some flasks of colored water. I am desperate, Mr. Trent. I need to understand what is happening here, and I need a way to defend against it if it should ever happen again."

"I am sorry, Inspector, but I am not sure if I can help you here," Lucas finally said.

"If you can? Or if you want to?" Corben asked.

"Can…" Lucas sighed. "There are a lot of secrets in the world I live in, but believe me, if I had a way of protecting you against this I would hand it to you without another thought. The truth is: I don't."

"But you must know something about those guys--about how they can do all this."

"I would assume that this group was mentored by one of the people you arrested a while back in that subway station. Based on that, I would further assume that they tried to break their mentor and his pack out, so whatever you do, you should try to lock them up as tightly as possible." Lucas thought for a moment about how much he should share with the Inspector before he continued, "With regard to how they did all this... Well... You might not like the answer, but the best way I have to describe it would be that it's a kind of magic. And just as a side note, be careful--the people you arrested, the mentor group, also have these kinds of abilities."

"So what are you saying? That they have access to some secret technology that is by far superior to us? So superior that they can smuggle it into a prison?"

"What I am saying is that there is a force at work here that is hard to understand--a force that can't be easily controlled and that is even harder to fight against. Believe me, I know. If you want to call that force 'technology', then so be it."

"You are not seriously trying to tell me that those clowns are some sort of real-world mages, are you?" Corben asked.

"You heard what I said. Make of it what you will." Lucas tried to be evasive.

"I knew that I would not like what you would have to say, but I have to admit that I dislike your words even more than I had anticipated." The Inspector sighed.

"I am sorry to hear that. Unfortunately, there is little I can do to change it."

"So what do you suggest I do?"

"I don't think that I am the right person to give you any suggestions on that. After all, I don't even know if this is what it seems to be."

"Do you doubt it?"

"Not really." Lucas sighed. "But I have been wrong before."

"Will you at least have a closer look, then? Please?"

"All right, I can do that. But I'll need help," Lucas agreed after a long moment of thought. He was very unsure if he wanted to get involved, but keeping a good working relationship with the Inspector seemed to be a good idea, especially if Cleric and his pack were still active.

"Sure, whatever you need." Corben nodded. "Can we go right away?"

"All right, all right. Let me see how quickly I can get the person I need."

Lucas would have preferred to wait a few days, but apparently Corben was anxious to move on it now. He quickly pulled out his cellphone and called Darien.

"Hi mate," he greeted him and immediately got to the point. "A pretty serious problem has arisen and I need your expertise to check it out. You wouldn't happen to have time right away?"

"Sure thing," Darien answered. "What do you need?"

"Can you come over here, please? I will fill you in on the way."

Darien agreed and hung up.

"I guess he will be here in 10 minutes or so. Do you have a car ready to take us to the prison?" Lucas addressed the Inspector.

"Sure. We could have picked your friend up too. That might have been faster." Corben nodded.

"Faster, yes. But that much time you must give me, for privacy's sake."

"Sorry, of course." He nodded.

A time of silence followed. Lucas used it to pick up the photos again and look at them. The sight was horrible, no matter which one he took.

"Do you know how many more of those guys we are facing?" Corben asked.

"Well, I can only guess." Lucas was somewhat happy to have an excuse to put the pictures back down. "The original circle was seven strong. Assuming that each of them has mentored another group, and assuming an average of seven people per group, that would be close to 50. Minus the one group you arrested with the main circle, and of course minus the ones here, that leaves somewhere between 30 and 40, I would guess."

"Jesus..." Corben looked very unhappy. "That's almost an army."

"I think it sounds worse than it is." Lucas tried to calm him down. "Not all of them will have this kind of capability. So most likely you are not looking at more than five to ten who could cause trouble. If my assumptions are correct, and that's a big if..."

"Let's hope for the best then."

Lucas just nodded in reply, with another awkward silence following that nod. This time it was a knock on the door that ended it.

"You have another visitor." His mother had stuck her head into the room.

"Thanks, Mum." Lucas smiled at her. "Shall we go then, Inspector?"

Corben nodded and they went downstairs.

"Thanks for coming on such short notice, Professor." Lucas shook hands with Darien.

"Anytime for you, mate." Darien smiled.

"Professor, I don't think you have met Inspector Corben yet?" Lucas did the introduction.

"Not in person, no, but we did speak on the phone once." Darien shook Corben's hand. "Where are we going?" he asked when he saw Lucas putting on his shoes.

"Wandsworth," Lucas replied. "I'll fill you in on the way."

When they were finally in the car and heading to the prison Lucas told Darien the entire story and showed him the pictures. It was easy to see that his friend was as stunned as he had been not too long ago.

"Can you hand me the flask please, Inspector?" Lucas waited for Corben to pull the little bottle out of his pocket.

"What do you make of this, Professor?" He handed it over to Darien.

Darien looked at it carefully, but without using any spells so far.

"Not as potent as some other stuff we have seen already," he said. "In fact, it's pretty mediocre grade at best. But still, very aggressive."

"Mediocre?" Corben repeated in disbelief.

"What is this?" Darien asked Lucas.

"Apparently that's the acid that gave short shrift to the door and the shield."

"It definitely has the patterns for something like it." Darien nodded. "And sorry Inspector, but my analysis stands: That stuff is mediocre at best."

"Could it be degenerated already?" Lucas asked.

"Yeah, it's degenerating as well, but that's not it. It's filled with more impurities than you have holes in an average Swiss cheese. Whoever made this shit didn't know the first thing about Alchemy."

"Alchemy?" Corben asked. "Our chemists say that this is water with food coloring. Are you saying that this is actually an untraceable acid?"

"According to those photos it does behave like an acid." Darien nodded. "Untraceable... Well, maybe your people were just not looking closely enough."

"And you just did? With no tools? No laboratory? Without even opening the vial?"

"Yes he did, Inspector," Lucas jumped in. "And let's leave it at that, please. We are trying to help, but there are limits to what we can tell you."

"All right, all right," Corben replied. "I am sorry. I am really grateful for your help, but it's all just a little hard to absorb right now."

They continued without further conversation until they reached the prison complex. When they approached the guard post, the carnage was still visible. The front door to the main building was half-open, smashed and broken like they had seen on the pictures. Lucas was once again shocked.

"Sorry, no visiting hours today," the guard addressed them.

"William Corben, SO-19." The Inspector showed his badge. "I need to inspect the crime scene again."

"Of course, Inspector." The guard nodded. "Can I please see some ID from you too?" he then addressed Lucas and Darien.

"No, you can't!" Corben almost shouted at him.

"But regulations..." the guard started.

"Regulations are the least problem you have here right now. They are with me; that's all you need to know," the Inspector responded harshly.

"All right, sir." The man looked intimidated. Lucas could see him writing "Corben +2" into his book as they were walking by his desk into the yard.

"What do you make of this, Professor?" he asked Darien as they approached the smashed door.

"The dissolved parts seem to match with the acid theory." Darien looked at it closely and carefully. "But look at how much the metal has flexed here on the sides. They didn't bother pushing it open after trashing the lock; they burst it open with something that had a hell lot of power. It looks as if a giant had hit it with his fist."

"Like a 'Repellum'?" Lucas asked.

"Yeah, exactly like that." Darien nodded.

"What is a 'Repellum'?" Corben seemed to be fascinated by Darien's analysis.

"Think of it as a repulsing beam, like an energy-based battering ram," Lucas tried to explain without telling details.

"Energy-based?" It was hard to determine if Corben was confused or just in disbelief.

"You will feel it, but you won't see it coming." Darien had finally stepped back from the door.

"Shall we go in?" Lucas quickly asked to avoid more questions.

Corben nodded and led them through the gate. Walking down the corridor, Lucas felt a cold shiver running down his back. He had never come into contact with a prison so far, and now that he was here he was very happy that this experience would only be temporary. Everything in here felt cold, unpleasant and, to a certain degree, dangerous.

"There is where it happened," Corben said when they walked around a corner.

"Jesus." Lucas felt another shiver roll down his back. Chalk outlines dotted the place, blood spills reinforcing the feeling that something terrible had happened here, and the burn marks and bullet holes on the wall told the rest of the tale. He could almost see the battle happening, could almost feel the pain in the air.

"What do you make of that?" the Inspector asked.

"I never thought that things like this really happened outside of action movies." Lucas slowly walked through the corridor.

"Sorry to disappoint you, Mr. Trent." Corben followed a few steps behind.

"Professor, any thoughts?" Lucas asked.

"Lots of them," Darien said with a shaky voice. "Those guys are worse than Cleric was."

"So they are one of us?" Lucas sighed. "Cleric's students? Or his masters?"

"They are one of us all right." Darien nodded. "I would guess students, but they sure as hell left a lot of carnage and even more residual energy, so I am not entirely sure."

"Residual energy?" Corben asked.

"Leftovers from what they did." Lucas nodded. "Unfortunately, it's hard to say much without having been there. The remains only tell so much."

"Would you like to watch the surveillance camera footage? Will that tell you more?"

"No harm in trying," Darien said after looking at Lucas. "There isn't much concrete I can tell you from what I see here."

They followed the Inspector to the security center. The room was filled with TV screens showing multiple angles throughout the prison complex. Looking at it, Lucas had the impression that there was not a single place in here that would give you privacy. And once more he was happy that he was only here as a visitor.

"We have three cameras in the corridor," the prison guard said. "I will let the replay of all three run simultaneously so you can get a good overview."

Lucas and Darien tensely watched the video.

"I've heard this voice before," Lucas suddenly said, pointing at the man throwing the flasks. "And I have seen the effect before too. That's Cypher's group."

"Where?" Darien and Corben asked at the same time.

"Buxton," Lucas answered and looked at Darien. "Remember the fight that Cougar and I had there?"

"You have fought against those guys before?" Corben asked.

"Unfortunately, yes." Lucas nodded.

"How? And where did you report it?"

"We were lucky. And they were for sure not as determined as they were here."

"And they used this same acid there?"

"Yes. Mad Man threw a flask at Cougar and me." Lucas nodded.

"Then how come you are still standing and the guard isn't?"

"Pure luck," Lucas said after thinking for a moment. He had for a second considered telling Corben the truth about how his shield had saved them, but there was little point. The Inspector would hardly have understood it and it would only have raised more questions.

"Can you tell me anything more about them?" Corben understood Lucas' evasion and decided not to press any further.

"What I can tell you with a fair degree of certainty is that they were after the people from the subway station. I don't know what else there is that would help."

"Maybe you can tell me why their protective shield failed in the end. Did we drain it with the flashbang?"

"Professor?" Lucas looked at him.

"No, you didn't drain it." Darien shook his head. "But you distracted the one who was providing it. The loss of focus made him drop the shield."

"Distracted him? How can distraction cause a shield to fail?"

"Keeping this kind of force field up takes a lot of concentration," Darien answered. "It's not like flipping a switch somewhere."

"I am sorry that we can't do more to help, Inspector." Lucas said.

"That's all right; you have actually done a lot already," Corben answered. "I might not understand all of it, but at least I now know who they were after. I will have the group transferred to Belmarsh, just to be on the safe side."

"If there is nothing else to look at, I would appreciate if we could get out of here again." Lucas was still not feeling any more comfortable.

"Of course." Corben nodded. "Let's go."

They walked out silently and stayed that way the entire ride back to the Trents' house. Lucas was watching the Inspector closely the entire time. He was under the impression that Corben was still unwilling to believe in the concept of magic and still had his mind centered on some kind of secret technology.

"Sorry again for intruding on you like this, and thank you for your time," Corben said when Lucas and Darien got out of the car.

"Anytime, Inspector," Lucas replied. "But next time please give me a call and let us meet somewhere else."

"Of course. Do you need any help in explaining my intrusion to your parents?"

"Thanks, but I think I can handle that myself." Lucas shook his head.

"As you wish. Let me know if you change your mind."

"Will do. Goodbye, Inspector." Lucas bowed and watched Corben drive away.

"What do we do now?" Darien asked him.

"Not much we can do, unfortunately," Lucas sighed.

"They killed police officers."

"And paid with their lives," Lucas interrupted him. "This is not exactly our fight. We are not the magical law keepers."

"But there must be something we can do to prevent it from happening again."

"And what would you suggest? Interfere and risk even more exposure than we already have? And where would you interfere to begin with? We don't know the first thing about their motives."

"That's bullshit, Guardian. I don't like it."

"I don't like it any more than you do, Professor. And I am open for suggestions if you happen to have any."

"I don't. But we can't just wait for them to start waging a full scale war against the public. That would cause even more exposure for us."

"Can't argue with that." Lucas sighed. "I will talk to JJ. Maybe he has some good ideas."

"Maybe the others have some good ideas too." Darien suggested.

"Let's see. We can tell them on Monday if you like."

"Sure thing." Darien nodded. "I better get going now. It's getting late."

"You are right." Lucas had only just realized that it was way past 8 p.m. already. "Have a good night, Professor."

CHAPTER 4

WEAK SPOTS

When Lucas approached his door he started feeling uneasy. He knew that he had to tackle his parents alone, but he had no idea what he was supposed to tell them. Walking toward that situation made him realize that right now he was only one inch away from having to give up his secret. If his parents somehow made the connection between Corben's visit and the prison break attempt, there would be no way out anymore for him, at least not without either stubbornly refusing to answer at all or seriously bending the truth, neither of which encouraged him in the least. Lucky for him the problem was postponed. When he opened the door the entire house was dark. He was unsure if his parents were already asleep or had just gone out, but it didn't matter much. He was glad that he could just get into bed and call it a day.

With heading to school early and returning late, Lucas managed to avoid the discussion with his parents for another day, but on Saturday there was just no way he could dodge the bullet anymore. And unfortunately for him, even after almost two days he had no idea what to tell them. He took extra time in the shower and got dressed at a speed that made even snails look fast in comparison, but at some point he had to walk downstairs. When he reached the bottom of the stairs he could see them sitting at the table. It looked as if they had been finished with breakfast a while, the plates empty and the tea kettle cooled down to room temperature.

"Good morning," Lucas said and walked into the kitchen to boil some more water.

He heard them mumbling a reply before it became completely silent in the dining room. Growing uneasy again, he took his time before returning and finally sitting down at the table. He then started eating his breakfast, trying to be as natural as possible, but the silence at the table quickly became extremely awkward.

"So what did you do?" his mother finally burst out.

"I am doing a lot lately," Lucas said while chewing on his toast. "What in particular are you referring to?"

"Don't play games with us, Lucas." His father's voice was unusually strict. "You don't have a police officer in your room every day. What did you do?"

"I helped him bring a criminal to justice a while back. He was here because there were some details that seemed unfinished. No big deal." Lucas tried to stay honest without revealing too much.

"And why did he come here, then, instead of calling you to the station? And where did you go with him afterwards?" His mother was obviously unsatisfied with his explanation.

"He apparently lost my phone number; otherwise, I am quite certain that he would not have come here all the way from London," Lucas said. "And we went to London with him to look at a few things."

"What things?"

"Mum, I am not happy that he was here, either. Nor am I happy that I am still involved in this thing. Please don't make matters worse by asking about an ongoing investigation. If you want more details, I can give you the Inspector's phone number, and you can call him and ask him yourself. I am not even sure what I am allowed to tell you, anyway."

"We are just concerned, son, you must understand that. If there is anything we can do to help, if you need anything at all, please tell us." His father's voice had calmed down significantly again.

"I do understand that, Dad, and I am sorry that this is causing you concern. But please take my word for it that there is nothing you can do to help. I have to see this through to the end myself."

Lucas could clearly see that his parents were still far from convinced, but apparently they had calmed down enough to leave it at that. After another awkward minute of silence, his parents even started chatting about other things again, finally relaxing the situation and giving him a chance to finish his breakfast in peace. He then helped his mother clean up before walking back up to his room to continue his schoolwork. But even though he was much calmer now than he had been before, he made no real progress in his work. His anticipation for the date with Kung Fu was already too powerful, his thoughts much too far away to focus. So after only an hour of work, he decided to put his books aside and try to relax.

When Lucas arrived at the mall a few hours later he felt butterflies in his stomach. He had never been on a date, except the one rather weird evening with the girls in Buxton, and he wasn't even sure if today's dinner would in fact turn out to be a date or just a casual pizza with a strange girl. He had no idea what to expect and no idea how to behave, other than "like himself", which right now seemed to be a hard thing to do. He walked through some stores on his way to the pizzeria, trying to free his mind a little, but it was no good. On the contrary, the longer he walked around, the more nervous he got about it. When he realized that his hands had started shaking, he decided to not stall any longer and head straight to the restaurant. Taking a deep breath, he entered and took a look around. He was still 15 minutes early, so he didn't expect Kung Fu to already be there. He was on his way toward an empty table when he recognized her sitting in the very corner of the room, at a table that was almost hidden behind some plants. He had to take another deep breath before he could approach her. When he finally did, she smiled at him.

"Told you I would be faster," she said without standing up.

Lucas thought for a moment how to great her, and how to respond to that line of hers.

"Faster is not always better, I've been told," Lucas finally said and gave her a kiss on the cheek as he moved by her.

"That's only true for boys." She grinned.

"So much for sex equality," he replied cockily.

"You know, Guardian, I really like you. You are about the only guy I've met so far who is not afraid to shoot back at me."

"I like you too. But I would honestly prefer not to be forced into a shooting duel with you. I am quite certain that I would not have the slightest chance to come out victorious."

"Don't worry, I will not bite your head off. Or at least I will try not to."

"That's reassuring." Lucas grinned. "Although I don't think you would be capable of it, anyway."

"And why would you think that?"

"Well, you do have a big mouth, but it's not THAT big."

They both had to laugh following this statement and luckily for Lucas, right after that the waitress showed up to take their order, giving him a little break. He made a quick decision and put down his menu. Kung Fu was still looking when he was done, so he waited patiently and used the spare moment to finally take a good look at her. This was only the second time he had seen her in civilian clothes, and the other time had been in a rather dusky bar. She was a little smaller than him, sporty to a degree that one could almost call muscular, but still very feminine with her long blonde pigtail and her really lovely face. She was wearing a tight yellow shirt and a track-suit top, tight blue jeans and some sort of fancy jogging shoes. Lucas was still uncertain about her age. He would have estimated her somewhere in her mid-twenties, but it was really hard to tell. Her face looked so young that she could also have been under 20, but on the other hand there was something in her appearance that made him believe that she was even older. In the end it didn't matter to him at all right now. She was just a beauty to watch and the longer he looked at her, the more breathtaking she became.

"What are you staring at?" She suddenly jarred him out of his thoughts. Obviously she had ordered too, as the waitress was already gone.

"Take an educated guess," he replied, amazed that such an answer would come to him spontaneously in such a situation.

"Shall I get you a magnifying glass so you can get the details too?"

"Thanks, but my eyes are quite good."

"And do you like what you see?"

"Want to take another educated guess?" he winked.

"I will take a third one as well: You would not mind at all having more to stare at, right?"

"I think there is no more need for me to speak; your guessing is spot on." He laughed. "But I think we need to stop this at some point, otherwise they will throw us out of the restaurant."

They continued joking and fooling around until their pizzas arrived. Lucas had the feeling that he was glowing by then, being happy as he had rarely been before. This kind of conversation was not his thing at all, but with her he really enjoyed it.

"Before I forget..." she started again after a few minutes of eating in silence. "JJ told me that you agreed to support us with this little black circle. I am really grateful for that."

"We are always happy to help. And besides, we do owe you one for Cleric."

"It still means a lot to me. It's hard to find true friends in our world."

"I couldn't agree more." Lucas nodded. "Which reminds me of something: I think there might be a complication that I need to talk to JJ about. Unfortunately, last time I gave him my cell number, but he didn't leave me one where I could reach him."

"I am sorry, but I don't think that I am at liberty to share it with you. JJ is very secretive about such things. And besides, he said that you should have a way to reach him if something important should come up. Was he wrong with that?"

"No, but it's not THAT important that I would go that route," Lucas said.

"I can relay a message if you like. I'll meet him on Tuesday."

"That would be nice." Lucas quickly told her about the prison incident and the dead mages there.

"That sounds majorly important to me. Shall I give him a call right away?" She looked disturbed.

"No, don't. Tuesday will be soon enough for sure; after all, they are already dead and unless we have a necromancer running around somewhere, I guess they will stay that way for a while."

"As you wish." She bowed a little

"And besides, we are not here to talk about Cleric and his goons, are we?"

"What are we here for then?" she winked.

"I don't know about you, but I am here for one reason only--and that reason is you."

"Oh how sweet." She smiled. "Be careful with such statements, though. I might take them as an excuse to come over and kiss you." She winked again.

"Damn, I knew I should have prepared more of those." He grinned.

"You are not seriously aiming at that, are you?"

"Why not?"

"Because I could almost be your mother."

"Get outta here." Lucas laughed. "You can no more be my mother than I could be Airmid's father."

"You have no idea how old I am, do you?"

"No, I don't." Lucas shook his head. "And frankly, I don't care either. You are just trying to get out of that impetuous statement of yours."

"No, I am not. I am dead serious."

Lucas knew that she was not joking right now, but something told him that this was not actually an attempt to get out but more a sign of insecurity on her behalf. Somehow he seemed to have hit a nerve with this direction, which was totally unexpected. He thought for a moment about what to do. He definitely didn't want to scare her off, but he also was rather intrigued by the thought of a kiss and didn't want to let it slip by. He finally decided to continue along the same line he had started: head on.

"Chicken," he said and leaned back, trying to look as if he was offended by her statement.

Lucas could almost see the thoughts running through her head then. She was engaged in a major struggle against herself. He was not exactly sure what the feelings were she had right now, but to him it looked like some kind of terror fighting against her pride. He could clearly see the tension in her muscles and at one point he could even spot the carotid artery pulsing, telling him that her heart rate was clearly skyrocketing right now. The moment seemed to take forever, and the longer it took, the more nervous and worried Lucas got, suddenly even more uncertain if this move had been a good one or if he had just succeeded in blowing his first real date. He was already thinking about how to get out of this awkward situation when Kung Fu suddenly jumped out of her chair, and before he had a chance to react, she had pressed a firm kiss on his lips.

For a moment Lucas was stunned. He had kissed a girl before, but somehow that just had felt a whole lot different, a whole lot better. When he finally pulled himself together again, Kung Fu had already returned to her chair and was now eagerly looking at him.

"I hope that was what you wanted," she said in her signature offensive voice. Lucas did hear the little difference in it very clearly, though. This time it was not a joke to her; she was very unsecure underneath that hard look.

"Sorry, you caught me off guard--can you do that again?" he replied, his heart still pounding heavily.

"You are impossible. You are even worse than me." Now she was leaning back and looked offended, although Lucas was under the impression that something within her was quickly approaching a breaking point.

"I hope I'm not," he said in a soft voice and now got up himself to press his lips firmly on hers.

When he sat back down, he immediately recognized that this had been the right move to make. He had clearly caught her off guard this time, leaving her even more uncertain about what was going on than before, but he was sure that the tension inside her was gone now. He watched her silently for a while, giving her time to regroup.

"Do you mind if I ask you something?" she finally said in a very serious voice.

"Of course not. Please..." Lucas replied calmly.

"Where do you want this to go?"

"Wherever you are comfortable with."

"You are aware that I was not kidding before? I really could almost be your mother."

"And I already gave you the answer to that: I don't believe you, and even if I would, it wouldn't change a thing."

Silence followed again. Lucas watched her eagerly, trying to read her thoughts.

"Can I ask you a question now?" he finally said.

"Sure." She nodded.

"Where would you like this to go?"

"I honestly don't know. But I would like it to go there for a long while."

"That makes two of us then." He smiled.

"Well, in that case, let's find out what else makes two of us." She grinned, her taunting voice back.

"I am sure we will find a lot."

"To us, then." She raised her glass.

"To us." Lucas followed the example.

"By the way..." he started after taking a sip. "You wouldn't want to tell me your name, by any chance? I think it will be a little weird if I introduce my parents to 'Kung Fu'."

"I would love to see their reaction to that." She laughed.

"I don't think you would get much reaction. They already know Psycho and the Professor... So Kung Fu is not too far off after all."

"Well, I am unsure if I would like to bear the consequences of it in the end, so if you ever introduce me to your parents, my name is Sandra."

"Well, it's my pleasure to finally get to know you, Sandra. I am Lucas." He bowed a little.

"The pleasure is all mine, believe me."

The evening went by faster than they both realized. They covered everything from their youth to their education, giving each other at least a little bit of the picture. Lucas learned that she was born and raised in London and was still living in the suburbs. She was a martial arts expert and made her living as a sports teacher at a high school in the city. She had as little knowledge of computers as he had of martial arts and other than action movies and magic, they seemed to have little in common at all.

"When do you want to meet again?" he asked when they were standing outside in the parking lot.

"Whenever you want," she replied. "The more interesting question is, though: Where do you want to meet next?"

"Well, when is easy from where I stand: ASAP. Where? Interesting question, actually." Lucas thought for a while. "We could grab something to eat again if you like. Alternatively, we could go see a movie. And I would also be good with more privacy if you like. So basically, it's up to you."

It took them almost ten minutes of back and forth discussion before they finally agreed to meet in a week and go watch an action movie that was due to start on Thursday. When they finally parted ways, Lucas made sure that it was not without an intense farewell kiss.

On his way home he almost felt weightless, hovering more than riding his bike. He felt a power inside him that he had never experienced before. It was somewhat similar to the evening he had had with Rachel in Buxton, but even though that evening had been more intimate, it had produced nowhere near as much joy as this mundane dinner just had. As he thought back to Buxton and all the differences today's date had provided in comparison, he for the first time realized that he was truly in love.

The following Monday Lucas had to face one of the most boring lectures that he had on his schedule this year: Philosophy & Ethics. It was not a particularly hard subject, but it was one that had no right answers, only different points of view, which made it very hard for him to grasp. He had a hard time not falling asleep, especially because he had worked through the entire Sunday in hope of making up some lost ground from the day before, but close to the end a discussion came up that caught his attention. The topic was revolving around tools, how they evolved and what the implications were with giving someone a powerful tool. The philosophical argument went along the line that handing somebody a tool that was beyond his own comprehension could distort evolution. The discussion itself was not particularly fruitful, but the topic had sparked an idea in Lucas: What if he could, based on Stephanie's new knowledge of Alchemy, build magical artifacts containing his shield charm? Maybe with that he actually did have a means to protect Inspector Corben and his men from another attack by Cleric's students. The ongoing discussion made him worry a little, because his teacher, after all, was right. Giving that artifact to Corben would be like handing a tool to somebody who was by far not ready to comprehend it. On the other hand, he was certain that the topic at hand with the Inspector was not about evolution, but about leveling the playing field. He continued weighing the pros and cons the entire remainder of the day, even on his way out to the shack. When he arrived there he was still so excited that he had completely forgotten about the primary reason for the thought, and that the others had no idea yet what had happened. He was last to arrive, the others awaiting him inside due to the bad weather.

"I have something I would like to hear your opinion on, guys," he said when they had all settled down around the table.

"The Professor already told us that something was coming our way," Jasmin said. "He wasn't that excited about it, though."

"Damn..." Lucas cursed as he finally remembered. "Sorry, I was so far ahead in my thoughts that I totally forgot about this."

He quickly explained the situation to the others in as much detail as possible, giving Darien a chance to jump in here and there to add more.

"After that, I am really looking forward to what else you have on your mind that could be more pressing." Stephanie was shocked.

"It can wait until we have finished this one," Lucas said. "So what's your take on this?"

"If they succeed in breaking Cleric and his lot out, all our effort will have been for nothing." Marcus spoke his mind first.

"Not necessarily, Cougar" Darien replied. "After all, if they break out they will be fugitives, which means that it's not just us who will be searching for them, but pretty much the entire law enforcement power of the planet. They are, after all, convicted murderers."

"What's their endgame?" Cedric asked.

"What do you mean?" Jasmin inquired.

"They might be stoned, but they are not stupid. They know this as well as we do, so if they risk a stunt like that they were either even more stoned than I thought or they have some kind of master plan that depends on somebody in this prison."

"Eagle..." Lucas said.

"They will still not be able to keep him out forever. What's the point?" Marcus asked.

"Whatever they need, it will be finished in a relatively short amount of time." Lucas nodded. "Either they need him to share a secret of sorts or they are planning to move soon."

"They are planning to move," Darien said.

"Why are you so sure?" Marcus asked.

"Because if they just needed information all they really would need is a lawyer. And it's by far easier to fake being a lawyer than to break somebody out of prison."

"I don't understand..." Marcus was confused.

"A lawyer can visit an inmate in a prison," Darien explained. "And more importantly, a lawyer has the privilege to speak to his client without anyone else monitoring. So if they wanted a secret passed out, that's the easier way to get it."

"So what do we do? We can hardly hang around the prison and wait for them to try again," Jasmin asked. "And even if we could, what good would it do? It wouldn't get us a single step closer to the underlying reason."

"We can also hardly spy on another circle as we obviously don't know any," Darien added.

"Not entirely true--JJ's mentees have one at their fingertips," Lucas replied. "But overall you are right; it's highly unlikely that we get to the root of it in time, at least not if we are starting from the lowest level."

"Then let's start higher up," Cedric suggested.

"Higher up like what?" Marcus asked.

"We actually have two possibilities at our disposal. First, we do know exactly where the highest ranking one we know is right now. And we do have access to him," he said. "And second, there still is the civilian side of the coin."

"Jackson..." Lucas nodded.

"Yep." Cedric nodded back.

"I still don't understand how this helps us," Stephanie threw in. "Cleric and his goons will hardly tell us anything, unless you send Psycho in and have her perform magic in prison. And this Jackson guy is not exactly somebody we can approach now, can we?"

"Cleric will be a tough nut to crack, and no, if we want to try it we have to do it without magic," Lucas said. "I will nonetheless try, if Corben lets me. With Jackson you might be right; we can't approach him directly. But given the trouble he went through to grab Harlington Research, I think it is fair to assume that the company will play some role in his plan. Professor, do you see any way to keep your eyes open without jeopardizing your job?"

"A lot of the projects at HRC are classified these days, but I will do my best. It should at least be possible to figure out what Jackson is pushing most," Darien said.

"That's settled then." Jasmin tried to smile. "Now spit out what else you have on your mind, Guardian."

"My other topic is actually related to the discussion," he started. "Inspector Corben asked me if there is anything I can tell him to help his people defend themselves against the next attack."

"So? You can hardly teach him how to cast a shield charm now, can you?" Marcus was confused.

"No, but maybe I can build him a shield in a box. A tool." Lucas grinned.

"An artifact," Darien said, speaking more to himself than the others.

"And how do you propose tackling that? We know squib about artifact magic, at least as far as I am aware," Marcus asked.

"I tend to disagree," Lucas replied. "After all, I have something like an artifact hanging around my neck." He pulled out Stephanie's vial.

"That's a potion, not an artifact," Marcus objected. "It only works once, and you have to actively use it to be any good."

"We are on the same page with that, but maybe that doesn't matter." Lucas was still excited about the idea. "Corben will most likely not walk into such a fight blindly, so he can activate the shield beforehand. And what's the problem with it only working once? Once might just be the edge SO-19 needs over those guys."

"I am not happy handing Corben and his people something magical," Darien said. "Have you thought about the implications? And about the responsibility you get yourself into, once you open that door?"

"I actually thought a lot about that yes," Lucas said. "I still think that it is a viable solution. At least until we have this situation figured out."

"I am sorry, Guardian, but I tend to agree with the Professor," Jasmin jumped in. "Giving the police a magical artifact is just wrong."

"We will not get on the same page with that, it seems," Stephanie said. "I am with you, Guardian; protecting life is my highest priority, after all."

The discussion continued for almost an hour. Marcus took sides with Lucas and Stephanie, while Cedric stood with Darien and Jasmin, leaving them in a tie. And even after discussing all arguments up and down for an hour, they were no closer to having a united opinion, other than that they agreed to disagree. It was, after all, philosophical, with both sides having valid arguments.

"We are not getting anywhere." Lucas finally sighed. "Why don't we do this: Let us find out if we even have the knowledge to build such an artifact, and if we do, we will create two or three and give them to the Professor for safekeeping." He then turned directly to Darien. "You are, after all, the most cool-headed person in this group. We will not hand them to anybody outside the circle unless we all agree upon it. I entrust that to you."

A short discussion followed, but they quickly agreed upon it. It was, after all, a fair compromise.

"So how do we tackle that now?" Jasmin asked,

"Airmid, Professor, that's your expertise." Lucas looked at them. "I have the spell. I am counting on you to come up with a way to bind it."

"I am sorry, but I think I am the wrong person for that, Guardian," Stephanie replied. "My approach would be to find an herbal combination that generates some kind of shield. From that we could brew a potion. Other than that, all I can add is that we will need magical fire."

"What we could try is brewing a potion and you just weaving your energy patterns into it. Maybe that will stick. But it is highly unlikely. If I compare Airmid's spells with her potions, I have to say that the energy pattern is totally different."

"Well, I would say we should try it. The worst thing that can happen is that we fail. Not much harm in that," Lucas suggested.

The others agreed, and so they started to follow the plan. Lucas provided the magical fire, while Darien and Stephanie tried to come up with a potion recipe that would not have an effect on its own, but would be able to store energy. The others tried to help out wherever they could. It took them more than four hours based on that approach before they finally came up with something that actually seemed promising. When Darien finally held up the flask with the green-glowing gel, Lucas was relieved. The process had drained him significantly.

"OK, that now looks exactly like your 'Seperatio' charm." Darien analyzed it. "How do we test it?"

"Let me pour it over something and then Whirlwind can try to blast it with his 'Ventus' charm," Lucas suggested.

"There is an old wood panel outside," Stephanie suggested.

"OK." Lucas smiled. "I will hold it like a shield, and let's see what happens."

They quickly grabbed what looked like an old door and tried to cover it with the gel. This unfortunately pretty quickly showed the first flaw in the idea: It took them a very long time to cover the whole panel, and it was a painstaking process. When they finally had it finished and Darien had confirmed that the energy structure still looked the same, Lucas took position and prepared to be blasted by Cedric. All of them waited eagerly for the result. When Cedric finally cried "VENTUS" they all held their breath. Unfortunately, the first thing they all heard after the endless moment of anticipation was Lucas' cry as Cedric's attack hit him frontally, threw him back a few meters and caused him to land in the grass with the panel on top of him.

"I would call that one an epic failure," Darien said unemotionally and walked over to help Lucas up.

"What went wrong?" Lucas asked after he had gotten rid of the panel and was back on his feet.

"Everything," Darien replied. "Your spell is just not made to be a potion. Sorry."

"Well, at least we don't need to think about the possible uses of our artifacts anymore." Cedric shrugged his shoulders.

"Maybe it's not possible at all to build an artifact," Jasmin suggested.

Lucas looked at his watch. He really wanted to prove them wrong right now, but he just couldn't. This was not meant for their eyes yet.

"Let's call it day then, shall we?" he finally responded.

The others nodded and slowly started packing up. Lucas continued thinking about the things that had gone wrong, but he just couldn't come up with a good explanation. And the only person he knew who really had experience with such things was someone who was not easy to reach. When he arrived home, he decided to put the topic aside for the moment and try to talk to Gremlin at the next Magus Major meeting.

CHAPTER 5

EXPOSURE

A few days later, Lucas was heading out of school on his way home. He had just unlocked his bike when he recognized a man standing just outside the perimeter fence. And even though the person was wearing a hat and dark sunglasses, he immediately recognized him and walked up to him.

"Greetings, JJ," he said.

"Greetings, Guardian." He bowed a little.

"What an unexpected surprise. What brings you here?"

"Kung Fu relayed your message, so I took the first chance I had to talk to you."

"You could have just called me if it was of so much concern to you. That would have been much quicker."

"This is not something I would want to discuss over the phone." JJ looked around. "Shall we walk? I don't like standing here in the open."

"Certainly." Lucas pushed his bike along as they slowly went away from campus.

"If they are really trying to break Eagle out of prison, it all starts to make sense," JJ started. "The herbs they are collecting would mean that he intends to brew quite a large amount of that potion."

"IF they are trying to break him out. And IF that circle of yours is actually related to that," Lucas replied.

"I thought you don't believe in coincidences?"

"I don't. But it strikes me as odd that they would go to such lengths for that. And even if that's their plan, I doubt that they would have enough time to finish it before the police caught up to them."

"I doubt that the police would ever catch up to them. Not unless one of us points them in the right direction. But tell me, what's your theory then?"

"I don't have one, unfortunately. It all makes little sense to me. But then, I never was able to catch their endgame in the first place."

"So what do you want to do then?"

"Jesus, JJ, how should I know? This is way bigger than me. I can't even begin to imagine what it is that would be important enough to come into the open like this."

"That strikes me as odd too. That looked more like desperation than a plan."

"You know what's even odder?" Lucas looked at JJ. "If they are so desperate to get out of prison, why don't they just break out themselves? They have at least three pretty powerful battle mages in their group, far more powerful than the group that tried the stunt. The police wouldn't stand a chance if they unleashed their combined force."

"You are right, that's weird. Could it be that the people inside didn't know about the breakout attempt?"

"It's all guesswork, JJ. They are either desperate and in a hurry, or they are just stupid. As long as we can't figure out their goal, there is nothing we can do."

"Shall we bring this up with the other Magus Majors? Maybe one of them knows more."

"I will not stop you if you want to go there. But given how they reacted to your last approach, I highly doubt that they would be of any help here."

"So we just wait?"

"There is little more we can do unfortunately." Lucas sighed. "I am planning on visiting Cleric in prison. Somehow I doubt that he will be willing to talk to me, but I will still try. Other than that, your mentees are our best bet right now."

"Hardly encouraging..." JJ sighed

"But unfortunately the truth," Lucas said.

"Let's hope the best then," JJ said and slowed down. "Let me know if you find out something new, please."

"Will do." Lucas nodded.

He took a few steps when he suddenly realized that he still didn't have JJ's phone number.

"Oh, JJ..." he said and turned around, but to his surprise there was nobody there anymore, just the birds singing all around him in the park.

The longer Lucas thought about the chat he just had had, the more the situation made him uneasy. The circle that had attacked the prison was the same that had tried to kidnap a girl during the camp in Buxton a year ago. And while their mentor, Cypher, had made him believe at that time that this was just pure stupidity and had never been intended by their masters, he somehow doubted that now. They might maybe have been dumb enough to pick a fight at the camp, but nobody could be stupid enough to attack a highly-guarded prison for no good reason. And if such a reason in fact existed it definitely had to be far bigger than what the Mages of the Round Fireplace had encountered so far. But no matter how long he thought about it, there was nothing that he could think of that would justify an approach that drastic. Lucas was very well aware of what they had already done in the past, but so far they had never exposed themselves and they had always kept their distance from law enforcement--except, of course, for the fact that one of them had actually been a policeman. After a while he shifted his focus to the one thing he did know for sure: The potion that Eagle had been brewing was meant to cause ecological damage. Combined with the forceful takeover of Harlington Research by Mr. Jackson, this would have suggested that they were trying to run some kind of eco-terrorism here in the UK. But even if that was true, which Lucas was very uncertain about, it still would not explain their behavior. He knew how ruthless all true believers--and he did consider eco-terrorists to be true believers too--could become over time, even up to the point that they would sacrifice their lives just to make a statement. That thought also had a flaw, though, in this situation: So far nobody had made a statement. It still all made no sense. There was no power to be gained, no money to be made, no greater good to be achieved, no matter how he spun the situation. When he went to bed that evening he decided to try his luck and visit Cleric the first chance he got. He was very aware of the fact that there was little chance to gain anything from such a meeting, but given the situation he at least wanted to give it a shot.

During a break next day Lucas decided to give Inspector Corben a call. Besides the fact that he knew nothing about prison visiting hours, he also didn't want to go behind the Inspector's back with this. A little to his surprise, Corben seemed happy about the call, even grateful for the idea. The Inspector even offered to pick him up after school and accompany him to the prison, an offer that Lucas more than willingly accepted. Even though the chance was there that Corben's presence would make the conversation more complicated than it already would be, he felt a lot safer having a veteran law enforcement officer at his side.

"Thanks for the company," Lucas said even before exchanging any greetings with Corben.

"Anytime. I would not want to miss this for the world," the Inspector replied. "Besides, I doubt that you would have gotten very far without me anyway."

"I think so too, actually." Lucas was a little surprised by the statement. "But why would you say that?"

"Well, because I somehow don't think that you know who to ask for." He grinned and handed him an envelope.

"Great point actually," Lucas had to admit. He had not even thought about that before. Without knowing any names, it would have been very hard indeed. He opened the envelope and took out a stack of paper. It contained pictures. Some looked like the typical prison photos he knew from movies; others looked as if they had been shot in the subway station where they had confronted Cleric.

"I don't know who you are talking about when you use your strange names and you most likely wouldn't recognize their real names if I had listed them, so our best bet to get to the right person is for you to point him out," Corben said.

"That's him." Lucas picked out a picture that showed the subway station in almost the same condition he had left it in, just with the bad guys no longer wearing their hoods.

"Lucius Preston." Corben nodded. "Strange guy. Doesn't talk much, always seems to be praying. I have never seen a person before who was so dedicated to religion."

"I am not sure if I want to know too many details about the gods he is praying to," Lucas said. "Do you know anything else about him?"

"Not much. As far as I remember he works for a bank. Completely clean before you handed him to us, just like most of the others."

"Where are we going, by the way?" Lucas looked out the window. "Isn't

Wandsworth in the other direction?"

"They are no longer at Wandsworth. I had them transferred to Belmarsh a few days ago."

"Oh, nice." He could feel a cold shiver running down his back again. Belmarsh was a renowned name in the area, a maximum security facility that was said to show little patience for inmates who stepped out of line. It was definitely a place that he was not looking forward to being in. When they approached the gate, he immediately felt intimidated.

"You are aware that you need to show your ID this time, right?" Corben asked.

"Sure." Lucas nodded. "I'm not exactly happy about it, but then, there are a lot of things right now that I am not happy about."

They signed in and headed for the visiting room. Entering the room, the cold shiver came back instantly. It looked just like you see in modern gangster movies. The room was divided by a wall of reinforced glass with no openings. Chairs were provided on both sides and phones were mounted as well, presenting the only way to interact with the other side. The room contained multiple cameras, covering every inch of it, and heavy duty steel doors on either side. Lucas tried to look as calm as possible, but he really was majorly nervous, almost frightened. They sat down and waited for a few minutes before the door on the other side opened and a man was led in. He was wearing orange overalls with a number printed on the front. The shackles on both his arms and feet, as well as the chains connecting them, shimmered in the neon light. Two guards had grabbed him tightly and were more or less dragging him along to the glass, where they connected the chains to a heavy-duty ring that was attached to the floor. They then walked back out, leaving the three alone in the room.

"What a pleasure to see you again, Guardian," Cleric greeted him with a despicable grin on his face after they had all picked up their handsets. "Finally gives me the opportunity to finish what I started before."

"Careful what you say, Preston," Corben shouted into the microphone.

"What? Do you really think you can protect him?" Cleric laughed loudly. "Or that this pathetic glass wall is any kind of obstacle?"

"I don't need protection, not from you," Lucas said coolly. "You had no chance last time; why should it be any different now?"

"Because I have had a lot of free time lately."

The frosty look on Cleric's face caused Lucas to intuitively fire up a shield charm. He was not exactly sure what was happening, but the energy he felt pounding his protection seemed to be enormous. For a moment he thought about shooting back, but then decided to just let it be. Lucas was sure that Cleric had no chance to penetrate his defenses. And anything he could have done to counter would have raised suspicion.

"You can't be serious." Lucas looked him directly in the eyes.

"Whatever you are doing, stop it," Corben commanded.

"Stay out of this, bobby," Cleric hissed back and gave him a short, vicious look before immediately focusing back on Lucas.

Lucas was still trying to relax and not counter, but now he started to rebuild his shield. He figured that the best way to stop the confrontation discreetly was to drain his opponent's energy. He was almost done reconfiguring his protection to a leeching device when a cough from the side caught his attention. When he turned his head he saw that the Inspector's face had turned red and he was obviously struggling for air. Without hesitating a moment he extended his shield, and to his relief he could hear Corben take a deep breath right after that.

"You can't be serious." Lucas said again in an angry voice, quickly finishing his original plan.

"You can't defend him forever," Cleric laughed.

"No, but you can't keep that up for much longer either." Lucas voice sounded cold. He could feel the new spell draining his opponent's energy almost instantly.

"Fool," Cleric suddenly shouted and started rattling his chains, trying to break free.

"Sit down," Lucas commanded. The reaction was a clear indication for him that his shield had done the trick.

"Why don't you fight back?" Cleric was still jumping around as much as his chains allowed. "Come on, try to kill me, you idiot."

"I don't kill. That's your business," Lucas' voice was completely cold now. "Sit down."

"What do you want?" Cleric finally complied.

"I want to know why those idiot students of yours tried breaking you out."

"That's true loyalty," Cleric answered with a triumphant look on his face after thinking for a moment.

"More like true stupidity," Lucas replied, but his thoughts had wandered off. The moment of silence that Cleric had needed before answering led him to believe that his opponent had not even been aware of the attempt so far. And that meant that either Cleric had never been the target to begin with, or he at least didn't know anything about the plan. And then there was a third possibility: What if they hadn't actually planned to get him out, but to make sure that he never got out again? Was it possible that they had had it wrong from the very beginning?

"He is useless, Inspector. Let's go." He shook his head and stood up.

"That's it?" Cleric shouted and his face immediately turned red. "You disturb my peace just to ask me one question? Fool!" He started to rattle his chains again, once more trying to break free. Corben seemed to be unsure for a moment, but then followed Lucas out of the room.

"What the hell was that?" the Inspector whispered when they walked through the corridor.

"What was what?"

"First I feel as if I am being choked by an invisible hand, then you walk out after only one question? What is going on?"

"Let's talk in the car," Lucas replied without even looking at him.

They left the prison in silence, the Inspector visibly agitated.

"Now talk," Corben almost shouted when they were driving out the parking lot.

"Cleric didn't even know about the breakout attempt. And about the choking thing--sorry about that. I should have been prepared for it."

"Prepared for what? How did he do that?"

"I told you that he had some tricks up his sleeve too."

"And so do you, it seems."

"Yes, that impression might arise."

"If Preston didn't know about the breakout, is it possible that we were talking to the wrong person?" Corben had decided to drop the first inquiry.

"Possible." Lucas nodded. "But I somewhat doubt that any of them knew anything about it."

"So who facilitated that attack, then?"

"That's the 500.000 dollar question, Inspector."

"500.000 dollar?" Corben was confused. "What's the million dollar question, then?"

"The million dollar question is: Why?"

"Who cares about that? If we get the facilitator, the show is over."

"If you get the guy, he will just be replaced by someone else. Only if you take away the reason for him to be there in the first place do you stand any chance of ending this mess."

"If you say so." Corben sighed. "So what now?"

"Now I will go home and continue my schoolwork. I am not a detective." Lucas thought for a moment before continuing. "And technically neither are you. Why are you still in this?"

"That's an easy question." The Inspector laughed. "The detective who is running the case is hitting one wall after another. And as I am the one with the only helpful CI in this matter, they asked me to help out."

"But that's certainly not your only reason. You seem to be taking this personally," Lucas said, following a hunch.

"Are you reading my mind now?" Corben paused for a moment before continuing, "One of my men is still in critical condition. The doctors have little hope that he will survive. He would be the first officer under my command that I have lost. I know staying with the case will not save him, but at least I want to get the bastard who is behind it."

"I am sorry to hear that. I'll keep my fingers crossed that your man survives. And that you catch the bad guy soon."

The rest of the way was filled with silence. Neither of the two had anything else to say and neither wanted his thoughts disturbed. When Lucas finally got out of the car he only mumbled a quick goodbye and closed the door without even waiting for a reply. He walked straight up to his room, his mind torn between two topics. On the one hand, there was Cleric and the prison break, which now made even less sense than it had before. On the other hand, there was Corben's injured man, whose picture Lucas could no longer get out of his head. It seemed so unfair that another man was about to die, a man who put his life on the line in a battle that he never had a chance to win in the first place. He juggled the thoughts for another hour or so before he suddenly burst into tears. He cried for half an hour, only stopping because he was too exhausted to produce any more tears. This whole thing just didn't feel right. It in fact felt so wrong that he was afraid it would tear him apart if he didn't at least try to make it right again. After a while of just lying on his bed, he finally decided to act rather than cry. He pulled out his cellphone and opened the address book. His first thought was to call Airmid and ask her for help, but thinking about the discussions they had had about the artifacts, he quickly decided against it. He just didn't want to force her into this dilemma too. After thinking through all the others in his circle, he finally came to the conclusion that there was only one person he could ask. And he now even had a way to reach her. He quickly jumped out of the address book and hit a speed-dial button.

"Hi Kung Fu," he said when she answered the phone and immediately continued, not even giving her a chance to reply. "I am sorry for dropping in on you like this, but I need your help."

"Anything. What do you need?" She sounded alarmed by his voice.

"I need to get hold of Angel. And I need her right now. Is there any way you can get her to contact me?"

"I will have her knock on your door in 10 minutes at the latest."

"No, please have her meet me at the Timestop. Can you do that for me?" Lucas was eager to avoid another awkward conversation with his parents.

"Consider it done. Anything else I can do to help? You don't sound particularly good."

"I am not feeling very good either. But no, right now that's all. I will tell you the details on Saturday if you like."

"Definitely."

"Thanks again."

He hung up and ran down the stairs, cycling to the Timestop as fast as his feet would pedal. When he entered the room Angel was already sitting at a table and even had his favorite drink standing ready for him.

"Thank you for being here." Lucas was still out of breath when he sat down.

"I can hardly deny a cry for help from an old friend, can I? Especially when the cry is that loud."

"Sorry, I didn't want to create that much noise."

"Don't be. And now go ahead. You definitely didn't bring me here just to be sorry for bringing me here."

"No, of course not." He quickly told her about the prison break, Cleric and Corben's injured colleague.

"That really sounds bad," Angel said. "But most of that I already knew a week ago, and so did you. Why are we here?"

"Because I just can't let that police officer die. It's breaking my heart."

"And you are waiting for me to support you in that? Or do you want me to oppose you?"

"I would like to know your opinion." Lucas sighed. "If I do this, I risk exposing me, Airmid and most likely the entire magic community to a certain extent. On the other hand, this is not exactly new. We have done this with Cougar before. And after all, that officer was injured by magic, so he does deserve having magic available for his recovery too."

"Interesting arguments. All of them. And no easy answer."

"What would you do?"

"I honestly don't know. But then, I don't even have someone at my disposal who could make a difference here. That's a privilege only few people have."

"Is there any rule about that? Any guidance from the council?"

"The only one that will apply here is: Make your own choice, and then live with it."

"Damn it, Angel. I just can't let this happen." Lucas was close to crying again.

"Then act."

"But I can't risk exposing Airmid and the others."

"That, my friend, is the problem every leader has to face at some point. There is no right answer here; there are just different consequences."

"Well, I guess we just found out why I never wanted to be a leader in the first place," Lucas sighed.

"And we already more than once found out why it still is a good thing that you are." Angel patted his shoulder as she walked by him. "Have faith in yourself; everyone around you does."

With that she walked away, leaving him sitting there alone, lost in his thoughts once again. Talking to her had not made his decision any easier, but somehow he hadn't expected that anyway. From the very first day she had always told them that as a mage you are in control of yourself and free to make your own decisions, with all the consequences that arise from that very fact. One other thing she had just told him was that he had a rare privilege in having Stephanie around to help in the first place. After thinking for a while, he realized another privilege, though, that none of their dark counterparts had: He had five other mages around him who were not afraid to speak their minds and make their own decisions. All those facts were not new to him and he could have cursed himself for the fact that he time and again needed to be reminded of them. In the end, the decision he really had to make was not whether they would help the police officer. The only decisions were if he wanted to bring the topic up with the others and if he wanted to wait until Monday. And those came easy to him. Yes, for sure would he bring it up with the others, and no, when a life was on the line waiting was not an option. Following those decisions he pulled out his cellphone once again and started calling the others, asking them all to join him at the Timestop. When he was through with the calls he made sure to extend Angel's courtesy, having all their favorite drinks ready for them at the table when they arrived.

Half an hour later they were all assembled around the table and Lucas quickly filled them in on the situation and his dilemma.

"If we go through with this, and I am not saying that we should, how would you do it without handing them our secrets on a silver platter?" Darien asked when Lucas was finished.

"There are two people in this that we need to trust for this to have a chance," Lucas replied. "One is Inspector Corben. He already knows some things; if we pull that stunt off he will know even more. The other one is Doctor Tackman. He already knows a lot too; after all, he backed us up when Airmid saved Cougar. What I propose is to have that officer transferred to Luton General and give Tackman a heads-up. But that's hypothetical right now, too. As I said before, I am not sure about this either. And then, it's Airmid who will do the work, so her opinion will count most in this."

"We saved a thief once without spending too much thought on it," Stephanie said. "If I can help that policeman I will. There is no question about it."

"I am with you too," Marcus said. "SO-19 has come to our rescue twice already, and they wouldn't even have this problem right now if it weren't for us in the first place."

"I am on your side as well, Guardian." Jasmin was next. "I would still not hand them artifacts, but saving a life is a no-brainer for me."

"One more gun on our side will never hurt. That's all I will say to that," Cedric added in his usual cold voice.

"Please don't get this wrong now, guys." Darien sounded a little tense.

"I am with you, but I just need to be the voice of opposition for a moment: What you are suggesting is extremely dangerous. It could easily expose us and what's even worse, it could lead to Corben thinking that we will be around whenever something goes wrong and fix it for him. Do you really want that?"

"You have a valid argument here, Professor, and there is not much I can say against it." Lucas sighed. "The exposure is obviously the most risky part of it. And there is really nothing to prevent that. Regarding Corben, you are also right, although I think that we can mitigate this. And then, there still is the fact that they have come to our rescue twice already."

"But that's their job, after all," Darien replied.

"So what are you suggesting then, Professor?" Jasmin asked.

"I am not suggesting anything. As I said, I am with you on the issue. But somebody needs to be the devil's advocate in this. We are all trying to do what feels right here, and although we might have different reasons for having that feeling, we all agree on it. All I want is to ensure that we don't rush into this headlong, without having weighed the consequences as well. After all, we will have to live with them."

"I have heard your argument, Professor, but my mind is set. I am still in favor of helping," Stephanie replied to him first.

"I know that you are right, Professor, but I am not wavering either. That is just a risk we have to take. And maybe in this case it is my risk to take, because if we really have to, I can always change their mind on things," Jasmin seemed even more convinced now than she had been before.

"I know how it feels to be dying. And I know how it feels to be saved. That's why I don't think that it will make the Inspector and his people more reckless in the future. If anything, they will get more cautious. I am still in too," Marcus said.

"You are right that we have different reasons for what we do. And while you somewhat challenged the others, you didn't challenge mine. I consider SO-19 brothers in arms, so one more is always better," Cedric said.

"You are right with all you say, Professor, and somehow every fiber in my body tells me to agree with you and stay as far away from this as we can. But I just can't. I just can't live with myself, knowing that somebody who was there for us, who has fought on our side, is dead and I could have done something to prevent that. I am sorry, I just can't." Lucas' voice was shaking.

"I can't tell you how glad I am that you all stayed with your original opinion." Darien seemed majorly relieved.

"Now I am confused." Jasmin looked at him. "First you argue heaven and earth against us; now you are relieved?"

"I am with you on that, Psycho. I couldn't agree more with all of you, and I believe I have already made that clear before," Darien replied. "This is the only right thing to do, the only way to go if we want to stay true to ourselves. But just as none of you could live with not helping, I could not have lived with running into this blindly. It is hard to be the voice of opposition if you actually aren't opposed to the thing in the first place, but somebody had to voice those concerns. Somebody had to make sure we had considered them beforehand."

"I am tremendously grateful that you took that burden, Professor," Lucas said. "I had the same concerns, but I just couldn't be as detached as you were. Thank you for that."

"Seems that is settled. Can we go ahead with it now?" Marcus asked.

"By all means." Stephanie nodded. "What do we do next, Guardian?"

"First we need to talk to the doctor. If he is not with us on this, the entire show is off," Lucas said. "Then we call Corben. He has to pull off the transfer somehow. And then all our hopes rest on you, Airmid."

"How quickly do you want to move?" Jasmin asked.

"As quickly as we can. The Inspector told me that the doctors have little hope of the guy surviving much longer, so we have no time to waste."

"Then what are we waiting for?" Marcus stood up.

"Airmid, how quickly can you prepare for this?" Lucas asked.

"I am always prepared these days." Stephanie smiled and pulled a flask out of her backpack.

"Very well, then let's do this. Psycho, Airmid, I will need your help at the hospital. For the rest of you, there is not much to do in this."

"We will still be there, just in case something unexpected comes up and you need backup." Darien smiled.

"Very well, let's do it then." Lucas stretched out his fist to the middle of the table, waiting for the others to put their hands on top.

"Brother to brother, yours to the end," they then said in unison.

CHAPTER 6

MIRACLE

When they arrived at Luton General Hospital it was already getting dark outside.

"I just hope that the doctor is still here today," Lucas said.

"If he is, and we want to do all of this tonight, somebody needs to call my parents and come up with a good excuse. Otherwise they will get concerned," Stephanie threw in.

"I guess that goes for most of us," Lucas sighed.

"Don't worry. I will take care of that. At least that keeps me from being completely useless here," Darien grinned.

Lucas left the others a few steps behind and approached the front desk.

"Can I help you?" an obviously bored receptionist asked him.

"I hope so," Lucas replied. "I need to see Dr. Tackman. Can you see if he is in right now?"

"I am sorry, kid, but at this time of day only emergencies are accepted."

"Well, that is exactly what I have at hand here." Lucas was quickly getting annoyed by her bored look and voice.

"Don't make jokes. This is no joke around here."

"I am not joking about anything right now. Could you please find Dr. Tackman for me?" He had raised his voice a little.

"Ok, ok, but don't say that I didn't warn you." She picked up the phone and dialed.

"Hey Jessica, I have a kid here who insists on speaking to Tackman. What shall I tell him?" she said after a few moments. "Hold on, I'll ask," she continued after a short while, before turning to Lucas again. "Who are you again?"

"Just tell the doctor that the goddess of healing is in need of his assistance once again," Lucas replied.

"Really?" The receptionist looked at him as if he was some kind of alien.

"Yeah, really. Can we please stop this game and get moving? I need to speak to the doc."

"Did you hear that?" she said into the phone, followed by some "ahas" and "sures" and other one-word answers to whatever the person on the other end was saying.

"Wait here, someone will pick you up in a minute," she then said and shook her head as she put down the phone.

"Thank you." Lucas bowed a little and took a few steps back.

Looking back, he could see that the others had scattered in the hall so as not to attract too much attention. He first thought about walking over to one of them, but then decided to just stay where he was and wait. He slowly scanned the lobby, trying to be as relaxed as possible in the situation, although given the circumstances, that proved to be very hard to accomplish.

It didn't take much more than a minute before a nurse came walking down a corridor hastily.

"You are the goddess of healing?" she asked as she approached Lucas.

"Let's just say that I am her assistant," he replied.

"I just hope you are not fooling around," she said and started walking back the way she had come, Lucas following next to her. "The doctor has had a long day already and he will not be in the mood for jokes."

"I would never joke about this," Lucas replied coolly.

"Good," the nurse said and opened a door for him. "You can wait in his office then. He will be with you shortly."

He walked past her into the familiar, small office and took a seat on a wooden chair that was placed close to the wall. The nurse closed the door behind him, leaving him sitting there alone. It took about five minutes before the door burst open again and the doctor entered the room. Lucas could see signs of sweat and blood on his white coat, accompanied by an expression on his face that clearly showed fatigue.

"This better be good," he said before even looking at Lucas. When he finally did see him after sitting down in his office chair, he was confused for a second. "I do know you, don't I?" he then asked.

"We met once already, yes. The circumstances were not exactly fun then either."

"They rarely are when people walk into my office." The doctor sighed. "So let's get it over with, please. I am tired. What sort of freak am I getting this time?"

"The 'freak' in question would be a police officer," Lucas started explaining. "To be precise, a member of the SO-19 armed response unit."

"Oh." Tackman's expression changed immediately from exhaustion to concern. "How bad is it?"

"Bad. The doctors in London are predicting little chance of survival. And I honestly don't even know if we can fix the damage that has been done."

"Well, we all certainly appreciate you trying." The doctor rubbed his eyes. "What do you need from me?"

"Actually, not much. When Inspector Corben brings him in, please just ensure that he gets admitted and we can get access to him. We'll handle everything from there."

"All right, I can do that, I guess." He nodded. "Is that officer one of your people?"

"No." Lucas shook his head.

"Then why would you care?" Tackman seemed confused. "Don't get me wrong," he continued, "I appreciate your help in such situations. I have just never seen any outsider being rescued by your group."

"Well, this man might not be one of us, doc, but he is to a certain extent in this bad situation because of us," Lucas said.

"Forgive me for being direct, but that has not stopped you freaks from ignoring such people before. And leaving me and my people with a mess to clean up."

"There is little I can say in defense of the people on my side of the line; you are absolutely right. Many of those 'freaks', as you call them, have quite an interesting way of looking at things. But then, so do a lot of 'normal' people as well. They tend to not help either."

"I grant you that." Tackman nodded. "But you didn't answer my question. Why do you care?"

"We all have our reasons, doc." Lucas turned his head, looking out the window. "For me, personally, I could not have looked in the mirror anymore if I hadn't at least tried everything in my power to save that man.

After all, he does put his life on the line for all of us every day. We owe him that much."

"Amen to that..." Tackman leaned back in his chair. "So when do you expect him to arrive?" he asked.

"I don't know yet," Lucas had to admit. "I wanted to talk to you first to avoid confusion. As soon as the details are worked out, you will be the first to know."

"Tell Jessica first, please. I will brief her and then get some sleep. Seems we could be looking at a long night..."

"Let's hope not." Lucas stood up and walked to the door. "Thank you, Doctor."

He then walked out and headed back to the lobby. Without stopping, he flashed a quick thumbs-up to the others and stepped outside the building, grabbing his cellphone. He quickly dialed Corben's number and waited.

"Good evening, Mr. Trent."

"Good evening, Inspector," Lucas replied, trying to sound as calm as possible.

"How can I help you?"

"I am sure that I will very soon regret having made this call." He sighed. "This time I can maybe help you."

"This time?" Corben laughed. "You have helped us a lot already. But please, go ahead."

"Let me get right to the point: Can you have your injured officer moved to another hospital without questions being asked?"

"Maybe. Why?"

"Maybe isn't good enough, Inspector. Can you get it done or not?"

"Yes, I can. It will not be easy, but there is a way. Why?"

"I can't promise you anything. But let's just say that his chances of survival might increase significantly if he gets there in time."

"I will gladly take any straw you can hand me. Unfortunately, nothing short of a miracle will make a difference in the end anyway."

"In that case you better hurry up. And pray for that miracle while you are at it."

"I'll get right to it. Where do I need to get him to?"

"Luton General. Doctor Tackman will be expecting you."

"I don't know what you are up to, or why, but thank you."

"Don't thank me just yet. I still don't know if the effort will do any good in the end. Oh, and please let me know beforehand when you will arrive."

Lucas hung up and walked back into the lobby. Now all he could do was wait.

It took about twenty minutes before the Inspector informed Lucas of his arrival time and another half hour after that before they finally brought the wounded officer in. He and the others tried to remain out of view and waited for Doctor Tackman to prepare everything for them. It was an agonizing time for all of them, especially for Stephanie, who was eager to get to work. When Tackman finally showed up with the examination results, his face clearly showed the bad news.

"The patient is almost dead," he said and handed the file over to Stephanie. "Most of his skin is burned, he is suffering from severe blood poisoning, many of his internal organs are already damaged beyond repair, and if none of that kills him first, the pain medication for sure will."

"I am not sure how much I can do for him, Guardian," Stephanie said without looking up from the file, her voice sounding a little shaky. "The doctor is right; there is excessive damage to almost all layers of his body."

"The patient is in room 153. Let me know if I can do anything to help," Tackman said and walked out.

"Do the best you can, Airmid. And let us know if we can do anything to help."

"You will need to do a lot here," she replied with a sudden change in her face. She was totally calm now, fully focused, and her voice was firm. "This will take at least four of us to even have a remote chance of keeping him alive."

Lucas took a quick look at Jasmin, who just shook her head in reply. They knew Stephanie's second personality well by now, but so far it had rarely come out without Jasmin giving it a little bump.

"All right then. What's the plan?" Lucas asked, relieved to have this part of her on the other side of the conversation.

"There are four parts to this, and we somehow need to fix all of them at once," she explained. "I can most likely clear the blood and repair the organ damage with a spell, but the skin damage is too severe for that. I can only work with my potion there. Unfortunately, we can only do this slowly; otherwise he will die from pain. And even more unfortunately, much of the poison in the blood is produced by the skin right now, so unless we fix that everything else will not matter. Oh, and of course, we need to get him off those painkillers before they completely destroy his body."

"What can we do to help?" Lucas asked again.

"You need to stop the poison in the skin. I will need some kind of a filtering shield; can you do that?"

"I will do my best. But I need a pattern to filter by." He nodded.

"Yes, of course. Professor, that's where you come in."

"Got it." Darien nodded.

"Psycho, you need to block his pain somehow. And trust me, it will be far more pain than anyone was ever in before."

"I will do my best." Jasmin nodded too.

"Cougar, Whirlwind, if Psycho fails to stop the pain completely, you need to make sure that our patient doesn't move too much."

"Aye, Sir." Marcus saluted.

"All right, then." Lucas looked at each one of them. "Let's work a miracle."

When they set off toward room 153, they made for a strange sight, Stephanie leading the pack with the file in hand and the others following behind her in a row, almost like a military unit on the way to combat. They didn't talk, didn't look left or right, no emotion was visible on their faces, just the pure dedication of a team on a mission. The corridors were all deserted; for them it almost felt like walking through a ghost town. When they entered the room they were all shocked for a moment, except for Stephanie, who still showed no emotion whatsoever. The police officer was lying on the bed, completely covered with bandages, multiple infusions hanging next to him and a lot of screens showing different vital signs. Stephanie took a quick look at the labels of the infusion bottles and then scanned through the vital signs. Lucas was amazed watching her. Once again she showed her skills in the field of medicine, working through the information like a seasoned physician would. It was almost surreal for him, watching that little girl outgrow herself time and again in such situations. Stephanie had already walked around the bed and prepared everything she needed before the others had even come out of their shock.

"No time to waste. Let's go," she said calmly and uncorked a bottle of healing potion.

What happened next closely resembled a seasoned veteran surgeon with his best team of aides. Her calmness brought the others out of their paralyzed state quickly and played a tremendous part in helping them focus, even though she didn't even notice them at that moment. Stephanie was standing in the center of it all, giving orders to all the others while working on the patient herself. They started off with Stephanie stopping most of the medication flows to the policeman's body and Marcus and Cedric cutting open some bandages. The sight they uncovered was horrifying. The uncovered areas looked less like a human body than a piece of charcoal. Lucas had to gasp for air when he first laid his eyes on the burnt face. He couldn't believe that someone in this condition could still be alive.

"Do your thing, Psycho," Stephanie said without looking up.

Jasmin immediately reacted and started focusing on the wounded police officer. Lucas could see the expression of pain on the burned face even as the magic started kicking in. He knew Jasmin's skills all too well from their own past experiences. Seeing now that no matter how hard she was working there still was pain in the policeman's body just was another grim reminder for him of how bad the situation really was. And it also was a wakeup call for him, showing him bluntly where the limits of their skills were. He would have loved to help her, share some energy with her, but unfortunately he also had a task at hand, and his was little easier than hers. With Darien's supervision he started testing shield patterns, trying to identify the best possible solution for blocking the poison. The biggest problem the boys faced, though, was that even with Darien's amazing skills, it was nearly impossible to identify what was poison and what was not, which made the already-hard task of designing a partially permeable shield even harder, as he had no clear indication of what to let through and what to block. While they struggled, Stephanie was ferociously running up and down the body, applying healing potion, mumbling things that almost sounded to the others like tiny spells and constantly monitoring the vital signs on the monitors while she was at it. Her pace was almost superhuman, reminding Lucas of moves he had only seen from Marcus so far, and even then only under the influence of magic.

"A mesh will not work, Guardian," Darien said, focusing on a spot where Lucas was trying out his shields. "Some of the particles we need to get out of the system are smaller than the blood cells."

"I am open to suggestions, Professor," Lucas replied, constantly trying to rebuild the shield matrix.

"Can you build some sort of pattern recognition into the shield?"

"I have no idea how I should do that. Shields don't work like that." Lucas shook his head.

"Then let's try a two stage approach here," Darien suggested. "Build a large mesh shield on top to filter out the larger particles and then build a very fine mesh shield below to only have the small things go through. With that the good stuff should be left clean in the middle."

Lucas nodded and pushed himself even harder, trying to work Darien's pattern.

"It's no good," Darien sighed in frustration. "All that gives us is clotting."

"Can't you use your repulsor spell instead of a shield here?" Marcus suggested while handing a clamp to Stephanie. "Somehow push the poison particles away?"

"That's actually a great idea, Cougar." Lucas almost smiled through the pained expression on his face. "I most likely can't use the Repellum, but I did manage to build an energy draining shield not too long ago; maybe I can come up with a poison magnet of sorts..."

Together with Darien he immediately started putting his new idea to the test. It proved to be a huge effort to do and even then it only worked partially, but it was the best result so far. He tried hard to focus and build up as much energy as possible for the full body application of the spell, but he felt the strain on his system by now too. He was almost at the point of calling it, when he heard a fatigued voice from the side.

"I can't hold this any longer. Whatever you want to do, you need to do it now, Airmid," Jasmin wheezed.

"Professor, how does the shield look?" Stephanie reacted almost instantly, shifting her focus away from what she had been doing before.

"Not good. We can filter most of the poison out now, but unfortunately the charm combination will also filter other stuff out, so there might be major side effects to it."

"Can't be helped; we are running out of time. Guardian, whatever you have, fire it up."

"Roger that," Lucas responded through his heavy breathing and started projecting his latest shield-magnet charm combination onto the entire body.

"Here it comes..." Stephanie stretched her hands out, holding them a few centimeters above the patient's body. "Stop your magic, Psycho; it's now or never."

Jasmin nodded, closed her eyes for a moment, and then sank to the ground. At the same moment an unnatural, vibrating voice came out of Stephanie's mouth.

"BALSAM MEDELA," she shouted and for a moment Lucas could actually see streams of white and yellow energy flowing from her fingertips into the policeman's body. Her body was vibrating wildly as she shot burst after burst of that healing force into the burnt body, with her face getting paler and paler with every passing second. After a short while the flow stopped and Stephanie sank to the ground, trembling in exhaustion.

Then a moment of silence followed, with only the heavy breathing of Jasmin, Stephanie and Lucas audible in the room. Darien, Marcus and Cedric were standing ready, waiting for a cry of pain, but nothing happened. Almost a minute passed with all of them eagerly watching their patient before they could finally see a reaction. His heart rate was slowly climbing and tears had started rolling from his still-bandaged eyes.

"What's happening?" Marcus almost whispered.

"He is in agony," Jasmin replied, slowly pulling herself up from the floor. "I don't know how he can even stand that amount of pain."

"Is there nothing we can do to ease his suffering?" Lucas looked at him.

"Unfortunately not." Stephanie shook her head slowly, still lying on the ground, only half-conscious. "He has to fight through that pain on his own. If he can do that, he will most likely survive."

"We should let him rest then," Lucas suggested.

"Yes we should." Stephanie nodded while standing up. "But first we need to close the bandages."

"How do you want to do that? Replace them all?" Lucas asked.

"No. Most of the surface wounds will start closing soon, so there is little point in doing that. Besides, it would mean that we have to move his body a lot, and we should avoid that if possible," she replied. "We have cut everything open cleanly, so we should be able to just patch them closed, maybe with some extensions here and there."

Lucas stepped back when he saw that Stephanie was already starting to work with the help of Marcus and Cedric. He was completely exhausted from the procedure and had to fight hard not to fall asleep on the spot. Leaning against a wall, he just watched with a faint smile. He didn't know if their huge effort had had any real impact, but he felt glad that they had given it their best. When Stephanie was finally done she led the others out of the room, turning off the lights as she passed by the switch. "Sleep well, be strong," she said to the officer and then closed the door behind her. Lucas was sure that he could still hear the patient moaning in pain even when they were already a good distance away from the room.

"Now all that's left to do is inform Doctor Tackman. And then we wait," Stephanie addressed the others as they were walking down the corridor.

"How long will it take before we know the verdict?" Marcus asked.

"A day or two, I would say." Stephanie shrugged her shoulders. "But I honestly can't tell. I have never done anything that extensive."

"Then let us get an update after the weekend. And keep our fingers crossed until then," Lucas suggested.

The others nodded silently before they parted ways. Lucas and Stephanie quickly filled in the doctor while the rest of the group was already heading out. After that they too were happy to be on their way, and so, it seemed, was the doctor. It had been a rough day for all of them, and they all desperately needed some sleep.

CHAPTER 7

POWER

When Lucas was on his way to the cinema the following Saturday, he could still feel the drain from the hospital experience. He knew that his energy levels were all back up to full capacity, but somehow the evening had left a deeper mark on him. Knowing that he would be meeting Kung Fu shortly raised his spirits a little, but even that was not capable of lifting the dark shadow completely. His thoughts kept racing around the whole time, wondering if they had done the right thing exposing themselves like that, wondering if they had made a difference and trying to understand why this obviously noble move would not let go of him for such a long time. He knew that part of it was the uncertainty that he was still in, but he had the feeling that there was something more at work here, something he couldn't quite put his finger on. He sighed when he got off his bike and walked into the building complex.

"Hey stranger." Sandra's voice almost made him jump. She had been standing in a corner, out of view from the entrance.

"Hi beautiful." Lucas tried to smile while giving her a welcoming kiss.

"What's up with you?" She gently pushed him back a little and looked right at him. "You look spooked."

"Is it that obvious?" Lucas sighed once again.

"At least to me it is," she nodded.

Lucas took a quick look around before walking with her to the other end of the hall, where he was convinced that they could talk without anyone else listening in. He then told her the entire story, including his second visit to the prison, as well as their hospital endeavor, of course.

"That is quite a story you have gotten yourself into there, Guardian." Sandra was stunned. "I will keep my fingers crossed for that officer."

"It is a never-ending story unfortunately," Lucas replied. "We were so sure that this chapter was over, but it always comes back to bite us. Not to mention that it also gets worse with every day that passes by."

"That seems to be the problem with these kinds of power struggles... They never go away; they only change appearances. I can see this almost every day in school, with the little gangs that form there in the classes. As soon as you dissolve one, somebody else will rise into the power vacuum that the last one left behind."

"And what's the solution to it, then?" Lucas asked.

"I wish that I had one. So far the only thing I could find was to fill the void myself, depriving the potential candidates of their space to maneuver beforehand. But that is very time- and energy-intensive. It is also not always achievable to begin with, unfortunately."

"That's not exactly a great perspective for the future you are offering me here, Kung Fu. On the contrary, if you are right, then that's very depressing."

"I fully agree." She nodded. "But that's all I have to offer. Sorry."

Lucas nodded silently, looking past her out the window, his thoughts wandering around.

"Hey, would you like to postpone the movie?" Sandra asked after over a minute of silence. "It seems that you could need the rest."

"I got some rest last night and it didn't really help. I think what I need more than that is distraction," Lucas answered. "And the one thing I definitely don't need right now is to be alone. So unless you are about to ditch me for bringing my problems to our date, I would really appreciate spending the afternoon with you."

"Having an open ear for problems is what friends are for, so even the idea of me ditching you for that is insulting. You better get that out of your head before I beat it out of there for you." She smiled and gave him a long, intense hug. "And now, let's go get tickets and popcorn, before we grow roots here."

Sandra locked her arm under his and started walking toward the counter, giving him no time to object and no other option than to walk with her. As they walked along, Lucas' mind started to ease up noticeably. He still could not fully comprehend this relationship with her and the effect it had on him, but right now he was happier than ever before that she was there, and that just having her close allowed him to draw fresh energy. By the time they had sat down in the theater he was already cheerful again, having all his problems shut out at least for a little while. The movie itself proved to be an additional distraction, with both him and Sandra enjoying it to the fullest. In fact, he enjoyed it so much that it was half an hour before he realized that they had been cuddling across the theater chairs in a quite uncomfortable position. For a moment he thought about sitting back up, but quickly decided against it. The joy of her being close seemed overwhelming compared to the discomfort of his awkward body position. So instead he laid his arm around her shoulder and pushed himself even closer to her.

After the movie they walked out of the building in the same tight hug they had maintained throughout the entire show. It was only then that Lucas started feeling the pain that the chair's armrest had caused.

"It seems that I am too old for this," Lucas said and rubbed his side.

"You are too old?" Sandra laughed loudly. "You are just weak, it seems. Do you hear me complaining? But hey, if that was too much to take for you, we can skip that part next time."

"Just because you are super woman doesn't mean that I am weak." Lucas gave her a friendly punch in the shoulder. "But maybe I should sit in your lap next time. That would certainly help avoid this."

"Me sitting in your lap would make more sense, don't you think?" she winked at him.

"Sure." He laughed after figuring out what she was aiming at. "But not in a movie theater that is filled to the brink, don't you think?"

"Why? Are you shy?"

"Yeah, a little..." Lucas said. "Aren't you?"

"Depends..."

"On what?"

"The opportunity, I guess." She grinned. "I would rather overcome my shyness than miss a once-in-a-lifetime chance."

"Did you just call me a once-in-a-lifetime chance?"

"Maybe..."

"Pah..." he said, trying to look insulted, and pushed her away.

"Hey, what's that all about?" She stopped and turned toward him. "I offer you a compliment and you push me away."

"Interesting compliment." Lucas still had his offended face on, but his voice conveyed clearly that it was only for show.

"Why's that?"

"A once-in-a-lifetime opportunity would mean that after taking it you would never have it again. And that implication is not exactly a compliment, don't you think?"

"I did not mean it THAT way." Sandra turned red. "I only meant..."

"I know." Lucas grinned and gave her a hug.

"You are impossible." Sandra now gave him a punch on the shoulder.

They walked on, continuing their back and forth jokes until reaching her car.

"So what do we do now?" Lucas asked.

"Whatever you like."

"I am not exactly very experienced at this... So maybe you can help me out a little bit and at least tell me what you would like?"

"I am not sure if I understand what 'this' means." Sandra laughed. "But if it's all the same to you, why don't we take a walk in the park? It should be fairly quiet there right now."

"Sounds good." Lucas nodded.

It quickly became clear that Sandra had been right with her assumption. The park was only lightly populated, giving them enough space to be almost alone. Still, there seemed to be someone around all the time, so they never had complete privacy. After a while Lucas started wondering if that had been intentional--if it was her way of keeping a little safe distance, or if it was just coincidence. For him it made little difference in the end. He still had no idea how to proceed in their relationship anyway, so taking it slowly was to a certain extent welcome for him. He was happy being with her and while taking walks in the park was not exactly his standard evening routine, he really enjoyed the time they spent there. And so the hours passed by with them wandering the area, chatting, joking, kissing and sometimes just being close and silent.

"You know, I would love to invite you to come home with me tonight," Sandra said around 10 p.m. "But there is a matter I have to attend to early tomorrow morning, and I don't want to be the one responsible for you losing your Sunday sleep."

"I am not sure if I want to let you use my Sunday sleep as an excuse here..." Lucas grinned. "But I do agree that it is better for both of us to go home separately. I don't like leaving you, but I would like it even less to have SO-19 storming your place because my parents reported me missing. But then, maybe I should also start thinking about the pros and cons of those once-in-a-lifetime opportunities." He winked at her.

"I think you can skip that part, at least in this instance. This will definitely not be a once-only opportunity."

"I will take you up on that promise, for sure." He gave her an intense kiss. "But now I will let you leave. I couldn't in good conscience accept being the reason for you oversleeping."

After some more intense goodbyes he watched her get into her car and drive off before he finally took his bike and started his journey home himself. The mild breeze and the total silence along the way let the other parts of his life trickle into his thoughts again slowly. But even the horrors of the hospital could not bring down his mood anymore. At least for tonight, in Lucas' eyes the world was a good place to be.

When Lucas was heading toward the shack on Monday evening, his mind was still to a great extent focused on the police officer at Luton General. Stephanie had been there to visit him the day before, but it had been too early to tell for sure, so the tension was still high. The one thing that did give Lucas some comfort was the fact that the man was still alive, which at least showed that their intervention had had a positive effect. The other side of the story, though, was that it had prolonged the pain for the patient as well, and besides that, there still was the exposure that Lucas and the others had opened themselves up to. Weighing all that still left him unsure if the decision he had made had been the right one after all. But no matter how he spun his thoughts, one thing remained clear at all times: The decision had been made, the action had been taken, and there was no turning back now. So he just hoped that Stephanie would come bearing good news today. Unfortunately for him, it was still too early, though, even after almost three days now.

"I visited the patient with Dr. Tackman just before I came here," Stephanie said when they were all sitting around the wooden table. "They are still keeping the bandages on mostly and have a lot more tests to run before we know how much damage will remain permanently. What we know so far is not encouraging, though. He is scheduled for surgery tomorrow because of a fracture in his arm that we seem to have missed.

Additionally, he is still in pain and might have to live with that for quite a while."

"Are they giving him medication for this?" Marcus asked.

"No." Stephanie shook her head. "They still don't know how much internal damage his body has. Giving him pain medication at this point would put him at risk, especially given the amount of meds they had given him in London before our intervention."

"Is there anything we can do?" Jasmin jumped in.

"Short of doing another full-blown magical session, I doubt that there is any option for us," Stephanie said. "As much as I hate to admit it, at this point our best course of action is most likely to just step back and wait. Hopefully we will know more soon."

"Let's all keep our fingers crossed then," Lucas said.

A minute of silence followed, as they looked at each other.

"If you don't mind, I would like to change the topic." Darien finally ended the awkward moment.

"By all means please do," Marcus replied.

"Well, actually it is still somewhat related," Darien started. "I tried to keep my ears open at HRC and see if there was anything that could help us make any sense of the prison break attempt."

"And what did you find?" Jasmin interrupted him eagerly.

"There are a lot of things going on in parallel right now, and I am still not sure what to make of them. We are still pushing extremely hard to get the crystal power plant running, although a lot of our managers are convinced that it will never be cost effective, because of the complexity of the process. And that's even without them realizing that there is a major flaw in their experiments."

"What's that?" Lucas was curious.

"Well, it's about the crystals," Darien continued. "We just got another bunch of them delivered, and they vary so extremely in quality that most of their measurements are totally invalid."

"Don't they see this quality problem?" Lucas was baffled now.

"How could they?" Darien looked at him. "The crystals are magical in origin. I doubt anyone even understands those things, let alone would be able to get solid data. And I can hardly speak up on that now, can I?"

"Fair point." Lucas nodded. "Where are they getting those crystals from anyway?"

"I have no idea." Darien shrugged. "Jackson's Logistics Company is delivering them. I have so far not been able to get hold of the paperwork."

"Weird..." Lucas said.

"Yeah. The project is weird all the way around." Darien nodded. "And it is being pushed so hard that HRC is cutting corners in other areas, delivering really sloppy results these days."

"What do you mean?" Marcus asked.

"There are a lot of environmental studies going on right now, much of them still coming as the aftermath of the potion incident in the woods, but a lot also coming in from other areas and even internationally. Such studies are the bread and butter of HRC; that's what they are good at normally. But at the moment I hear a lot of chatter internally saying that reports are finished prematurely, based on half-ass data at best."

"So they are trying to hide the problems?" Lucas asked.

"That's the weird part... They are not." Darien shook his head. "On the contrary, they seem to overstate a lot of the problems. The scientists think that someone upstairs is just trying to be cautious, but I am under the impression that there is more to it than that. It almost looks systematic."

"That's certainly weird." Lucas nodded. "Why would they want to do that?"

"I have no idea. All I can tell you right now is that people are becoming unhappy on both ends," Darien said.

"So where does this leave us? Or Cleric?" Stephanie asked.

"I have no idea," Lucas answered. "It still makes no sense. But my guess would be that they are somehow involved in those crystals. It's the only direction I can see so far that could actually have an endgame."

"And what would that be?" Darien asked. "If this product is financially unviable there is little point in pushing it, don't you think?"

"Unless causing those ecological problems is meant to drive the rest of the power production industry into even higher cost, blaming the effects on them and forcing the government to push new measures on them," Lucas suggested. "In combination with the unrest in Libya, the revolt in Egypt and the sanctions against Iran, which are already leaving the fossil fuel market in an unstable state, it could make a huge impact that will put this whole thing in a different light for alternative energy solutions."

"Bold statement, mate," Darien said. "And it has two tiny problems attached to it: For one, the crystal thingy still is not sustainable unless you have a factory full of mages. So the endgame there can only be a quick gain, which hardly seems worth the effort. And for the other, if they push back on fossil fuels, as you are suggesting, people will just look more favorably toward nuclear energy again. After all, the greenhouse effect doesn't really apply there..."

"You are right, as always." Lucas sighed. "But unfortunately there is nothing else I can think of. And we have nothing more to go on than that."

"Oh, actually we do." Darien grinned and started searching through his backpack. "Here we go," he said a minute later, putting a fist-sized, dark blue stone on the table.

"What is that?" Marcus immediately picked it up and looked at it closely. It didn't look like much and could have just been any regular stone picked up from the ground, if it weren't for the blue color that seemed out of place.

"That's one of the energy crystals," Darien explained. "They considered it broken after some tests and threw it away. I took the liberty of taking it with me."

"May I have a look?" Jasmin suddenly asked with a strange look on her face.

"Sure." Marcus nodded and handed the crystal over.

"What is it, Psycho?" Lucas had noticed her spiked interest.

A long moment of silence followed, with Jasmin turning the stone in her hand and inspecting it very closely.

"I have seen one of those before," she finally said.

"Where?" Lucas and Darien said almost at the same time.

"In a forest outside of High Wycombe."

"What were you doing there? And how come this stone stood out enough for you to recognize it again?" Lucas was curious.

"Well, first of all because it was not one stone; it was a pile of them," Jasmin said. "And it did not stand out to me, but to the youngsters I am mentoring. They picked them up after a confrontation with another circle there."

"Come again?" Lucas was not sure which topic to jump on first, the fact that she knew about the crystals, the fact that she had witnessed a magical fight, the fact that she was mentoring another circle, or the fact that she had not mentioned any of this to them thus far.

"When did you become a mentor?" Stephanie seemed amazed by the fact, and from their faces so were all the others.

"A little while ago," she answered. "It's a quite interesting experience, I have to say."

"And why didn't you tell us?" Marcus was curious.

"Well, because I am still not sure how to handle the whole situation." She sighed. "I have to protect the circle's privacy; that's my first priority there. And quite frankly, so far they have not done much that would have been interesting enough to tell you in the first place."

"A fight between two circles is not interesting? Interesting way to look at it," Marcus replied.

"There was no magic involved, so it was nothing more than a semi-violent conflict. I am certain that you witness things like that as well from time to time. And I had no clue about the stones at that point, either."

"Magical crystals. In a struggle without magic. Interesting combination." Darien looked at her.

"But not unfeasible," Lucas jumped in. "If your guys can't do magic yet, Psycho, and the others were specifically trained to do only one kind of magic, that being the creation of the crystals, then a fight would not be magical, as both sides lack the means for it."

"Interesting theory." Darien nodded.

"And here comes your factory full of mages," Marcus threw in. "If they really are able to train adepts to learn specific spells."

"Which would also explain why the quality is so unpredictable. They are still learning," Lucas said.

"Then we finally know what their endgame is." Darien looked at Lucas.

"I am not convinced yet." Lucas shook his head, looking back at Darien. "There is still your argument with nuclear power, and in the end you also need to have a way to keep this production up, which will prove incredibly difficult for them. But at least the possibility is open again."

"Right now it's all guesswork anyway." Darien sighed. "I will keep my ears open. Let's see what comes up."

"So Psycho, how did you end up becoming a Mentor?" Stephanie changed the subject, as it seemed that nobody wanted to add anything more to the discussion.

"That was quite interesting, actually," Jasmin replied, still playing with the blue stone in her hand. "I was at an esoteric exhibition in London a while back. One guy there was selling herbs and potions. Nothing serious, I guess, mostly old natural recipes that have been around for ages. One thing seemed off, though, which is why I was interested in the first place: He had one pack of herbs lying there, almost in the center of the table, that according to the sign was not useful at all. Still, that one pack was held together by some sort of bracelet with a shiny, nacre stone worked into it."

"Odd... The bracelet would be worth more than the herbs. Unless of course there was something more to that pack," Darien said.

"Yes, I thought so too; that's why I asked him about those, and also if he was willing to sell the bracelet. His reaction was quite weird. He had no intention of selling it, but handed it to me anyway to get a good look. And while I was holding it he was watching my hands constantly, as if he was afraid that I might switch it out or something."

"That's odd." Stephanie was fascinated.

"The really odd part came when I handed it back. He then suddenly smiled at me and said 'Ah, so you are one of us after all.' I was totally stunned by that statement." Jasmin paused for a moment before continuing. "Then he basically asked me if I was interested in being a Mentor. And that's that." She grinned.

"Who was the guy?" Marcus seemed fascinated by the story too.

"He goes by the name Ranger," Jasmin said. "He said that he is some sort of coordinator for Mentors in the London area."

"So he knows Angel then?" Stephanie asked.

"I honestly can't tell," Jasmin replied. "I have not asked him."

"You are awfully quiet, Guardian," Darien suddenly addressed Lucas. "What is it?"

"Nothing," Lucas quickly answered, caught completely off guard by the question. He had remembered Ranger from the Magus Major meeting, and he also was pretty sure that he knew what the bracelet actually was all about, but he could hardly tell the others. "The council made a great choice approaching you for mentoring, Psycho. Congratulations."

"Approaching me?" Jasmin looked at him. "I approached him."

"Do you really think this was a coincidence?" Lucas looked at her.

"Are you saying that it was staged?"

"No, Psycho, not staged, but carefully planned, I would say. You do recognize details, which is what brought you there in the first place," Lucas said. "And that's the first thing a good Mentor needs in order to follow the progress of a group. We all know that by now. But anyway, my statement stands: You are the perfect choice for that job."

"I am honored by your confidence, Guardian. I wish I saw it that way too."

Lucas just smiled at her, without answering that statement.

"Can we now have a closer look at that crystal?" she asked after an awkward moment of silence, handing the stone to Darien.

"What do you want to know about it?" he asked, putting it down on the table.

"Well, you are the analytical mastermind in our group," Jasmin replied. "You tell me."

"Can you find out if this thing has a 'hidden agenda', like the potion in Buxton did?" Lucas asked.

"Interesting question." Darien nodded. "Can do."

Darien picked up the stone, holding it up with both hands right in front of his face. He then started humming a weird, low frequency melody and fell into a deep trance. Lucas was watching him curiously. He had never seen Darien in a state like this before. Darien's humming changed its pitch time and again for a few minutes before it finally stabilized. Lucas watched carefully, still fascinated by Darien's focus. It looked to him as if Darien's hum was tuned in to the frequency of the stone, almost as if the stone had started vibrating in his hands due to it. Then, after what seemed to be ages of constant, motionless staring Darien finally made a move.

"Explorare Magica," he said in a totally calm, slow voice.

Then his eyes started moving around rapidly, jumping from one spot on the stone to another in a totally random pattern. Another five minutes passed, with Darien's eyes being the only thing moving in the shack at all, before he finally exhaled noticeably and put the stone back on the table.

"Holy shit," Marcus said. "I have never seen you like that before, Professor."

"That was a new one for sure." Lucas nodded.

"Just a little evolution of my previous spell," Darien laughed. "At some point I had to start doing something better, don't you think? After all, you do that all the time."

"So what's the verdict?" Jasmin looked at him eagerly.

"Nothing much to say, unfortunately." Darien's face turned serious again in an instant. "The crystal is an energy store, magically crafted almost from scratch, it seems."

"Energy store? Like the weird potion?" Marcus asked.

"No, not like that. At least not exactly." Darien shook his head. "The potion is built to enhance the magical capabilities of the user. The energy stored in the crystal is not meant for enhancing magic. It's meant to produce electric power."

"Like a battery?" Jasmin had picked up the stone.

"More like a fuel rod," Darien explained.

"What's the difference there?" Marcus looked confused.

"A battery is a container that stores the energy. When you drain the energy from it, the container still stays more or less intact. A fuel rod gets consumed when drained. Or at least significantly altered.

"So you are saying that they have to burn that thing in order to get the energy out? Wouldn't that be just as bad as burning any other kind of fuel?" Marcus said.

"Not every release of energy is based on oxidation, Cougar," Darien laughed. "And although I am not sure exactly how the process is supposed to work, my guess would be that there will be little left over after the 'burning' of that fuel. And whatever is left over will most likely not be exactly toxic. But then, that's just an educated guess."

"What exactly is this thing made of?" Lucas had taken the stone, now examining it closely.

"It has many of the plants in it that Eagle used for the potion, some sort of clay, copper and some other metals that I can't clearly identify. Plus salt and a lot of hydrogen, so there most likely is also some sea water in the mix."

"No granite or anything like that? How did they end up getting a stone to form out of it?"

"Interesting question indeed, Guardian," Darien said. "I would assume that the stony shell results from the clay being burnt, but there is most likely more to it than meets the eye."

"Do you see any hidden agenda in the crystal?" Lucas asked.

"No. If there is something else to that thing then they hid it much better than they did in the potion." Darien shook his head.

"So this thing really is a solution to the world's energy problems then--is that what you are saying?" Stephanie was pointing at the crystal that Lucas was still holding in his hand. "No waste, no hidden agenda, and almost unlimited availability, as long as you can get the manufacturing right."

"If you put it that way..." Darien thought for a moment before continuing. "Yes. That's what it seems to imply."

"Well... Is it just me, or does anyone else in here have a hard time believing that?"

"You are right, Airmid." Lucas nodded. "Where is the catch here?"

"Well, for starters it seems that harnessing that energy is not exactly trivial. After all, the HRC experts have still not figured it out," Darien said. "Plus we still don't know how much energy you can actually get from one stone, and in comparison, how much energy would be necessary to make one."

"The first seems to be a technical problem only," Jasmin said. "That would still keep the idea noble and worth pursuing. That by itself seems farfetched coming from those people."

"Yeah, and the energy balance problem would maybe make this fraud, which would fit better into the picture, but would also make this totally useless and a waste of time." Darien nodded. "And I doubt that anyone in their right mind would do that."

"We are talking about Cleric here. He has never been in his right mind." Marcus grinned.

"But the Professor is right," Lucas said. "We are still missing something here. This is currently either too good to be true or too stupid even for them."

"Professor, could we harness the energy from that crystal using magic?" Stephanie asked.

"Interesting question." Darien started thinking again. "Right now I wouldn't know how to do it, but it might be worth trying."

"Then let's do it," Lucas suggested. "Any ideas where to start?"

"As with all fuels, I would suppose that we need to jumpstart some sort of chain reaction," Darien said. "But the only suggestion I would have toward that would be to push some additional energy in and hope that we push the crystal structure over the threshold with that."

"How should we set this up? Just leave the crystal lying here and push?" Marcus asked.

"We should build some sort of rig to hold the crystal in place," Darien said. "And we should have at least some kind of safety net around it."

"And what would that look like, Professor?" Lucas asked.

"Well, I don't exactly know," Darien said. "But as we are trying to generate electricity here, I would suggest we put some metal spikes into the ground around the crystal, to act as lightning rods, just in case we really manage to get this going."

"OK then, let's do it," Lucas said and stood up.

The others nodded and followed him outside, Darien picking the stone up as he left the table. They decided to use the fireplace as their center point, as it was pretty isolated within the area already. They quickly started gathering material, Marcus and Jasmin centering around getting wooden sticks and cords to build up the rig while Stephanie and Cedric looked for leftover nails, metal rods and similar stuff to build the protective surrounding. In the meantime, Darien and Lucas removed everything flammable from the proximity of the fireplace, creating a five-meter perimeter. The construction ended up looking quite weird from an outsider's perspective. The wooden frame they had built looked almost like a box on stilts, with cords holding the crystal in place in the middle, strapped to each corner of it. In addition to that, Darien had decided to run wires from the crystal to the metal spikes, and also to connect the spikes themselves to each other to form a circle. He was convinced that this would further reduce the risk of an uncontrolled electrical discharge. On the other hand, it meant that they would have to rely on his magical eyes to see any success, as having the crystal now wired directly to a grounding spike meant that there was little to no chance anymore to see a spark or lightning discharge from the crystal to the ground. But they all agreed that safety had to come first.

"Now, how do we jumpstart this?" Marcus asked.

The others remained silent, first looking at each other randomly, hoping that somebody would come up with an answer, then all ending up focusing on Lucas.

"I have no idea," Lucas finally had to admit.

"Can't you just push an energy shield into the middle of the crystal? Maybe that does the trick," Marcus suggested after another agonizing period of silence.

"Sure can." Lucas nodded and starting focusing on the stone. "Are you ready?" he then asked, addressing Darien without looking at him.

"Always." Darien nodded.

"Then let's get this going," Lucas said and increased his concentration. "Seperatio," he finally said in a calm, quiet voice.

The others eagerly watched the crystal, looking for any kind of reaction, but it quickly became apparent that nothing whatsoever was going to happen.

"Your energy doesn't interact with the structure of the crystal," Darien analyzed. "We need something more aggressive here."

"Hey Whirlwind, how about your counter-spinning tornados? Could you fire those into the stone?" Lucas asked, causing the others to feel cold shivers running down their spines. Cedric had come up with that idea a while ago and had tested it on Lucas back then. The idea had been to let two tornados spin below the skin of a person, causing massive pain in the process. It still was one of the darkest spells they had in their arsenal, and one that had never actually been used so far.

"Sure thing." Cedric nodded and focused on the stone. "CONDOLESCO," he then said in a loud, firm and very low voice and stretched his hand out toward it.

The others again waited eagerly, but nothing happened.

"Do that again, please, Whirlwind, but focus it a little lower," Darien requested.

"Sure." He nodded and repeated the spell.

The others again watched carefully, and this time they all were convinced that something had happened, although it was very short and very uneventful.

"What was that now?" Lucas asked, looking at Darien.

"Not much," Cedric commented and shrugged his shoulders.

"But at least something," Darien said. "You generated a short discharge within the crystal. Not much, but it did the trick."

"But it did not start a chain reaction," Lucas said. "So it didn't exactly do the trick after all."

"What can we do to improve this, Professor?" Marcus asked.

"The internal structure of the crystal seems to have pockets of denser energy. If we can ignite one of the bigger ones, maybe that will generate enough power to keep it going."

"Then guide me to one of those," Cedric said.

"The biggest one I can see is right in the bottom spike of it. Just two millimeters or so from the end, in the center. Can you aim for that?"

"I can sure try." Cedric grinned and started focusing again. "CONDOLESCO," he then cast with a voice that suggested he had put more energy into it this time.

A short moment of eager waiting followed that spell, before things started to get hectic. Lucas could see a few sparks flying from the bottom spike of the stone, then a lightning discharge followed from there into the ground below. Even more lightning followed, before Lucas heard a cry from the side.

"Guardian, shield us!" Darien yelled and jumped back, trying to duck behind whatever cover he could find.

It took Lucas a moment to grasp the apparent danger that Darien had noticed and come up with a plan to counteract it. After he had pulled himself together, he reacted in a split second. He quickly started weaving an energy ball around the entire contraption they had built, including the grounding spikes and the wires.

"GUARDIO," he finally shouted, firing up the charm. Then he immediately started reinforcing it and weaving additional layers of protection onto it. What happened next came as a shock, even for him. Lightning bolts started flying from the crystal in all directions, impacting on his shield and making it glow in a mysterious, icy blue color. At the same time the grounding wires started glowing as well, but red hot, making Lucas assume that there was at least as much power flowing through them right now as was being unleashed against his shield. He was just about to reinforce the shield close to those wires when the first one, a connection wire between two of the grounding spikes, snapped with a loud bang, shooting the ends through the air. One end impacted Lucas' shield, causing sparks to burst from the tip with an intensity that was almost blinding. Through those sparks Lucas almost didn't recognize the other end impacting their wooden rig, cutting it in half and setting the sticks on fire at the same time. The vibration caused by the crumbling rig proved to be the final nail in the coffin for the rest of the contraption. The wires now all snapped, causing more cuts through the rig, and the entire system crashed in a big ball of flames and lightning. Lucas watched the scene with rising horror, pushing himself to the limit to keep the shield stable. He was so extremely focused that he didn't even realize that all the others had ducked for cover, leaving him standing alone next to the inferno. When the system finally came to rest, the carnage was clearly visible. The spikes were still growing red hot, partially fused with the remains of the wires, the wooden structure was burning slowly in the fireplace and in the middle of it all was the crystal, now lying there innocently, like a regular blue stone. Lucas was breathing heavily, drained significantly by the experience. He dropped his shield and sank down into the grass, gasping for air. It had not even been two minutes since the first spark had flown, but that short period of time had been very intense for him. He could see the others jumping in now, extinguishing the flames and cooling down the remaining metal with water. After taking a few more deep breaths he finally stood up again.

"Holy cow, that was a hell of a chain reaction this time." Marcus almost looked frightened, staring at the blue stone.

"The only problem with that is that this was no chain reaction at all." Darien was standing right next to Lucas now.

"What do you mean?" Marcus turned around, facing him.

"What we witnessed here was just the one pocket of energy that Whirlwind set off. It did not jump to other areas of the crystal."

"If that was only one pocket, then I am scared of the potential that this damn stone might actually have," Lucas said.

"Me too, mate." Darien nodded. "But at least there seems to be no way to actually harness that potential."

"Do you have any idea why that is?" Lucas asked. "I mean, after all, the amount of energy the crystal emitted definitely by far exceeded whatever Whirlwind shot in to start it in the first place."

"I can only speculate," Darien replied and thought for a moment. "First of all, you are right, of course. While Whirlwind's energy blast was quite significant, it was nothing compared to the inferno that he initiated with it. But then, Whirlwind applied his energy right into the hot spot, giving it a very focused burst there. The energy unleashed from the crystal went all over the place, so maybe there never was enough in one spot to ignite any of the others."

"So we were lucky then?" Marcus looked at the stone.

"Seems so, yeah." Darien nodded. "The only alternative I could possibly think of is that the type of energy emitted was not right to start the reaction to begin with, but I doubt that."

"And that would make little sense anyway, don't you think?" Lucas said.

"Why?" Marcus asked.

"Because it would imply that the stone can only be triggered magically, and that would not exactly help when you try to revolutionize the energy sector," Lucas answered. "Besides, HRC must have had some successes in using this stone already, right Professor?"

"Yes, they did." Darien nodded. "Although I never heard of a burst like the one we had just now. But your theory has a flaw anyway, Guardian: Just because the energy that comes out of the crystal can't spark the next cell, it doesn't mean that only magic can. After all, there are many more forms of energy than just those two."

"Additionally, the big output we received from the one cell that Whirlwind ignited would suggest that at least within the cell we were able to initiate a chain reaction," Jasmin threw in from the side.

"Yes, that's a very valid point, as well." Darien nodded.

Lucas nodded silently, looking at the crystal. Darien's first explanation still seemed to be the most viable and he had nothing else to offer that could trump it. He was unsure, though, what the implications of that would be. After all, if a homogeneous crystal could be formed, it would make the whole project viable. That was a good thing on one hand, as it seemed to imply that there was a reasonable chance to actually solve a global problem with this. But it also implied that the group around Cleric and Mr. Guthridge had something positive in mind, and that was hard for him to grasp. The past had so far only shown a streak of violence and destruction wherever those guys had appeared. Of course, there was the fact that a system like the crystal would bring in a lot of money if it could be built reliably, and money always had been a strong enough motive to commit violent acts. But that by itself made no sense either. The risks the group had taken had been quite high, and had backfired on them more than once already. And for the end goal of generating the crystal, those risks seemed totally unnecessary. After all, they could have built all of this in their backyard, without raising any flags whatsoever. Lucas sighed. No matter how he spun it, the situation still made no sense. He was certain that there was something more to this, something they had missed so far. But that something was eluding him, at least for tonight. He stood there as if paralyzed, watching the others clean up the mess the experiment had created, feeling exhausted both physically, from his shield charm, and mentally, from trying to find the missing piece to the puzzle. He didn't even hear what the others were saying, didn't realize anything that was going on anymore. There was no energy at all left in his body.

CHAPTER 8

PLAGUE

When the sound of the alarm clock pulled Lucas out of his dreams the next morning, he needed a moment to get his bearings. He was at home, in his room, but right now he could not recall how he had gotten here. He did remember yesterday's adventure very clearly and in vivid detail, but only to the point where he had shielded the crystal. Whatever had happened after that eluded his memory, even though he tried hard to fit the missing pieces together. It was a weird feeling for him, almost scary, having this blind spot in his memory. He had heard stories of such periods from his classmates, but normally those stories always involved lots of alcohol or other, less legal, substances. As he had avoided such "experiments" in his life so far, the feeling was totally new for him, and completely unexpected, given the circumstances. He continued rerunning last evening's events in his mind until he arrived at school. Unfortunately, even after dozens of repetitions, there was not one shred of additional information exposed, so he finally decided to stop. He would have to rely on the others to fill in this void when they met next time. Looking at today's schedule he was certain anyway that he would have little time to tackle the issue. There were lots of hard topics coming up that all required his full attention.

Three hours later he was just packing up his things after one of those taxing classes when a phone call pulled him back toward the other part of his life.

"This can't be good," he mumbled and walked out of the classroom before answering the call.

"Greetings, Inspector," he said after picking up. He continued walking down the hallway, looking for a quiet spot.

"Hello Mr. Trent," Inspector Corben said. "Would you have a minute, or is this a bad time?"

"I can spare a minute or two for sure, but not much more than that right now, I'm afraid," he answered.

"Understood, so I will get right to the point," Corben said. "One of the guys we arrested in the subway station has reached out and requested to talk."

"That's a new one." Lucas was surprised. "What does he want to talk about?"

"I don't know yet. I just got the news half an hour ago myself."

"I appreciate you keeping me in the loop, Inspector, but why am I getting the feeling that this is not actually a courtesy call?" Lucas asked.

"Well, most likely because it isn't," Corben said in a grim tone. "I am a little reluctant to say this, but it seems I need your help again."

"There is no need to be reluctant about that. But why would you need my help interviewing a prisoner?"

"Because he refuses to talk to the detectives. He said that he will only talk if one of his kind is present too. And while I am still uncertain exactly what that means, I am somehow sure that you would fit that request."

"I am not so sure about that, but let's see. Who is it, anyway?" Lucas was curious.

"Murphy," Corben answered.

"Detective Murphy?" Lucas was stunned. Murphy had been the last one on the list that he had expected to be cooperative.

"Yeah, that one," Corben said.

"Well, ok..." Lucas thought for a moment. He had a lot of schoolwork to do and didn't want to delay it with another trip to Belmarsh. But curiosity about what Plague had to say was just too strong in the end. "I have classes until three today. If it fits your schedule, I would be available after that."

"Fine by me," Corben replied. "Where shall I pick you up?"

"You can pick me up directly from College, I would say. Just text me when you arrive."

"Sounds good. I will be there at three," Corben confirmed and hung up.

Lucas walked back to the classroom, not sure what to make of the situation. He couldn't find any good reason why Plague would want to talk. The black circle had been a tight-knit companionship so far, so one of them rolling over and betraying the cause seemed to be a highly unlikely scenario. But why else would he request 'one of his kind' to be present? And what would he hope to gain from such a meeting? There was little chance that whatever he knew would bring him out of his murder sentence. But then, Lucas knew so little about the real goals of that circle that it wouldn't have surprised him at all if Plague actually had something of value to offer. He decided to bench the topic for now. It was all pure speculation, after all, at that point, and he would get his answers soon enough anyway. Besides, Professor Cooper had just entered the room, ending his leisure time abruptly.

When classes finally ended that day, Lucas took his time packing up his stuff before walking out. The Inspector had already texted his arrival a while before, but he did not feel like hurrying right now. Looking through the parking spaces, he needed a moment before spotting Corben's car at the far end. He was still not very happy about having agreed to the trip; after all, even now thinking back about his last visit to the prison still made a cold shiver run down his back. The Inspector started the engine when he saw Lucas approaching.

"Good afternoon, Mr. Trent," he greeted him after he had sat down in the passenger seat, putting his backpack next to his feet.

"Greetings, Inspector," Lucas replied.

"Thank you for taking the time," Corben said and pulled out of the parking lot.

"Let's see if it does any good," Lucas answered with an almost emotionless look on his face.

"Well, there must be something of importance on Murphy's mind; otherwise he wouldn't have approached us in the first place."

"True..." Lucas nodded. "But I am not so sure if I am the person he will want to share that something with. After all, I am part of the reason he is in there in the first place."

"He chose not to talk to the detectives, so I doubt that he will send you away too. You are one of 'his kind' anyway, aren't you?"

"As close to 'his kind' as he can expect to get from the police, I guess."

"What does that mean anyway, 'his kind'?" Corben was curious.

"That's a little hard to explain, Inspector." Lucas sighed. "I am sure you understand part of the picture by now, but I'm afraid that this will be what you are stuck with. At least for now."

"And that doesn't make me very happy, to be honest with you. But I will respect it, of course."

Lucas let a faint smile cross his face, but didn't respond. They drove silently for a short while, giving him a few moments to let his mind wander. He was not happy about the charade he had to put up with the Inspector either, but everything he could have said to fill in the blanks would have posed the risk of revealing things that weren't supposed to be revealed to an outsider, at least not in his way of looking at the magical community. And even though by now he trusted the Inspector more than any other non-mage, he still was not willing to take that chance. When he put his focus back on the upcoming encounter, Lucas realized that he had no idea how to approach the situation correctly. That was not exactly a new feeling; after all, when he talked to Cleric he had walked in without a plan too, but this time it felt like a bad idea. Plague wanted something, and he wanted a mage present for the discussion, so it seemed imperative to him that they got this right from the beginning, or they would risk losing vital pieces in the puzzle. He was just about to address Corben when the Inspector broke the silence first.

"I almost forgot," Corben said. "I have still not thanked you and your friends for saving the Constable."

"Actually, you did thank me, even before we had done anything," Lucas replied, letting his thoughts wander back to the horrors he had witnessed in the hospital. "And we haven't saved him yet. The last I heard, his condition was still critical."

"Aside from the fact that he would surely not be alive anymore without your help, which is more than enough to be grateful for from where I stand, your information actually seems to be outdated." Corben almost seemed to smile. "The doctor told me this morning that his condition has improved drastically over the past few days and they classify his status as stable now. He might still need a while before he is back on duty, but he will live to fight another day."

"That's incredible news." Lucas was relieved to hear that. The days of uncertainty had been weighing heavily on him, and that weight now got lighter with every second that passed. "I'll keep my fingers crossed that he makes a full recovery soon."

"Thank you. I'm sure he will," Corben said. "And I am also sure that he would like to thank you all personally too."

"I am not sure I feel comfortable with that, but I will talk to the others about it, of course. Let's see what they think."

"Fair enough." Corben nodded. "I will go visit him first chance I get. If you want to join me, let me know."

"Will do," Lucas said. "Please convey my best wishes to him."

Having heard this news gave him additional energy for the upcoming meeting with Plague. The risk they had taken with their interference had paid off. They had not only beaten all odds with it, but also--and that right now was much more important for him--again gained ground on the black mages to a certain extent. He was just about to return to his original topic of logistics when he realized that Corben had turned off the engine. Taking a quick look outside, the cold shiver came back as he recognized the massive wall of Belmarsh right in front of them.

"Shall we?" Corben asked.

Lucas just nodded in reply, stepping out of the car, leaving his backpack behind. They walked together, getting thoroughly checked at multiple guard posts they passed, until he could finally see the visitors' room ahead at the end of a long hallway.

"How do we proceed?" Lucas asked.

"I would say we let Murphy talk. I have no idea what he wants, so I also have no concrete plan."

Lucas was not happy about that answer, but just nodded in reply. When they finally entered the room, he immediately spotted a man leaning on the side wall.

"You are here to talk to Murphy?" the man addressed them.

"That would be the idea, yes." Corben nodded.

"You don't mind if I sit in?"

"I might mind, actually," Corben said in a slightly unfriendly tone. "Who exactly are you?"

"Detective Constable Raoul McEntire, Internal Affairs," the unknown man introduced himself. "And you are?"

"Inspector William Corben, SO-19," Corben replied, still keeping the unfriendly tone. "And he," he pointed at Lucas, "is with me."

"What relationship do you two have with the prisoner?" McEntire asked.

Lucas didn't like the tone in the detective's voice and was just about to say something when Corben responded first.

"SO-19 was the unit that made the arrest. Other than that, I have only had the pleasure of meeting Murphy once before, during an operation. And that meeting was very brief. And he," Corben once again pointed at Lucas, "is with me."

"Then why are you so hostile?" the constable inquired, scribbling frantically in his notebook.

"Because interrogating those people is your job, not mine. And if you had done your job, rather than interrogating me now, I might not have to be here in the first place. Now unless there is something terribly important you need to know from me right now, I would suggest you go stand in the corner over there and be quiet."

"We are on the same side here Inspector," McEntire said while walking toward the corner of the room that Corben had indicated. "And besides, we have to wait anyway. The guards have to get Murphy from the medical wing."

"Medical wing?" Lucas was surprised. "What happened?"

"Well, apparently, police officers are not exactly well-liked inside these walls. It seems that Murphy has met some old acquaintances of his, people he put behind these bars and who seem to bear a grudge because of that."

"That's weird." Lucas shook his head in disbelief. He had of course expected that Plague would have enemies in here, and that those enemies would not hesitate to harm him. But on the other hand, he was a mage after all, and a very capable one as far as Lucas could tell from their past encounters. He should have easily been capable of defending himself against attacks.

"Are you ok with the detective being here?" Corben asked.

"Yeah, sure. I don't care." Lucas nodded.

They both sat down next to the glass wall, just where they had been sitting when they had talked to Cleric. It took another five minutes before the guards finally appeared and led Murphy into the room. The sight was not pretty. Lucas almost didn't believe it at first. There were blood stains on multiple parts of the orange overalls that he was wearing. His face was bruised top to bottom, stitches next to his eye suggested a recently attended to cut, and his hands also showed major swelling and abrasions.

"What happened to you?" Lucas asked when they all had finally picked up their handsets, including McEntire, who had sat down next to Corben.

"I won a popularity contest, and this was the prize." Murphy laughed in agony. "What do you think?"

"What a pity," Corben said in a stone-cold voice, with a matching look on his face. "But this is not a social visit. You wanted to talk, so talk."

"I told you that I will only talk if you bring one of my kind here," Murphy replied harshly.

"And I am as close to that as you will ever get, Plague." Lucas jumped in, now with the same cold voice that Corben had used before.

"I know you, don't I?" Murphy looked straight at him now.

"You definitely do. After all, I was the one who put you in here," Lucas grinned.

"Ah... Guardian... I knew I had heard the voice before." Murphy laughed again, only this time it sounded despicable. "Well, a fitting response to my request, I have to say."

"Then talk," Corben demanded impatiently.

"Not so fast." Murphy tried to sit up straight before he continued. "I have some demands to make."

"You are hardly in the position to make demands." Corben was getting angry very quickly. "Or do you really think that we will let you out of here after being an accessory to murder?"

"I am not stupid, Inspector," Murphy said, his voice sounding a little sore. "I don't want out; I just want to be transferred somewhere else, where I am less well-known--maybe back to a standard facility, rather than this maximum-security shithole. I have done nothing so far to deserve this treatment."

"I can't make concessions like that," Corben replied.

"You can't. But he can." Murphy pointed at McEntire.

"And why would I do that? What do you have to offer that would justify that?"

"I know a good chunk of the bigger picture," Murphy said before he had to cough loudly. "Can you please bring me some water? My throat is burning like hell. Damn medicine," he addressed one of the guards.

"What bigger picture?" McEntire asked. "You killed a man. What more could there be?"

"Let him talk," Lucas interrupted the detective. "And can someone please bring him some water?" he continued as he realized that neither of the guards was moving.

"Do you believe that he has something to offer?" Corben asked Lucas.

"I'm not sure yet, but I would at least like to hear a bit more," he answered before turning back to Murphy. "Why would you betray your own people?"

"Because now that I understand what they are actually doing, I don't want any part of it," he replied, continuously coughing.

"Jesus." Lucas turned to Corben, as it seemed that Murphy's cough was getting worse by the minute. Corben gesticulated the guard on the other side to get some water in, and he responded by speaking into his radio.

"You are just looking for an easy way out," McEntire almost shouted into the phone. "There is nothing more to that."

"You know that there is more," Murphy addressed Lucas, breathing heavily.

"I might. But why would I believe that you know anything about that?" Lucas was curious, but cautious. Something seemed to be very wrong here, but he couldn't quite put his finger on it. Plague rolling on his circle seemed weird, especially after all the things that they had done together so far. He had been on the brutal end of the scale from the very beginning, so it was very hard to believe that there could be an endgame involved that was so extremely horrifying for him. Getting beaten up also sounded a little too convenient under those circumstances, almost like the perfect story. Plus there was this weird cough that he had all the time. On the other hand, the demands he had made were reasonable. He had not tried to get free or even negotiate a reduced sentence; all he had asked for was another prison.

"The blue stones don't work," Murphy said, his face turning slightly red from the constant coughing. "They knew all along."

"Oh, now you blame everything on stones," McEntire said from the side. "What kind of delusional story is that? For that bullshit you wanted a kid in here?"

"Yeah, because the kid apparently knows something you don't, McEntire. Now shut up," Corben yelled at him after seeing Lucas' facial expression change when Murphy mentioned the stone. "Is there something to what Murphy is saying?" he then asked him.

"Yes." Lucas nodded and turned toward the Inspector. "I am still not sure how much Murphy has to offer on that matter, but if he has something then it's worth hearing it."

"You are not seriously suggesting that I give in to his demands because of a blue stone?" McEntire asked Lucas in disbelief.

Corben was about to respond when they heard a thud through the handset. Lucas quickly turned toward the glass wall. The handset was hanging in the air, the chair had tumbled over and Murphy was now lying on the ground with no sign of movement.

"What the hell?" Corben jumped up to get a better view.

One of the guards had approached Murphy and was feeling his pulse. The other was yelling something into the radio. They couldn't hear what was being said, so they could only watch and wait. More guards came rushing in moments later, followed by two medics with a gurney. Lucas could only see bits and pieces of what was happening, with all the people running around on the other side. It looked like they were performing CPR for a while before loading him onto the gurney and rushing him out of the room. Only then one of the guards that had stayed behind picked up the handset and addressed the three.

"It seems the prisoner had some kind of an allergic reaction to the medicine he got earlier today. They are rushing him to the hospital now, but it doesn't look good," he said.

"This can't be a coincidence," Lucas mumbled.

"Please let us know the outcome," Corben said to the guard and then turned toward the detective. "And in case he dies, make sure that this gets looked into thoroughly. I agree with my young friend here; that's a hell of a coincidence."

"I will, Inspector." McEntire nodded with a pale face and shaky voice.

Corben hung up the handset and walked toward the door, pulling Lucas, who had still not fully recovered from the scene, with him. They quickly moved through the corridors and checkpoints out of the complex toward the Inspectors car. Lucas was almost in a trance, his mind trying vigorously to sort out what had just happened and make any sense of it whatsoever. How could somebody have managed to kill a former police officer right in front of his eyes, within the walls of a maximum-security prison? What was it that he had discovered about the plot that was so extremely disturbing that he would come forward in the first place? And what had he meant with his last statement? Who had known all along?

"What the hell was that?" Corben's question pulled Lucas back into reality after they had sat down in the car.

"I honestly don't know," Lucas answered slowly. "And unfortunately the only person who was willing and able to tell us seems not to be talking anymore."

"What was that about the blue stones? You seem to know what he was talking about."

"I also only know bits and pieces about that so far, unfortunately." Lucas sighed and thought for a moment. "There is this idea of a new form of energy that is based on weird blue crystals. I first stumbled on it a few years back on a field trip with school. And somehow it seems that those goons are connected to that project, although I can't really tell how."

"And how exactly is this related to the murder we booked Murphy for in the first place?"

"I am not sure about that either, unfortunately. But then, there is so much that I don't understand when it comes to this group," Lucas said.

"Maybe we should let the detectives run with that blue stone thing, then?" Corben suggested.

"I would hold off on that for now if I were you."

"And why's that?" Corben was surprised.

"So far all we know for sure is that there is this crystal thingy, and it doesn't work. If there is a larger agenda here and it really is bad enough to make Murphy turn on his friends, then we should be very careful where we poke around. Those people have been very elusive so far, disguising their true intentions. They might get scared off and go into hiding if they feel threatened. Or worse, they might go on the offensive. After all, the group has shown its ruthlessness already in the not-too-distant past, and that was apparently a small detail if we trust Murphy's comments. So whatever the big picture is that we are not seeing here yet, it seems to be worth killing for."

"So what would you suggest then?"

"First let's wait and see if Murphy survives this, whatever it was," Lucas said. "If so, we will know more then. If not, it will at least give me a little time to put some pieces together. Chances are quite high that this group will show up on our radar again. Higher at least than them showing up on yours. And if not, then your detectives can still go and poke around JDC or Harlington Research and see what they uncover there."

"All right." Corben nodded. "I will keep this between us, then, for as long as possible. But if Detective McEntire starts asking around, it might be made public pretty quickly."

"Things are never really secret once more than one person knows about them." Lucas shrugged. "That's a chance we have to take and in the end couldn't influence anyway. I doubt, though, that he can make the connection."

"I just hope this doesn't blow up in our faces," Corben said and started the car. "After all, if you are right, then this has to be pretty big. And I for one don't like unknown, big things hitting me unprepared."

"If that's the case then you should consider a career change, Inspector. But I agree with you, I don't like such situations either."

Lucas let his gaze wander across the objects passing by, trying to calm his mind a little. He knew that Corben had made a very valid point, and that asking him to keep this under wraps would put a huge responsibility on the Mages of the Round Fireplace. He was sure by now that Plague's collapse had not been a drug allergy, but rather was foul play of some sorts. And if that was true, then it added a new layer of danger to the story. Cleric and his group had killed a man, but that had been in a combat situation--brutal, unjustified and with no remorse to that point, but at least in a provoked situation. The attack on Plague had been methodically planned and implemented. That was not the doing of a strong-headed lunatic, but rather that of a strategically-thinking mastermind. Lucas considered for a moment that this attack might have been an act of desperation, but quickly discarded the thought. Whatever Plague would have told them might have shed some insight into the plans of the larger group, but it would hardly have stopped them. After all, he was very unlikely to have any proof and almost certainly wouldn't even have known any real names. Additionally, even if this attack had been planned out of desperation, it still had to have been carefully planned. Once again a cold shiver ran down Lucas' back. The struggle with Wolfman had been bad, taking on Cleric had been by far worse, but compared to whoever they were facing now, both seemed like children's birthday parties to him at the moment. And that implied that they were almost certainly in over their heads once again, a thought that he didn't like the least bit.

"Shall I drop you off at the College or would you like me to drive you home?" Corben's question pulled Lucas out of his thoughts. They had already made it all the way back to Luton without him realizing it.

"College would be better. I need to get my bike from there," Lucas replied, trying to bring his attention back to his current surroundings.

The Inspector nodded. It was only a few more blocks until they got there, leaving no more time for conversation between the two.

"Thank you for your time," Corben said when they arrived and shook Lucas' hand.

"Anytime, Inspector." Lucas tried to put on a faint smile, although he was not at all feeling like it. "Please convey my best wishes to your colleague when you visit him at the hospital. I hope he makes a full recovery soon."

"I will, thanks." Corben nodded. "Have a good remainder of your day."

"You too," Lucas said as he exited the car. "Godspeed, Inspector, until we meet again."

As he rode his bike back home, Lucas thought about the bigger picture again. He knew that in order to solve this he would need more help than his circle could provide on its own, but he was very uncertain who to approach with it. The Magus Major meeting seemed to be the most prudent idea, but with the few bits and pieces he had gathered so far, he knew that going there was futile. JJ had made a much more compelling argument last time, with a far more concrete and imminent threat, and got nowhere fast. Bringing it to JJ's attention was another option, and given that they were looking into this as well, at least as far as the environmental problems were concerned, it seemed like a valid approach. The only problem he saw was that he was uncertain if both their circles together would be enough to figure this out. But as there were no other feasible options to go with, he decided keep it at the top of his list. Maybe the others had more good ideas, or had discovered something else in the meantime. Maybe they would find enough information in time to stand a chance with the Magus Majors. And then, of course, there still was the slight possibility that all of this was much less of a problem than he was imagining it to be right now. For today there was little more he could do, so he decided to leave the topic alone and wait until next Monday to discuss it with the others. Until then he had other obligations as well that needed to be considered and would require all his attention.

CHAPTER 9

CO

When Lucas was heading to the shack the following Monday a lot was going through his mind. He had dedicated the majority of his previous week to schoolwork and had been so preoccupied with it that he hadn't even realized how quickly the days had gone by without any news regarding the crystal power, Plague or even the injured police officer. In the aftermath, he was very happy about it, as it had really given him the opportunity to catch back up with his workload, which made him far more relaxed now than he had been last Tuesday. The only thing that weighed a little bit on his mind was the fact that he also hadn't seen Kung Fu for a while now. He had had plans to call her and see if she was free on the weekend, but had totally forgotten about it during the week, and when he finally had remembered on Friday she had already made other plans. And while this development had provided him with even more free time to do something for school, it was still somewhat bothersome for him. And even now he was struggling a little with the feeling that he had had throughout the weekend because of it. It was a weird combination of jealousy toward whoever or whatever she was spending time with, yearning for her, sadness and queasiness that mixed together into a mental state that he did not find at all enjoyable. From a logical point of view, it was somewhat ridiculous for him. After all, their relationship had never been exactly a well-defined one to begin with, and they had not spent that much time together so far, so missing a weekend should not have been unexpected at all. But then, logic did not count a whole lot when it came to him and Kung Fu, and he was only slowly coming to terms with that fact. He time and again thought this through in an epic internal battle to regain his sanity and come up with a plan on how to move this forward. But while he was uncertain of how to deal with the situation, there was one thing he was not, and that was worried. And for that he was infinitely grateful right now. It was one of the things that had changed drastically in his life due to his pursuit of magic. Granted, it had been a gone-wrong party with Stephanie and a computer challenge that had mostly contributed to his epiphany back then, but it was the use of magic that had made it possible. And even with his internal conflict now, there was a spark of joy in all of it, as all of this felt more like a friendly rivalry than an all-out conflict. In the end, he was certain that whatever the outcome was, it would be a good one, and that he would only grow stronger from it. Unfortunately though, it was not the only thing on his mind. The progressing recovery of the police officer was good news, too, of course, but it was somewhat overshadowed by the whole situation with Plague and the missing pieces to the puzzle with Jackson, Guthridge and the mysterious others that were lurking somewhere in the dark, almost certainly including more mages.

When he arrived at the shack he could see smoke coming out of the chimney. He had not expected anyone else to be there yet, as he was quite early, but he was happy have company early on, and also happy that he would not be the one who had to start the fire. He got off his bike and walked toward the side to stow it when he first heard the sounds coming from there. It took him a moment to make sense of what he heard, but then quickly realized that it was the sound of someone splitting wood. When he finally walked around the corner he was a bit surprised to see Marcus there with a long pole axe, hacking away like a professional lumberjack.

"Howdy, Guardian!" Marcus greeted him while taking a swing at a block of wood.

"Greetings, Cougar," Lucas replied. "I hadn't expected to see you here so early."

"I had some time to spare. And since I remembered that we disintegrated a lot of wood last week, I thought it might be a good idea to replenish the supplies a little bit. After all, we don't want to get cold here." He laughed and split another block.

"I am sure the O'Briens will appreciate it." Lucas grinned and stowed his bike.

"I think the six of us will appreciate it much more than the rest of the O'Briens." Marcus laughed and stepped away from the chopping block, approaching Lucas.

"Brother to brother, yours to the end," they both said simultaneously, laying their hands on each other's shoulders.

"How long have you been here?" Lucas asked and looked around. There was already a considerable amount of split wood lying around all over the place, suggesting that Marcus had been at it for quite a while.

"Half an hour or so," he answered and picked up another block.

"You did all this in half an hour?" Lucas was impressed.

"Yeah. Good practice." Marcus laughed. "But I think it's about enough now. Can you help me collect all the pieces and pile them up under the projecting roof?"

"Sure thing." Lucas nodded and grabbed a pair of heavy duty gloves before starting to pick up the chunks. Marcus was also already at it; he just didn't seem to care about gloves. They chatted about inconsequential things and both enjoyed the relaxed time. The hour of the meeting approached fast and they were almost finished with their work when Darien showed up with a large bag dangling down the left side of his body.

"How can you ride a bike with that thing?" Marcus asked him after they exchanged their greetings.

"Carefully," Darien laughed. "But I couldn't fit those things in my backpack, so I had little choice."

"What did you bring anyway?" Lucas was curious.

"My laptop and some newspapers."

"Newspapers? You are aware that we have enough of those left in the shack to get the fire going, right?" Marcus said.

"Those are not meant for the fire, Cougar. And as far as I remember, you can even light fire without them, so I wouldn't have bothered about that to begin with."

"So what are they for, then?" Lucas asked.

"I will show you when the others arrive, Guardian, if that's all right. It's quite interesting, actually."

"As you wish." Lucas nodded. "Let us quickly finish up here and go inside, then."

Marcus and Lucas stowed the remaining pieces and the tools and walked into the shack, Marcus carrying a few blocks with him to feed the fire inside. They had just gotten comfortable when Stephanie showed up, closely followed by Cedric. When Jasmin finally arrived ten minutes later, they assembled quickly around the table. Lucas waited for someone to say something, but it quickly became clear that they were once again looking at him, expecting him to break the silence first.

"So, who wants to start?" he finally asked.

"How about you?" Jasmin suggested.

"How about the Professor?" Lucas countered. "After all, he brought the big bag."

"Very well," Darien said after a long moment of silence and pulled his bag up onto the table. The others watched him eagerly as he took out newspaper after newspaper and laid them out on the table. Lucas was still not sure where Darien was going with this, so he started browsing through the headlines of the newspaper. This proved difficult though, because he quickly realized that many of them were printed in languages he didn't understand. When Darien was finished, he put his bag back down on the floor and looked at the others as if he had just made some kind of very strong statement and was waiting for replies.

"Are we supposed to understand what this is all about?" Jasmin looked at him.

"Look at the headlines," Darien replied.

"I did," Jasmin said and bent over the table to look at some more papers. "But I barely understand ten percent of them."

"Neither does anyone else at the table, except for you, Professor. So can you please fill us in?" Marcus looked a little annoyed.

"Oh sorry, I didn't realize that..." Darien looked contrite. "I gathered these papers from pretty much all over the world, and all over the last two months or so. Apparently, the thing we see here in the UK is not a local phenomenon."

"What 'thing'?" Jasmin asked.

"The degradation of the environment. There are tons of studies worldwide that seem to confirm the exact thing that Harlington Research has been suggesting for a while now. That we have a rapidly progressing problem with plants dying and animals following not far behind."

"That is more or less common knowledge, Professor. It's called 'global warming'. What are you getting at?" Jasmin looked at him.

"Global warming is a fact, yes. But global warming progresses slowly, not as harshly as this. And you are missing the point."

"The point being?" Cedric now asked.

"That other labs worldwide confirm HRC's results."

"Why is that a big deal? Harlington Research is a renowned company in this sector. Wouldn't it be natural to assume such an outcome?" Stephanie jumped into the discussion.

"Not if the results were wrong." Lucas had picked up one of the English papers, apparently one published in Australia. "Holy shit, Professor."

Darien nodded vehemently and pointed at Lucas.

"Why would the results be wrong?" Stephanie looked, confused.

"The Professor told us not too long ago that HRC was cutting corners and that it looked as if they were exaggerating the statements," Lucas answered, his voice sounding as if he was deeply engrossed in his thoughts. "So either the results were correct in the first place, and the concern about the corner cutting was unfounded, or there is a method to this madness and someone is actively pushing this rumor."

"I would opt for the latter," Darien said and pulled a sheet of paper out from between two newspapers. "Look at this." He handed it to Lucas.

"What am I looking at?" Lucas asked and looked through the printed spreadsheet, trying to hold it in a way that the others could read it too.

"Those are all the studies that have been quoted in the papers and the companies that published them," Darien replied. "Look at the owners of those companies."

"Hmm..." Lucas looked through the list, but none of the names sounded familiar to him at all. Then, after reading it back and forth a number of times, he finally spotted the pattern that Darien seemed to be aiming at. "You can't be serious." He pulled the sheet closer to confirm his thought.

"What is it, Guardian?" Stephanie asked.

"All those companies have the same structure that Harlington Research now does," Darien explained with a victorious grin on his face. "There is always a 'Co' in there who holds a pretty big share."

"Are you saying that this is the same 'Co' that we have here in the UK, this Guthridge guy who is hiding behind Jackson?" Jasmin said.

"I doubt that it will be the same one in every company, but it is a hell of a coincidence, don't you think?" Darien replied.

"But I still don't get what this is all about." Lucas had put the list back on the table. "We all know that humanity is harming the planet, why are they risking diluting this message with fake studies?"

"Why would overstating the problem dilute it?" Marcus looked lost.

"Because if someone proves any of those studies wrong the conspiracy theorists will be all over the place, denying global warming again," Lucas replied. "And that would hardly help."

"I have a thought on that actually," Darien jumped in. "If you look closer at the newspapers you will find another thing lurking in the background here." He took one of the Canadian papers and screened through it before putting it in the middle of the table, opened to page 7. "Based on the now widely-accepted study results, governments are starting to act and increase the pressure on fossil fuel companies, especially on caloric power plants. They are introducing new taxes all over the place to finance alternative energy sources."

"Which is not a bad thing, right?" Stephanie seemed unsure.

"It is a good thing for sure; after all, it will solve the problem in the long run." Darien nodded.

"Then what's the problem?" Marcus asked.

"The problem is that we are missing the point." Lucas was still reading through the article. "The governments did not act on the truth; after all, they knew about the problem for decades now. They acted only when a probably-faked series of studies showed up. A series that cost the ones generating it millions of pounds to get done. There must be something more to this."

"And there is." Darien grinned once again. "Or did you forget that the mysterious 'Co' also happens to own a revolutionary new power source that supposedly does not harm the environment?"

"A power source that does not work..." Lucas threw in. "There has to be an endgame here somewhere, but we are still missing the point."

"What will be the effect of this, if the crystal energy never starts working?" Stephanie asked.

"That's a great question, Airmid." Lucas nodded. "Who will benefit the most from this?"

"To a certain extent it will be renewable energy, like wind or solar," Darien commented. "But those sources are not reliable enough to be a global solution. So if you take all the experimental stuff, like the crystal, out of the picture, it will most likely be the nuclear sector. After all, they also don't have the problem of greenhouse gases."

"We are missing something here, people," Lucas repeated. "If our assumption here is correct then this 'Co', or the 'Cos' for that matter, is spending lots of money to discredit conventional energy. Additionally, this guy is spending even more millions to push a magically-fueled power source that doesn't work. That sounds like a bad choice of investment if all he gains is a push toward nuclear power."

"That is true, but only if this 'Co' is aware that the crystal energy does not work," Darien threw in.

"They are aware," Lucas replied and told them about the prison visit.

"If 'they' actually means the 'Co' and not someone even higher up, playing puppet master for that 'Co'," Darien suggested.

"This global conspiracy is getting too much for me to follow. Sorry, guys," Jasmin said and rubbed her head with both hands.

"I agree." Marcus raised his hand.

"So do I." Stephanie nodded.

"Unfortunately, Guardian is most likely right. It all makes little sense because we still have no clue what this is all about in the end." Darien sighed.

"Then how do we figure this out?" Jasmin asked.

"The more pressing question is: Do we even want to?" Lucas leaned back with an exhausted look on his face.

"Do you suggest we let those magical lunatics run unchecked?" Marcus looked shocked.

"I am not suggesting anything so far, Cougar. But look at the picture here: There is something going on on a global scale. There are multiple corporations involved, most likely a lot of money, and almost certainly more mages. And we, on the other hand, are nothing more than a bunch of kids who happen to have stumbled into this because we chose to help a girl in trouble. What are our chances?"

"If this were about chances then we would never have taken on Cleric and his goons in the first place, Guardian, you know that," Darien said. "But you are right; the chances are getting worse with each passing day, it seems."

"I would still not want to bail out, no matter the chances," Marcus said. "This is about the environment, and I care a lot about that. And hell, I refuse to believe that we are the only ones fighting for this. We might not be able to solve it, but maybe we can help at least a little bit toward a solution."

"Well said," Cedric nodded.

"So we continue with this?" Lucas asked.

"The question is purely rhetorical, right?" Darien looked at him.

Lucas looked first at Jasmin then at Stephanie, who both nodded in reply to his look, before replying to Darien. "It seems to be, yes," he then said and nodded.

"So what's next then?" Marcus asked.

"We need to figure out what their plan is," Lucas said. "And I am open for suggestions, because so far that beats me..."

"Maybe we should go back to Jackson's house again. It did not help last time, but there has to be something there, other than a nice façade," Marcus suggested.

"Maybe we should install a camera there somewhere? That would give us a better chance to actually see something," Darien added.

"You know that that's illegal, right?" Stephanie asked.

"So is breaking and entering, but that didn't stop us last time," Marcus reminded her.

"Sounds like a good plan to me." Lucas nodded. "How would we go about that, Professor? I doubt that we will have any useful Wi-Fi signal out there that we can piggyback ourselves onto."

"I would go for cameras with motion detection and a memory card," Darien said. "Install them, let them run for a while, come back and swap the card. It is more work, but far more reliable. And it is cheaper too, because I do in fact own two such devices."

"Then let's do this," Marcus said and clapped his hands. "What else do we need?"

"A few power tools might help." Darien thought for a moment. "And I think that's it."

"The three of us should be able to get this done. What do you think, Cougar?" Lucas asked, pointing out himself, Marcus and Darien.

"Sure thing. Weekend?" Marcus nodded.

"Sounds good." Lucas nodded back, and so did Darien.

"That's settled then." Jasmin stated after a few moments of silence. "What else do we have?"

"What about your circle, Psycho? Is there any chance that they have a handle on this as well? After all, they stumbled over a pile of crystals a while ago," Darien asked.

"Good thought, actually." Jasmin nodded. "So far they have not come into contact with that black circle again, and I hope that it stays that way for a while longer."

"Why's that?" Marcus asked.

"Because they are far from ready for another fight," Jasmin replied. "And I don't want to pick up the pieces if they challenge those guys again and lose."

"Let us know if something should boil up. They might not be ready for the fight, but they are also not alone here," Marcus said.

"I appreciate the assistance, but you know the rules here, right? We can't interfere unless someone higher approaches on the other side," Jasmin said.

"I know the rule, but I still think it's stupid," Marcus mumbled.

"At least we should be watching from somewhere close if the conflict should arise. Maybe their mentor will show up after all, and if not, we can at least pick up the pieces together," Lucas suggested.

"On another thought," Marcus said, "We could also go to High Wycombe ourselves and see what we find."

"You are aware how large that area is?" Stephanie threw in.

"Yeah, but we have a good starting point," Marcus replied. "Psycho has already been at one location before."

"And nobody has been there since," Jasmin said. "My mentees made sure of that so far."

"It still can't hurt to look at the area on a map and see if there are any obvious places close by that we should check out. I like the idea," Lucas said.

"I'll take care of that after we have mounted the cameras," Darien volunteered. "Psycho, can you please assist me in finding the spot where you saw the crystals?"

"Sure." Jasmin nodded.

"OK, that's settled then too." Lucas smiled. "Do we have other leads that we could follow up on?"

"How about JJ and his circle?" Stephanie asked. "Is their conflict related?"

"Hard to tell." Lucas thought about it for a moment. "I will fill him in on our plan when I next see him. Let's see what he thinks."

"Is there any way to figure out if this 'Co' character is actually in charge or if there is someone behind him?" Darien asked after a moment of silence.

"For that we would need to find that 'Co' in the first place, don't you think?" Stephanie replied.

"To be sure we would, yes." Lucas nodded. "But I think there are some things we can deduce based on what we already know."

"Like what?" Marcus asked.

"Let's start with Cleric," Lucas said. "I highly doubt that a mage of that level would do the bidding of a business man. And even if one or two mages would follow the temptation of the money, it would surely not be as many as they need to pull a worldwide stunt like that off."

"Why would you think that? After all, money is a great motivator." Jasmin looked at him.

"Because I think that every mage has the power to make money on his own," Lucas replied. "Think about it... If Airmid offered her services even on a small scale, she could make tons of profit in a very short time. Same goes for you, Psycho. And pretty much for all of us, I would suppose, with a little more or less effort, that is."

"So what are you saying then? That Cleric was the one calling the shots?" Marcus asked.

"No." Lucas shook his head. "If that were the case then it should be over now. I am saying that we are most likely looking for another mage who was guiding Cleric and his bunch. And based on that, I would assume that either this mage is in charge of the 'Co' guys himself, or there is someone above him who is. Although the longer I think about it, the more I am convinced that the top of the chain has to be a mage."

"Unless it's a conglomerate," Darien suggested. "But I agree, even in that case a mage is most likely part of it."

"So how do we find this mage then?" Stephanie asked.

"The better question is: What do we do once we find him?" Marcus looked grim.

"Good questions, both of them." Lucas nodded slowly. "Unless this mage, or mages for that matter, comes out of his shadowy hiding place we have little chance of ever finding him. And if we do, we better duck for cover, because I honestly doubt that we are in any position to fight such a person. At least not openly."

"What do we do then?" Marcus asked.

"I would say we do the best we can," Lucas said. "Try to figure out the endgame, and while we do, chip away the low-level support structure wherever we uncover it. The best way to solve a big problem in the end is always to slice it into smaller pieces."

"Which still does not get us any closer to the head," Darien said.

"No. But I guess only patience will," Lucas replied. "We have Psycho's circle, we have JJ's circle and we have Jackson. Let's take care of those three first and see where we stand then."

The others nodded silently.

"Is there anything else to discuss?" Lucas asked after over a minute of silence.

"Only what we do with the rest of the evening," Marcus replied after another awkward minute had elapsed with everyone just looking at everyone else.

"I would suggest we get some training going," Lucas said. "Chances are that we will face another fight down the road. We should be prepared."

The others nodded and followed Lucas outside. There they took turns practicing everything they thought might help during a conflict situation. Lucas and Cedric pushed their attack spells further out, Marcus focused on his agility, Jasmin focused on her illusion spell and even Darien and Stephanie found ways to participate, with Darien training his skills as a magical detector and using his sight as an aiming aid for Lucas and Cedric and Stephanie trying to develop a sedation spell of sorts, to at least have a means of self-defense. They all were so focused on the training that they totally lost track of time, continuing their session until late into the night. When they finally packed up, they were all exhausted and in dire need of a bed.

On the way home Lucas started thinking about Kung Fu again. With their upcoming plan for the weekend he would again be blocked at least half a day and schoolwork would at least take another half day away, so the timeslots he had available were already becoming scarce. And while he still had a little wiggle room when it came to when exactly they would head for Jackson's house and when to do his schoolwork, he was somewhat feeling uneasy about it. The question that ran through his head was all about priorities. Was it more important to get to the bottom of this situation with Cleric and Jackson, or was his own life, his slim chance of getting into his first meaningful relationship, the thing that should take precedence? And what was it exactly that he was hoping for here, anyway? This relationship was hardly something that could last. The age difference was too large and the gap between the two of them was too wide when it came to their hobbies and interests. He couldn't help but feel that he was clinging on to a pipe dream here, one that was hardly worth pursuing, and even less worth putting above saving the world. But there was something there that made it seem different. He of course knew by now that his emotions were mostly in charge when it came to the topic, but there was one thing that made him wonder right now: Was he pushing this illusion of a future so hard because of his emotional attachment, or was there also some colder, more logical reasoning in the background? After all, even if this relationship lasted only a short while, he definitely had much to gain from the experience. And while he tried to enumerate all the things that would be beneficial, all of a sudden a thought struck him like lightning: Had she thought this through too? And that thought proved to be very discomforting for Lucas right away. It quickly introduced questions about her motives and the things that she would most likely benefit from in this kind of relationship, and it suddenly made him feel like a toy to her. There was little he had to offer to any girl, and even less that he could present to someone like her. His thoughts started racing around the topic, trying to come up with all the logical reasons that would make him interesting to her. But the longer he thought this through, the more reasons he came up with and analyzed to the end, the more he ended up realizing that there was nothing of value there. With every new thought his ego grew smaller and smaller, finally reaching a state where panic started to spread in his mind and tears were rushing into his eyes. At one point, he even had to stop his bike because he was unable to clearly see the road anymore. He stood there, hunkered down on his bike's handlebars, and started crying. His thoughts faded into the background, panic still being the predominant feeling he had. He knew that kind of feeling from his past and he was preparing himself for a long, hard journey through this emotion, but to his surprise it didn't take more than a moment. Almost immediately after his thoughts had gone silent, a voice popped up in his head.

"Are you done?" he heard that voice asking, and he could feel a hard push of anger running through his veins. He knew that voice by now; it was the same one that had popped up before when he had transitioned to Magus Major. But right now he had a hard time putting it in perspective.

"What should I be done with?" he mumbled to himself. He wasn't even done mumbling when his inner voice already came back with the answer.

"Done with logical pessimism," it said.

He needed a moment before he realized what he had just done. He had fought so hard to get on par with his feelings, had benefitted so much from listening to them in the recent past, and now, when they mattered most, he had shut them out again and left the stage open solely for his logic.

"Yes," he said and took a deep breath, trying to open himself up as much as he could. And immediately it started hitting him: All the joy he had felt so far when being with her, all the fun they had had so far, including their first run-in at the Timestop bar that had not felt too warm at the time, but now was as cheerful a memory as all the others were. And all the pain he was in when she was not around for too long. The burst of emotions was so strong that it made him feel warm and comfortable in just a few seconds. Indulging in those feelings a while longer even made his doubts fade away slowly, including all his previous thoughts about her possible reasons for being there. It took him a few moments before he realized why he was willing to let go of those doubts: Immersing in the situation so fully almost allowed him to feel her emotions too, and from all he could perceive, there was nothing other than joy in her too when they were together, and that feeling just wouldn't fit his earlier thoughts. After calming down again a few minutes later he resumed his ride home, feeling cheerful again and looking forward to seeing Kung Fu more than he had done ever before. As he rode along there was a weird thought in his head, though: Why had it been so hard for him to realize this? He had not shut out his feelings before ever since he had come to terms with them a while ago. Why now? But no matter how much he tried to wrap his head around this, nothing seemed to make any sense. And even his emotional side had nothing meaningful to offer on the subject, at least nothing that would hold up to scrutiny. After a while he decided to shelve the topic for now and maybe ask Jasmin about her thoughts on it when he had a chance. At that moment, a seemingly unrelated memory popped up in his mind, so strong and clear it was as if the situation had just happened yesterday. He suddenly saw himself back at the Duke of Summerset, sitting at the corner table, talking to Gaia. It was just one brief moment that had surfaced, but he could hear her voice as clear as day: "Unity. And belief," she had said. He could not make any sense of it right now, but somehow he realized that he had just hit another weak point in his personality and that Gaia somehow had known about that too. He was painfully aware that he had just proven his lack of unity. But he still was unable to understand that second part. What was it he was supposed to believe in? And why would this pop up right now? The thought continued circling his mind for the rest of the evening, not clearing out even when he already lay in bed. This weakness was bugging him so much that it actually was the only thing he could think about until he finally fell asleep. He knew that it was a problem, and he knew that he needed to solve it sooner rather than later. But it would have to wait for another day.

CHAPTER 10

CONSEQUENCES

When Lucas woke up Tuesday morning he was feeling energized and happy. He was still not fully to terms with his relationship and the issues of unity and belief were also still pounding in his head, but neither could affect his positive attitude too much right now. Since he had actively pushed his logic back yesterday evening and had allowed his feelings to have their say again in an equivalent position, things had started to fall into place again in his mind. The uncertainty of the relationship was still there of course and he was, more than ever, aware that it would be a tough nut to crack all the differences, but now it felt more like a challenge than a problem. What he had realized now was that there was nothing to lose for him in this, but a lot to win. And even the thought of being wrong about Kung Fu and just ending up being a toy for her didn't bother him anymore. He was more than convinced that this was not true anyway, but even if it were, it would still end up being a win-win situation to a certain extent, and that felt good. A similar pattern emerged when it came to priorities. He knew that he had been capable of juggling all the responsibilities so far, and he would certainly still be able to do that with this one additional point in his life. Contrary to yesterday's thoughts, he now was even convinced that his relationship would help in some of the matters. After all, having a mage as a girlfriend would put him in the great position of not having to have the shroud of secrecy in that area. And after seeing in multiple cases of what that secrecy was able to do, even for someone like Jasmin, it felt like a really big bonus point.

When Lucas arrived in school that morning, he still had almost half an hour left before his first class. He quickly looked through the schedule to see if there was anything he still needed to prepare for the day, but like almost always he soon saw that everything was in perfect order already. Happy about this fact, he decided to use the time in a meaningful way and try to set up a date with Kung Fu for the weekend. He pulled out his cellphone and walked out to the end of the corridor, where he always went when he wanted to be more or less undisturbed in school. He was just in the middle of writing a text message to her when the phone rang.

"Déjà vu..." he laughed after he had picked up the call. "I was just about to text you."

"Shall I hang up so you can finish?" she asked and laughed too.

"And a very good morning to you too," Lucas said.

"Hey sweetheart, I feel bad for not having had time last weekend and I would like to make it up to you."

"There is no reason to feel bad, Kung Fu, so there is also no reason to make up for anything," Lucas said. "I didn't give you too much lead time, after all."

"Still... I feel bad, and unless you want me to continue to feel bad for longer than necessary, I would like to make it up to you," she replied.

"As you wish." Lucas had to smile. "What did you have in mind?"

"Are you free late Friday afternoon?" she asked.

"Hold on," he said and looked through his watch calendar. "I am out of school around two on Friday, so yeah, later Friday afternoon sounds great. What's the plan?"

"That's a surprise," Was her short answer. "We have to meet in downtown London for it though. I hope that's OK for you?"

"Sure." Lucas nodded. "As long as I have a decent way to get back home afterwards, I am happy with any place you choose."

"I will take you home if necessary," she said. "And of course, there is always the guest bedroom in my apartment if you want to stay over."

"That's settled then." Lucas again had to smile. "Just text me a time and meeting point, and I will be there."

"Will do. See you soon."

"Looking forward to it. See you," Lucas said before hanging up.

When he walked back to the classroom he was whistling without even realizing it. He had no idea what Kung Fu was planning for Friday evening, but he was definitely eager to find out. He was a little unsure about her offer to stay overnight though. The way she had presented it sounded like a kind of last resort idea, but he couldn't help wonder if that was just his interpretation. He rarely slept anywhere other than in his own room, and normally when he had to, it was not something he liked very much, but somehow her guest bedroom sounded like a very welcome alternative. After thinking about it for a while, he decided to preventively get his parents' permission for it and pack his backpack accordingly, just in case. He added the entry to his watch calendar and also added a reminder for the evening to talk to his parents about it, before he finally stowed his phone and started preparing for the first lesson of the day.

Lucas' schedule was packed until noon, leading to him not even checking his phone once. When he finally did during his lunch break, there were three texts waiting for him. Sandra had texted him an address for Friday, Darien had texted asking for details on the Jackson house visit and Stephanie had texted about the improving conditions of the police officer.

"Damn it," he said to himself when he opened the last message. Due to the lively discussion about the articles in the papers, he had totally forgotten to tell the others about his discussion with Corben and the good news he had received. He quickly texted Darien and Marcus, asking for their preferences on the weekend excursion before walking to his famous corridor spot and calling Stephanie.

"Hey Guardian. Didn't expect your call," Stephanie greeted him.

"Hi Airmid. Well, after your text I just had to call to say sorry," he answered.

"Why would you be sorry?" Stephanie was confused. "We made it. The officer will recover."

"Yeah, and that's a good thing." Lucas was still a little contrite. "But I already knew this a few days ago and forgot to tell you guys on Monday. I could have saved you the trip to the hospital."

"Actually, I haven't been to the hospital yet." Stephanie said. "I met Dr. Tackman in the city earlier today and he told me. But I did plan on visiting the patient later on. Do you want to join me?"

"I am not so sure if that is a good idea," Lucas said. "We have exposed ourselves quite a lot already with that little stunt. I am not sure if additional exposure will do us any good."

"I disagree with you, sorry," Stephanie replied very calmly. "Yes, the exposure might be a concern, but ensuring the patient's wellbeing is a bigger concern for me."

"And there are plenty of doctors to take care of that," Lucas reminded her.

"True, but none of them understands what we did. And I don't want to risk a relapse because of my over-carefulness with our privacy."

"Fair enough. You are, after all, the expert on this," Lucas admitted. "Do you want me, or maybe Psycho, to accompany you? Or would you prefer to be alone with the policeman?"

"I would prefer the company, but I understand if you don't want to be there. I am the healer, so the risk should be my burden to bear," Stephanie said.

"But as long as we are together in this circle, nobody has to bear their burden alone. So if you want me to tag along, I will. I could be at the hospital around four, if that's all right with you?"

"Sounds good." Stephanie sounded happy. "See you there."

Lucas was not at all happy about this development, both because it took away some valuable time and more because he still thought that this kind of exposure was way too risky in the long run. But Stephanie had already made her mind up when he called, and he knew her all too well by now to try changing that. And if she went there, it was not even a question if he would go there with her. He had brought that mess onto them when he suggested helping that officer in the first place. And he was the Guardian, after all, which meant that letting her walk all alone into a situation that he deemed to be risky was way against his nature. He quickly finished up his lunch and used the remainder of the break to get as much work done as possible, so at least the backlash in school would be minimal.

When he arrived at the hospital a few hours later he saw Stephanie's bike at the bike slots already. According to his watch he was ten minutes early, but seeing Stephanie there before him came as no surprise. When he walked into the lobby he could see her standing near the side wall, talking to Dr. Tackman. The situation looked very relaxed to him, so he decided to walk up to them right away.

"Good afternoon," he said and nodded a little toward both of them.

"Hey Guardian." Stephanie immediately turned toward him and gave him a hug.

"Good afternoon to you too." Dr. Tackman smiled. "It is a very rare thing to see your kind around here without a catastrophe following close by."

"It is most likely a rare thing to see anyone around here without a catastrophe, I would assume," Lucas laughed.

"Fair point." Tackman laughed too. "But I think you know what I meant."

"Yes, of course." Lucas shook Tackman's hand after Stephanie had finally let go of him. "And I apologize for taking up more of your time now."

"Please don't," Tackman said. "You have done a lot of good in the short time we have known each other, and I do appreciate that more than you can imagine."

"Most of the good we do is for our own 'kind', as you like to call them, so I doubt that you would appreciate that all too much," Lucas replied. "And the one exception my friends and I made so far is hardly impressive."

"And you think it makes a difference who you help?" Tackman seemed a little stunned. "You were right the other day, you know. People generally don't care all too much what happens behind them. Your kind normally is little different; after all, you are just human too. But you and your friends are. You do care, and you do try to help, even if the odds are stacked against you. You two being here today is the living proof of that, in both regards. You pulled that officer out of a definitive death sentence. I am sorry, but if you call that 'hardly impressive', then you are delusional. And coming here now tells me with 100% certainty that you do care after all."

"Well, we might have different points of view when it comes to the facts at hand, but you do have a good point when it comes to the medical condition we had to deal with." Lucas nodded. "But has it ever occurred to you that we might not be here because we care, but rather because we are hoping to gain something? That would be the more human reason, after all."

Tackman laughed loudly and needed a moment to regain his voice to answer. "That's the most ridiculous statement I have heard you make yet. I'm sorry, Guardian, I might not be able to fully comprehend what it is you are doing, but I do understand that coming here now poses more risk than it could ever pose reward for you. So yes, I might have thought about that angle, but I dismissed it pretty quickly too."

"Well, your high opinion honors me and my friends a lot. Let's just hope that we are worthy of it," Lucas said without any emotion slipping onto his face.

"If you doubt that, then you are the only person here who does." Tackman grinned and patted his shoulder. "But you are once again not here for small talk, unfortunately, so shall we get going?"

Lucas nodded and followed Stephanie and the doctor through the corridors of the hospital. It was weird feeling such support from someone who was not into magic himself. He had always been worried that people who didn't understand their gift would be reserved at best and aggressive at worst and had always done his very best to avoid letting anything slip. But Tackman seemed to not care about their weirdness. He had never made tried to find out more, had never tried to push other problems onto them, and still seemed to be appreciative. His logical side cried foul in every direction and urged him to be as careful as possible with the doctor, but his emotional side totally disagreed. There was not a shred of feeling in him that would doubt Tackman's intentions. Nothing other than trust in someone he knew little about. And this time, the emotions had the upper hand so clearly that even he, as a logical thinker by trait, could not deny following their lead.

When they finally entered the patient's room Lucas had a hard time coming to terms with what waited for them inside. The policeman was almost sitting upright in his bed, wearing a typical hospital nightgown and a brown bathrobe on top. His face looked like something out of a horror movie, scarred from left to right, hair growing only on parts of the head, with even more scars filling up the rest. A piece of his right ear was missing, and even more scars were visible on his hands. Next to his bed a woman was sitting in a guest chair, chatting with him. She was in her mid-thirties, had long brunette hair and was wearing a shiny red dress. The chat seemed mundane, but they both looked very cheerful, which to him seemed out of place, given the extensive damage that the man's face had.

"Excuse our intrusion, Constable Wainwright, but you have some more visitors," Dr. Tackman smiled as he entered.

"And why would nice young kids like you want to visit a worn-out bobby like me?" Wainwright turned towards them and smiled. "You are not by any chance thinking about joining the service as well?"

He then laughed and made an inviting gesture toward them. Lucas and Stephanie walked up to his bed, the doctor staying back.

"Hold on..." The officer's look became serious all of a sudden. "I have seen you before." He looked at Stephanie.

Lucas was unsure what would happen next, so he instinctively stayed half a step back and made sure he was focused and ready to react.

"Don't worry, kid. I am not going to harm her. I am just having a hard time believing my eyes." The policeman addressed Lucas, obviously having interpreted his reaction correctly.

"What is it, Marc?" The woman in red looked alarmed now too.

"You remember the dream I told you about?" He turned toward her. "The dream I had when they first brought me here?"

The woman nodded in reply.

"Well, it seems that my dream wasn't one after all," he continued. "Madeleine, meet my guardian angel."

"What?" The woman was now totally stunned, and so were Lucas and Stephanie.

Wainwright turned toward Stephanie. "When I was brought here everyone had told me already that I was about to die," he stated. "And then your face appeared, with all that confidence and beauty, and you pulled me back from that cliff. It made no sense to me then, and frankly it still doesn't, so I assumed it was a dream and that you were some kind of a guardian angel, watching over me. So please forgive my surprise. I had not expected to see you walking up to my bed."

"Well, I can assure you that I am no angel." Stephanie smiled at him. "And it was no dream. I was here with you that night."

"And I do know you too, right?" Wainwright had turned toward Lucas.

"Yes." Lucas nodded. "I was the one who got you into this mess to begin with."

"That can't be true..." He was looking more closely at him now. "The retard who shot me with the flame thrower was killed shortly after he hit me. And you don't look very dead to me. In addition, you don't exactly look like a retard to me." He laughed.

"That's not what I meant." Lucas had to laugh because of the officer's statement, but he didn't really feel like it. "You will most likely remember me from your operation in the subway station a few months back. I was the one tipping you off on that."

"The sting where we arrested DCI Murphy, yes. I remember now." Wainwright nodded. "But what does that have to do with me being here today?"

"Well, it's our assumption that the people who burned you were after Murphy and his friends. So if we hadn't pointed you toward them, this would never have happened," Lucas sighed.

"That makes you as guilty for this as the guy who sold me my shoes." Wainwright's look had gotten serious again. "That's my job, after all."

"Still..." Lucas started.

"You stop that," the woman in red interrupted him harshly. "There is nobody to blame other than the people who belong behind bars. Marc's job is dangerous; he knows that and I know that as well. But neither of us would have it any other way."

"Forgive my confusion, ma'am, but aren't you the least bit angry about the condition Mr. Wainwright is in right now?" Lucas was stunned. If that had happened to someone he loved, he would have blamed the whole world for it.

"What condition would that be? Alive?" Madeleine looked at Lucas. "The guy who meant my husband harm is dead. And yes, I am angry at him. But at the same time, I am grateful that Marc is alive."

"But he will never be the same again. I mean, the miracle might have kept him alive, but I doubt that all those scars will ever go away." Lucas still had a hard time believing the woman's calmness.

"Scars tell a story, my young friend," Wainwright said. "In my case, the story of a policeman not being careful enough. And while they certainly don't make me all too happy, the fact that I can sit here now and talk about them is something that makes me infinitely happy. And you are of course right; I will never be the same again. I will be more cautious in the future. But I will still be standing at the front line, upholding the law."

"You almost died doing that. Haven't you at least thought about taking it slowly after this experience?" Stephanie asked.

"I almost died, but I didn't. Justice did prevail in this case, and that is a good motivator to continue. Besides, if I step aside now then someone else would need to step into my shoes. And do you really think I would prefer letting someone else get into harm's way while I am still standing?"

"I admire your perseverance," Lucas said. "It really seems that this is more than a job for you."

"It is what I love to do." Wainwright nodded.

A minute of silence followed that Stephanie used to look through the constable's medical record.

"So, if you are not a guardian angel, what are you then?" Mrs. Wainwright asked Stephanie. "And what brought you to my husband?"

"Those questions are not so easy to answer," Lucas took it upon himself to respond. "As I said before, we were the ones who helped get Preston and his gang arrested. And when Inspector Corben approached me and told me about the prison break attempt and the consequences it had had, we decided to at least try to help."

"That explains what brought you here, but not what you are exactly," she continued poking.

"We are complicated," Lucas said. "We also have our passions and our skills, just like your husband does. Ours are just not so easy to explain."

"Why don't you try?" she asked.

"You are the Inspector's CI, right?" the constable jumped in before Lucas had a chance to respond.

"Yes." He nodded toward him.

"Then please accept my apologies for the questions. Neither my wife nor I want to diminish our gratefulness for what you did by our natural curiosity," he said.

"What?" His wife seemed confused.

"Bill told us a while ago that there was a CI out there who valued privacy over everything else. And that we should do nothing to compromise that wish if we ever came into the situation," Wainwright addressed his wife before turning to Lucas. "I am not sure how you came to be in the position you are in right now, but I am more than sure that I owe you my life. And so does Bill Corben. And I can fully assure you that I will never, ever jeopardize the integrity of a CI. I do respect your wish for privacy. I hope you never need our help again, but if you do, rest assured, we will be there for you." He offered Lucas his hand and he immediately shook it.

"I appreciate your understanding, Constable." Lucas smiled. "I also hope that our paths do not cross again anytime soon, but I somewhat doubt that, unfortunately."

"Once you start poking into those areas they rarely let you go again, it seems" the constable said and nodded. "But as I said, we will have your back."

They continued chatting a little longer, while Stephanie looked at the records and some of the scars.

When she took a step back Lucas turned toward her. "Have you checked everything you wanted to check?" he asked.

"Yes, everything looks far better than I expected, except for the scars. Those will need a long time to heal, and most likely never fully will," she replied.

"Don't worry about the scars," Wainwright laughed. "They will be a good reminder for my colleagues."

"Well, we should let you get some rest again," Lucas said to Wainwright. "Get better quickly."

"I might check back with you in a few days," Stephanie said as she shook Wainwright's hand. "I doubt there will be any more complications, but I'd rather be sure."

"Be safe, you two" the constable said as they walked out the room.

"Godspeed, Constable. Until we meet again." Lucas waved on his way out without turning back.

Lucas was happy when they finally approached the front entrance of the hospital. Stephanie discussed a few more details with Dr. Tackman before joining him on the way out.

"That went well," she said with a smile.

"It was a close call," he replied. "We are lucky that the constable stopped his wife from asking more questions. Anything more than what we told them so far would have been compromising in my eyes."

"That's true unfortunately." Stephanie nodded. "Now I begin to understand what you were trying to say earlier today. We really need to be even more in the background in the future."

"Yeah. Stunts like this can blow up in our faces pretty quickly, unfortunately" Lucas said. "But it paid off this time; let's keep it at that."

Stephanie nodded silently as she got on her bike.

"Have a good week, Airmid. See you on Monday," he said when he got on his.

"You too. Good luck at Jackson's house," she replied and rode off.

"Thanks," he mumbled back and got on his way too. It was again time for him to get back to his other life and deal with all the schoolwork that was waiting for him. He sighed when he thought about it. It would be a long evening.

CHAPTER 11

COMFORT ZONE

When Friday came, Lucas was as cheerful as he could possibly be. The school week had been uneventful after Tuesday's visit to the hospital, the workload he had left for the weekend was pretty light, and the one exam he still had coming for today was not something that took him out of his comfort zone. The visit to Jackson's house had been scheduled for Saturday afternoon, so no matter what Kung Fu had in store for him today, he would have plenty of time for it. And his parents had agreed to him staying elsewhere for the night, without asking too many questions. It felt a little weird to him that they didn't even want to know where he was going. The only thing his mother insisted on knowing was if an adult would be somewhere around in case of any problems. In hindsight Lucas felt a little bad for only answering the question with a short, "Yes, of course." The answer had been a correct one; after all, Sandra was an adult by all standards, and technically so was he, having his eighteenth birthday behind him already. It had just not been the whole truth, because he did 'forget' to mention the fact that he was involved with her. But as his mother had not asked any further he had just remained silent, which for now had to be good enough.

The last exam in the end proved to be more of a problem than he had anticipated, not because of the topic, which was something he knew plenty about, but because he could hardly focus at all. The anticipation of the evening was too strong, as were the emotions that raged through his body. In the end he had to rely on a sort of short meditation that he had thus far only used when casting spells in order to calm down enough to not fumble the test. In this mental state of total calmness, he quickly finished everything and even was able to complete it a few minutes ahead of time. When he walked out of the classroom the burst of emotions and thoughts came back almost instantly, which made him wonder if that calmness really had been the product of his meditation or if he had in fact cast some sort of emotional magic without realizing it. The thought kept bugging him for a while longer, but in the end, he had to admit that there was just no way to tell the difference. Especially since he had come to terms with his emotions and consequently ascended to Magus Major status, the lines had gotten seriously blurred. Magic was part of his life now, and there was just no way anymore to truly do things without it. Thinking back to the exam it, for a brief moment only, felt like an unfair advantage to him. But he quickly dismissed that thought. There was no level playing field in school; he had known that long before he had started using magic. It was just a question of focus and effort, and he was convinced by now that those who struggled in school were lacking either one or the other. Lucas kept thinking about the topic until he had reached the train station.

When he boarded the train to London he finally put the topic to rest and started looking ahead. He had spent quite some time trying to figure out what Sandra was up to, but could not produce a single useful clue. The meeting point was almost in the city center, leaving the area around it packed with potential destinations to consider. Looking at his watch, he saw that he had plenty of time left. The train ride would take about three quarters of an hour, plus another estimated 30 minutes in the tubes, which would have him arrive about half an hour early. He kept looking at the map printout that he had brought with him until he exited the train at St. Pancras station, but he was as wise then as he had been before. When he finally got off the tube and was walking towards the set meeting point, he started feeling queasy. He knew that there was nothing to worry about at all, but still he couldn't shake it, no matter how hard he tried. And as much as he was looking forward to this date, he was dreading that next half hour of waiting, because he was quite certain that this feeling would only intensify. To his surprise, this worry was taken from him quite quickly, though. When he walked around the final corner Sandra was already there, sitting on a bench, talking to someone on the phone. Lucas had to take a deep breath as he approached her. He had seen her quite a few times by now, but she still looked stunning to him. Wearing tight black jeans, high end jogging shoes and a bright yellow jacket, she looked like the sun itself with her big smile. When she recognized him she waved in his direction and her smile got even bigger.

"Seems I have less time to chat than I thought I would," Lucas heard her saying into the phone. "I will call you tomorrow if that's all right with you, Beck."

Lucas stopped a few steps away to let her finish her conversation.

"Hey gorgeous," he smiled when she had finally put her phone away and was approaching him.

"Hey sweetheart," she replied with a grin. "Are you shy?"

"No, I just wanted to give you some privacy for your conversation."

"Do you really think I would have a phone call requiring privacy in a public place like this?" She laughed and gave him a kiss.

"Are you really in the position to choose where you are when the sensitive phone calls come in?" Lucas said and kissed her again.

"Fair point," she had to admit. "But that was just my sister Rebecca. So no state secrets."

"I didn't know that you have a sister," Lucas said. "Is she into magic as well?"

"No. And she doesn't know about my involvement either." Sandra had put her arm around his waist and started walking. "But unless you want to hit on my sister, I would suggest we change the subject."

"There are enough hormones floating through my body from your presence alone. I doubt that I could handle two of your kind," Lucas laughed and pulled her closer. "Where are we going anyway? You still haven't told me what you are up to."

"I know that you are not into sports that much, but I still wanted to take you to one of the many that I enjoy a lot. And if I am not totally mistaken, you will like it as well," she answered. "Remember you once said that you would not want to get into a shooting duel with me? Well, you might have to reconsider that wish."

"Shouldn't I have brought sportswear for that, then?" Lucas had not expected this kind of afternoon activity.

"No. All you need is good shoes. And you wear those all the time, so we are good." She grinned. "And actually, we are already here."

Lucas looked ahead at the location she was pointing at. It looked like a multi-story warehouse of sorts, with no apparent sign out front but a lot of flashing lights visible through some windows. When they came closer Lucas saw that many of the windows were actually covered from the inside in dark curtains and only one block had been left open. Sandra pulled the door open and they both stepped in. The room they walked into was not at all what Lucas had expected. The outside of the building was shabby, but inside everything was state of the art. Computer screens hung on the walls, a nice large counter was at the far end of the room and there were a lot of smaller tables with chairs. It resembled a bar at first glance, but with a weird, futuristic style, almost like on a space station out of a computer game. The counter was made of metal with a lot of lights built into it, the tables had touch screens fabricated in, apparently for placing orders, and there were multiple doors leading to other areas that all looked like those you would see in space movies. Lucas took quite a while to overcome his awe and get back to reality.

"Sandra, how nice to see you again. I did not expect you back so soon." A man with a strong French accent had approached the two from behind the bar.

"Francoise, good to see you too." She smiled and let go of Lucas to shake his hand. "I actually did make an appointment for today. And as you can see, I did not come alone."

"Ah... You are finally presenting your boyfriend." Francoise smiled and shook Lucas' hand. "This will make a lot of men in here sad, you know?" he then said to him.

"Hey! Don't put me in an awkward position here." Sandra hit him lightly on the shoulder with her fist. "Lucas, meet Francoise, Francoise, Lucas," she introduced the two.

"Pleasure meeting you." Lucas was still stunned because of his surroundings.

"Same here." Francoise smiled. "Welcome to the warzone."

"Warzone?" The comment pulled Lucas back to reality immediately.

"Oui. Didn't Sandra tell you what you were getting yourself into?" He grinned and pointed toward an array of monitors mounted on a wall.

So far Lucas had only looked at the screen above the bar, which apparently showed the menu, daily specials and the news. The array on the side wall showed a totally different picture. Some screens showed scoring lists, a few of them seeming to capture some kind of event that was currently in progress and others more resembling a high score overview. The other monitors presented a look into a weird kind of maze with different markings and strange contraptions all over it. And in that maze Lucas could see people running around, wearing some kind of weirdly futuristic-looking body armor and rifles that were connected to that armor.

"Actually, she didn't," Lucas grinned while still following the action on the center screen. "At least not in detail."

"You are in a state-of-the-art laser combat arena," Francoise explained. "We offer team skirmishes as well as one-on-one duels."

"That sounds like fun." Lucas turned around to face the others again. "Where do I sign up?"

"Well, then let's go." Sandra smiled and pulled him with her toward one of the large side doors. "Lock us in for the next team match for starters, will you please, Francoise?"

"Sure thing." Francoise nodded and went to the counter.

Lucas followed Sandra into what seemed to be a locker room. They locked their jackets and bags up before she stepped over to the wall and pulled two random bags off that were hanging there in a long line of similar ones. When Lucas opened the one she handed him, he found a set of armor and gun in it, exactly like the ones he had seen the players wear on the screen. He was still looking at the high-tech jacket when Sandra had already finished putting hers on. With her help he also got into his armor and secured his laser gun in a holster that was mounted up front on the armor plate. Then they walked into another room together. This one was smaller, with benches on each side and two doors exiting on the far end.

"This is the staging area," Sandra explained. "Once the teams have assembled here the referees will come and explain all the rules before we go in for a 10-minute game."

"Do you do this regularly?" Lucas asked her.

"Yes." She nodded. "Helps sharpen the senses and improve the reflexes. But you will see that when we head into a duel later. Then you can find out which of us actually does have the upper hand." She winked.

Lucas had so far only known this kind of game from his computer, and even there he had not played them very often. But even though the equipment here looked lame compared to the high-resolution pixel art of a computer game, the surroundings, the atmosphere and the fact that there was no pause button in the arena made this far more immersive than any game he had played so far. When the referee, a man in his early twenties, walked in a few minutes later he made sure to give the briefing his full attention. The rules were fairly simple and so was the technology, but it was still fascinating to listen. When they finally stepped through the door into the arena and the game was about to start, Lucas could feel the adrenaline pumping through his veins. He had been tagged into the blue team, together with Sandra and four others he didn't know. Judging from the way they handled the gear it seemed that they were veterans, which pushed him to the edge even more, being the only rookie in the team. He spent the first few minutes staying close to Sandra and trying to steal some tricks from her, but he quickly got the hang of it and started making his own way around the arena. It was a fun experience and he even managed to score a few points throughout this first match. But in the end his team lost by quite a significant gap of hits and they had to clear the arena again.

"That was awesome," he said when he was finally back in the locker room with her. "Thank you for bringing me here."

"I'm glad that you like it." She smiled. "Shall we go again?"

Lucas nodded and so they went back into the staging area. The second round was a blast too, so much so that they added another three rounds after that. By the end of the fifth match he had managed to achieve scores comparable to the other players already, making the experience even more enjoyable for him.

"Do you feel ready to take me on?" Sandra asked with a grin.

"What do you mean?" Lucas was still catching his breath after the last encounter.

"The team matches were just the warm-up," she said. "There are some duel arenas in the building too, where the two of us can go head-on without anyone else interfering."

"I doubt that I will stand a chance against you in a match like that," Lucas laughed. "But I sure as hell will try."

"Great. I don't date quitters, so I wouldn't have accepted no for an answer anyway." She winked and led the way upstairs to another staging area.

The arena they entered there was smaller than the one they had played in before, but it was still big enough to get lost in it. And in contrast to before, it was totally silent in here, combining the duel itself with an element of hide and seek. Lucas tried to tread as carefully as possible, avoiding making noise at all cost. And apparently Sandra was doing the same, as after five minutes he still hadn't heard a single sound anywhere. It was a weird feeling in here, almost scary. Nothing moved, no sounds, no shadows other than the flickering of the neon lights, no soul around. And still, he knew that somewhere in this maze she was hiding and waiting to get a shot at him. The tension almost made him mad as he walked through the corridors until his armor finally lit up, signaling that he had been hit. He quickly turned around, but couldn't see her. Only when the second shot hit him did he spot her at the far corner. But before he could aim his gun she had hit him for the third time, ending the game.

"Damn, you are way too good at this," he laughed when they walked out of the arena together.

"Don't stay at the center of the aisles; that's a rookie mistake," she said. "Other than that, I was just lucky that I spotted you first. Shall we do it again?"

"Sure thing. I will not leave here without a rematch." He grinned.

They entered the arena again and this time Lucas was even more careful. It again took them about five minutes before they encountered each other, but this time Lucas managed to take cover before she was able to score more than one point. He tried to circle around her twice and even the score but both times she anticipated the move and was waiting for him, scoring another point. Only when he doubled back on the third attempt was he able to get in behind her and score a point too. Doing another zigzag and using the cover of a small opening in a wall he even managed to tie the score. Fueled by that lucky break, he made another move, hoping to surprise her again. And he was already aiming for his final shot when she recognized him.

"Levipes," he heard her hiss before she jumped in a sort of barrel roll, avoiding his shot and getting one off herself, scoring her the final point and with it, victory in this round.

"That was unfair." Lucas tried to make an annoyed face, but had to grin. "But it was a great move."

"It would only be unfair if you were a commoner." She grinned. "But given that you are a mage too, I see no ethical problem with that move."

"Oh, THAT is how you want to play that game..." He laughed. "You should have told me; maybe I would have done it differently then too."

"Well, in this case... I told you now, so let's go again." She made an inviting gesture.

Lucas nodded and they stepped into the arena for a third duel. But right after the door had closed behind them he realized that there was not much that he could do. He had no idea if his shields were capable of deflecting the infrared lasers of the guns, and other than that he had little in his magical arsenal that would make a difference. He walked around the corridors with his shield fired up, constantly thinking about his options to level the playing field. About three minutes into the game Sandra scored her first hit, making it apparent that his defense was not working in this kind of scenario. He dropped it and quickly retreated to think the situation through again. And then suddenly an idea struck him: He was more than capable of weaving energy lines and nets; he knew that. Maybe with his emotional side he would also be sensitive enough to detect his own energy, which would allow him to build some kind of magical radar, comparable to Darien's eyes. He quickly started building an energy beam that would deflect back from objects and tried to open up his senses as much as possible.

"Deprehendere," he then cast, once again having no idea where the word had come from. And to his astonishment it worked instantly. He could feel the energy being bounced back from the walls and objects within the arena and was able to build a map in his mind based on that. But that by itself was not helping him either, so he started rebuilding the energy patterns, for them to penetrate walls and objects and only be reflected by a human body.

"Deprehendere," he cast again. And this time he had done the trick. It only took him one quick look around to see where Sandra was hiding, and as he got closer he could even recognize which direction she was looking. Armed with that information, it was now all too easy for him to sneak up behind her, fire off a shot and get back into cover before she even knew what had hit her. And even her agility magic could not help her out of that anymore. When she got the second hit and apparently realized that she was outgunned, she started leveraging her spells to move around the arena quickly, trying to not give him a good way of sneaking up. But all that did was delay the inevitable. With Lucas now being aware of her position and direction all the time, it was easy for him to avoid her and wait for the perfect situation to score his third point.

"I have no idea how you did that, but you are officially the fastest learner I have ever seen in this arena." She was still gasping when they walked out the arena together.

"I am not a fast learner in this sport. I could have never beat you fair and square, but I might be the more powerful mage." He grinned.

"You did almost beat me in the last game," she replied. "So don't be modest. And whatever kind of magic you were using in there seems to beat all that I had to offer. And I do think that my magic is very helpful in situations like this."

"Your magic is great for open encounters," Lucas replied, "but not for stealth games. That's where I seem to have had the better plan."

They walked down to the locker room again and finally took the gear off. She was exhausted physically from the last game and he felt the mental drain from his spell too, so neither was up for another run.

"That was really fun. Thank you," Lucas said when they were walking to the subway station. He only now had realized that they had been in there for almost three hours.

"We should do that again at some point." She smiled. "I have a score to settle now, after all."

"Anytime. It's totally worth traveling to London for," he said.

"You are not intending to go home already, are you?" Sandra had a strange tone in her voice that Lucas couldn't really make sense of. She almost sounded freaked out to him.

"I do not want to intrude on you." Lucas was careful as he responded. "But if you have more plans, then by all means bring them up."

"Well, I had one more plan for the evening, but I am not sure if you will be up for it." Her smile had faded.

"After you let me beat you at your own game, I think I am up for almost anything you could present me." He smiled. "So what's on your mind?"

"Well, it is almost dinner time, and I wanted to invite you home and cook for you," she said. "I know, it's a little bit on the edge of cliché, but I do enjoy cooking and rarely have the opportunity to do it."

"I accept. But with a condition," he said.

"And what would that be?" Her voice sounded somewhere between insecure and alarmed.

"That you allow me to help you," he said with a grin and pushed a kiss onto her cheek. "Otherwise it is a little too close to cliché for my comfort."

"Sure thing." She laughed, obviously relieved by his answer.

"But I have to warn you," Lucas said, "I am a terrible cook."

"Well, let's see if I am any better," she replied. "But in any case, it will definitely be fun."

They got onto the tube and hitched a ride to the outskirts of London. The neighborhood there looked far less inviting than the area that he lived in, but it still felt safe and quiet. Sandra led him to a large apartment complex just two blocks off the station. Her condo was almost in the middle of the building, on the sixteenth floor. It was quite spacious, with a small, open lobby that led directly into a large living room which included the kitchen. Multiple doors on three sides seemed to lead to other rooms and a large window front on the fourth presented a stunning view of the surrounding area. The room itself was very clean and very open. A dining table near the kitchen area and a sofa in the other corner were about the only things standing in it, leaving a wide area in the middle that was covered with mats on the floor. A TV set was hanging opposite the couch and the cable dangling loosely on a chair next to the dining table revealed that a laptop was most certainly used there regularly.

"Wow, this is quite a residence you have here." Lucas was still looking around the room and out of the window.

"Thank you. I was lucky to get it, and I try my best to make the most out of it." She had walked into one of the side rooms, which Lucas quickly identified as the bathroom. He followed her in, after taking his shoes off, and washed his hands thoroughly. The bathroom also was spotless-- not very large, but very well organized. It had a basin that was surrounded by cabinets with mirror fronts, a washing machine in the corner and a large bathtub with a glass shower curtain lining the back wall.

"Why do you have mats in your living room?" Lucas asked as they walked back out.

"Because I like to do sports at home too." She grinned. "And I would not want to do something like this without a mat below." She stepped to the middle of the mat and teetered a little before performing a standing flip right in front of his eyes.

"Well, I would not want to do something like that at all," he laughed. "The risk of serious injury would be overwhelming in my case. But I get the point."

They walked into the kitchen area and she started taking some pans and pots out of the cabinets.

"If you really want to help me, you could start by boiling some water." She pointed toward a water cooker on the back shelf. "But I am totally fine if you leave the cooking to me and have a look around in the meantime."

"I will help you," Lucas replied. "I hope there will be enough time afterwards for me to have a tour through the rest of the apartment."

From the corner of his eye he could see that Sandra had pulled a large wooden board out and was now hacking away on some vegetables. The speed with which she did this with was awe-inspiring, almost like a seasoned chef. Lucas watched her for a moment, still amazed that she was able to do that without chopping her fingers off in the process. When she pushed some carrots aside with her knife, he for the first time recognized the weird shape. It was almost symmetrical, sharp edges on both sides, and instead of a normal handle it just had a steel tang to hold it on.

"Interesting cooking knife you have there," he said as he filled the water cooker.

"That's not a cooking knife," she grinned. Then she took a swing and threw the knife across the room. Lucas almost dropped the canister he was holding when he followed the path of the knife. On the other side of the room he only now recognized a small wooden target board, with the knife now sticking out right in the middle circle.

"Remind me to never get on your bad side," Lucas said, whistling.

"You do know that I am a martial artist, right?" Sandra laughed and walked through the room to get her knife back.

"I assumed so." He nodded. "But I never realized how advanced you actually are."

"I can show you some moves if you like," she said and continued hacking the vegetables.

"I would love that." Lucas smiled. "In light of recent events, it would be a great idea."

"Recent events? Is that your way of saying I can get even for the laser game earlier today?" She winked.

"Not THAT recent," Lucas laughed.

They continued joking around while they prepared dinner. Sandra had put some sort of mixed salad with strips of white meat and roasted vegetables on the menu and she proved to be a master in preparing all of it. Lucas tried hard to help at least a little bit, but it felt as if for every one thing he got done, she had finished ten in the same time. When they finally sat down at the dinner table the entire room already smelled like it, which strengthened Lucas' appetite even more.

"This tastes awesome," he complimented after the first few bites.

"Amazing how much difference organic food can make," Sandra smiled.

"Amazing how much difference the right chef can make," Lucas grinned. "Thanks again for the invite." With that, he leaned over and gave her a kiss.

"You know what?" he started again after a few more bites. "This is the first time the two of us have ever been alone."

"Yes." She nodded. "That's why I was a little reluctant to invite you at first. I was not sure if you would feel comfortable with that."

"You are kidding, right?" Lucas stopped eating and looked up.

"Why would you think that?" she asked, also stopping to eat.

"Show me one guy in his right mind who would not want to be alone with you." Lucas laughed and took another bite.

"That's the thing with you, Guardian," Sandra replied slowly. "You are not like all those guys."

"What are you saying? That I am insane?" Lucas looked up again with a grin.

"Well, I think we both are to a certain extent." She had to laugh at that thought, but then quickly became serious again "But no, that was not my point. I think that you are far more mature than any of those guys you are referring to, and certainly far more mature than I am."

"Jesus, Kung Fu... I am as far away from mature as I possibly could be in that topic." Lucas shook his head. "The truth of the matter is that I don't have the slightest idea what I am doing. And all I am really trying to accomplish is to get along without making any major mistakes."

"You know what, you are just as weird in this as JJ is," she said. "Everyone around you knows how far ahead you are, in every aspect of life. Everyone around you believes in you blindly. Why don't you?"

"Because everyone around me believes in the part of me they know," Lucas sighed. "And that is only a small portion of who I really am."

"And you think that's any different from the way all other people are?" She spiked a piece of chicken with her fork and waved it in Lucas' direction. "You better think again. Everyone only presents one of their faces; that's normal. There is a Japanese saying: Everyone has three faces: the first that he shows the world, the second that he shows only to his truest friends, and the third that he shows to nobody but himself. Whether you like it or not, you might be more of a saint than any of the ones that the church calls by that name."

"That still doesn't make me mature. And it still doesn't explain why you would think I have a problem being here alone with you," Lucas replied.

"Well, let's just say that I don't want to scare you away. And I am still afraid that I might do that somehow tonight," she said and looked down at her plate.

"You should know by now that I am not scared easily. So don't worry too much, please." He gently stroked her arm. Somehow he still had difficulty wrapping his head around the situation. Why would she be scared about that? He was definitely more scared of getting punched in the face for doing something inappropriate. He continued to search for any clues about possible dark secrets she could have while they finished dinner, but there was nothing whatsoever that he could come up with. When they were both done eating, Lucas stood up and carried the plates back into the kitchen.

"What's that supposed to be?" Sandra jumped up and walked after him.

"Well, we had great dinner; now I would assume that we clean up the mess we made. Or do you have some magic lined up for that?" He grinned.

"The 'magic' is called a dishwasher, yes." She laughed. "And I can get that one filled up myself. You are the guest here, remember?"

"I guess I have to be an impolite guest, then." Lucas had to laugh too. "Because I will not get out of your kitchen until we have cleaned everything up. So... Where is that dishwasher of yours?"

"It seems you are even more incurable than I thought." She gave him a light punch in the ribs before finally helping him with the work at hand.

"Are you happy now?" she asked snappishly when the dishwasher was finally running.

"Yes, I am, thank you." He smiled and walked out into the open living room space.

"What would you like to do now?" she asked and followed him.

"Well, I know it's most likely a bad idea right after dinner, but if your offer is still good I would really like to see your martial arts in action." He had stepped onto the mats.

"Well, we should be careful what we practice, but the dinner was light, so a few slow moves should be doable." She smiled and stepped up next to him.

They then worked out for almost an hour, starting with a warm-up and some basic techniques around falling down and rolling off, some explanations about stability, center of gravity and other stuff that sounded more like physics than martial arts, and finally she showed him some attack and defense moves. Throughout the session Lucas had to focus completely on what he was doing. Everything looked so easy when she showed it to him, but the longer he trained the more he realized the minute details in the moves and the importance those had. And while his mind was rather quickly able to grasp the concepts behind those details, his body had a very hard time following that lead. He stumbled a lot, especially trying to get a stable stand or recovering from a fall, and he more than once saw how wrong he did things, but was unable to correct his moves and get them right. It was frustrating for him, acting like a newborn child in some areas, but he tried his best and kept on it as well as he could.

"You are a quick learner," Sandra complimented him when he managed to land on his feet after avoiding a punch.

"I don't feel like one right now," he laughed and prepared for another round. "I feel like a total idiot."

"You should see others when they have their first training session." She patted his shoulder. "You are way better than most. But this is an art, and learning arts takes time. No matter how good the student is."

"I still feel like I'm not getting anything right," he sighed.

"We did a lot of very specific exercises. Let's do some combinations now; you will see the difference immediately," she suggested.

Lucas nodded and they continued. And he immediately saw what she meant. The format now was to defend against multiple, subsequent attacks and rebound whenever possible. This kind of 'real fight' had him leveraging all the things they had trained before, but in this more free-flowing, chaotic way of moving the minute details didn't count that much anymore. In one situation he managed to pull Sandra off her feet with a move that he had been unable to perform before. The reason was that she had been standing out of balance to begin with, because of the previous move she had made. That allowed even his flimsy technique to become successful in the end. With more time and more runs through the routine, he even freed up some of his mental capacity and started realizing the situation as a whole again, instead of the very technique-focused outlook he had had before. And while this made the fighting even easier, as it allowed him to spot more opportunities, it also made him realize some other details he had missed so far.

"I'm sorry," he said after another move, causing her to stop dead in her tracks.

"What are you sorry about?" She looked totally surprised. "I was the one who just hit you in the ribs."

"Which was the point of the exercise, I guess." He laughed for a moment before becoming serious again. "I am sorry because I just now realized that I have been touching you in a pretty inappropriate manner time and again throughout the training. And I hadn't even realized it so far."

"Are you serious?" She took a step back.

"Yes... Why?" Now Lucas was surprised.

"First of all, body contact is part of martial arts, so if you want to train in it, you have to get used to that," she said. "Second, I have gotten used to this a long time ago, and I did receive my fair share of beatings and injuries over the years, so don't worry. And third, 'inappropriate' touching, as you called it, happens during such moves. It will happen in a real fight too. It's part of the sport, and not something that needs an apology, not from anyone, and definitely not from you."

"Why definitely not from me?" Lucas was still struggling with the situation.

"Well, I practically invited you into a sparring match with me, so I can hardly complain about the outcome now. But more importantly, if you want to touch me, then please just touch me. You don't need the excuse of a martial arts training session or any other excuse, for that matter. I know that you still feel uncomfortable with the situation we are in; that's why I always try to be cautious. But I don't, at least not at that level. So take all the time you need and feel free to act on your impulses whenever you want."

"You really don't mind?" Lucas asked a little shyly, still not sure if he should believe what she had just said.

"No, I don't. On the contrary, I do want you close to me." She shook her head.

"I think I will need a moment to let this sink in." He had stepped off the mats.

"Take your time." She approached him and gave him a short kiss.

He hesitated for a moment before taking her in his arms and giving her a much longer, more intense, second kiss.

"Thank you," he said and smiled at her.

"It is getting late by the way." She smiled back and pointed at the kitchen clock. It was after 11 p.m. already. "Shall I take you home now, or do you want to stay here?"

"I would prefer to stay, if that's all right with you," he said.

"Of course it is." She seemed happy about the decision. "I think we should get a shower then, unless you want to continue with the sparring. I'll let you go first. There are fresh towels on the heater and a bathrobe under the sink."

"Good idea, thanks." He nodded and walked off toward the bathroom, grabbing his night shirt and his toiletries from his backpack on the way. He took a long time in the shower, giving his mind room to sort through the evening. After brushing his teeth, he got dressed for the night, put the bathrobe on and walked out again. Sandra had turned on the TV and was sitting on the couch, watching the news. When she saw him come out she jumped up to take her turn in the bathroom. Lucas took her space on the couch and let his mind roam freely, looking at the TV, but not really following the program. About ten minutes later Sandra stepped back out, wearing a similar bathrobe to his. Her hair was bound into a pigtail again, and she looked really relaxed. She made her way over to the couch and sat down next to him. He turned over and smiled at her.

"You are really beautiful," he said. "I am a lucky guy getting to be here with you."

"That makes both of us lucky then." She smiled and gave him a kiss. "Do you want to watch some movies now? Or do you want to go to bed?"

"I doubt that I could really follow a movie right now," he said and looked down at her leg that had become visible under the bathrobe. "So maybe bed is a better idea."

"Sure thing." She grinned and stood up, walking toward one of the side doors. "This is the guest room. I have prepared the bed for you already."

He got up too, walked up behind her, putting his arms around her waist and giving her a long, gentle kiss on the neck.

"If you don't mind, I would rather join you in your bed tonight," he said and gently pulled her with him toward the master bedroom, turning off the lights as he walked.

CHAPTER 12

OVERDUE

When Lucas was on his way to the subway station the next morning he felt like a different man. Happiness had crawled into every inch of his body, combined with a feeling of relaxation the likes of which he had never felt before. It felt as if his mind and his emotions had fused into one interwoven block of unity, a block that made him a new version of himself: stronger, smarter, better. He was not totally sure if this had been caused by the events of last night, or rather by the events that had led up to those in the earlier evening, but he assumed that the latter was true. He hadn't gotten too much sleep that night, but he still didn't feel the least bit tired. During the entire ride back to Luton he smiled and watched his surroundings. He enjoyed the feeling a lot, and did whatever he could to immerse in it as much as possible. When he arrived home, he had little time to spare. Sandra had invited him back for the evening, which was an offer that he didn't want to let pass. He knew that there was still some schoolwork to do, but he reckoned that he would be able to get it done in time, and if not he would just have to take some of it with him and do it on the train. To his surprise, when he asked his parents' permission for the night out, they didn't even ask about his school duties. "So you finally have a real girlfriend," his father had said and laughed loudly before he had nodded his agreement and wished him a good time. His mother had been a little bit less euphoric, but had also seemed ok with it. She just had insisted that Lucas bring Sandra home at some point so they could both meet her. But what surprised him even more than his parents' open and welcoming response was the way he felt about their comments. Lucas remembered how annoyed he was when they had asked to meet the rest of the circle and how much it had bothered him in general when they stuck their noses into his affairs, but this time he had no such feelings at all. On the contrary, he was happy about the approval and saw his mother's request as a sign of true interest, rather than a means of control, and he was more than happy to do as she had asked, provided that Sandra was ok with it too. On his way over to the meeting with Darien and Marcus, he thought about the reasons for that. At first he presumed that it was a side effect of the strong feelings he had for her, but he quickly realized that this was not at all true. He quickly came to realize that this newfound unity inside himself was the real reason for his revised point of view. While his emotions had already had their say-so in the past, and had provided him valuable insight already, they had now become an integral part of his thoughts. And while often in the past his thoughts had dictated the emotions, like the annoyance he had felt with his parents, now his emotions formed together with the thought, making the picture by far less biased and more reliable. When he cycled around the last corner and saw the others already waiting, he smiled and centered his attention back to the task at hand.

"You look different today, Guardian." Darien looked at him as he jumped off his bike, even before exchanging greetings. "Almost like a different person."

"It doesn't need your eyes to see that, Professor. That one is obvious." Marcus laughed and approached him. "Our fearless leader has had an eventful night."

He then laid his hand on Lucas' shoulder. "Brother to brother, yours to the end," they greeted each other.

"I can see that too without needing any special gift." Darien replied. "But there is far more to it than you can spot."

Lucas had walked over to Darien now and they exchanged the greeting too.

"Is it THAT obvious?" he then asked and looked first at Marcus, then at Darien.

"Yeah, it is." Marcus laughed again. "You have a smile like a rocking horse. Who is the lucky lady?"

"I would love to let you see through my eyes for once." Darien nodded. "Your energy pattern looks totally different, way more structured and aligned. You don't morph that much just because of a night, no matter how great it was. So I second the question: Who is the lucky lady?"

Lucas thought for a moment, a little unsure if he should tell them the details.

"You have both actually met her at least once," he then said. "Although I doubt that you spent much time making her acquaintance. Her name is Kung Fu. She is part of Angel's circle."

"The fighting lady in the yellow robes?" Marcus seemed surprised. "I would have never dared ask her to be my training partner, let alone anything else. How did you pull that off?"

"How come that you remember her that well?" Darien asked Marcus. "Do you know her better than the rest of us?"

"No." Marcus shook his head "I just happened to fight side by side with her during our encounter with Cleric. And boy, that girl has skills... I have rarely seen a martial artist like her ever. Fast, precise, well trained. She is WAY out of my league, man, I can tell you that."

"Then she is in the right league for Guardian." Darien winked at Lucas. "Whatever she did to you, I am happy for you, mate." He patted Lucas' shoulder.

"Thanks, Professor." Lucas smiled. "But we didn't come here to celebrate my happiness, unfortunately. We have work to do."

The others nodded and got back on their bikes. It was only a short ride to Jackson's house, with some traffic along the way that forced them to cycle behind each other, leaving no chance for conversation. When they arrived, everything looked quiet. The house lay there just like they had left it last time. Nobody was to be seen anywhere, no cars outside the house, no neighbors on the street, only the occasional birds in the trees. The boys chained their bikes to a lantern a few houses down the road before they entered the garden. When they had reached the side corner they stopped and pulled out their robes. The hedges were high enough so nobody could see them from the street anymore, giving them the privacy needed. They slowly continued down the house to the backyard.

"They didn't even repair the window," Lucas said and shook his head when he walked around the corner.

"They have most likely not yet discovered that it is broken," Darien replied.

"That's good. At least we don't have to worry about our footprints inside this time," Marcus said and reached through the broken pane of glass to unlock the frame.

"Lucky us." Lucas nodded. He had just now realized that they would have had no way to disguise their entry this time, without Cedric around.

Marcus pushed the window open and quickly swung through it. After he listened at the door for a moment he gave them the all-clear, so Lucas and Darien climbed in as well. Their technique was still far from the elegance that Marcus had shown, but they at least both managed to get in without hurting themselves. They then slowly inched their way through the hallway toward the main lobby door, listening carefully as they walked. But as expected, there was no movement in the house whatsoever; it was abandoned, just like it had been last time. When Marcus pulled the hinge bolts and hoisted the door out they heightened their senses one more time, but it once again proved unnecessary.

"Where do you want to place your cameras now?" Marcus asked as he stepped out into the lobby.

"I would place one upstairs in here." Darien pointed at the very corner of the staircase, just above the door they had just come through. "That will give us a great view of the lobby and everyone who comes into the house. The second one I would put in one of the meeting rooms, and the last in the 'restricted' area somewhere."

"I thought you only had two cameras?" Lucas addressed him.

"I did until recently. But now I own three." Darien grinned. "They are quite cheap and I didn't want to leave any of those places out."

"OK, that sounds like a plan then," Lucas said. "Thanks for the foresight, Professor."

Darien and Marcus cautiously ascended the staircase and started trying different angles for the camera. Lucas stayed back in the lobby to assess if the camera would be visible for someone entering the room. It took them a few tries before they decided to drill a hole in a handrail pole and stick the camera lens through that. With Marcus' battery-powered tools it proved to be quite easy and very effective in the end. Neither the lens itself, nor the recording box it was attached to, were visible from any angle in the lobby. They then moved on to the meeting room. Unfortunately hiding a camera there proved to be far more difficult. The room was rather small, compared to the lobby, and people would most likely move around in here quite a lot, so there was no safe spot to place the camera. In the end it was Marcus who came up with an idea.

"Isn't there a cabinet in the other meeting room just like this one?" he asked and walked over to the second room.

"How does a cabinet in the other room help us hide a camera in this room?" Darien asked and followed him over.

"We can drill a hole into the wall here," Marcus pointed at a corner spot in the second room, "and then hide the recording unit in the cabinet. That should give us a view of the first meeting room."

"Great idea." Darien applauded. "The camera will sit pretty low, so we will most likely not see too much, but it will be good enough to hear at least, and it will surely not be recognized on either side."

"It's a risk though. If someone uses the cabinet in this room then we are screwed," Marcus threw in.

"That's a risk we have to take," Lucas said. "I doubt that anyone will do that anyway."

They carefully put Marcus' plan into action and mounted the second camera before moving on to the restricted section. After dismantling the code lock and looking around inside they unfortunately had to admit that it was even harder hiding a camera in those rooms. There was no furniture at all, no crates, no panels on the walls, nothing that would allow them to disguise the lens, let alone the small recording box. After discussing various ideas that all proved to be useless, they finally decided to hide the camera in a room across the corridor that nobody had been in for a long time. It would limit their visibility to the corridor only and at best a portion of the room behind, if the door was open, but it was the best they could come up with. When they were done Darien quickly rechecked that all cameras were set correctly and were in fact recording before they wiped all the equipment to remove their fingerprints and made their way out again, trying to leave everything as undisturbed as possible.

"Now all we can do is wait," Lucas said when they were back at the street, picking up their bikes.

"We should come here once a week and replace the memory cards," Darien said. "And I can't do that alone, unfortunately. I doubt that I can get in and out of the rooms by myself."

"I will accompany you, Professor," Marcus said. "We can do this between the two of us."

"Are you sure that you don't want me to come along?" Lucas asked.

"If you have time, then feel free to join us." Marcus made an inviting gesture. "But I doubt that we will need you."

"I am not sure if I feel good leaving you alone in this house. It's a bit risky," Lucas said.

"I doubt that any more mages will enter that place, mate. And I can definitely defend the Professor from a civilian or two," Marcus said with a grin. "So don't worry."

"OK," Lucas sighed. "But still let me know when you plan to come here. If I am free, I will join you."

The others nodded before they rode off, back into town. It had taken them quite some time after all to get this done, making them all happy that it was over now, especially Lucas, who was looking forward to a nice evening.

A few months had passed since the boys had been at Jackson's house, and nothing new had turned up. The video surveillance proved to be un-eventful; there only rarely was anyone coming to the house, and those people mostly seemed to be assigned to custodial duties, like emptying the mailbox or cleaning the few useable rooms to keep up appearances. Only once had they seen Jackson himself show up, but even he had only been there for appearance's sake. All other leads had also proven worth-less or at least gone cold by now. They had even followed Jasmin to the clearing near High Wycombe, but it was no good. Whatever clue might have been there in the past, it was gone by now. Inspector Corben also did not bring them any new insight. The only news Lucas had gotten from him was the confirmation of Plague's death and that the death was now officially ruled to be by natural causes or at best an allergic reaction to medicine, closing the investigation in that area too. The detectives had not discovered the link to the power plant by themselves and Cor-ben had stayed silent by Lucas' request, leaving that scene undisturbed at least. All in all, the group grew more and more frustrated with their inability to progress and with that frustration quickly lost their interest in the topic. For Lucas the upside to it was that he had more time for schoolwork and a lot of free evenings and weekends that he could spend with Sandra. He had spent a lot of nights at her place during this time and even had her over at his place a few times. So far his parents had never been around though, so his mother still bugged him once in a while to be introduced. But they still seemed to accept the new situation pretty well, as they had even offered him the use of their bedroom for the one night that she had stayed there so far, while they were away.

It was the first Monday in February, the semester was coming to a close and schoolwork was slowing down significantly for now. Lucas had just grabbed his bike and was about to head home when he saw a man with a long, green coat leaning against a tree just outside the school perimeter. He smiled and walked up to him, pushing his bike along.

"Greetings JJ," he said as he drew close.

"Good afternoon, Guardian." JJ bowed a little and started walking toward the park.

"Long time, no see," Lucas said. "What brings you here today?"

"I would like to ask for your assistance, if the offer you made a while back is still good," JJ replied.

"Of course, it is." Lucas smiled. "Is this about Kung Fu's circle?"

"Yes." JJ nodded. "It seems they have found some kind of hiding place of the dark circle they have been opposing for a while and now plan to go in and throw them out for good."

"Why does that idea sound familiar?" Lucas laughed. "When and where do you need us?"

"Their plan is to strike on Saturday somewhere in the early afternoon. Apparently the dark circle has a ritual scheduled that day. As far as we know the place is somewhere south of Beaconsfield." JJ pulled out a map with a rather large circle drawn on it and an arrow pointing at a location just north of that circle.

"That's just east of High Wycombe, right?" Lucas was stunned when he saw the map.

"Yes, why?" JJ asked.

"Well, Psycho's circle had an encounter there too, a while ago. That seems like an odd coincidence," Lucas said.

"Do you think they have both encountered the same black circle?" JJ asked.

"I hope so," Lucas sighed. "The alternative is that we have a nest there somewhere. And I don't like that prospect."

"Agreed." JJ nodded. "And in light of that fact, I am even happier having you around for that."

"Let's hope the best," Lucas said. "Where shall we meet?"

"Right where I pointed the arrow to." JJ pointed at the map. "There is a bus stop there with a waiting room where we can assemble. Pretty much nobody goes there around that time of year, so we will have our privacy. One o'clock would be good if you can make it."

"We will be there." Lucas nodded. "Let's see what they have in store for us. What shall we prepare ourselves for?"

"Good question..." JJ thought for a moment. "I hope we can handle the situation on our own, so I don't really know. So I guess there is nothing really, other than you being there and backing us up."

"Well, that's a given anyway. I will discuss it with the guys in the evening and see if we come up with something more to prepare." Lucas grinned.

"Thank you," JJ said and slowed his walk, falling behind Lucas.

"You are welcome, my friend." Lucas smiled without looking back. He knew that once JJ had left his sight he had disappeared, a trick that he had pulled before in similar situations.

Once Lucas had cleared the park he swung onto his bicycle and rode home. There was plenty of time to get his schoolwork done before he had to depart for the shack. He even found some time to familiarize himself with the terrain that JJ had pointed out on the map. It was within the same forest as the clearing that Jasmin's circle had had their run-in before, but almost on the opposite corner. Given the limited size of the patch of wood, that by no means was an assurance that the two were not connected; on the contrary, it rather suggested that the same people had been at work on both occasions. But the possibility was still there that there were multiple black circles in play here and Kung Fu's mentees would be in way over their heads on Saturday. On his way to the shack he continued to think about the possible scenarios for that encounter. He was almost certain that this would not go down without a fight. The only question was how big a fight would it turn out to be? Even if there were two or three circles in play, they would hardly pose a problem for JJ and his group; after all, the black circles seemed to be pretty low level. So the only unknown was the person or persons behind those circles. He started drawing up worst-case scenarios and in the end came to the conclusion that the risk of a major fallout was pretty small, leaving him in a happy mood when he arrived at O'Brien mansion.

"There is finally something new happening," he said when they had all sat down around the table, enjoying the warmth of the fireplace. When he looked at them one after the other, it quickly became obvious to him that this announcement had lit a spark in all of them once again. They all were staring at him, waiting eagerly for him to continue.

"JJ contacted me earlier today," Lucas said after a few moments. "Kung Fu's mentees are on the warpath. And you won't believe where they have stirred up a dark circle's lair."

"I hope you don't want us to guess now?" Marcus said as Lucas remained silent for a short while.

"Beaconsfield," Lucas grinned.

"That's the area near High Wycombe where we had already been before, right?" Stephanie asked.

"Yes, exactly. And not only the general area, but the same patch of forest." Lucas nodded.

"Is it possible that Kung Fu's guys are fighting my guys?" Jasmin asked.

"That's an interesting question." Lucas had not yet thought about that option. "I doubt that somehow, but I guess we can easily find out."

"How?" Jasmin was looking at him.

"You know where your circle's home base is, right?" he asked.

"Yes." Jasmin slowly nodded.

"Well, then let's see if the area matches." He pulled out JJ's map printout and put it on the table.

"OK," Jasmin sighed in relief. "That's far away from where my guys are."

"I would presume that both circles have stumbled upon the same dark group, Kung Fu's guys were just faster in following up." Lucas smiled and patted her shoulder.

"And when is this supposed to go down?" Marcus was obviously eager to get into the action.

"Saturday," Lucas explained. "And we are supposed to meet JJ and his friends here." He pointed at the meeting location.

"Finally..." Cedric grinned.

"Hold your horses, guys," Lucas said. "This is their raid. It is Kung Fu's place to watch over them and JJ's place to lend support. We are only there as an additional line of defense. So don't expect too much action for us."

"I will still make sure that we have enough healing potion and bandages available," Stephanie said and stood up, walking to her backpack. "Maybe we could use the evening to brew some more?"

"Sure thing." Lucas nodded. "I assume that you will be the main attraction from our end anyway, Airmid. As far as I know, JJ does not have a healer in his circle, and I doubt that the youngsters have one either."

"Not a position I like to be in. But certainly a new one." Stephanie grinned.

"Not so new either. I remember at least three occasions that had you center stage, Airmid, and one of those was actually pretty painful," Marcus said.

"What else do we need to prepare for, then?" Darien asked.

"I don't know actually," Lucas replied. "I am thankful for all ideas you guys have."

The others thought for a while, but couldn't come up with anything useful, other than just being well rested and bringing clothes fitting the surroundings. Jasmin suggested bringing a few blankets, just in case they had to treat someone outside, which ended up being the only good idea they had. Being more or less satisfied with the discussion, they moved their attention to preparing more healing potion, which took them the remainder of the evening.

"Where are we going to meet?" Darien asked as they were already outside, locking up the shack.

"Beaconsfield train station seems like a good idea," Lucas suggested. "It is not far from the point where we will meet JJ and the others, and I guess that at least some of us may have different routes to get there."

"I will most likely go there by car," Jasmin added. "If any of you have a hard time finding a route, I am more than happy to pick you up."

"We will not all fit in your car, though," Darien said and pointed at her blue Suzuki.

"Don't worry about that," Lucas said. "I will most likely come with Kung Fu anyway, so I am good."

"I will find my own way too," Cedric threw in. "But thanks for the offer."

"So it's the four of us then?" Jasmin looked at Marcus, Stephanie and Darien.

"If you really want to go that extra mile, it would be highly appreciated,"

Darien said with a little bow.

"But we can at least all get to Luton station, so you don't have to run circles through the city," Stephanie proposed.

"Sounds like a plan." Lucas smiled.

They quickly performed their greeting ritual before getting on their ways home. The anticipation was still noticeable. They would finally be able to do something meaningful again in the matter.

Lucas was so amped up about the upcoming encounter that time just seemed to fly by. When his school day ended on Friday he almost ran to get home more quickly. There was now only one thing that he still needed to take care of before the big day, and that was introducing Sandra to his parents. It seemed like a weird coincidence that the first chance for that presented itself right before such an important day, and he had even suggested postponing that once more and spending the night at her place rather than having her over at his, but she had politely but definitively declined that proposal. When he arrived home he quickly pushed through schoolwork before revamping his room for the night. It was the first time he had her over and didn't have his parents' bed at his disposal, so he had to build a mattress encampment on the floor to have enough sleeping space for the both of them together. Unfortunately, that meant reducing the free floor area in his room to almost zero, making it impossible to even sit at the desk chair anymore. The whole setup felt a little weird to him, almost unworthy of her, but it was the best he could come up with. And in the end, it definitely beat having her sleep in the guest room downstairs. He wasn't even finished putting covers on the mattresses when he heard the doorbell.

"I'll get that," he yelled through the house and hastened down the stairs to be at the door first. When he opened it, he almost had to laugh, looking at the big duffle bag that Sandra was carrying. It almost looked as if she intended to move in with him.

"Hey, my love," he said with a big smile and gave her an intense kiss after closing the door behind her.

"Hey sweetheart," she replied with a grin.

"Let me get that up to my room," he said and took the bag out of her hand.

"Thanks," she said. "I hope I have everything we need for tomorrow."

"It sure feels that way." He laughed when he realized the weight it had. When she had carried it, it had looked so easy to him, leaving him once again impressed at her strength. He had to use both hands to have even the slightest chance of getting it upstairs, but he gave his best to get it done without using magic. He tossed the bag on his bed and ran back down. To his surprise there was no sign of his parents yet. He had expected at least his mother to show up instantly, remembering how it had been when Jasmin had visited for the first time.

"Jesus, did you have to dress like that today?" he laughed when she had taken her jacket off. She was wearing tight black jeans, an even tighter sports top and a training jacket that she had opened. "How shall I introduce you to my parents if you take my breath away?"

"I'm not sure if you have noticed those past months, but I always dress like this," she replied and gave him another kiss.

"I have noticed, but the effect has nonetheless not diminished yet." He grinned and put his arm around her waist. "Let's go find my parents, shall we?"

She smiled and made an inviting gesture, walking into the living room together with him. His father was sitting on the couch reading a rather large newspaper; his mother was just stepping in from the kitchen with a tea kettle in her hand. The dining table was set with four cups and a plate of homemade biscuits.

"Mom, Dad, may I introduce you to my girlfriend Sandra?" Lucas said, trying to keep a neutral face. "Sandra, these are my parents."

"Finally we get to meet you." His father had jumped up and put the paper on the couch table. "I'm Charlie." He shook her hand.

"Emilia." His mother followed his example after putting the kettle down.

"It's a pleasure to meet you both. I heard a lot of good things about you," Sandra said.

"Not all of those will be true unfortunately," Charlie laughed. "And unfortunately I can't say the same about you. Lucas has, as always, been a little secretive. But please, have a seat."

"I am sure that they all will be true. After all, you managed to raise Lucas to be an extraordinary man, so you both are certainly extraordinary parents." Sandra smiled and sat down.

"Don't flatter us too much," Emilia said and sat down too. "You don't need to earn points here."

"And I have no intention to do that," Sandra said. "I am only speaking my mind."

"That's a good start," Charlie grinned.

Lucas had sat down next to Sandra and was observing his parents with interest. They both were examining her closely, but while his father did so in a very subtle way, his mother was almost blunt doing it. A few months ago he would definitely have been majorly annoyed by that, but right now he wasn't. He was totally calm and enjoying the experience a lot.

"I hope I fall within acceptable standards?" Sandra had obviously noticed his mother's behavior too, as she addressed her directly now.

"You are not quite what I expected," she replied. "But in the end it's not my standards that are relevant here."

"That sounded mean," Lucas said and tried to have an annoyed look on his face. But once again there were no hard feelings. He knew what his mother was aiming at, and so did Sandra. And he knew that she had no problem with that, so neither did he.

"I have to agree," Charlie nodded. "You should apologize for that, Emilia."

"No, you shouldn't." Sandra smiled as she looked at Lucas' mother. "I am 30 years old, and I am quite certain that this was not what you expected to get as your son's first long-term girlfriend."

"Then you understand my skepticism here?" she asked.

"Actually, I don't," Sandra replied. "This is the twenty-first century. The biological clock no longer expires at 30; it ticks way past 40 these days. And besides, I think all of us at this table are aware that the first relationship someone has is hardly ever the one that lasts 'til lives end."

"Well put." Charlie nodded in agreement. "But tell me then, what is it you see in our son that made you agree to this relationship?"

"If I compiled you a list of all the reasons that come to my mind right now, I would need a lot of time and paper," Sandra said. "And besides, wouldn't it be far more obvious to ask Lucas that question?"

"Humor me with a few of those, will you?" Charlie asked again.

"Lucas is the smartest guy I have ever seen," she started. "He is polite, forthcoming, but also capable of defending himself when someone crosses lines. He is far more mature than most 30-year-olds I know, let alone any people his age, and of course he is good-looking as well. But most of all, he knows how to push my buttons in almost every aspect of life, and that makes him unique."

"Mature is an interesting description of Lucas," Emilia said with an emotionless look on her face.

"But you have to admit that it's a true one." Charlie turned toward her. "Just remember the party he went to with the O'Brien girl."

"Her name is Stephanie, Dad." Lucas shook his head. "And that was not mature, that was just necessary."

"Exactly my point." Charlie pointed at him. "Everyone else your age would have loved being there, but you stayed true to your word and watched out for her. And that is the very definition of mature."

"If you say so…" Lucas was still shaking his head.

"What is it that caught your attention with Sandra?" His mother looked at him now.

"What kind of answer do you expect from me now, Mom?" Lucas returned the look. "That she is the hottest chick I know and I just couldn't control my hormones?"

"Well…" his mother started but couldn't get any further because both Sandra and his father had started laughing loudly.

"That would be the answer nobody expected from you." Charlie had a hard time getting his laughter under control. "And for sure not the real reason either."

"It's been quite a while since you have called me a chick." Sandra also had a hard time speaking. She was obviously enjoying the conversation a lot.

"Well, it might not be the main reason, but it's nonetheless true," Lucas said with a very calm voice and look on his face. "There is nobody else who is as beautiful as you are." He turned to her and gave her a kiss. "But to answer your questions, Mom," he then continued and turned back to his mother, "she is the first girl that I've ever met who accepts me the way I am. She has never pushed me, other than in sports competitions, has never expected anything from me and in the end also knows how to push my buttons. And I like that a lot."

"Yeah, I know how to handle kids." She winked at him.

"What's that supposed to mean?" Emilia had been caught off guard again.

"Not what you think," Sandra laughed. "I am a teacher."

"Then maybe you can teach him some things while you are at it." Charlie winked at her.

"I think he can teach me more than I can teach him," Sandra grinned. "But I will try."

"Well then, welcome to the family." He extended his hand and Sandra shook it.

"Thank you. I am glad that you approve of me being here," she said.

"Just don't do anything stupid, you two," Emilia added and shook Sandra's hand too.

"We will try not to be any more stupid than all other kids." Lucas grinned.

"I'll take your word for it," his father said and started pouring tea for everyone.

They continued chatting for quite a while longer while drinking tea and eating cookies. For Lucas the experience was still feeling great. It was like Sandra had been part of the family for ages already. He kept close to her all evening long, and at some point even was under the impression that their behavior had led to his parents also staying a bit closer to each other than normal, almost as if their love for each other had inspired them to feel theirs again more strongly too. When they walked up to his room and bid his parents good night, they were both happy. No matter what awaited them tomorrow, this evening had been the perfect way to get their minds focused and their bodies relaxed.

CHAPTER 13

LAIR

On the ride over to Beaconsfield Sandra and Lucas had a great time discussing last night's meeting with his parents. During the night they had heard some explicit sounds from their bedroom and were now speculating if her meeting them was part of the reason for that.

"My father definitely thought about you last night," Lucas was just saying.

"Are you saying that he has a crush on me?" Sandra asked.

"Maybe not a crush, but for sure some fantasies," Lucas laughed. "You saw how he looked at you earlier."

"And you have no problem whatsoever with this because...?"

"Why would I have a problem with that?" Lucas asked.

"Well, aren't you at all jealous?" Sandra replied. "Maybe I have the same fantasies about your father. Some girls like older men, you know?" She winked at him.

"Well, being jealous in my situation would just be stupid, don't you think?"

"And why's that?" She was curious.

"One of the 'problems' that arise with dating the hottest girl in the greater London area is that there will be many men of all ages who have you as the centerpiece of their wet dreams. If I were to be jealous at every one of them, then I would not have time for anything other than being jealous, and I think that might be a waste of my resources. Besides, it was me who was lying next to you in my makeshift bed last night, not my father. So even if your comment were true, I guess he drew the short straw," Lucas said.

"I finally get a really young boyfriend, and then he doesn't behave like one. Can't you at least act like an 18-year-old once for a change?" She laughed and hit him on his thigh with her palm.

Lucas stuck his tongue out in reply, accompanied by a mad grimace, making them both laugh for a while longer.

"Seems we are here," he then said and pointed ahead at what looked like the parking lot of the train station.

"And you are plenty early," she said and pointed at the car's clock. It was just past twelve. "Sorry for that; maybe you should have ridden with Psycho."

"I knew that you would need to be here earlier. And I'd rather spend my time with you and have a little time left than ride with anyone else," he said. "Let alone with Psycho. She drives like crazy," he then added and laughed.

Sandra stopped at the side of the road. He gave her a kiss before jumping out.

"See you in a bit," he said as he pulled his backpack from the rear seat and pushed the doors closed. Sandra waved in reply and drove off. For a while he just stood there and watched her disappear around a bend before walking over to the station. When he entered the waiting room Cedric was already sitting there, discussing something on the phone. The conversation looked agitated, so Lucas decided to stay back and give him some privacy. It took about five minutes before he hung up and came walking over.

"Hey mate," he said and shook Lucas' hand. The area was a little too crowded for them to great in their traditional way.

"Good to see you," Lucas replied and patted his shoulder. "Why are you in so early?"

"Better ten minutes early than one minute late." Cedric shrugged his shoulders. "What's your excuse?"

"JJ's circle is meeting earlier already, so Kung Fu had to be here earlier too. And as I came with her, that made me early too," he said.

"Fair enough." Cedric nodded and sat down.

Lucas knew that having a conversation with Cedric was bound to be one-sided, so he decided to remain silent and watch the other passengers. He had just focused on a group of teenagers who were playing ball on the platform when he heard a jarring sound out in the parking lot.

"That sounds like Psycho," he said and turned around.

"Definitely." Cedric nodded without moving an inch.

Lucas walked over to the window and watched his friends get out of the car. Each of them was wearing a backpack. Stephanie seemed a little stressed out, Jasmin looked cheerful and Marcus and Darien were wildly gesticulating in some sort of heated discussion.

"Greetings, everyone," he said and held the door open for them to enter.

"Can you tell Psycho to adopt a more passive driving style, please? She seems not to listen to me," Stephanie said and gave Lucas a hug.

"I doubt that she will listen to me either," Lucas laughed. "Maybe you should ride back with Kung Fu and me instead. Although... then you might need to endure our weird discussions."

"Anything is better than her driving," Stephanie grinned.

Lucas quickly greeted the others before they sat down in a corner of the waiting room.

"The Professor brought another one of his cool gadgets," Jasmin said to Lucas.

"Total overkill if you ask me..." Marcus replied before Darien had a chance to say something.

"What is it?" Lucas was curious.

"A wireless door camera," Darien said and pulled it out of his backpack. "Take a look."

"That's a great idea actually. Might prove to be overkill, but it is good to have it around," Lucas complimented.

"How does this work?" Stephanie had taken one of the pieces.

"You put that little thing where the action is, and then you can watch what's going on here on the screen," Darien explained and turned the device on to show her.

"That's awesome," Stephanie said and started waving the camera around. "What's the catch?"

"There are two actually: One is that we need to get this camera to the action; otherwise there is nothing to see. The other is that this was built for monitoring a front door. So the monitor is supposed to be within a short distance of the camera, meaning that we have to be relatively close too," Darien replied.

"Let's see if the chance arises to set this up," Lucas said. "If not, we need to rely on your eyes, Professor, or whatever means of communication JJ is bringing to the table."

They quickly checked through the gear that the others brought and divided up some of the things to share the load. Especially Stephanie had been packed heavily with bandages, patches and flasks over flasks of healing potion. Ten minutes before the set meeting time they walked out of the waiting room and got on their way toward the bus stop that JJ had pointed out. It only took them a few hundred meters to get from the more or less populated train station to a totally deserted area of fields and patches of forest.

"Good time to get our robes, don't you think?" Lucas said and opened his backpack while walking.

The others nodded and followed his example, quickly transforming the innocent-looking group of teenagers into a circle of mages. To look a little less weird for any possible drivers-by they decided to leave their hoods down for a while longer, only pulling them up when they had the bus stop in sight already. As they approached the small closed waiting room next to it they saw three people standing in there already. All three were wearing robes; all three had their hoods pulled deep over their faces. Lucas could recognize a green robe, a red robe and one that was either black, or at least a very dark shade of grey. He was a little disappointed not seeing Kung Fu's yellow robe there, but he quickly realized that she had to stay close to her circle somewhere and could therefore not be at the bus stop now.

"Good afternoon, my friends," Lucas greeted the three when he entered the room, followed by the others.

"And a good afternoon to you, old friend," Angel was the first to reply, shaking Lucas' hand.

"Everything set?" Lucas asked JJ when he greeted him next.

"Seems like it." JJ nodded. "But we have to see. So far nothing has happened."

"This is Dread, by the way. I am not sure if you have been introduced before," JJ said a moment later, pointing at the man in the dark robes.

"I believe we have had the pleasure before." Lucas approached him to shake his hand. The robe was a very dark grey, revealing little more than the hands of the wearer.

"Buxton, yes." Dread nodded.

Lucas remembered now. When he had visited Angel during the summer camp it had been Dread who had welcomed him to the A-zone and led him to her. It had been the same occasion where he had met Kung Fu for the first time.

"What do we do now?" Marcus asked after they had all shaken hands.

"We wait for Hopper to return and give us an update. He is with Kung Fu right now," JJ said.

"What's your plan for communication?" Lucas asked. "Using a messenger seems to be a little slow."

"We have no cellphone service out here, so our options are limited," JJ replied. "The idea is to see where this lair is and as soon as we know, move in closer to reduce the roundtrip time."

"Maybe we should add some technology to that?" Darien asked Lucas.

"Totally..." Lucas nodded before turning back toward JJ. "The Professor brought a wireless camera. If we have a chance to set that up next to the lair, we might have a better way to stay up to date."

"That's great." JJ smiled. "But if this encounter goes sideways you might lose the camera--you are aware of that, right?"

"Cameras can be replaced; people can't," Darien said in an almost cold voice and handed JJ the sender. "We still need to move close though; the range is very limited."

"Your help is highly appreciated here." JJ patted Darien's shoulder and took the camera. "And if we lose the device we will replace it for you."

"We will not lose the device," Cedric said with a confident look on his face.

"Let's hope not," JJ replied.

He had just finished examining the camera when another man in green robes entered the hut.

"I see the cavalry has arrived," he said with a grin on his face.

"What's the verdict, Hopper?" JJ asked.

"The youngsters are on the move," he replied, his face becoming strict again. "That's the area they are heading toward as far as we could tell." He pointed out a part very close to the border of the forest, less than a kilometer from where they were standing right now. "We should know more details soon. I will make my next run now."

"Take this with you." JJ handed Hopper the camera. "Our friends brought it for us."

"Nice," Hopper grinned. "Always prepared, I see."

He had already opened the door when he turned back toward Stephanie. "Oh, by the way, I have never had a chance to say thank you. You stitched me up pretty well after our last encounter. I owe you one."

"You owe me nothing, Hopper," Stephanie smiled. "You came to our rescue, so at best we owe you one."

Hopper smiled and walked out. Lucas had to giggle a little when he saw him running down into the forest. Hopper's moves looked more like jumping than running, but he moved very efficiently that way.

"Now you know why we call him Grasshopper," JJ laughed when he saw what Lucas was giggling at.

Darien had switched on the monitor and was watching Hopper move into the forest. Unfortunately, the limited range struck quickly, leaving them blind again less than a minute later.

"Now we wait again," Marcus sighed. "I should have gone with him. Two messengers are better than one."

"But two messengers are also more obvious than one," Lucas replied. "It's their show, Cougar, not ours. Relax."

About ten minutes later Hopper approached again from the forest line.

"We found the lair," he said hastily and pointed out the exact spot on JJ's map. "One large wooden cabin with multiple rooms as far as we can tell, a dirt road leading up to it and plenty of dense forest around to hide in."

"Then let's move in closer," JJ said.

The others nodded and followed Hopper out of the waiting room and into the forest. They walked carefully and tried to make as little noise as possible. For Hopper, JJ and Marcus that seemed to come naturally, but the others had quite a hard time keeping up. About ten minutes into the forest Lucas could finally spot the hut through the thick trees. They had approached it on an almost perfect, straight course, until now. All of a sudden Hopper made a sharp right turn and walked parallel to the dark circle's hiding place. It took Lucas a while to see where he was going. It was an area with a few big rocks between the trees that gave perfect cover. The hut was about hundred meters away, so there was no way to see what was going on inside, but it was still close enough to move in quickly. There was still no sign of Kung Fu or her mentees, so they took cover and waited again. It took another ten minutes before Darien tapped Lucas on the back. When he turned around Darien was holding his monitor up for him to watch. The camera had come back in range, but so far there was little to see. The person holding the device was moving quite quickly and erratically, leaving them with nothing but glimpses of the surrounding areas. When the movement finally stopped, they had a quite clear view to the hut. It looked as if Kung Fu had set up camp a few meters within the forest, next to the hut's front entrance.

"There they come," Darien whispered, pointing at a group of people approaching the hut. Lucas counted five, but was unsure if that was all, or if some had slipped by the camera. They all had gathered around Darien, watching eagerly as the group entered the hut, closing the door behind them. When the camera started moving again Lucas looked up through the trees. He could see Kung Fu move to the hut carefully and put the camera into the corner of a window. Then she made her way back into the forest.

"Good girl," Lucas smiled and looked back at the monitor. The camera had no microphone attached, so they could only watch, but not listen in. There were in fact five people who had walked into the hut, facing a group of six in black now.

"Bad situation." Lucas shook his head.

"Don't underestimate my kids." Sandra had approached them without anyone noticing. "And besides, they have picked that fight; they have to live with it now."

"Good to see you." He gave her a quick hug before focusing back on the screen.

"Nice toy you brought here," she said when shaking Darien's hand. "Makes our lives a little easier."

"Always at your service," Darien grinned and bowed.

"And so it begins..." Cedric pointed at the screen, where one of the black robes had just been tossed through the air and crashed into a wall.

Chaos followed, both groups throwing spells and engaging in hand-to-hand combat, trashing parts of the furniture in the process. Lucas could see a bench splintering as one of Kung Fu's mentees was thrown into it. Shortly after that a table was reduced to ground level when a black robe landed flat on top and the table's legs gave way.

"Who is that guy?" Stephanie asked and pointed at a man who had walked in through a side door.

"That's my cue," Sandra grinned and ran off toward the hut.

"It seems to be the mentor of the dark circle," JJ explained to Stephanie. "Now Kung Fu can go in and level the playing field again."

"I doubt that this playing field will be level..." Marcus laughed. "Old man versus martial arts master. My bets are on her."

"Don't underestimate the power of magic, Cougar," Angel said.

A moment of quiet followed at the scene of the action when Kung Fu entered the room. She was apparently talking to the black mentor, giving both sides time to regroup. Then all of a sudden spells started flying again and the fight was back at its original ferocity in seconds.

"Jesus..." Lucas said when he saw Sandra just barely leap out of the way of a lightning bolt that the dark mage had shot at her.

"This is getting crowded..." Darien was the first to spot three more people entering the room.

"Mentees or mages?" Hopper tried to get a good look at the screen.

Darien looked up, focusing directly on the hut. "Judging from the energy patterns I would say they are mages," he said.

"Then it's time for us to go," JJ said and started a hasty walk toward the scene, followed by Hopper, Angel and Dread.

"What shall we do now?" Jasmin asked Lucas.

"We better get prepared for some injuries. This doesn't look too good right now," he replied. "Other than that, we just stay and wait."

The hut was now almost cramped full. Some fighting had moved to adjacent rooms that Lucas and his friends couldn't see through the camera, and the main room right now looked like a battlefield.

"Shit..." Marcus pointed through the trees. It took Lucas a moment to recognize the car that had just pulled up from the dirt road.

"How many more, Professor?" Lucas asked Darien.

"Two, and one of them has an even more massive energy signature." Darien almost sounded freaked out.

"That's not good," Lucas said. "Cougar, Whirlwind, are you ready for some action?"

"Hell yeah." Cedric nodded and was already on his feet.

"Professor, Psycho, Airmid, stay back here. This will get messy," Lucas said to them. Then he ran off toward the hut, followed by Marcus and Cedric. Arriving at the door, they could for the first time hear the battle noises, which made the situation sound even messier. When Lucas kicked the door open and set foot into the hut he could just from the corner of his eyes witness someone wearing a green robe being tossed back, through the window and out into the forest.

"Say goodbye to your camera, Professor," Marcus mumbled and side-stepped to avoid being hit by a frying pan that came flying his way.

Lucas tried to get hold of the situation quickly. The room of the hut they had come into was a total mess. Whatever furniture and equipment had been in here before was trashed by now, bodies from both sides lining the walls, unconscious or at least no longer capable of fighting. There were at least three more rooms that Lucas could spot, plus a staircase that led up to an attic. The attic seemed to be abandoned; at least there was no movement there that he could spot at first glance. The room directly to his left seemed to be a kitchen of sorts. Dread was fighting in there with one of the mages, together with one of Kung Fu's youngsters and two more black robes. The second room on the far-left corner seemed to be a laboratory of sorts. Weird apparatuses were standing on a large table, surrounded by a large number of flasks, kettles, potions and a pile of the energy stones. The two remaining youngsters of Kung Fu were duking it out in there against two black robes. The third room, with its entrance just opposite of the main entrance, seemed to be a bedroom of sorts, with a back door to the hut visible through the opening. Kung Fu and her first opponent were fighting in there vigorously. In the main room Angel and a second person in green robes--from the movement he assumed that this was Hopper--had been fighting three opponents. And finally the last arrival was standing right in the doorway between the main room and the bedroom. Lucas tried to assess the situation as well as he possibly could in the split second he had. He could see that Hopper was pressing his left hand against his chest, suggesting that he had been injured. Angel was also visibly bleeding from her right hand. Dread seemed to be doing best of them all, but even he looked as if he was fighting a lost cause. But beyond all the damage that had already been done, and beyond the fact that most of them were fighting hopeless battles, the biggest threat right now seemed to be the man standing in the doorway. He was small; Lucas estimated him at under 170 cm, with quite some weight around his waist, and he was wearing thick, round glasses. But as unimpressive as this stature looked, his facial expression and his cool movement suggested the opposite. When he saw the man raise his hand and point at Angel, he reacted immediately.

"SEPERATIO," he yelled and fired up a protective barrier between the man and his former mentor.

"COLLIDO," he heard the man yell almost at the same moment and felt the ripple of energy hitting his shield. Lucas immediately realized that his opponent was at least as powerful as Cleric had been, making him wonder if his shield could withstand this kind of attack. But when the full force of the spell hit the barrier something felt different than it had before, in the battle against Cleric. His shield was far stronger than it had ever been, and he hadn't even pushed it to the limit yet. Only at that moment did he realize the true potential that Kung Fu had unlocked in him months ago. That one day, when he had felt like a totally new person, had made him a new person indeed. The unity between his mind and his emotions was so natural by now that even a simple, mind-crafted spell like his Seperatio was now fueled by his emotional magic as well.

"Unity..." he mumbled and almost froze in awe of this realization. He realized quickly that something was still missing for him to unlock his total potential, but what he had at hand right now was more than he had ever had before, and he would have kissed Kung Fu right now for that gift, if circumstances weren't so grim to begin with. When the second spell from his opponent hit his shield, his mind focused back on the tasks at hand. Even though his shield was stronger than ever, the second hit had almost nullified it. He weighed his options and quickly decided to go on the offensive.

"INCENDIO," he yelled and stretched his hand toward the man with the glasses.

A stream of fire emerged from his palm, shooting at the opponent. But he was not short of replies either, casting a protecting shield that deflected the flames. Lucas pushed as hard as he could, but he couldn't break the defense. He dropped the flames and rebuilt his own shield charm, trying to be ready. Marcus and Cedric had in the meantime taken on two of the mages in the main room, giving Angel and Hopper some space to move. And while Hopper was still fighting one of the mages at full steam, Angel on the other hand looked pale and exhausted.

"Angel, get out!" Lucas yelled at her. "Take care of JJ; we can handle this."

Angel nodded and stumbled out the main door, covered by Lucas' shield charms. He tried to fire a spell here and there to help out the others, while still protecting against the man in the doorway, but he quickly realized that this man needed his full attention. He was just about to start another attack when he heard a loud cracking sound and a body came flying through the wall from the bedroom. It was the man with the long beard that Kung Fu had been fighting who was now lying in the middle of the room, unconscious. Lucas quickly refocused, but before he had a chance to cast, Marcus jumped at him from the side, pushing him out of the way of another pot that had come flying from the kitchen.

"Thanks mate," Lucas said and quickly looked over. Dread had pushed his ally back out of the kitchen into the main room and was covering his retreat. The situation didn't look good at all.

"My pleasure," Marcus grinned and jumped back into the action, attacking another of the black mages in hand-to-hand combat.

Lucas rebuilt his shield, which had already taken another hit from the man, and was just getting ready for a third attempt when he saw Kung Fu attacking the black leader from behind. The opponent seemed totally surprised, tumbling forward as she jumped into his back, feet first.

"You are getting annoying!" the man yelled with a massive Spanish accent. "COLIDO." He stretched his hand backward and hit Kung Fu head-on, tossing her through the back wall of the hut, out into the forest.

"That was a big mistake." Lucas was fully focused now. "REPELLUM," he yelled and stretched his palm forward, focusing as much energy into the spell as he could muster. The attacker was lifted up and tossed back into the bedroom, but with little to no permanent effect on him. Dread was now back in the main room too, bringing three more opponents to deal with, and Hopper was on the retreat as well, looking badly wounded. Lucas was just about to start a desperate counteroffensive when he heard a loud bang from the laboratory room. One of Kung Fu's guys had pushed his opponent into the center table with a force that had made the table tumble over, and all the things that had stood on it before were now lying on the ground, shattered and in disarray. And just as all things had come to a final rest on the floor the other youngster had tossed his opponent over the table, smashing him directly into what was left of the devices and potions. Lucas could hear a lot of glass shattering and saw liquids flowing through the room. A punch from the main attacker that had partially penetrated his shield and made him stumble backward brought his attention back to matters at hand for a moment. But before he could do anything, he spotted something in the laboratory room that looked even more dangerous.

"Everyone fall back! Find cover! NOW!" he yelled and quickly built up another shield to cover the retreat and ran through the main door out into the forest. He could see from the corner of his eye that the two youngsters in the laboratory had reacted instantly and were jumping out of the window there, while Dread, Marcus and Cedric came running right behind him, Marcus carrying one of the unconscious mentees of Kung Fu out with him. They hadn't even reached the tree line yet when Lucas heard the first electric discharges firing in the hut, shortly followed by an explosion that made the ground shake violently, almost knocking him over. He turned back to see if any defensive action was needed on his behalf, but none of the opponents seemed to have followed them. The hut was burning, clouds of colored smoke came out of the windows and he could hear things falling down inside. When he took a look around, he could see some of the black mages assembling on the far end, close to the dirt road. He couldn't tell if his adversary was with them, but right now it didn't matter. They were in no condition to continue the fight, so the best he could do was try to organize a structured retreat. He took position close to a tree, but still in the open, and looked for the others. The direction he had chosen was almost opposite where Darien and the girls were camped out, luring possible followers away from them. Cedric had taken position to his left, Marcus to his right. Dread was also still with them. Lucas looked at them, quickly trying to assess the situation. Dread was shaky, Cedric was bleeding from his forehead and Marcus looked exhausted too.

"You two, move out," he said to Cedric and Dread. "Cougar, are you up to covering the position with me for a bit?"

"Sure thing." Marcus nodded and tried to look as confident as possible when he handed off the person he had been carrying to Dread.

When Dread and Cedric had disappeared into the thicket, Lucas looked around for other members of the group. He quickly spotted the two boys from the laboratory and signaled them to come over. One was limping, the other trying to support him as they ran toward him. Marcus looked around eagerly, scanning for potential threats, but to their relief nobody seemed to care about them right now. When the two boys had vanished into safety too and nobody else was to be seen, Lucas took a last look around. He could spot movement in the hut, suggesting that their opponents were scrambling to save whatever they could from the lair. Other than that, the scene was quiet.

"Let's go," he said to Marcus and led him back into the forest, moving in a wide circle before finally heading toward their earlier hideout.

When they arrived back at the rocks, only Angel was there. Her hand was covered in a bandage. She still looked pale but otherwise she seemed to be all right.

"The others have retreated to the edge of the forest," she said and immediately started walking in that direction.

"How many of ours are we missing?" Lucas asked when he had caught up with her.

"None. You two are the last ones to make it out," Angel replied.

"That's a relief," Lucas sighed.

"We were lucky that you were there," Angel said. "If you hadn't come in, they would have crushed us."

"They still sort of did," Lucas said. "That was quite a bunch we had to fight there."

When they finally arrived at the edge of the forest, after an agonizing ten-minute walk, Lucas had to gasp for air. He had expected some injuries to come out of that encounter, but what he saw there looked more like a field hospital than a few minor bruises. Darien was building a splint for the boy that had come out last before them, Stephanie was just dripping healing potion on Hopper's chest and Jasmin was kneeling next to JJ, performing some kind of magic on him. The rest of Kung Fu's mentees were sitting or lying nearby, most of them having bandages somewhere or patches of their clothing soaked with healing fluid. Dread was sitting next to a tree looking as if he was in agonizing pain, which suggested to Lucas that Stephanie had cast a healing spell on him, and Kung Fu was lying in the grass with her sleeve rolled up, healing potion dripping off her arm.

"Holy shit," Lucas said as they walked through the ranks.

"I am glad to see you back in one piece, Guardian," Stephanie sighed in relief when she spotted him. "Are you injured?"

"Not that I can tell." Lucas shook his head. "Cougar?" He looked at Marcus.

"I am fine. Just caught some shrapnel, but I can deal with that myself."

He shook his head too and sat down.

Lucas walked over to Sandra, kneeling down next to her.

"That healing potion hurts like hell; has anybody ever told you that?" she said with a painful grin.

"I know. That's Airmid's way of telling you that you should be more careful next time," he said and gave her a quick kiss. "I am glad to see you back here."

"I was glad to see you in there," she replied. "That fight was a nightmare."

"Yeah. There were an awful lot of pretty powerful mages present at this lair." Lucas nodded. "So either your youngsters have really bad timing, or they hit a nerve center here."

"At least we now know where they are," she said.

"I doubt that they will be there much longer. Your boys trashed the place pretty good. But let's worry about one thing at a time. First of all, we need to get everyone to safety and ensure that nobody suffers permanent damage from this. Then we all need to get some rest. And THEN we will think about our next steps." He took her healthy hand and pressed it firmly.

"How are you feeling, Kung Fu?" Stephanie had approached them.

"Better by the minute," Sandra said with pain in her voice.

"The wounds seem to be healing well. I assume that it will take another ten minutes until you are fully recovered." She looked at the arm carefully. "Shall I send Psycho over to help you with the pain?"

"I can handle it, thanks. Psycho is needed elsewhere more urgently." Sandra tried to smile.

"How are we doing overall?" Lucas asked.

"Pretty well, given the circumstances. Most wounds are superficial; they should heal before we leave here. There are three that are a little bit more concerning. Hopper had a long splinter in his chest and I am not sure how well my spell will do there; the Professor is monitoring him now. Kitten has a concussion; there is nothing I can do--we need to have a doctor look at that. And JJ has received a bad blow to the head. I dealt with the wound, but Psycho is still at it, trying to assess the situation. He is conscious, but unstable."

"Should we take him to Dr. Tackman?" he asked.

"That would most likely be a good idea, yes." Stephanie nodded.

Lucas stayed with Sandra, watching Stephanie as she was making her rounds. They remained there for another half hour before Stephanie called it. The majority of the group had recovered from the wounds; only a few needed extra attention. Dread was still in pain, but Stephanie assessed him as stable. Hopper had fully recovered too but was also still in pain. Only JJ and Kitten were still in no shape to be left by themselves.

"We should take them to Luton General right away," Lucas said. "Kung Fu, are you up to driving us there? Or should we call an ambulance?"

"I am good," Sandra replied. "Thanks to Airmid. So yes, let's do that."

"I will make sure that Dr. Tackman is available for you on arrival," Angel said from the side. "Let's hope for the best."

They carefully moved the two patients into Sandra's car, placing Stephanie in the middle. Darien took charge of the remaining group and started organizing their return to civilization. Lucas took his robes off before getting into the passenger seat next to Sandra. He was not looking forward to another visit to the doctor, but they had to play it safe; he knew that. She drove cautiously the entire way to Luton, trying to avoid abrupt maneuvers and hitting potholes as much as possible. Stephanie constantly kept an eye on both their passengers, keeping them comfortable in the cramped space. When they finally arrived at the hospital Lucas took a deep breath. He was totally unsure what to expect and even more unsure how he should explain the situation to anyone inside. He opened the back door and offered Kitten his hand, helping her out of the car. When she stood up it quickly became apparent to him that she would not be capable of walking by herself, so he put his arm around her and supported her up the stairs to the main entrance. A quick peek back revealed to him that JJ was doing only slightly better. He was walking on his own, but it was not the least bit a straight path he was on, so Kung Fu und Stephanie both offered their hands. Stepping through the large door, Lucas immediately spotted Dr. Tackman standing near the side wall together with a nurse. When he spotted them he hastily walked over.

"What do we have here this time?" he asked.

"I am quite sure that she bumped her head majorly, but I can't tell you any details." Lucas answered.

"Sometimes I hate your people's secrecy," Tackman said grumpily and pulled out a penlight from his pocket, examining Kitten's eyes.

"There is no secrecy in this case, Doc," Lucas said. "I honestly don't know the details. When I arrived at the scene she was already lying there."

"Jessica, please get me a gurney for her," the doctor addressed the nurse.

"Better get two," Lucas said. "We have a second patient coming in right behind us."

"Great..." Tackman sighed and continued to work.

About a minute later Sandra entered, followed by Stephanie and JJ.

"What took you so long?" Lucas asked before turning toward the doctor. "Here they are."

"JJ doesn't know forward from back right now," Sandra said. "So we had to take some detours."

When Jessica arrived with two other nurses and the gurneys, Lucas helped Kitten lie down on one, while Sandra and Stephanie did the same with JJ on the other.

"There is no visible damage to her, except for the obvious signs of a concussion," Tackman said. "But we should get a CT scan and a spine X-ray, just to be on the safe side."

One of the nurses nodded and pushed her away, down a side corridor.

"Now, what happened to this one?" The doctor had walked over to JJ, again pulling out his penlight.

"He crashed through a wooden window frame and most likely had a hard landing on the other side," Lucas replied and stepped back to give him room to maneuver.

"He definitely has a concussion, and a mighty one, I might add." Tackman shook his head. "But I would expect pretty heavy bruising or other visible impact traumas to come with that. Did he wear some kind of helmet?"

"No, he didn't." Stephanie shook her head before looking first at Jessica and then the other nurse standing next to them.

"Give us a minute please," Tackman said to them and signaled them to move away. They both nodded and walked a few steps off, staying in range if their help should be required, but getting out of hearing distance.

"So?" Tackman asked Stephanie.

"He had a skull fracture and some wounds on his face and shoulders, presumably from wooden splinters and the broken glass," she said. "I took care of all of those before we came here."

"Do I want to know the details?" The doctor shook his head and checked JJ's head with his fingertips.

"I doubt it." Stephanie shook her head.

"Did you ease his pain too somehow?" Tackman asked. "I would assume that he still has some brain swelling from the impact, but he should be in agony if that were true."

"We eased some of his pain and I also tried to prevent the swelling as much as I could. Unfortunately, that's not as easy as dealing with some splinters and cuts," Stephanie said.

"OK. Let's get some tests done, then, and hope for the best," the doctor said and signaled the nurses to come back. "Do you want to stay and see the results firsthand?" he then asked Stephanie.

"I sure do." She nodded.

"We will leave you to it then." Lucas understood Tackman's intentions. "Call us when you are done; we will pick you up."

He took Sandra's hand and walked out of the building.

"Why are we leaving?" she almost yelled at him.

"Because the doc wanted us to," Lucas replied. "And because there is nothing we can do now anyway. Let them do their job."

"But I can't just abandon Kitten and JJ. I am the one who brought them into this mess." She had lowered her voice. Lucas could see that she had tears in her eyes.

"We are not abandoning anyone," he said and stopped walking. "And you didn't bring them into it; you just ensured that they both came out alive."

He turned toward her and watched her closely. The tears had started running down her cheeks and it was clear that she was fighting not to cry. When she opened her mouth to respond, he gently pressed her against himself, letting her bury her head in his chest. He could hear her sniffle and almost feel her desperation. He fondled her hair and just kept her close, waiting for the emotions to flush out. They stood there like this for over ten minutes before she finally managed to pull herself together.

"I still can't just let that stand," she then said with a much firmer voice. "This was not supposed to end up like it did."

"Life never is," Lucas said. "Next time we will prepare better."

"If we get another chance," Sandra replied. "I am not sure how my kids will handle that setback."

"They will be just fine, believe me." He stroked her shoulder. "Nobody who has the stamina to learn magic lets one setback get in his way. They will continue to learn, they will continue to practice and they sure as hell will be back to kick those goons out of their territory."

"Let's just hope that we didn't all bite off more than we can chew here," she sighed.

"Isn't that what we always do?" Lucas grinned.

"You maybe. But you are insane to begin with." She grinned back.

"Yes, but I am also insanely good." He winked at her.

"You are pathetic--you know that, right?" She had to laugh.

"Yes, of course. And I guess that's part of the reason why you love me." He kissed her.

"True." She nodded. "But sometimes it's just a bit much to bear."

"Well, you are a strong girl; you will manage," he said and took her into his arms again. "And now it might be a good idea to grab a bite to eat. We have to wait for Airmid to call anyway."

They walked to a nearby restaurant and tried to keep the topic off the bad guys for the duration of the meal, which proved to be a hard task for both of them. Luckily, they didn't have to wait too long. Stephanie's call came in when they were in the middle of their main course.

"That was quicker than I expected," Lucas greeted her on the phone.

"And with good reason," Stephanie said. "They are both more or less fine. Dr. Tackman ordered both of them in for a follow-up in a week, but they will both be able to leave the hospital today."

"That's great news," Lucas said and then quickly repeated to Sandra what Stephanie had just told him. "We are just across the street in a restaurant. Do you want to join us?" he then asked her.

Stephanie arrived at the restaurant just a couple of minutes later. The good news had significantly reduced the tension they had all been feeling so far, making the rest of the stay almost comfortable again. They decided to wait for the release of JJ and Kitten right here and see to it that everyone got home safely. Kitten made her way out first, shortly followed by JJ. When Lucas looked at them carefully, he was amazed at the recovery. If he hadn't known about their endeavor he wouldn't have been able to tell.

"You did a great job here, Airmid," he complimented Stephanie on their way to the car.

Lucas again took his seat next to Sandra, letting the others cramp together in the back. They dropped off Stephanie first, then drove to Hemel Hempstead to drop off JJ at a park, before heading into London. At a subway station they parted ways with Kitten and then finally continued on to Sandra's apartment. Lucas was glad when they finally arrived and he could get a long, hot shower and a long and relaxing night's sleep.

CHAPTER 14

DEATH

When Lucas arrived at the shack Monday evening the frustration was still clearly visible on some of their faces, most prominently Marcus and Cedric.

"We haven't gotten our butts kicked like this in a long time," Marcus said.

"Unfortunately, I have to agree." Lucas nodded.

"This was our one chance to get back into the game against those black mages, and we screwed it up," Jasmin said.

"We did the best we could. We can't always win, unfortunately." Lucas sighed and sat down. "I just hope we get another shot at this."

"Our chances are getting slimmer on that," Darien said.

"Why would you say that, Professor? Is there more bad news?" Lucas looked at him.

"Well, first of all, the video surveillance on Jackson's place has not turned up anything so far. And I doubt that it ever will. I mean, the house is literally only a front; he can't have any meaningful meetings or anything there. Everyone who stays there for longer than an hour will recognize the charade for sure. And second, yes, there is more bad news. HRC announced a short while ago that the crystal energy project was a big success and that it is now ready for the next step," Darien replied.

"I totally agree with you on the Jackson house topic, although I still believe that there has to be some kind purpose for the house; otherwise he would hardly go through the effort of keeping the front." Lucas was looking down at the table as he spoke. "On the HRC topic... Why would that be bad news? I mean, if they really figured it out, then that's great."

"The primary bad thing is that it's just not true. Everyone I talked to who was in that project so far said that they were no closer to cracking this than they had been when they first started. They still believe it's not viable," Darien said.

"So why would they announce the success then?" Stephanie looked confused.

"Rumor has it that they wanted to cut their losses and call it a success only for accounting reasons," he said.

"Accounting reasons?" Lucas was baffled now too. "What is the 'next step' they are planning?"

"The announcement was that they are founding a special company to pick up from the success and build the first full-size version of the plant, in the countryside close to Harlington. And apparently, they can only found a company if they claim a possible economic viability. I brought the announcement press release; take a look for yourself," Darien explained and started searching through his jacket pockets. When he finally found the piece of newspaper he handed it over to Lucas, who quickly read through it. "Clean energy breakthrough in Harlington," the headline said. "Harlington Research Corp. announces spinning off 'Whineberg Alternative Powers LLC' after major breakthrough in a classified clean energy source project. Investors plan to have the first commercial power plant ready for full production before the end of the year," the article began, continuing with lots more details about the build site and success statements from multiple scientists.

"I hadn't realized that you had so many senior scientists working on that thing. Look at all the testimonials here," Lucas said and showed the paper around. "Are you saying that they are all lying, Professor?"

"I am not sure," Darien replied. "What I am sure about is that I haven't ever heard most of those names before. So whoever they are, they are not working for HRC."

"Are you saying that all those statements are hoaxes?" Lucas was stunned.

"Not all of them, no. Dennis Whineberg, the guy who will apparently take over the new company, was one of the project leads within HRC. And some others they are quoting are also real. But most of them are not," Darien said.

"Why would Whineberg lie about his project? And some of his people too?" Stephanie asked.

"Because apparently, it leads to a great job opportunity," Darien said. "Whineberg was a low-level project manager in HRC; now he is co-owner and CEO of a new company. And all the people I know from the ones quoted are also getting new jobs in Whineberg's company. I have a picture of the bunch somewhere from the press conference. They all look like children on Christmas Eve." Darien searched through his jacket pocket again, pulling out another piece of newspaper with a picture on it.

Lucas looked at the group of around 15 people and had to agree with Darien. They all looked overly enthusiastic about the whole thing. When he scanned through the group one by one, he suddenly spotted something alarming.

"Who is that?" he asked and pointed at a person in the back row.

"That dude? He was not HRC... Hold on..." Darien took out his phone and scrolled through what looked to be a list of names. "Here it is," he finally said. "They stated that he was brought in by one of the investors. He is supposed to be an expert in the field of alternative energy from Spain. His name is Francesco Delmonte. Why? What about him?"

"Holy shit." Marcus had looked at the person now too. "Is that..."

"Yes," Lucas cut him off in mid-sentence. "At least it looks like him."

"Looks like who?" Stephanie was looking closely now too, but didn't recognize the man.

"That is the mage who tossed JJ through a closed window on Saturday," Lucas said. "That is the leader of the black circle."

"That's bad..." Jasmin looked alarmed.

"Bad, yes. But it explains a lot," Darien said.

"What does it explain, Professor?" Stephanie asked.

"It explains how they can call it a success. With a mage in their midst, they maybe really have the possibility to make this work, at least for a short time," he replied. "It's for sure not sustainable that way, but at least they won't be called on their fraud right away."

"That hardly sounds like an endgame to me, Professor," Lucas said.

"I am aware of that, Guardian," Darien sighed.

"Wouldn't a short success in real life increase the value of that company dramatically?" Jasmin asked.

"Sure." Darien nodded. "But only for the short period until someone figures out the scam behind it. What are you getting at?"

"Maybe the short time is enough. Maybe this all is a sort of investment scam," she said. "Push the price up, get more investors on board, and run away with the money."

"Interesting plan." Darien nodded. "But they would have to run very far, because everyone will sue them once this comes out. And I doubt that there will be enough money in it to justify that."

"Still, it's the best idea we've had so far," Lucas said with a complimenting look toward Jasmin.

"What do we do about it?" Stephanie asked.

"I am open for suggestions," Lucas said. "I have no idea."

"Maybe we should tip off the police about the hut?" Marcus suggested.

"And tell them what exactly? That we raided an opposing group who did not do anyone any harm so far?" Lucas asked. "That sounds like a bad idea."

"Then don't tell them," Darien said. "Just tell them that we saw suspicious activity there and that we think it might be related to the prison break attempt. Most likely the black mages are gone by now anyway, but what do we have to lose?"

"OK, fine," Lucas said and stood up. "I will call Inspector Corben right away."

He walked out of the hut and pulled his cellphone from his pocket. When he had selected Corben's name from the address book he paused for a moment. There was one thing they had to lose in this, after all, that he hadn't thought about yet. Those mages had just two days ago proven to be potent enough to beat three circles, including two Magus Majors. If they were still there when the police arrived the officers would hardly stand a chance against that force. He weighed the options for a while before hitting the call button.

"Good evening Mr. Trent," Corben greeted him.

"Good evening, Inspector," Lucas replied. "I have something for you, but to be quite honest I am a little reluctant to share it."

"I am all ears," Corben said.

"I believe that we found one of the hideouts of the people who were behind the prison break attempt," Lucas said.

"That would be good news," the Inspector replied. "Why would you be reluctant to share this?"

"Because one of the guys we expect to be there is even more powerful than Cleric was, and you have felt that power already," Lucas said cautiously.

"Cleric? Who is Cleric?"

"Sorry..." Lucas had to think for a moment. "Preston, I think the name was... the guy we visited in prison."

"So you are reluctant to talk because the situation could be dangerous?" Corben asked with surprise in his voice.

"Yes." Lucas nodded. "We already had one of your men close to death because of this group. I don't want to face that again."

"Danger is our business, Mr. Trent," the Inspector said. "Our unit exists for no other reason than that."

"Still..." Lucas replied. "I don't want to send your people into harm's way."

"Don't worry," Corben said with a firm voice. "We have all learned from the prison incident, and now that we are warned too, we will be extra careful."

"Very well," Lucas said. "I will text you the GPS coordinates of the location. Please watch your backs."

"We will," Corben said. "And I will keep you in the loop."

"Thank you, Inspector," Lucas said. "That's highly appreciated."

Then he hung up and quickly texted Corben the location of the hut before walking back into the shack. When he came in he saw that the others were just preparing Stephanie's cauldron.

"That's done. Now all we can do is wait," Lucas said.

"Not correct," Darien grinned. "All we can do is try to be prepared. That's why we decided to help Airmid brew some more healing potion. We used up quite a lot on Saturday."

"Great idea." Lucas smiled and walked over to help them.

They spent the entire evening replenishing their supplies, until Stephanie finally ran out of raw ingredients for the brew. The yield was not as plentiful as they would have hoped, but it was a start. They agreed to help her find more herbs throughout the week and resume the brewing next Monday.

Wednesday afternoon when Lucas was riding his bike back from school, he spotted a familiar car parked in a side alley a few houses down. He turned into the alley and stopped right next to it.

"Good afternoon, Inspector," he greeted Corben.

"Good afternoon, Mr. Trent." Corben looked tense. "Can you get in for a few minutes, please?"

"Sure." Lucas nodded and stepped off his bike. The Inspector's voice made him majorly worried. When he had sat down in the passenger seat and closed the door behind him, Corben handed him an envelope.

"You were right to caution us," he said.

Lucas slowly pulled the pictures out, expecting the worst. And what he saw surpassed his expectations. The picture showed the main room of the hut, even more destroyed than they had left it, burned in some areas, blood all over the floor and a corpse nailed to the wall, like in a crucifixion.

"Holy shit..." Lucas said with a cold shiver running down his spine. "That's REALLY bad."

"I agree," Corben said. "Your bad guy seems to be a real psychopath. We found three more corpses in the house, all of them brutally murdered. And we are not one step closer to finding him. All the blood is from the victims; they didn't even have a chance to defend themselves."

Lucas was looking through the rest of the pictures, getting paler with every single one he looked at.

"I was hoping that you had more information on your guy. We are observing the hut, of course, but I doubt that he will come back," Corben continued, as Lucas still wasn't able to say a word.

"You don't realize the magnitude of the problem here, Inspector." Lucas had a hard time talking.

"What can be worse than a dangerous guy murdering four people?" Corben was getting alarmed now too.

"This," Lucas handed Corben the picture of the man nailed to the wall, "IS the bad guy."

A minute of silence followed, with Corben having to let the statement sink and Lucas still looking through the pictures. The other corpses were the mages they had battled on Saturday, including the elder one that Kung Fu had engaged first.

"Whoever did this is even more powerful than this man was," Lucas finally said. "And if they didn't stand a chance to defend themselves, then he has to be far more powerful."

"What am I looking at here? Some kind of gang war?" Corben was still trying to make sense of the situation.

"I don't have a clear picture of this either, unfortunately," Lucas said. "But I have no hints whatsoever so far that we have a rivalry aspect on our hands here."

"Could any of your friends have done that?" the Inspector asked.

"There are some who would be capable of it, but I doubt that any of them has anything to do with this. This was not a simple murder. This was either a ritual, or a statement, and I would opt for the latter."

"What kind of statement?"

"My assumption would be that this guy's boss, or whatever you want to call him, was majorly angry about his performance. And he set an example here," Lucas said. "But that's just an unfounded assumption."

"So we have to assume that there is someone out there who is even more dangerous than the guy you were already reluctant to let us face here?" Corben asked.

"There is always a bigger fish, Inspector, yes." Lucas nodded.

"Great." Corben was unhappy. "I hope the detectives figure out who the dead guy was. Maybe that will lead us to his boss."

"His name is Francesco Delmonte," Lucas said. "As far as I know he is a Spanish citizen."

"How do you know that?" Corben asked.

"I know because I saw his picture in the paper on Monday," Lucas sighed. "He is somehow part of this new alternative energy company in Harlington." He was careful not to share too much with the Inspector.

"I will pass that on to the investigators, thank you." Corben nodded and scribbled down the name. "Appreciate your help."

"Sorry that I couldn't be of more assistance," Lucas said, still looking through the pictures.

Now that he had gotten past the horrors of the corpses, he was focusing on the background. Two of the pictures caught his attention right away. The first showed one of the corpses, lying in the corner of the laboratory. Looking through the remaining shelves, as well as some burst open canisters, he could see a lot of herbs and other raw ingredients. Looking at the second picture of the scene, showing a different angle, he saw what looked like a burst open storage cabinet with a lot of empty bottles in it and, scattered between them, a select few that were filled.

He immediately recognized the bottles, as well as the liquid in them: It was Eagle's environmental damage potion.

"Hold on... I believe I just found the reason for that prison break attempt..." Lucas said and browsed through the other pictures, looking for more shots from that room.

"What is it?" Corben took the two pictures and looked at them.

"Do you see the flasks in the cabinet?" he asked and waited for the Inspector to nod before he continued. "This liquid was manufactured by one of the people who is now spending his time in prison. And apparently, they are running short on supply."

"What makes you think that? Maybe they have the rest of the stash somewhere else," Corben suggested.

"The things you see lying around here in large quantities," Lucas pointed at the other picture, "are the raw ingredients for that liquid. They wanted him out to make some more of that."

"What kind of liquid is this? More of this acid we encountered at the prison?"

"No." He shook his head. "It is some kind of environmental poison. I still don't know what they are doing with it exactly, but if they are desperate enough to risk a prison break for it, there must be something more to it."

"Well, if they are running out of stock, and the maker is still behind bars, then we are good," Corben smiled. "One plan foiled."

"Not necessarily." Lucas felt uneasy. "If they run out of stock it could mean that they are also running out of time. And that would mean that something big is coming soon."

"Maybe they will make a mistake. Happens a lot when people are rushing things," the Inspector said.

"Hold on..." Lucas said and focused on another picture.

It showed the rest of the laboratory, which had not been visible in the first two shots. There was a lot of glass lying on the floor, from where Kung Fu's mentees had tossed the table over and thrown the low-level black guys. But to his surprise, the pieces of the weird apparatus that had been on the table, and shattered with the vials, were gone.

"Did your men remove anything from the room?" he asked.

"No." Corben shook his head. "What are you missing?"

"There was this weird machine standing on that table." Lucas pointed at the picture. "I know that it got destroyed when the table got knocked over, but apparently someone removed the pieces."

"Do you know what the device was for?"

"No. I assumed it was lab equipment, but it seems I was wrong." Lucas shook his head.

He was almost certain that this contraption had something to do with the crystal energy plant, but he didn't want to let the Inspector in on this just yet. The evidence was too scarce and the idea too far-fetched to start with.

"Once again, sorry that I couldn't be of more help" Lucas said and got out of the car.

Corben said his thanks and started the engine. He watched him drive off before making his way home. The whole situation had him majorly worried. The fact that someone had just murdered a Magus Major and three more Magus Minors without them having the remotest chance of defending themselves was a very bad sign. Whoever this was, he was not someone that he and his friends would have any chance to defeat. When Lucas arrived in his room he pulled out his cellphone and called Sandra.

"Hi honey. I didn't expect your call," she said with a happy tone in her voice.

"Sorry, Kung Fu, I know that you are busy right now, but we have a major problem," he said.

"What is it?" Sandra's voice changed instantly, her concern audible.

"I can't tell you on the phone. Is there a chance that we can meet and that you can bring JJ too?" Lucas asked.

"I will call him and ask. When do you want to meet?" she replied.

"Right now is a good time," Lucas said.

"OK." She said. "I will call you right back."

Lucas hung up and started pacing up and down in his room. It took Sandra only five minutes to call back and confirm the meeting, but for Lucas it seemed like hours. JJ had asked for a meeting place out of town, about 20 minutes' bike ride away for him. It was a small patch of wood, where they would most likely be by themselves. He quickly got dressed, packed his robes and raced off toward the location. When he arrived he saw Sandra's car already parked nearby, so he decided to put on his robes and walk a few steps into the forest. Looking around there, he could quickly spot his girlfriend a little deeper in, wearing her yellow robes as well.

"Sorry to summon you out here on such short notice," he said and gave her a hug.

"You sounded almost terrified on the phone. What happened?" she asked.

"Let us wait for JJ, please. I don't want to tell the story twice," he replied.

They had waited for about a minute when Lucas heard some unusual bird songs. A moment later JJ came walking out of the thicket toward them.

"Greetings, my friends," he said.

"Greetings JJ." Lucas bowed a little.

"This is the first time you have asked for a meeting like this," JJ said. "What happened?"

Lucas quickly filled them in on the things Corben had shown him.

"OK, now I understand why you are worried," Sandra said.

"What do you suggest we do?" JJ asked.

"I have no idea," Lucas said. "But this seems to be one nudge too big for us. We need help."

"I still don't get this. Why would someone from the dark side kill one of their own? Especially someone as powerful as this guy?" Sandra asked.

"I don't get this either. But if I had to guess, I would assume that this someone was majorly pissed off by that guy's failure to protect the lair," Lucas said.

"Is it possible that they were not killed by a dark mage, but rather one of the white ones?" she suggested.

"Do you really think anyone on the white side would make a statement like this?" Lucas asked.

"Do you mean if someone on our side would be capable of murder? Sure I do." She nodded.

"I am not talking just about murder," Lucas said. "This guy was crucified. I doubt that a good guy would do that."

"I disagree on that, Guardian," Sandra said. "The good guys are not exactly good either all the time. If the black robes hit one of them on the wrong foot, something like that could for sure be the result."

"You might be right to the extent that there are good guys who would be short-sighted enough to do something like that, but I doubt that any of those would be capable of committing this crime in the first place." JJ was fiddling around with his sleeve as he spoke.

"What do you mean?" she asked.

"There are only so many mages powerful enough to actually get this job done, and to get that strong you need to be extremely focused. Someone capable of that kind of focus will not just drop all his principles and do something like this." JJ had pulled his sleeve back now, uncovering a golden bracelet.

"But wouldn't a dark mage of that power level have the same kind of self-restraint?" Sandra threw in.

"True," Lucas replied to that. "But for a dark mage, murder would come more naturally than for a white one, I would presume. And making violent statements also sounds more like the doing of a dark one than a white one, don't you think?"

Lucas watched JJ from the corner of his eye. He had turned a little to hide his arms from Sandra's view and had opened a compartment on the bracelet. He could see him press his thumb on a nacre surface that was hidden below the lid, turning the surface purple for a short while, then switching to green. Lucas was glad that JJ had taken the step to summon the Magus Majors. He had thought about it himself already, but was uncertain if that was a good idea in the first place.

"What do we do now?" Sandra asked. "We can hardly let a murderer roam freely, but we can hardly engage him head on either."

"And even if we could from a strength point of view, we wouldn't know where to find him to begin with." JJ had stowed his bracelet again and turned back to face her.

"I might have a lead on that actually..." Lucas said. "But I also don't think that we are capable of winning that fight right now, so we should be extra careful what we do."

"So what do we do?" Sandra asked again.

"We wait," JJ said. "The lair is obviously gone, so your mentees succeeded in their quest after all. Everything else should not be our concern right now. At least not until we are ready."

"I don't like the sound of that, but unfortunately I agree." Lucas nodded and Sandra in the end did too, although it looked like a very reluctant nod.

"We will be in touch," JJ said and turned around, walking into the thicket.

"I hate this," Sandra sighed. "The situation doesn't feel right."

"I agree." Lucas nodded. "But right now there is little we can do."

"What did you mean when you said that you might have a lead?" Sandra asked.

"You remember that whole energy crystal thing that we were tracking?" Lucas started and waited for her to nod before continuing. "The dead guy was involved in that. He was part of the company that allegedly had the key to running this energy form commercially."

"And how does that help us find his master?" Sandra inquired further.

"The position this guy was in was the one that Cleric and his goons had before. So whoever brought him into this was also the one controlling them before. This was not his brainchild; there is a bigger picture here. And I am quite sure that his master is in the very center of this picture," Lucas said.

"And what are you doing about it?"

"Jesus, Kung Fu," Lucas sighed. "We are still trying to put the pieces together. Until we manage to figure out what they are really after, there is little we can do. We are watching the company. Maybe they'll bring someone else in now, to replace the dead guy. But other than that, we are also just trying to lay low and wait."

"That's hardly encouraging," she said.

"I totally agree with you on that." Lucas nodded. "The situation is somewhat frustrating for all of us. But JJ has a valid point, you know? Everything that was important to us and the people we are bound to protect has been achieved. Everything else is out of our direct influence."

He looked at his watch, recognizing a familiar message popping up. "A Magus Major meeting has been scheduled, requested by JJ," the message read, followed by date, time and location. The set date was almost two weeks from now, a Tuesday evening, again at the same restaurant downtown London. Lucas sighed and acknowledged the message.

"Are you in a hurry?" Sandra asked.

"Not particularly, no." Lucas shook his head. "And even if I were, I would still prefer spending more time with you and being late than having to leave early." He winked.

"It's a good sign that you still see it that way after multiple months." She grinned.

"Good, as long as you see it the same way," he replied.

"Believe me, I do," she said and gave him a long and intense kiss.

"I think I should let you get back to your work again now. Although I'd rather not," Lucas said with a smile. "But we will see each other again anyway on Friday."

"I unfortunately really don't have all too much time left today." She sighed. "But if you don't mind I would still like to spend every last minute of it with you, now that we are together already."

"Sure thing." Lucas nodded "The more the better."

They spent another half hour together, having a good time in the forest, before they finally parted ways. On his way back Lucas' mind was drawn back to the dark mages. He knew that there was little he could do at the moment, but somehow he felt the urge to do something nonetheless. It had not really been a calm time lately, but still he had the calm-before-a-storm feeling and just couldn't shake it. But no matter how hard he thought, there was nothing productive he could do right now that would aid the cause. So he tried to focus on the one thing that he could maybe do something about, and that was himself. He knew that there was still room for him to grow, still something holding back his true potential. Like so many times before, he could see the picture of Gaia again in his mind. "Unity. And belief" was what she had said. He had forced his mind to rethink that statement over and over again already, but he still was nowhere closer to understanding it. Then, suddenly, another picture rushed in. It was Angel, standing next to him in the Timestop bar. "Have faith in yourself; everyone around you has too," she had said. And before he had a chance to think it through, his mind presented him another memory. This time it was with Sandra, in her apartment. "Everyone around you believes in you, blindly. Why don't you?" he heard her saying. At that very moment he realized that this had been the key all along. But even with that new knowledge, he had no real idea how to leverage it. Belief had always been a central cornerstone of magical work. He remembered all too well his first-ever feat of magic, casting a kind of shield charm in the train, protecting himself from the spilling drink of another passenger. That also was made possible through belief, or rather the absence of doubt. And ever since then he had worked his magic based on that trust in it, which for him was equivalent to belief. After spinning the thought for a while longer, he sighed in frustration. He was convinced that he had found the key, but it still made no sense to him.

CHAPTER 15

ARCHEVEQUE

When Sandra arrived at Lucas' house Friday evening they were both exhausted from the week, as well as from the fact that they had not had any other insights in those two days, even though they had both kept their minds at it involuntarily. They decided to keep the day short, just get a quick dinner and then go to bed. They had no plans for the weekend, other than spending it together, and Lucas' parents were out visiting some friends, giving them the entire house to themselves, including the comfortable large bed, which they both vastly preferred over the makeshift camp in his room.

When they finally got downstairs on Saturday to have breakfast, it was already close to noon.

"Sleeping in really helps," Lucas smiled and whistled a happy tune.

"I agree." Sandra nodded. "Especially if you have company." She walked up to him and gave him a kiss on the cheek.

They enjoyed an extended breakfast and took their time cleaning up afterwards.

"What shall we do now?" she asked when they both were back in the living room. "It's 12:30 already; we missed half the day."

"Yeah, it's getting late. Maybe we should go back to bed," Lucas laughed.

Sandra was just about to answer when suddenly the terrace door, located on the far wall of the living room, burst open with a loud bang. They both turned around immediately, seeing a man walk into the room slowly. He was wearing a black robe and had his hood pulled over his face, leaving few identifying marks visible. Lucas was certain that the man was taller than himself and slim. He could see dark hair hanging from the hood, which at first suggested that it was a woman, but the aging hands without a doubt belonged to a man.

"Who are you?" Lucas shouted at him. "And what are you doing here?"

"I am your worst nightmare," the man in black answered with a weird-sounding French accent. "Who of you is known by the name Kung Fu?"

"What does it matter to you?" Lucas was agitated. "Get the hell out of my house."

"I want Kung Fu," he said in a calm, cold voice. "I don't care about anyone else right now."

"And I don't care what you want." Lucas was staring at him. "Get out, before I throw you out."

"You should not threaten me, kid." The man laughed, his voice filled with anger and hatred. "I know far more about violence than you do."

"Am I supposed to be afraid now?" He was getting angry now too.

"If you are not yet, then for sure you will be shortly." The man in black laughed and raised his hands. "URGUERO," he shouted.

"SEPERATIO," Lucas shouted back at the same moment.

He could feel the two energy streams colliding in the middle of the room. The power that this man exerted was tremendous, far more than he had ever seen anyone use before. His shield caught a lot of it before crumbling and letting the rest of the spell through, hitting Lucas right in the chest. He got lifted up and tossed back, crashing into the wall. Sandra immediately went into the offensive.

"LEVIPES," Lucas heard her cast before she jumped right onto the intruder.

A fierce few seconds of hand-to-hand combat followed before she was hit by another spell from the bad guy and tossed back into the sofa. Lucas had just returned to the fight, being relatively unharmed, thanks to his shield. The attacker showed him his side at the moment, focusing on Sandra, so he decided to take his chance.

"REPELLUM," he yelled and pushed his hands out.

The energy hit the dark mage spot-on in the side, but the only effect it had was that he had to make one step to the side.

"Is that all you have?" The man turned, facing him now. "URGUERO," he shouted again.

"SPECULUS," Lucas countered, focusing all his energy into his hand.

Once again, he got tossed back into the wall, this time a little harder than before, but still without taking too major a hit. His defensive charm had reflected a lot of the energy back to the attacker, making him stumble back a few steps now too. Lucas got on his feet as fast as he could, moving back to the center of the room. Sandra had by now also jumped back up and took position right next to him.

"You are getting annoying, you know that, right?" the man in black addressed them both and was about to raise his arms when a voice from behind Lucas' position made him stop.

"And you have always been annoying, you know that, right, Archeveque?" a man said.

Lucas had to resist the temptation to turn around and see who had joined them, but in the end stayed focused on his opponent.

"As have you, king of the dwarves." The man in black turned slightly, facing towards the kitchen entrance.

Lucas could see a man in shining red robes stepping up to them from the corner of his eye. Judging from the accent, he also was not native to England.

"Why don't you just leave and we call it a day?" the man in red asked.

"Because I still have unfinished business here. And you will not stop me from finishing it." Archeveque raised his hands again. "FULMINICTUS," he shouted.

"REFLECTO," the man in red responded.

Lucas and Sandra took one step back. A stream of lightning had emerged from the fingers of the black mage, meeting some sort of mirror magic cast by the man in red in the middle. The blue lightning from Archeveque and the orange lightning from the new arrival met in the middle, crashing into each other with a loud cracking sound, causing a very bright light and sparks flying everywhere. Both mages seemed to be constantly reinforcing the spells, making the mid-point move closer to one or the other, depending on who currently had the better focus. The cast only went for a few seconds before it became apparent to Lucas that the mage in red had drawn the short straw. When the lightning bolt from Archeveque was about to hit him, he stepped in.

"SEPERATIO," he cast again, trying to shield off the attack spell, but once again his shield was too weak to totally withstand the massive amount of energy. The man in red shook violently when the remainder of the lightning struck his body, before tumbling over and hitting the floor with a loud thud. Sandra reacted instantly and jumped back at the man in black, dealing some punches before being tossed back again by another spell. Lucas shot another Repellum at the man, shortly followed by an Ascius axe blow, but neither showed much effect.

"ANIHILAT," he suddenly heard a voice from the side.

The man in red had come back to his feet, his robes burned in several places. The spell caused the man in black to cry out in pain for a moment, before he rebounded with his push spell. The man in red tumbled back and fell to the ground again. When Archeveque turned to him next, Lucas fired up another Seperatio charm, this time trying to have a Speculus ready too, hoping that the two charms together could block the damage. Unfortunately, even two of his charms were no match for the attacker's strength, making him fly back again, with only little counter-effect on the man in black. When he jumped back up he could just see Sandra casting another Levipes charm and preparing to run toward the black man, when a spell hit her frontally.

"OCCIDERUS," he heard Archeveque yell before he saw smoke-like green energy emerging from his hands, shooting at her. When the energy arrived at her face she was stopped dead in her tracks and looked almost frozen for a moment, before she collapsed to the ground. Lucas' eyes started filling with tears. He had no idea yet what had happened to her, but he somehow felt that it had been a bad blow. He fired three Repellums in quick succession while making his way toward her body, falling on his knees right next to her. When he turned her over he saw his worst nightmares come true. Her face was pale, her eyes wide open and totally lifeless, no breath, no pulse.

"NOOOOO," he yelled and pulled her up toward him, sobs wracking his body. The whole world around him seemed to stop while he held her tight, tears soaking both their clothes quickly. From the corner of his eye he could see that the man in red was back on his feet, shooting spell after spell at the adversary, but it was all too clear that he didn't stand much of a chance. Archeveque blocked almost all spells and in turn threw attacks of his own. Lucas knew that his supporter would soon be out of the fight and most likely as dead as Sandra was, and that he himself would almost certainly follow shortly thereafter, but right now he didn't care. With her being dead, he wanted to die too, rather than running away and leaving her behind. He knew that he had nothing in his arsenal to slow down the intruder, let alone defeat him. The situation was hopeless anyway. When another burst of his tears had run down Sandra's face, Lucas suddenly saw a shadow behind her, sitting on the armrest of the couch. When he raised his head slightly he saw her sitting there, looking at him. Her body was translucent, her contours blurred, but he could see her clear as day. She had her yellow robes on and was wearing her hood, just like she had that first time they met in Buxton.

"Kung Fu, is that you?" he said with a shaky voice, looking at her.

"You know what I am," she said and stood up, walking toward him slowly.

"You are a ghost, right?" Lucas still had tears in his eyes, blurring his vision.

"Yes," she said.

"So you are really dead?" He started crying loudly again.

"It seems that way," she said and nodded. "But you are not. And I hope I trained you better these past months than to give up and let others follow my faith, just because you can't get your act together."

"But there is nothing I can do. I am just not strong enough." He had buried his head in her body.

"Everyone around you believes in you, blindly. Why don't you?" he heard her say, and when he looked up he could see her standing there in civilian clothes now, just like she had been in her apartment that evening.

"How can I believe in myself after letting this happen?" he almost shouted at the ghost, pointing at her body.

"Because if you don't, my death will be in vain. And you are better than that," she almost yelled back.

"But I don't know what to do." He had buried his head in her body again.

"Because you still believe in magic, rather than in yourself." Her ghost had come close to him now, back in her original form, wearing the robe. "There is no magic in the world; there are only mages being capable of channeling energy. Believe in yourself. Everyone else does."

Lucas was still crying, but his mind had suddenly realized the mistake he had made thus far. When he raised his head, all of a sudden the world started to change around him. The air seemed to be filled with colored streams, every object was now a web of energy patterns, and even Sandra's ghost looked fuller now. He could only imagine that this had been the way that Darien had seen the world all these years, recognizing all the portions of magical power floating around freely everywhere.

"Now get the hell up and fight," Sandra's ghost yelled at him.

He carefully laid her body to rest before getting back on his feet. The man in red was lying in the middle of the room, more burn marks lining his robes, but at least he was still moving. The man in black was standing a few feet away from him and just getting ready to cast again. Lucas pulled his hands up close to his chest, focusing on his next spell. He drew all his energy and all his emotions into it, and in addition started pulling in all the energy from the surrounding area, channeling it through his body and his arms into the spell that was building in his palm. When he finally stretched out his arm and yelled "REPELLUM" he almost had to close his eyes. The amount of energy pulsing through his arms was so massive that it hurt him badly, making him feel as if they were about to explode. The point on his palm where the energy emerged felt as if it was burning white hot, and the stream of pure force that hurled toward his enemy now was so bright that it was almost unbearable. He could see the defensive shield that Archeveque had established around his body, but when the first pulse of energy arrived, Lucas had not a shred of doubt in his mind that he was the stronger one this time. The first wave crumbled the intruder's defenses like a sheet of paper, letting the rest of the energy pass through unchecked. When the second pulse hit the black mage in the chest he was lifted up and tossed back violently. Lucas could see him crash into the frame of the terrace door, and then, to his big surprise, crash right through that frame, flying through the entire garden, crashing right through the wooden fence and finally, with a loud thud, hitting a tree out on the street. He could hear another thud when Archeveque fell down on the ground, but he was out of Lucas' view at that point.

"Now THAT is what I expect from my boyfriend." He saw Sandra's ghost smile at him for a moment before vanishing into thin air.

Lucas was still gasping for air after that spell, but when his mind came to rest even a little, and he realized that the imminent danger was over, he started crying again and let himself fall back down to the floor, pushing his head into Sandra's body.

"This can't be happening," he mumbled, thoughts racing through his mind. He needed to do something; he needed to find a way to get her back. Anguished and seeking ideas, he remembered the necklace he had been wearing for a while now. It had a vial of healing potion attached to it, a gift that Stephanie had given all of them back when she had finally learned the art of potion making. He quickly wiped the tears from his eyes, ripped the necklace off and dripped the potion into Sandra's mouth.

"Please, please, please..." he mumbled, watching desperately for signs of the potion making a difference, but nothing happened. Over a minute passed before the tears came back, his hopes shattering even more. He threw the necklace into a corner, the glass vial shattering on impact. Then he drew out his cellphone and hit a speed dial button.

"Hey Guardian," Stephanie greeted him, but he didn't even listen.

"Airmid, help me." He had major problems even getting those words out through his crying.

"What is it? Where are you?" Stephanie's voice changed immediately.

"Home." he replied and then buried his head in his hands, crying loudly.

"Hold on, I am on my way," he heard her say before she hung up.

Lucas tumbled back, letting himself slide down a wall, still clenching his phone. He just now noticed that the man in red was still here. He had run outside, obviously checking on Archeveque, and was just now coming back to the terrace door. Lucas saw him stop just outside the house, looking around, but right now he couldn't have cared less. He sat there, looking at Sandra, crying like he had never cried before in his life. It seemed to him like time was standing still; all he felt was overwhelming pain. When the man in red finally entered the room again he was not alone anymore. Someone in green robes had joined him.

"Not another one," the person in green, a woman, said. "The boy was lucky that you arrived in time; otherwise he would have joined her."

Lucas knew the voice from somewhere, but he couldn't make the connection right away.

"I am the lucky one here, Gaia," the man in red replied. "If it weren't for that boy, we would all be dead now. Archeveque has grown much stronger."

"Are you saying that he did this?" Gaia pointed at Lucas.

"Yes." The man in red nodded.

"I'll be damned," she said. "Seems that Archangel was right after all."

"I hope that your healer will arrive soon. We definitely caught some attention," the man in red said.

"She will be here as quickly as she can, Laurin," Gaia said and looked at Sandra's body. "But I wouldn't hold my breath if I were you. We couldn't save any of the others either."

"We have company," Laurin suddenly said and got into a defensive stance, a sword appearing in his hand out of thin air.

Gaia immediately followed his move, standing ready.

Lucas was in no mood for another fight, but he still jumped up to be ready. Just at that moment Marcus came running around the corner into the living room, stopping dead in his tracks as he saw the others and taking a defensive position right in front of Lucas.

"Who are you?" he yelled at the other two.

"Stand down, Cougar. They are on our side," Lucas said in a shaky voice and sank back on the floor.

"My name is Laurin," the man in red introduced himself. "And that is Lady Gaia."

"You are German, right?" Marcus identified the accent instantly. "I am Cougar."

"Yes I am." Laurin nodded. "Pleasure to meet you. I just wish it was under better circumstances."

"What is a German mage doing in Guardian's house?" Marcus was still unsure of the situation.

"I was trying to protect them, and as you can see," he pointed his open hand towards Sandra's body, "I failed."

"Protect them from whom?" Marcus asked.

"A very bad person, known as Archeveque," Laurin said and looked back toward the terrace. "Someone else just arrived," he then said.

A moment later a woman in a bright white robe came running into the house.

"Sunshine... Finally..." Gaia said and pointed her toward the dead body.

"What are you doing here?" Lucas addressed Marcus.

"What do you think? Airmid cried mayday, so I came as fast as I could," he replied. "What the hell happened here?"

"I don't know yet." Lucas was on the brink of crying again.

"Calm down, mate." Marcus patted his shoulder. "Airmid and Psycho should be here any minute now."

He then turned around and walked toward Gaia and Laurin.

"Now someone tell me what the hell is going on here, before I do something we all will regret pretty quickly," he said.

"I can't tell you for sure," Laurin sighed. "Archeveque unexpectedly came out of hiding last Sunday. He killed some of his minions in a hut not too far away from here and then started running around on a vengeance spree. It seems to have taken him a few days to find everyone he wanted to find, but this morning he finally went on the move again, killing another six people, this girl included. And he for sure would have gone on with it, if your friend over there hadn't stopped him."

"The hut near High Wycombe?" Marcus was stunned.

"Yeah, that one." Laurin nodded. "Do you know something I don't?"

"Shit..." Marcus took a step back and leaned against the couch. "Her mentees attacked that hut on Saturday. We got our asses kicked, but we did some damage before they repelled us."

"That place must have been pretty important if it lured Archeveque out in the open like that." Gaia jumped into the discussion.

Laurin was just about to respond when Stephanie came running into the room.

"This scene is getting crowded," he said and shook his head.

"It will get more crowded soon," Marcus replied.

"Guardian, what happened to you?" Stephanie had run straight toward him.

"Nothing happened to me." Lucas was still crying. "But everything happened to her." He pointed at Sandra. "Please, Airmid, do something."

"I will do my best," she said and turned around.

Gaia approached her, putting her hand on Stephanie's shoulder.

"I am afraid there will be little you can do to help," she said.

"And I still will try whatever is in my powers," Stephanie responded aggressively. "Now get out of my way."

"As you wish." Gaia bowed and stepped to the side.

"Who are you?" Stephanie asked the woman in the white robes, who was now kneeling next to Sandra's body.

"My name is Sunshine. I am a healer, just like you I presume," she said calmly.

"Seems so." Stephanie nodded. "I am Airmid."

"Then let's see if our combined powers can achieve what mine alone couldn't in the other cases." Sunshine made an inviting gesture.

They worked together for over an hour, but nothing they did made any difference. In the meantime the rest of the circle had arrived, as well as someone else who apparently was with Gaia. Jasmin had taken care of Lucas as well as she could, but even she had no cure for his grief. When Stephanie and Sunshine finally called it, they were both exhausted.

"I have no idea what this attacker did, but there is nothing we could do," Stephanie said and took Lucas in her arms. "I am truly sorry, Guardian, but she is gone."

Lucas cried for another ten minutes or so before Laurin approached him and laid his hand on his shoulder.

"I am truly sorry for your loss, Guardian, but there are things we need to take care of," he said.

"And what would that be?" Lucas let go of Stephanie and turned toward him.

"We have four dead black robes and six more of our own," Laurin said. "And unless you want to tell the police exactly what happened here, we need to make sure that we have a fitting alternative story available."

"And what would you suggest we tell them?" Lucas asked. "The police already know about the black-robed guys; they told me a few days ago."

"We can paint the six deaths of today as home invasions gone wrong," Laurin said. "In the end that's what they were anyway."

"Six deaths?" Lucas hadn't realized the magnitude of the problem so far, although he had heard them talking about it. "Who else did this maniac kill?"

"Five teenagers--three boys, two girls. We believe that it was the circle Kung Fu was mentoring." The last man to arrive jumped into the discussion.

"This is Chameleon, by the way," Laurin introduced the man to Lucas. "He is the one who will be selling the story to the authorities."

"We need to warn JJ," Lucas said. "If he came after the mentees and their mentor, it's only a matter of time before he comes after the supporters. And that would be both Kung Fu's circle and mine." The feeling of imminent danger had brought Lucas' focus back. He was still grieving internally, but the bond his emotions had with his mind and his heart by now was so strong that they were without a fight taking a back seat to make room for the bigger picture.

"I doubt that he knew about the supporters," Laurin said. "From what I could gather it was only Greybeard who had talked, and he didn't have any contact with the rest of the group. But you are right, we should be cautious."

"The question really is what any of us will be able to do." Darien had joined the discussion. "You are apparently a powerful battle mage, Laurin, and if Guardian and you working together can hardly beat this guy, what are the low-lives like me supposed to bring to the table?"

"You have a valid point unfortunately." Laurin nodded. "The best thing you can most probably do is run."

"Hardly a great idea if this guy comes storming into my home," Darien replied. "After all, my parents live there too, and they can even do less."

"We have to face the fact that we are outgunned here," Lucas said. "And all we can do is try to avoid confrontation until we can level the playing field again."

"Do you have any suggestions?" Chameleon asked.

"I hope that our beloved Council will have some. After all, isn't that what it is there for?" Lucas said and pointed at Gaia.

"The Council also doesn't have an army at its disposal unfortunately." Laurin sighed. "And that would be what we need in this case."

"But there must be someone strong enough to take Archeveque on," Lucas said with a hint of despair in his voice.

"Unfortunately, there is not always a bigger fish, Guardian. Sometimes the only thing you can throw at a really big fish is a large number of smaller fish," Laurin answered.

"People, we need to move." Chameleon tapped his foot. "I expect the police to arrive within the next ten minutes max."

"What do we need to do?" Lucas asked and took a look around.

"First and foremost, we need to get all the people out, except for yourself and me," Chameleon said. "Then you should call your parents, and whoever else you would call if someone invaded your home. I will take care of the regular officers and the medics. The rest is up to you."

"OK." Lucas nodded and quickly rallied his friends around him. "Thank you all for coming here on such short notice," he said. "But Chameleon is right, there is nothing we can do anymore, so please go home and stay safe. If anything comes up, give me a call; otherwise we will meet again on Monday."

The others nodded reluctantly. None of them wanted to leave Lucas alone, but they knew that their staying here would have raised more questions than it would have helped. They packed up and headed on their way, leaving Lucas standing there with Sunshine, Chameleon, Laurin and Gaia.

"I am sorry that I couldn't do more for your girlfriend, brother." Sunshine gave Lucas a long hug. "I truly am."

"You have nothing to be sorry for, Sunshine," Lucas said in a firm voice. "Thank you for trying. That's more already than I could have asked for."

"I will take care of the bodies, as usual," she then said to Gaia before walking out into the garden.

"I will be back once the police are finished here," Gaia addressed Lucas next. "There is little I can bring to the table, but I can at least help you restore some of the damage."

"I appreciate the help, milady." Lucas bowed before her.

"Stop doing that please," she said as she turned around. "If anyone in here deserves to be bowed before it's you, not me." With that she walked out into the garden as well.

"I will keep an eye on your friends, Guardian. I'm not sure what I can do if Archeveque attacks again, but I will nonetheless stand my ground and fight," Laurin said and bowed a little. "I owe you my life. I will never forget that."

"You don't owe me anything, Laurin. If it weren't for you I would be dead now too," Lucas replied. "And I will never forget that either."

"I hope next time we meet will be under better circumstances," Laurin said and took a step back. "Godspeed, Guardian, until we meet again."

"Godspeed, Laurin. Stay safe," Lucas said.

He expected him to walk out too, but Laurin didn't move. Lucas watched him carefully. He stretched out his arm and all of a sudden a sword appeared in his hand. Laurin kissed the blade, then stretched out his arm again and mumbled a spell. Without any sound or warning, his body turned into a cloud of smoke, starting at the feet and continuing up. Lucas watched in awe as the smoke was sucked into the sword until there was nothing left but the very sword hanging in mid-air. And then, with a vague "puff", it disappeared.

"Now THAT is great magic." Lucas was still amazed.

"What next?" he then said and turned to Chameleon.

"Now you call whoever you would normally call if you had a break-in," he said.

"Well, that would be Emergency Services first, my parents next, and in this special case, most likely the Professor and Inspector Corben," Lucas said "What do you think?"

"You can skip Emergency Services; they would have your call on record. I think it is also best to skip the Professor; after all, you already know the details. That leaves your parents and Corben. I am good with both."

"And what do I tell them?" Lucas asked.

"Whatever you see fit. Especially in the case of the Inspector. You do have a standing relationship after all," he answered.

"All right, I will get right on it." He nodded and stepped away.

When he called his parents, his emotions took the upper hand again. It felt totally weird though, as he was fully focused, even though he was crying during the call. But he quickly realized that this would be the expected behavior for someone who had just witnessed his girlfriend die, and that until recently he had been in that mode completely anyway. As expected, his parents decided to pack immediately and come back home, which would give Lucas about four hours before their arrival. When he called Corben next, he had turned the emotions down a few nudges. The Inspector ended the phone call pretty quickly after hearing the main facts and announced his appearance at the scene. When Lucas pocketed his cellphone and walked back into the living room the first responders were just arriving outside. Looking out the window, he could see a police patrol car pulling up. Two officers stepped out and were hastily walking to the front door. Lucas wanted to go and open it, but Chameleon had already passed by him.

"Don't you want to take off that robe?" Lucas asked. "Don't you think that looks suspicious?"

"They call me Chameleon for a reason, Guardian." The man grinned and walked on.

"Luton Police Service, Constable Miller," he heard the officer introduce himself as Chameleon opened the door. "We have reports of a home invasion at this address. Can we come in?"

"Detective Inspector Cornbridge, Major Crimes Unit," he heard Chameleon respond. "Please come in."

When they walked around the corner, back into the living room, Lucas had to smile for a moment. Chameleon had transformed his robes into a trench coat, looking a little bit like the movie detective Columbo.

"This is the surviving victim, Mr. Trent," Chameleon introduced him to the officers. "I have already taken his statement, so all that is left is to wait for forensics to arrive."

"That makes our lives a little easier, if that is appropriate to say in such a terrible situation," one of the officers said. "We will secure the scene and interview the neighbors. Maybe someone saw something."

"Thank you, Constable." Chameleon nodded.

A few minutes later an ambulance arrived. The medics checked out Lucas, but couldn't find any obvious signs of injury. And as Chameleon wouldn't allow them access to Sandra's body they were gone again pretty quickly. With the living room blocked off by police tape, Lucas had sat down on the stairs. He was just dozing off a little bit when the sound of a siren made him focus again. A car with a single blue flashing light on top had stopped in their driveway with squeaking tires. The vehicle had not even come to a full stop yet when the passenger door already swung open and another police officer jumped out running toward the still-opened front door. He was wearing a uniform and body armor, as well as a hand gun strapped to his right leg. Chameleon made a step forward to introduce himself, but the officer just ran past him when he saw Lucas sitting on the stairs.

"Corben, SO-19, get out of my way," he yelled at Chameleon as he ran by.

Lucas stood up slowly. He was just approaching the Inspector when a second police officer, dressed just like Corben, came running in. He immediately recognized the scars on his face.

"Good afternoon, Inspector. Good afternoon, Constable," he said with a slightly shaking voice. "I am sorry that we never meet under better circumstances."

"Are you all right?" Corben asked and looked at him.

"I am." Lucas nodded. "But she is not." He pointed at Sandra's body.

"What happened?" the Inspector looked around.

"You have seen the pictures from the hut in High Wycombe too..." he replied. "Take an educated guess."

"Are you saying that this was the same perpetrator?" Corben was stunned. "What did he want from you?"

"Nothing," Lucas sighed. "He was not after me; he was after her." He pointed at Sandra again. "Apparently he holds her responsible for what happened at the hut."

"Did he come through the terrace door?" the Inspector was carefully examining the scene.

"Yes, he came in that way and we threw him out that way again; unfortunately, way too late for her." Lucas' face was cold.

"I will make sure that we have units posted in the neighborhood until we find that lunatic." Corben had walked back to Lucas.

"I will take first shift, Inspector." Constable Wainwright, who had been standing guard next to the front door so far, said immediately.

"Don't bother. I doubt that he will come back, and even if he does, I doubt that an officer or two would make much of a difference." Lucas sighed. "This guy has killed at least ten people within a week; he will not have any problem continuing that streak."

"Ten people?" the Inspector was stunned. "Where are the other five?"

"They just happened a few hours ago; you will soon hear more about it," he said.

"Here are the names." Chameleon passed a piece of paper over to Corben. "But please keep this to yourself for now; we don't want the killer to know that we have made the connection already."

"Thank you, Detective." Corben nodded before turning back to Lucas. "Is there anything I can do to help?"

"Not right now, but thanks for the offer, Inspector." Lucas shook his head. "But I am convinced that this is not over yet, so that might change pretty quickly."

"You know where to find me. I have little patience for murderers. We will be there whenever you need us." Corben offered Lucas his hand. "I'm sorry for your loss. I am sure I can't talk Constable Wainwright out of staying close, so I will not even try."

"Thank you, Inspector, I appreciate that. Although I would rather have your constable somewhere safe than nearby. But you both seem to have made up your minds, so I will not try to convince you otherwise." Lucas shook his hand and bowed a little. "Have a good day."

Over the next two hours Lucas watched the forensics team go over his living room with a fine-toothed comb, before the coroner finally was allowed in to remove Sandra's body. When the remaining officers had left, he was happy to finally be able to get to work himself. Chameleon had transformed back into his robes and was just arranging some glass shards when Gaia stepped back in.

"Now let's restore the mess," she said and drew some kind of wand.

Lucas was just about to ask what she had planned when she cast her first spell.

"NASCOREA," he heard her hiss.

For a moment he was unsure what was supposed to happen, but then it became apparent pretty quickly. The shattered wooden frame of the terrace door had come to life and was now growing back into form.

"Now I know why you are on the Council, milady." Lucas watched with his mouth open.

"You are impressed way too easily," Gaia laughed. "Growing a tree is not exactly rocket science for a witch. The glass would be trickier, though."

"That's why you don't bring a witch to do a druid's job," Chameleon grinned. "DEFLUOSO," he then yelled and pointed at the glass shards that he had laid out before.

Lucas watched as the pieces started to glow red on the edges and magically move together, fusing into a single pane of glass again.

"CIERUS," Chameleon then cast, making the newly-formed sheet take off and hover back into position.

"NASCOREA," Gaia hissed again, having the wood grow around the edges of the pane, forming a perfectly new door.

"You two are amazing," Lucas whistled in acknowledgement.

"There are things that none of us can fix, but those we can, we definitely will." Gaia smiled. "I will take care of the fence now. That should be the last thing we have left to restore your home to its original state."

"Thank you both." Lucas bowed before them.

"Godspeed, Guardian. May you find peace on your journey," Gaia said as she stepped out into the garden.

"Godspeed, milady, until we meet again," he replied and shut the door behind them. Now that he finally was alone, he walked up to his room to let his emotions run freely for a while again. He was still in a lot of pain and he was sure that it would stay that way for a very long time. Lying on his bed, he cried for several hours, before exhaustion made him fall asleep.

CHAPTER 16

JACKSON

When Lucas was riding his bike to the shack Monday afternoon, he was still just a shadow of himself. The news of Sandra's death had spread pretty much everywhere, everyone he knew had offered condolences and most people were still looking at him in a weird way, as if they were expecting him to always hunker down in a corner and cry when time allowed. Most of the time that would actually have been what Lucas felt like doing in the first place, but his united self had kept him from following that urge on most occasions. Arriving at the shack, he looked at his watch and realized that, for the first time ever, he was late. He stowed his bike and put on his robes on his way to the entrance, but before he reached the door he spotted somebody up near the forest line. He opened the door slightly, just enough to throw his backpack in and stick his head through.

"I'll be with you in a few minutes," he said before closing it again and walking towards the trees.

The person had walked a few steps into the forest to remain unseen by any spectators, a move that Lucas was used to by now.

"Greetings, Guardian," the man said. He was wearing light blue robes and had a familiar voice.

"Greetings," Lucas replied. "What can I do for you?"

The man pulled out a keychain from his pants pocket, singling out a small key fob shaped like a globe. The piece looked very beautiful, apparently made from gold with some carved, translucent stones worked into it that formed the continents. He pulled slightly on the chain that was anchoring the fob to the keys, making the globe pop open. Then he thoroughly pressed his thumb onto the nacre surface that came to light inside and showed it to Lucas. To his surprise the surface didn't flash up purple, like he had been used to so far, but it flashed up in blue, almost identical to the color of the man's robes. Lucas acknowledged the gesture by pulling out his watch and also presenting the nacre surface to the man. And his also lit up blue when he put his thumb onto it.

"I am Thor." The man bowed a little. "We have met before."

"It's a pleasure meeting you again, Thor, although the timing is not exactly the happiest for me right now." Lucas returned the bow. "I recognized the voice, but couldn't connect it to you."

"That's quite all right," Thor said with a smile. "And I am sorry that tragic circumstances accompany our meeting."

"What made you come all the way out here?" Lucas asked. "You could have waited for the meeting next week if you wanted to talk to me."

"Actually, I wanted to talk to you in private. The meeting would not have been appropriate for that," he replied. "I presume that you have recognized the changed behavior of your locket?"

"Yes. Why is it blue now?" Lucas nodded.

"It shows purple to identify a Magus Major to his equals. It will show blue to do the same for a Magus Superior. But again, only when facing an equal counterpart," Thor explained. "Which also reveals why I am here."

"You have got to be kidding me..." Lucas said. He had felt the step he had taken during the battle against Archeveque, but he had thus far not realized that it had been the full step to the final level.

"Once you unite all three aspects of yourself, the mind, the heart and the soul, toward one common goal, you are addressed as Magus Superior," Thor said. "Very few are capable of making this step, so there will not be too many times that you see your locket light up in blue."

"What does that mean now for me?" Lucas asked.

"Like the other levels before, it only means what you make it mean," Thor answered. "Only a select few will know the difference, even amongst the Magus Superiors, and those will not impose anything upon you. The one change it brings to your life is that your locket now holds one more feature: You know that by pressing the nacre surface for a while it will turn green, and a Magus Major meeting will be scheduled on your behalf. If you keep your finger pressed on it for a while longer, the green will turn into red, which in turn will lead to a meeting of the Magus Superiors being scheduled the same way. That meeting might be further away though, so it might be that someone will come and pick you up, rather than expecting you to travel there yourself."

"Like a magical cab service?" Lucas had to grin at that thought.

"Actually, we all prefer some form of teleportation, but in essence it is just that, yes." Thor nodded. "That's what I came here to tell you, so now I will let you get back to your circle. Unless of course you have any questions that I might answer?"

"I actually have one, if I am allowed to ask it." Lucas was curious. "Who was the other one?"

"The other, what?" Thor looked at him.

"At the last Magus Major meeting Gaia told me that there were only two Magus Superiors in the room. I now know that you were one of them, but who was the other?" Lucas rephrased the question.

"That's hardly a secret." Thor laughed. "Gaia, of course."

"Really? I had assumed that she had excluded herself." Lucas was stunned. "That makes the group even smaller..."

"Like I said..." Thor smiled.

"How many are there then when you call a Magus Superior meeting?" Lucas asked.

"If you call upon the group you call upon the entire community in Europe. I don't know the numbers exactly, but I presume it's a dozen or so. Normally the meeting will see six, or maybe seven," he answered.

"In the entirety of Europe?" Lucas couldn't believe it. "Holy shit..."

"Like I said..." Thor repeated with another smile.

"I think I need to let this settle for a while," Lucas said. "I hope we will find the time to talk again at some point."

"We will meet in a week, I presume?" Thor said. "You have your next chance there most likely."

"Looking forward to it." Lucas smiled.

"Ditto." Thor grinned. "It's good to have another one close by. That's a luxury that not many of us share. Godspeed, Guardian; may your life be long and safe." He turned around and took a few steps into the forest, before vanishing into thin air.

"Godspeed, Thor, until we meet again." Lucas bowed after him before walking back down to the shack.

When he arrived, the others were eagerly waiting for him.

"What was that all about?" Jasmin asked.

"I had a visitor," Lucas answered. "Sorry for keeping you waiting."

"How are you feeling?" Stephanie asked.

"As well as can be expected," Lucas replied. "Kung Fu's funeral is on Wednesday and I can tell you that I am not looking forward to it."

"Is there anything we can do?" Jasmin looked at him.

"You have all done a lot more than I could have expected already. But thank you for the offer." Lucas smiled.

"We did nothing more than you would have done for all of us. And if there is anything more that we can do, then we certainly will. That's what friends are for," Marcus said.

"Amen to that." Darien nodded.

"I have something for you," Cedric said to Lucas and started searching through his pockets. He pulled out a chain with a brand-new vial attached to it. "Seems that you broke yours during the fight. Airmid, if you please." He handed it over to Stephanie.

"So that was healing potion in Kung Fu's mouth, after all," Stephanie said while opening her backpack. "Good move, Guardian. And very unfortunate that it didn't work."

"That 'good' move made me trash the most valuable gift I ever got. Not very worthy of me I would say," Lucas sighed.

"The most valuable gift used for the most valuable person in your life. I could not have asked for a more fitting cause," Stephanie said and re-filled the vial. "And I am still sorry that my magic was not strong enough to make a difference."

"Your magic already made more difference than anyone else's did," Lucas said. "We are lucky that we have you in our midst."

"We are lucky that we are together in this group." Marcus had stretched his fist to the middle of the table. The others followed his example instantly.

"Brother to brother, yours to the end," they all said in unison.

Stephanie handed Lucas the chain with the now-filled vial.

"Thanks, Airmid. And thanks, Whirlwind." Lucas bowed a little.

"If you are up to it, I have news..." Darien said after a moment of silence.

"I think we are all eager to get our feet back on the ground after the encounter in the hut. So please, go ahead," Lucas said and turned toward him.

"Let me start with two minor things first: I heard last week that HRC is rushing another batch of environmental reports. The scientists are furious right now, because after the outsourcing of the crystal energy thing, they would have had enough resources to do it right. But management intervened and pushed the half-done work out prematurely. And once again they are overstating problems, at least according to the scientists."

"This is driving me crazy. I still can't make any sense of it." Lucas shook his head.

"Especially with all the bad things that are going on right now environmentally..." Jasmin nodded.

"What do you mean?" Lucas looked at her.

"Haven't you heard the news? There was a breakdown of an oil drilling platform close to the US coast. They say that it's the most significant ecological disaster in a long time," she said.

"I have not heard that yet, no." Lucas shook his head. "But then, I have heard pretty little those past days."

"Maybe that is why they are rushing. To emphasize the point of that oil spill," Stephanie suggested.

"In any case, the fossil fuel industry is getting its fair share of beating these days, that's for sure," Lucas said. "What else?" He looked at Darien.

"Second, I heard that this Delmonte guy has been let go from Whineberg Alternative Power and they are contracting an external resource for this now. I have no idea why they would do that, though; after all, it has only been a little over a week since they announced the team," Darien continued.

"Maybe they were unhappy with his performance?" Marcus suggested.

"I know the real reason actually, and it is far more mundane," Lucas said. "The guy is dead."

"How do you know that? And how come you didn't tell us?" Darien was stunned.

"Inspector Corben told me last Wednesday. I didn't think it would be important in the short term, so I decided to tell you at our next meeting. Which happens to be today." Lucas said. "Archeveque killed him, and another three of his minions. At least that's what Laurin thinks."

"That explains it for sure." Darien nodded. "But why would he kill his own guy?"

"My best guess is that we destroyed something important when we raided the hut and Archeveque was so furious that he killed the people who were in charge of protecting it. Plus, he then killed the people responsible for it too, including Kung Fu," Lucas said.

"That must have been some important piece, if he killed someone as powerful as Delmonte for it." Marcus sounded shaken.

"Seems so, yes. Laurin said that it was very unusual for Archeveque to come into the open like that." Lucas nodded. "Maybe we are spoiling his plans far more effectively than we thought."

"That might also explain the other thing I wanted to show you." Darien sounded anxious when he reached into his backpack and pulled a laptop out. "We finally got something meaningful from watching Jackson's house. Take a look."

Darien started up a video showing the lobby area. Lucas was standing behind him, watching eagerly. The door swung open and two men entered the room, one of them carrying a roll of paper.

"That's Jackson." Lucas recognized the one without the paper instantly. "But who is the other one?"

"What is so important that we have to meet in person?" Jackson asked the other man.

"We have been given a high priority task, directly by the boss," the other said without even taking his cigarette out of his mouth. "And it is a messy one."

"Another hostile takeover?" Jackson asked.

"No, far messier." The other one shook his head and started walking toward the conference room. "We need to blow a building up."

Darien stopped the video and opened another file. It was the one from the conference room camera.

"Why doesn't he contract a construction company then?" Jackson was just asking as they walked into the room.

"Because the owners will hardly let us do this voluntarily," the man with the cigarette said and unrolled the paper on the table.

"You can't be serious," Jackson said after looking at the drawing. "I am not a terrorist."

"You are in this shit as deeply as I am," the other one almost yelled at him. "You falsified the HRC reports, faked financial statements and were an accessory to those fools who helped us take over the company in the first place, and that is just covering HRC, not all the other companies that came before. So don't tell me what you are or are not."

"But this is madness." Jackson seemed in shock. "How are we even supposed to pull this off? There will be massive amounts of security at the site."

"We will get our eco-terrorist friends back out in the open and stage a demo at the site. That should distract security enough so we can get in position over here," he pointed at the paper, "and shoot an RPG right into here." He pointed at another spot on the map. "That should do the trick."

"I will not be any part of that," Jackson said. "This is not what I signed up for."

"You will not only be part of it; you will be the one pulling the trigger," the other one said.

"Are you out of your mind, Guthridge? There is no way in hell I will be anywhere near this when that RPG goes off." Jackson turned around and stormed out of the room, Guthridge following two steps behind.

Darien once again switched the video file, playing another one from the lobby. Jackson was storming past the front desk when Guthridge appeared in the picture, holding a pistol with a silencer attached to it. Jackson was about three steps away from the front door when Guthridge fired two shots right into his back.

"Bad choice, Jackson. I told you from the beginning that there is no halfway with this project. Seems I have to do things myself then," Guthridge said as he approached the body. He then pulled the trigger again, shooting him straight in the head. Then he put the gun away and pulled a cellphone out.

"It's me," he said after a moment. "I need you to clean something up at the Import-Export HQ. I'll leave the front door unlocked for you."

He hung up, put the cellphone away and stepped out of the house. After that Darien stopped the video.

"What the hell was that all about?" Lucas was still stunned, and so were most of the others.

"Something big is going to happen, and it's going to happen soon," Darien said. "An hour after that, two men arrived and removed Jackson's body, cleaning up pretty thoroughly after themselves."

"They must be getting close to their goal." Lucas had sat back down.

"Why do you think that?" Marcus asked.

"They have been very methodical and very stealthy in the past. But since the raid on the hut, they have introduced pretty desperate measures," Lucas said. "I mean, look at that. What could be bad enough for a guy like Jackson to cry foul?"

"I agree that they are getting desperate, but that doesn't mean that they are getting closer to their goal now, does it?" Marcus said.

"I agree that desperation might be their primary motivator here. With Eagle gone, their supply of the potion is drying up and now with us trashing the lair, they apparently lost something else that was vital. But even with that, if they still had a long road ahead they would not voluntarily kill their closest allies, not after losing so many already in the past. And both Delmonte and Jackson played a vital role in this somehow. I mean, think about it... How long can Jackson stay missing before people will start asking questions? He owns shares of a lot of companies that are involved here," Lucas replied.

"We need to figure out what the plan is," Darien said.

"Did I miss something or did Guthridge leave the paper on the conference table?" Jasmin asked.

"He did." Darien nodded and pulled up more footage from the empty conference room. "Shall we go in and get it?"

"We should not get it, but we should get in and make some pictures of it." Lucas said. "And this time that should be easy... After all, the front door is still unlocked, right?"

"I will go there tomorrow," Marcus said. "Taking a few pictures should be easy enough; no need to drag anyone else there."

"Actually, there is," Lucas said. "We need to get the video equipment out of there."

"Why's that? It has just started paying off that we installed it." Darien was surprised.

"Because at some point in the near future we need to tell the police about this. And we better not leave too many traces of our presence if we can help it," Lucas replied.

"I still think that I can manage this by myself," Marcus said. "I am not going to plug the holes or anything, so it should be an easy enough task."

"I am not happy letting you be there alone," Lucas said. "I will go with you."

"You have enough on your plate already, Guardian," Marcus said.

"I will back him up," Cedric threw in. "Not everything needs your attention, fearless leader."

"OK, fine," Lucas said reluctantly. "Let's hope we can figure this out before it's too late."

"We will go tomorrow afternoon. That should be soon enough," Marcus said.

Lucas nodded. He still was not happy about not being there with them, but he had a funeral to prepare for, and he still needed time to think about what Thor had said earlier.

The next evening, Lucas was just finishing dinner when his cellphone rang.

"Hi Cougar. What's up?" he answered the call.

"Guardian, we are in deeper shit than we thought," Marcus said. "I just sent you the pictures we took from the plan that Guthridge took to Jackson's house. You need to see this."

"All right, slow down." Lucas excused himself and ran up to his room, opening Marcus' email. "What am I looking at?"

Lucas opened all three pictures and tried to make sense of what he saw. It was some kind of area blueprint of a big facility with multiple buildings and connections between them. It would have looked like any other factory if it hadn't been for the weird, round buildings on one side, which had one spot on them marked with an X.

"Look at the title," Marcus said.

Lucas scrolled to the bottom of the first picture. "Sizewell" the label said.

"No way..." Lucas held his breath. Sizewell was a nuclear power station just about 100 kilometers northeast of London. "What are those lunatics trying to do?"

"Apparently they are trying to blow up a power station," Marcus said. "No wonder Jackson chose to not participate in this. That's plain terrorism."

"I need to get this to Inspector Corben," Lucas said. "Great job, Cougar."

"I hope the police can stop this. I don't want Chernobyl coming to the UK," Marcus said. "I'll keep my fingers crossed."

Lucas hung up and hit a speed dial button.

"Professor, I need you to send me those videos," Lucas said without even waiting for Darien to say hello.

"Right away," Darien replied. "What is it?"

"They are planning to blow up a nuclear power plant," he said.

"They... WHAT???" Darien seemed shocked.

"Exactly." Lucas nodded. "I need to get this to the police ASAP."

"The videos are on their way. I sent you the cut versions to avoid questions."

"Thanks Professor. I'll keep you posted," Lucas said and hung up, to immediately dial another number.

"Good evening Mr. Trent," Inspector Corben answered the call, obviously chewing on his dinner at the moment. "What can I do for you?"

"Good evening, Inspector," Lucas replied. "I need to talk to you right away. We have a problem."

"It will take me about half an hour to get to Luton," Corben said, putting down some cutlery. "Is that good enough?"

"It has to be." Lucas nodded. "Can we meet in the parking lot at the mall?"

"Sure thing. I'll be there in 30," Corben said.

"Thank you, Inspector. See you soon," Lucas said and hung up.

By now the videos had arrived in Lucas' inbox as well. He quickly reviewed them for anything that could reveal their identity before copying them over to a thumb drive, together with the pictures. He also made some printouts of the photos and put them into an envelope, together with the USB stick. He then copied all the files over to his laptop too, stuck it into his backpack together with the envelope, and cycled to the mall at his best speed. The place was almost empty at this time of day; only a few employees were still there finishing up and getting ready to go home. Lucas chained his bike to a lantern and started walking around the parking lot. He knew that he was ten minutes early, but he just couldn't stand still right now. When he finally saw Corben's car pull into the lot, he was relieved. He signaled the Inspector, who drove over and stopped in an empty space right next to him.

"Thank you for coming here on such short notice." Lucas shook his hand as he sat down in the passenger seat.

"I promised I would be there whenever you need me." Corben tried to smile, but was obviously agitated too. "What is so important?"

"Before we start we have to clear one thing up," Lucas started. "Some of the things I am about to show you have not come into my possession entirely legally. I still think the information is important enough to risk the exposure, but I need your guarantee that you will treat this absolutely confidentially."

"As long as the things you are telling me are not outweighed by the crimes you committed to get them, I will protect you. If that's the case or not, you have to decide for yourself," Corben replied.

"Fair enough," Lucas said. "Then let's do this. It paid off that you did not have your detectives poking around in HRCs business just yet. Unfortunately, some bad things happened, though."

He pulled out his notebook and showed Corben the videos, including the one from the cleanup crew.

"You know, I think you are safe with whatever you did to get this material." Corben was stunned. "Murder outweighs pretty much everything else."

"I am happy to hear that," Lucas said. "But I did not ask you to come here to present you a murder scene."

"What could be more important than that?" Corben was getting a little queasy.

"You heard that they want to blow up a building with an RPG," Lucas said and waited for Corben to nod. "We know their target."

"I doubt that a single RPG can cause a lot of damage to a building." Corben was getting more curious by the minute. "So what could they possibly target that has you so majorly concerned?"

Lucas opened the picture and turned the laptop toward the Inspector again.

"A live nuclear power station," he said.

"They want to blow up Sizewell B?" Corben was getting a little bit pale now too.

"Looks like it." Lucas nodded. "And I guess you understand now why I am concerned."

"Indeed." Corben nodded. "I need to cycle this to all relevant authorities. But I will of course protect your identity."

"Thank you, Inspector. Here is a copy of everything I just showed you, and I included the address of the murder scene as well." Lucas handed Corben the envelope before opening the door. "I hope you can stop those bastards. I don't want more death in my neighborhood anytime soon."

"I will see to that." Corben nodded and started the engine, driving off as soon as Lucas had closed the door behind himself.

"What the hell is Archeveque planning?" he mumbled to himself as he got on his bike. There were still pieces of the puzzle missing, and he just couldn't fill in the blanks.

CHAPTER 17

REVELATIONS

When Lucas arrived at the funeral next day, accompanied by both his parents, he felt majorly uncomfortable. Not only did going there bring back the memory of Sandra's death, and all the pain that came with that, but it also brought an unexpectedly large group of people to the scene that he didn't know. There was her family, a group of children, obviously from the school she taught in and a lot more, who Lucas presumed were friends and colleagues. He could not spot any of her friends from the circle, which made him feel even worse, as they at least would have been people he could have related to. The burial was planned out in the open; the coffin had been put on a stand a few meters away from the future grave, with half the lid opened for people to pay their final respects. Lucas could see three people standing a few feet away from the coffin, an older couple and a girl that was somewhere between his age and Sandra's, and a line had formed toward them. He was sure that these were her parents and her sister, so he got in line to express his condolences. The wait was agonizing, but seeing their grief as he came closer made him feel not as alone anymore in his feelings. When it was finally his turn, tears had filled his eyes.

"I am sorry for your loss," he said when he shook her mothers' hand, tears running down his cheeks.

"Thank you," she said. "Are you one of her students? You must have liked her a lot." She dabbed away his tears with her handkerchief.

"I liked her more than you can imagine," Lucas replied, having a hard time not starting to cry. "But I am not her student. I am... well... was... her boyfriend."

"You are Lucas?" Her sister had stepped up to him and taken him into her arms. "She spoke a lot about you these last months. She was lucky to have you."

"She died in my living room." Lucas finally couldn't hold it anymore and started crying. "I am not sure if lucky is the word to describe that."

"That was a tragedy indeed, but not your fault." Her mother now took him into her arms.

"Please, Lucas, stand with us," her father said and made a step to open a spot between himself and her sister. "You are family too."

"Thank you." Lucas nodded and took the place.

A lot more people had joined the line, all conveying their condolences to the four of them now. Lucas had to fight his tears almost the entire time, but he tried his best to stay focused and strong. When they finally were through, he walked over to the coffin to take a final look at her. She lay there, dressed in a nice white blouse, with a smile on her face, looking as beautiful as she always had. When he saw her he burst out in tears again.

"I will get the bastard who did this to you, I promise," he said.

"I am sure you will," he heard a voice saying from the side.

When he turned around, he had a hard time recognizing anything through his tear-filled eyes. Someone was sitting on her gravestone, a few meters away, but his vision was blurred too much. He walked over to get a better look, but as much as the surroundings became clearer, the person didn't. It was just a shadow, sitting on the stone, smiling at him.

"You are back," he said when he finally recognized her translucent image. "Why?"

"Because you brought me back, just like you did in your house," she said.

"Will you stay with me?" he asked.

"Is that what you would want?" she replied.

"I want you back," he said. "But I don't know how. Help me, please."

"My body is not coming back, Guardian," she said. "You are a Magus Superior now, you surely have realized that too."

"I don't want you to leave," he said, tears running down his cheeks again.

"I will stay here as long as you fuel my presence." She smiled.

He was just about to answer when he heard someone approach from behind. The ceremony had begun. They had closed the coffin and were carrying it over now to the grave. Sandra's sister was first in line, taking her place next to him.

"Thank you for being here today, Lucas," she said, taking his hand. "It means a lot to my parents."

"There is nowhere else I would rather be, Rebecca," Lucas replied. "I am just sorry that we didn't have the chance to meet under better circumstances."

They stayed there, holding hands, until the ceremony was over. He was still in a lot of pain, but having her next to him made it feel a little easier than it had before. When people finally started flocking toward the nearby restaurant for the traditional burial meal, Sandra's parent's approached them.

"We have reserved a place for you at the head of the table. Will you join us there?" her father asked.

"I will for sure, thank you, Mr. Granger." Lucas nodded. "Just give me a few more minutes. I would like to be alone for a while."

The Grangers nodded and walked away, leaving him standing there all by himself, next to the open grave. He just stood there for a while, looking back and forth between the coffin down below and her translucent image sitting on the stone. He was just smiling at her when someone approached him from behind.

"Greetings, Guardian," a familiar-sounding voice said.

When Lucas turned around he saw a man wearing green robes walk up to him. He was not wearing the hood, so he recognized him instantly.

"Greetings, Ghosthunter," Lucas said and wiped tears from his eyes. "What brings you here?"

"Isn't that obvious?" he said and gave Lucas a hug. "My condolences, old friend."

"Thank you," Lucas replied. "So you see her too?"

"I don't see ghosts, no." Ghosthunter shook his head. "But I do feel their presence. And quite frankly, with you here, it does not come as a surprise."

"Why is that?"

"Spirits don't want to stay here with us, so if they do, they either have very important unfinished business to take care of, or there is someone, or some ones for that matter, with a lot of energy anchoring it."

"Are you saying that I am keeping her here against her will?" Lucas was stunned.

"That might indeed be the case, yes." He nodded. "And while I do understand your grief, especially given the circumstances, I would encourage you to make your peace with her and let her move on."

"What do you know about the circumstances?" Lucas had turned toward Sandra's ghost.

"Robbery gone wrong, I heard... It was all over the news after all," Ghosthunter said and turned too.

"That's not exactly the truth, unfortunately," Lucas sighed and told him the high-level version of the story of the hut and the real encounter in his living room.

"Even worse, especially if she was killed by magic," Ghosthunter sighed. "But nonetheless, you have to let go. It's not healthy for either of you."

"Maybe I will be able to, once I have brought this Archeveque character to justice." Lucas started crying again. "She meant the world to me, G... I can't just let her die and move on like this."

"In your heart she will live forever, Guardian." He put his hand on his shoulder. "But let it be the real her, all the good memories and feelings you have, and not a residual energy pattern that feeds off your strength."

"I will try..." Lucas said, doing his best to stop crying.

"If you need my help, give me a call." He handed him a business card. "But I have every confidence that you will be able to deal with this on your own."

He turned around and walked away, leaving Lucas standing there alone again, looking at the silent smile of Sandra's ghost. After a minute or so he finally started crying again and sank down to his knees, hiding his face in his hands. All the pain unloaded at once, making his body shake violently in the process. He continued crying for almost half an hour, until he was too exhausted to produce any more tears. Then he finally stood up and looked at the ghost again.

"I guess this is goodbye then," he said and tried to smile.

"It is never goodbye, sweetheart; it is always just safe travels," she said.

"You are right, of course." He wiped his eyes. "Godspeed then, my love, until we meet again."

"Godspeed, Guardian. I will watch over you from the other side." She bowed a little before jumping up from the stone and drifting off into the skies.

"I will always love you," he said, looking down into the grave, before he finally turned around and walked toward the restaurant.

Next Monday, Lucas was just finishing up his lunch break at school when his phone rang. He looked around to make sure that he was undisturbed before picking up the call.

"Good afternoon, Inspector," he said.

"Good afternoon, Mr. Trent," Corben replied. "I am sorry that I didn't call before, but I didn't want to bother you on the weekend."

"Bother me about what?" Lucas was curious.

"Your tip paid off, in both areas," the Inspector said. "That weird house you sent us to... Forensics found enough evidence to confirm your videos. We still haven't found a trace of the body, but we were able to arrest the two cleaners."

"Nice." Lucas smiled.

"And more importantly... There was a demonstration at the power plant on Saturday, just as your videos predicted. Local armed police were able to intervene before any harm was done, securing not one but three RPGs and as many people who apparently wanted to use them, including your smoking friend, Mr. Guthridge. The case is with the district attorney now, but I think it's safe to predict that they will get him for both attempted terrorism and first degree murder."

"I am really relieved to hear that, Inspector," Lucas said. "That's really great news."

"And we have you to thank for it," Corben replied. "Let's just hope that it is over now."

"It is not over yet, I can guarantee you that," Lucas said. "The guy who killed my girlfriend is still out there, and he will definitely not take another setback lightly."

"We will get him too, don't worry," the Inspector replied. "I will make sure of that."

"I appreciate that, Inspector, I really do." Lucas sighed. "But I am not quite certain that he will be so easy to get."

"Nobody said anything about easy..." Corben laughed. "But we will still get it done."

"Let's hope so. This dude has me majorly worried," Lucas said.

"Let me know if you find any trace of him. We will be ready when you do."

"Thank you, Inspector, I will for sure. I wish you a good afternoon," Lucas said.

"Same to you," Corben replied and hung up.

Lucas quickly grew uncertain about his feelings after that call. It was definitely a great achievement having caught Guthridge and foiled the plan to blow up the power plant. But Lucas was still all too aware of the consequences such interference had had in the past, making him wonder how Archeveque would react this time. There was, of course, the slim chance that with the arrest of Mr. Guthridge and the death of Marcel Jackson, and with that the loss of direct control over the companies they had owned, his nemesis would have finally suffered a crippling blow and would return into hiding again, but somehow Lucas doubted that. Too much had happened, the still-elusive goal that the bad guys had seemed too close and the impact that one move could have made on a game that was played on global scale seemed too little.

When Lucas told the others about Corben's success they were all cheerful. They did share his concerns, but for them the momentary triumph was by far stronger.

"Something big is still cooking here, and I just don't get it," Lucas said.

"We need to rethink this," Darien said. "We always assumed that hitting on fossil fuel technologies with those studies was futile because it would only play into the hands of nuclear power. Their plan to blow up Sizewell B might very well mean that our primary assumption was right after all."

"I still don't get it, Professor. What are you aiming at?" Jasmin asked.

"I am not sure yet either. But it is apparent that Archeveque was targeting the entire mainstream energy sector from the get-go," Darien replied. "If Sizewell had been a success, there for sure would have been major pushes against nuclear energy now too, just like after every nuclear disaster."

"But how would that help them?" Jasmin still seemed unconvinced.

"Let's assume for a moment that the Professor is right," Lucas jumped in. "What would the effect have been if the RPG attack had succeeded?"

"Stricter laws for the plant operators, higher taxes most likely, and another push towards alternative energy," Stephanie said.

"More funding for alternative energy would mean a paycheck for the Harlington guys," Marcus said.

"But only for a short while," Lucas replied. "Unless they can get the plant running, which seems to unrealistic, at least long term."

"Maybe they can get it running long enough to find investors and then just bail out with a huge profit," Darien suggested.

"We have been over this scenario time and again." Lucas sighed. "I doubt that there is enough money in that to justify all the effort."

"What if the crystal power plant is not the endgame, but just another step toward it?" Cedric threw in.

"What do you mean?" Darien looked at him.

"What if Whineberg is just supposed to create another ripple effect?" Cedric said.

"I don't follow..." Jasmin looked at him too.

"You have a valid idea here, Whirlwind." Lucas said. "Let's assume for a moment Sizewell had blown up and all the predictions we have made actually had happened."

"OK..." Darien said and watched Lucas curiously.

"Let's further assume Archeveque has the means to get the crystal plant up and running for a day or two, just to demonstrate it publicly and have it put under enough scrutiny that experts will actually believe him. What effect would that have on the situation?"

"It would attract investors, for sure," Marcus said.

"And it would lead to business for Whineberg Alternative Power. There would be many countries that would like to get a plant like this," Stephanie suggested.

"But if it only holds for a few days, that profit would be short-lived, and everyone involved would get sued right after the plant stops," Jasmin sighed.

"We are looking at this the wrong way," Darien said, with a suddenly changed facial expression. "And I believe I finally understood what you were aiming at, Whirlwind."

"Then spit it out, Professor. You look excited about it, after all" Marcus said.

"There is one more effect that this presentation would have," Darien started. "It would put additional pressure on the conventional power industry."

"Why's that?" Jasmin asked.

"Because so far they always survive because of the fact that there is no alternative." Lucas nodded. "If they have a bad reputation because of the environment, and an alternative is available, they are doomed."

"But only until people figure out that there is no alternative after all," Jasmin reminded them. "And that will be the same short period that they would have to gain profit from the plant in the first place."

"What if this is not about selling?" Darien asked.

"What else would it be about? You make money by selling things, right?" Marcus asked.

"Remember that I told you a while ago that there were investors in the background who held back large amounts of money?" Darien asked.

"Vaguely." Jasmin nodded.

"What if it is about buying?" he continued.

"That would actually make a lot of sense." Lucas nodded thoughtfully. "And it would fit their method of operation."

"Buy what?" Stephanie asked. "I still don't get what you are aiming at."

"Guthridge and Jackson have in the past already taken over companies by pushing them into a bad position. We have witnessed this form of hostile takeover with Harlington Research," Lucas said. "What if they are trying to do the same thing with conventional power plants?"

"Drive an entire industry to the brink of bankruptcy, just to buy it?" Jasmin asked. "Isn't that a huge risk to take?"

"Not if you know that the reason the sector is approaching bankruptcy will go away in a very short time," Darien replied. "Once the crystal power fails, prices for conventional energy will rebound pretty quickly. After that, all you need to do is publish more environmental studies that contradict the impact that these forms of energy have, and BAM... You bought yourself the planet's power supply for pence on the pound."

"That's quite a conspiracy theory..." Marcus whistled.

"Yes, one that is worth trillions of pounds if it's executed correctly," Darien nodded.

"Wouldn't the Monopolies and Mergers Commission jump in when someone tries to buy that much stock in one big chunk? Or the stock market authority?" Stephanie asked.

"We are talking global scale here. Not all markets have such mechanisms in place," Darien answered.

"And don't forget that we are not talking about one person doing the buying. There will be multiple, seemingly unrelated, investors. I doubt that the authorities will be able to see the common denominator behind those people," Lucas added.

"Assuming you are right, what do we do about this?" Jasmin asked.

"Right now, we don't need to do anything. By foiling the Sizewell plan we bought ourselves a lot of time. Without killing the reputation of the nuclear sector too, the plan doesn't work. And after Saturday nuclear plants everywhere will be under heavier guard, so they will have a hard time trying that again," Lucas said.

"But time is all we bought," Marcus said. "Archeveque is in no hurry, after all."

"He might very well be," Darien suggested. "With Jackson dead, Delmonte dead and Guthridge in prison, he will most likely lose his grip over HRC and the other companies shortly. By the time he gets that back the storm will have calmed again already, people will have forgotten about all the studies and problems and he will have to start all over again. And with Eagle still in prison, he would have to do that without his environmental harming potion."

"So you are saying we have won?" Marcus asked.

"If he plans to finish what he started he needs to do it soon," Lucas said. "So either he will, or we might very well have won after all."

"What do we do now?" Stephanie asked.

"We wait... And stay alert, in case something should happen," Lucas said. "There is nothing more we can do, unfortunately."

A few days later Lucas was on his way to the Duke of Summerset for the Magus Major meeting. It had been quiet so far, but he was still under the impression that it was the calm before the storm, rather than Archeveque having given up on his plan. Sunshine once again greeted him at the front entrance, striking his name on the list after identifying him through the nacre surfaces. The group was pretty similar to last time, some new faces, some people missing, but many of the same that he already knew. Merlin was here again, so was Ranger, and both Gaia and Thor. JJ was still nowhere to be seen, but this time Lucas was early, so there was still plenty of time left. He sat down at an empty table and ordered something to drink. He was just about to pick up a newspaper when Thor approached him.

"Would you mind if I join you?" he asked.

"I never mind friendly company, Thor. By all means," Lucas smiled.

"How are you holding up?" Thor asked after sitting down.

"I am doing OK, thank you. I still miss her a lot, but the funeral helped to bring some closure at least," he replied.

"I know it's hard to accept, but others will come that you hold as dear as you did her," Thor said with a faint smile on his face.

"I know that, Thor, I'm not a child anymore." Lucas sighed. "But it will not make the pain go away any faster."

"For sure not." Thor nodded.

"There is something I wanted to ask you, by the way," Lucas said.

"By all means, please." He smiled.

"You said something about teleportation last time, and apparently you've mastered that pretty well yourself. Is this a common skill amongst high level mages?"

"Depends on the definition of common..." Thor said. "I tagged along for the ride a few times before I came up with my own version. Some have it naturally, even in lower levels, and some don't do it at all. I know, for example, that Lord Ashur thinks yielding that power is cheating on the gods, so he doesn't."

"Your own version? What do you mean by that? And who is Lord Ashur?" Lucas asked.

"Lord Ashur is a member of the Council. He is a Frenchman as far as I know, very weird guy, and very strong on principles. Regarding the teleportation, well, except for those of us who have it in their standard repertoire, we try to make them fit into the repertoire." He grinned. "Lady Gaia opens a staircase into the earth and emerges at her destination that way. The Beast engulfs himself in a windstorm that carries him where he needs to go. I chose to use a lightning portal as my means of transportation."

"So you are saying that I can master this too? Maybe with some sort of shield cocoon? Like a planetary-bound warp bubble?" Lucas asked.

"I doubt that there is anything that you can't master, Guardian," Thor laughed. "And yes, the idea sounds solid, actually. I would test it in the open, though. I have heard stories of people who teleported into a wall."

"Thank you for that advice." Lucas bowed a little. "I will try that."

A moment of silence followed before Lucas had another topic pop into his mind.

"One more thing..." he started. "Have you ever heard of split personalities in mages?"

"Split like what? Like schizophrenia?"

"Not as pathologic as that, but in that direction, yes." Lucas nodded. "We have a healer in our circle; her name is Airmid--a cute, very shy young girl. But in some situations she just seems to flip a switch and presents herself as a very focused, almost coldly professional person."

"Well, that kind of split is easy to explain, and you should be able to do that yourself, actually," Thor said.

"Humor me, please, because I really don't get it."

"Mind, Heart and Soul..." Thor started. "You united them; she hasn't."

"So you are saying that she is normally working with the power of her heart, and in those situations she is jumping into her mind?" Lucas was stunned at the obvious explanation.

"Yes. Just like you started off working with your mind, before you opened your heart." He nodded. "For a healer it is pretty common to leverage the heart first. It's a pity, though, to hear that kind of split."

"Why's that?"

"Because if you do that jump multiple times without realizing the connection, and making peace between your power sources, you most likely never will," Thor said.

"Are you saying that she is stuck being a Magus Minor forever?" Lucas was unhappy with the statement.

"Not necessarily, but most likely." He nodded. "There still is the chance that she will work her way through her soul and find partial unity that way, and of course, there is also the chance that she will learn to channel both sources separately at will at some point, which both would pull her up to Magus Major level, but she has a handicap there."

"I don't like that at all..." Lucas sighed. "She has so much potential."

"They all do..." Thor said with a faint smile. "And still only very few ever make the leap. You know that by now."

"Unfortunately, I do." He nodded and was just about to sink into his thoughts when he heard a voice speak up in the center of the room.

"Brothers, Sisters, welcome to our meeting." Sunshine's announcement made them turn around. "JJ has called upon the group, but before

I hand it over to him, I would ask all of you to pay your respects with a minute of silence. Six mages died unnatural deaths a little over a week ago, and one of them, Kung Fu, was very close to two of our friends present here today."

A minute of silence followed, everyone looking at the floor, before she finally continued.

"Thank you for that. And now the stage is yours, JJ," she said and sat down.

"Brothers, Sisters, thank you for answering my call." JJ had walked into the center of the room. "Last time I called you because I assumed a threat lurking in our backyard. Today I am standing here because that threat seems to be bigger than we all expected."

"Your eco-idiots again?" Merlin didn't seem too impressed.

"Two weeks ago, Kung Fu's mentees found and raided the lair of those guys," JJ continued. "The adepts were accompanied by a full circle of mages, including at least one Magus Major. If it hadn't been for Guardian and his friends, they, as well as me and my circle, would most likely not have survived that encounter." He bowed toward Lucas. "A week later someone broke into the homes of those kids and murdered them in cold blood, including Kung Fu."

"That's what happens if you get involved in such fights," Merlin said and shrugged his shoulders. "It gets messy."

"Do you know what they were after, JJ?" Ranger asked.

"No, unfortunately we don't." JJ shook his head.

"I might be able to add some information to this point." Lucas stood up and walked toward JJ. "We believe that there is a larger plan behind all this. Just last Saturday we tipped the police off to a planned attack against a nuclear power plant, committed by people we think are connected to the group. Luckily, police foiled the attack before they could go through with it, but that was only the latest coup they had attempted."

"If the attack was stopped, what are we doing here then?" Merlin asked.

"The mage behind this killed six of our friends and four of his own and he is still at large," Lucas replied. "Do you really want to let it stand like this?"

"If he killed four of his own he most likely is a total idiot and not exactly a major threat. He will need a while to rebound, no need to do anything." Merlin leaned back.

"I see no reason, either, to get into this fight, guys. Sorry." Ranger shook his head.

"I am a healer, not a fighter," Sunshine said. "I will offer my help in your endeavor, but only to pick up the pieces. I will not harm someone deliberately."

The other mages in the room also mostly declined to help, which hardly came as a surprise to Lucas. Most were under the impression that the threat was over anyway; others just seemed not to care in the first place. What struck Lucas' curiosity, though, was that neither Gaia nor Thor had participated in the discussion. While he had not expected either of them to offer their services, he had expected that they would have voiced their opinions, just as they had done last time. He decided to wait for the discussion to end before approaching them and asking them in private. It took almost half an hour before JJ finally gave up and sat down, looking exhausted and frustrated. Lucas approached his table but didn't sit down.

"This group is utterly useless." JJ almost had tears in his eyes. "Kung Fu was a good friend, and even that doesn't mean anything to them."

"It means everything to you and me, JJ." Lucas patted his shoulder. "And we will figure this out without them. I promise you that. You are, after all, not the only one who held her very close to his heart."

"I know, Guardian, I know." JJ nodded. "I admire your strength in this matter."

"Believe me, I spilled my fair share of tears over this, but right now I want to get this bastard before he hurts somebody else. That is the only thing that keeps me focused," he said.

"That thought is also the only thing keeping me sane." JJ nodded. "I doubt, though, that we will be of much help in the near future. The people who had the connections are dead and my own circle is a member short."

"We are in this together, old friend. We will make it through." Lucas patted his shoulder again.

"I am grateful for that, Guardian." JJ bowed a little. "Here is my business card, by the way, with my phone number on it. Let me know when something comes up."

"Will do." Lucas nodded.

"Thank you," JJ smiled.

"Anytime. And now excuse me, please. I need to talk to Lady Gaia."

Lucas walked over to the corner table and bowed slightly.

"Good evening, Guardian." Gaia looked up at him. "What can I do for you?"

"Good evening, Lady Gaia," he replied. "May I join you for a moment?"

"Sure." She nodded and made an inviting gesture toward a chair.

"Thank you," Lucas said and sat down. "I was wondering what your thoughts on the issue at hand are. After all, you were very quiet during the discussion."

"I don't have many thoughts at the moment," she replied. "Archeveque is a major problem, and not just in this case, but right now it seems that you have gotten the situation under control pretty well."

"What do you mean, not just in this case?" Lucas was curious.

"We have been tracking him for a long time now, pretty much ever since he turned his back on the Council." Gaia sighed. "But for the most part he stayed in hiding, and when he did come out once every other year or so, he left a trail of carnage before vanishing again. So chances are that he will just stop once more."

"Why didn't you stop him when he last appeared?"

"It was not for lack of trying." Gaia laughed in agony. "You have fought against him; you know how powerful he is."

"But isn't that what the Council is here for? Being able to oppose even such powerful adversaries? Why didn't the Council intervene?" Lucas was almost a bit angry now.

"What more intervention did you expect from the Council?" Gaia looked upset now too.

"What do you mean?"

"All Magus Superiors can stand their ground in a fight, but only very few are actually training battle magic as their primary skill set. And the one member of the council that fits that direction actually fought alongside you, if memory serves," she said.

"Hold on... Laurin is a Lord of the Council?" Lucas was surprised.

"Yes." Gaia nodded.

"Are you saying that he is the strongest mage we have on our side?" Lucas had to gasp for air. "He didn't look very on par with Archeveque that day."

"Laurin is not the strongest mage on our side, no, but he is close. And he for sure is the strongest when it comes to battle magic. If he was as outclassed by Archeveque as you say, then there are very few who might stand a better chance," Gaia said.

"Like who?" Lucas asked.

"Well, apparently you, for starters." Gaia laughed. "And there might be one or two more that come to mind that you haven't met so far."

"Me? I highly doubt that I am stronger than someone on the Council." Lucas shook his head.

"Evidence is contrary." Gaia shrugged her shoulders.

"Doesn't that defeat the very definition of the Council?"

"I think I already answered that last time, my young friend. The strongest ones are not always the ones that we have there. And besides, strength is rarely measured on the battlefield these days," she said.

"So what do we do now about the situation?" Lucas was still unhappy.

"Right now the ball is in Archeveque's corner. He has to make the next move," Gaia answered. "Once he does, we will try to react accordingly. I will convey the issue to the Council, you can be sure of that, but I doubt that they will have any other plans. The best we can hope for there is the support of one or two more members."

"Not very encouraging..." Lucas sighed. "But still highly appreciated, of course."

"You are close to the top now, Guardian; the air is thin up here. You better start getting used to that," she replied.

"There are too many things these days that I need to get used to, milady. This will most likely take a while." He sighed and stood up. "Thank you for your time and your insight. Godspeed, until we meet again."

"Godspeed Guardian; may you find peace on your journey." Gaia bowed a little.

CHAPTER 18

PLANT

It was Friday morning. Lucas was sitting in class when a text arrived on his phone. He was eager to read it but decided to wait until the break. When he finally had a chance he went out on the corridor and pulled the phone out. The text was from Darien, asking him for a call-back. There was little information in the text itself, but somehow he was under the impression that there was some urgency involved, so he decided to follow the request right away.

"Hey, Professor. What's up?" he asked as Darien answered.

"Things are moving again in the crystal power plant topic," Darien stated. "And they are moving unusually fast."

"Slow down please..." Lucas said. "What is going on?"

"WAP has called for a press conference on Tuesday at the power plant location outside Harlington. A bunch of experts from universities world-wide will be flying in on the weekend and inspecting the plant on Monday. Whineberg plans to announce the full production readiness of the system at the press conference then, supported by the testimony of said experts."

"WAP?" Lucas was confused for a second.

"Whineberg Alternative Powers," Darien said. "Sorry, we use the acronym internally by now."

"OK, and they are moving on Monday? So the plant is ready now?"

"Apparently not yet. The internal memo said that all personnel have to clear the facility by Saturday noon, because an external expert is coming in on Sunday to install the last necessary component, which apparently is still top secret."

"An external expert? Do you have any idea who?" Lucas asked

"No," Darien replied. "But the order came from Jackson directly, with signoff from Guthridge, saying that nobody is to disturb that person."

"Jackson is dead, Guthridge in prison," Lucas recapped. "Do you think this is Archeveque himself?"

"With Eagle still in prison and Delmonte dead, I would think so, yes. But it could be one if his minions again," Darien replied. "But the order has to come from him; who else would have access to the company like that?"

"Yeah, it sounds like he had a fallback plan, in case Guthridge and Jackson were indisposed." Lucas nodded.

"If they move now it means, though, that our assumptions were wrong" Darien said. "After all, the nuclear thing has blown up in Archeveque's face, so even full success of the plant will not have a major impact on that area now."

"No, but it will still send the fossil fuel industry into a downward spiral. Maybe he has opted to cut his losses and aim only at them?" Lucas suggested.

"So what do we do?"

"I would say we all meet tomorrow and discuss it. From where I stand, we should make sure that the plant does not run on Monday. Unless, of course, they really have figured it out with the crystals and have a genuine energy solution in their hands."

"I agree. Where do we meet? Timestop?" Darien asked.

"I would go for the shack. And maybe we should invite JJ as well," Lucas suggested.

"Sounds good," Darien replied. "Two o' clock? I'll call the girls? You call the boys?"

"Perfect. I'll call the boys and JJ. See you tomorrow." Lucas nodded and hung up.

During the next break Lucas called Cedric and Marcus, as well as texting JJ that he needed to talk to him. He didn't want to call him directly, not knowing where he would be at that time of day. When he walked out of school shortly after noon he saw him standing there, next to a tree, waiting for him. He quickly filled him in regarding the general topic and tomorrow's meeting, asking him to join it with his circle. JJ seemed eager to participate, so the discussion stayed quite short. When he arrived home, Lucas decided to bring one more party in on the topic.

"Good evening Mr. Trent," Inspector Corben greeted him when he called.

"Hello Inspector," Lucas replied. "I will get right to the point, if you don't mind."

"By all means," Corben laughed.

"We believe that the culprit who murdered my girlfriend, and nine others, and who was most likely also the mastermind behind the Sizewell coup, will be at the Whineberg Alternative Power facility in Harlington on Sunday."

"That's great news. We will be there with a welcoming committee then." The Inspector seemed excited.

"It would be better if you stayed in the background until we call you," Lucas disagreed. "We are not sure yet about his presence, and we also assume that he will be extremely dangerous. So I'd rather face him together with my friends first and hand him over to you afterwards, just like we did with Preston and his gang last year."

"I am not happy to let you go in there first. After all, we are the ones who get paid to put our lives on the line, but I trust that you have good reasons, so I will do as you ask," Corben said. "But we will be close by and ready, just in case."

"Thank you, Inspector," Lucas said. "See you on Sunday."

"Good luck, Mr. Trent. Stay safe," Corben said and hung up.

Saturday afternoon Lucas arrived at the shack right on time. There were several cars parked outside and several bikes next to it, suggesting that pretty much everyone was already here. Walking by the window he saw Angel, Hopper, JJ and Dread, as well as Marcus, Cedric and Darien. Stephanie's horse was also present, so she was apparently also here already, which meant that only Jasmin was still missing. He walked in and greeted the others with a smile.

"Last time we met at your request; this time it's us again who call for assistance," he said into the round.

"This fight is personal for all of us," Dread replied. "We are glad you brought us in on it."

"We are just waiting for Psycho, then we can start," Lucas said and looked out the window. "And here she comes already." He grinned as he saw her car approaching. He continued to watch until she had shut down the engine, before turning around to the others.

"I believe we might have a shortage of chairs today," he said, looking around.

"That will be the least of our problems," JJ laughed.

They squeezed as many people on the bench as could possibly fit, leaving the three chairs they had for the girls. Lucas and JJ remained standing. Darien started pulling out charts printouts and a map, laying them out on the table so everyone could see the important parts. Five minutes passed by, with them looking silently at what Darien brought up, before Lucas got uneasy.

"What's happening with Psycho?" he said and walked back over to the door. When he opened it, she was just halfway through the yard, walking in hastily.

"Are you all right?" Lucas asked, but the expression on her face clearly indicated otherwise. When she came closer he could see that she was pale as a ghost.

"What's wrong?" he asked as he let her pass by him into the shack, closing the door behind her.

"You were right; that's what's wrong," she said in a shaky voice.

"Slow down, sit down and then tell us what's happened." Lucas led her to the empty chair.

"Professor, do you have your laptop with that fancy mobile-internet-thingy with you by any chance?" She addressed Darien.

"The hotspot." Darien nodded. "Sure I have." He pulled the devices out of his backpack and powered them up. "What do you need?"

"Open a news site," she said.

"Which one?" Darien started clicking around.

"Any one. CNN, BBC--pick one."

"What's going on, Psycho?" Lucas was still concerned, given her uneasy voice.

"Jesus." Darien had turned pale now too and turned around the laptop for Lucas and the others to read.

They didn't have to search too long. The very first headline sprang immediately to Lucas' eyes: "Flood wave hitting mainland Japan. Nuclear power plant leaking radiation. Tokyo within the danger zone," the article read.

"No way..." Lucas took two steps back and sat down on the floor. "How the hell did they do that?"

"I get that a nuclear accident is bad," Angel said, reading through the details of the article. "But what has that to do with us?"

Lucas quickly summarized the events of the last weeks to the larger group, including their thoughts from last Monday, without standing up from the floor. After he had finished, silence prevailed in the room for several minutes.

"You are aware what this means?" Darien finally broke it.

"It means that you were right." Jasmin nodded.

"It actually means more than that," Darien said.

"And what's that, Professor?" Marcus asked.

"It means that tomorrow is our last chance to stop this. All pieces are in play; if the demonstration on Monday and the press conference on Tuesday go all right then Archeveque has won."

"You are right, Professor." Lucas nodded, slowly standing up now. "We better not screw this up."

"If they can pull a flood wave off, how do we know that they don't have another energy source available as a backup? So far no matter what plan we torpedoed, they always had another one up their sleeves," Stephanie threw in.

"You are right, unfortunately." Lucas nodded again. "We have to stop Archeveque for good. That seems to be our best chance to break this apart once and for all."

"Then let's hope he is actually there," JJ said.

"If he is not there at the beginning, he will definitely show up once we start interfering. There is no way in hell he is leaving this to his minions again. Not after all the screw-ups he has had to deal with already," Lucas said.

"Then let's screw him up once again, shall we?" Dread bashed his fist on the table. "What's the plan?"

"Professor?" Lucas was looking at Darien.

"I don't know exactly when this 'installation of the secret part' will take place, so I would suggest we take positions outside the plant in the morning and wait. Once the bad guys arrive we can act," he said.

"We will assess the situation as well as we can before we enter," Lucas said. "I don't want any major injuries, so anyone who starts getting weak or has anything exceeding a superficial wound gets out immediately--are we clear on that?"

He waited for the others to nod before continuing.

"Airmid, Professor, Psycho, you have to deal with the carnage again. I hope it will be less than last time."

"We will be ready," Stephanie said.

"I also informed my friend at the police about our plan. They will stay in the background until we call," Lucas said. "Professor, I will leave the Inspector's phone number with you, in case something goes wrong."

Darien nodded again.

They continued discussing the details of the plan, including studying the plans of the building Darien had brought. The location was larger than their previous battlegrounds, making it highly likely that they would have to split up for the fight, which made Lucas very unhappy. It also had multiple emergency exits, making it hard to contain the fight within, but on the other hand this gave them an easy way out pretty much everywhere in the building. The upside was that the building was located quite a bit outside the city, making it unlikely that other people would be close by. One problem that also presented itself due to that, though, was how they would get to the location. Harlington itself was easy to reach, but the plant was outside the city with no public transportation to speak of. Dread and Angel jumped in for the rescue and offered to pick them up from Luton.

"Is there anything else?" Lucas asked about two hours later, when they had finally all leaned back from the plans.

The others shook their heads silently.

"We have never done this with outsiders present, but I think the situation is fitting to bend that rule--what do you say?" Lucas looked at his circle, seeing them all smile and nod. He then stretched his fist to the middle of the table, waiting for the others to follow his example, including JJ's circle.

"Brother to brother, yours to the end," they then said in unison.

When Dread picked Lucas up downtown Luton the next morning, the tension was already in the air. They were all eager to get this done and apparently none of them had gotten any meaningful sleep last night. The drive was quiet, Lucas trying to meditate, Stephanie looking through her backpack time and again to ensure she had everything available, Cedric just looking out the window with his cool, emotionless face and Dread fully focused on the road, even though traffic was light. When they finally arrived at the meeting point, about a kilometer away from the plant, the others were already there, wearing their robes, with the hoods pulled into their faces. Darien was just unloading a pile of blankets from Angel's car, bringing them to an area they had chosen as their point of retreat.

"Good thought," Lucas said when he approached him for their greeting.

"Yeah, it's pretty cold today." Darien nodded. "I hope we don't have to stay outside for all too long."

"Yeah, I don't want anyone to get killed by Archeveque, but I also don't like the thought of someone freezing to death out here." Lucas nodded.

"That won't happen," Darien grinned. "Cougar brought a butane-powered heater and enough gas cartridges to last the day."

"It always pays off to have a Boy Scout around," Lucas laughed.

When they finally had unloaded everything and prepared a makeshift shelter in an old barn ,Lucas looked over to the power plant.

"Now, how do we spot our friends?" JJ had approached him.

"That will actually be a problem." Darien had come too. "Whatever they built this building out of, I can't make out too much on the inside. Maybe I will see when they fire up the crystal, after all it is pretty potent, but I cannot tell if a person is inside."

"Let me try something..." Lucas focused on the building. "Deprehendere," he whispered slowly.

"There is nobody in there yet," he said after about a minute. "I will keep the grid up; let's see how much power it takes over time."

"Have you developed my eyes now too?" Darien asked.

"To a certain extent." Lucas nodded. "But more importantly, some sporting activity I had with Kung Fu a while back forced me to develop a magical radar."

"Nice one." Darien grinned. "At some point you will not need me anymore."

They waited until way past noon before Lucas finally felt a presence at the plant.

"Five people just entered, and they brought some equipment with them," he said to the others.

"Mages? Or workers?" Hopper asked.

"Mages. For sure," Lucas replied.

"Then what are we waiting for?" Dread had stepped up to them too.

"All right." Lucas nodded. "Everyone stay safe."

They made their way down from the barn, approaching the perimeter of the plant.

"What about the security systems?" Angel asked.

"According to the Professor they should be disabled. The mages don't want prying eyes in there when they work," Lucas said.

The gate was unlocked, so they continued in toward the side entrance. A keycard-based lock was installed on the door there.

"Seems we have to kick in the door." Marcus grinned.

"Or not." Angel pushed him aside and tapped the lock twice with a long stick she had been walking with all time. "Disserus," she hissed and suddenly, with a barely audible hum, the door opened.

"Nice one," Marcus complimented.

"Two of them are upstairs in an office area, most likely the control room," Lucas said. "The other three are in the main hall right now."

"How do you want to play this?" JJ looked at Lucas.

"You take your group and go upstairs," Lucas replied. "We will take the guys down here."

"Is that wise? You are three, we are four. Shouldn't we take on the larger group?" Dread asked.

"I think it would be better if you deal with the smaller group quickly and come back down to assist afterwards," Lucas said.

"As you wish." JJ nodded and walked on, Dread, Angel and Hopper following him.

"Are you ready for this?" Lucas then addressed Marcus and Cedric.

"Always." Cedric grinned.

"Hell yeah." Marcus nodded.

"Then let's go." Lucas led the way through the corridor.

Before they had even entered the main hall they could hear cries from upstairs and things shattering all around.

"Seems our friends are having fun already." Marcus grinned, when all of a sudden a man in a black robe came running around a corner about 30 meters down the corridor. When he saw Lucas and the others he stopped dead in his tracks.

"What are you doing here? Who are you?" he yelled.

"You mind?" Cedric stepped past the others and smiled at the man.

"They call me Whirlwind." He bowed a little. "And here's why. VENTUS," he then shouted and sent the guy flying backwards until he hit the wall and fell to the ground, not moving anymore.

"That was easy..." Marcus said.

"Too easy..." Lucas was concerned. "I don't like this."

They moved on toward the main hall. When Lucas looked around the last corner he immediately had to duck for cover, as an arrow came flying his way, soaring just barely past his face into the opposite wall of the corridor. He quickly wove a variation of his Seperatio charm that he could push in front of himself like a shield before he entered the room. Four more arrows came flying in quick succession, as well as two shuriken, all impacting his shield and falling to the ground.

"Repellum," Lucas cast in an almost bored voice and sent the bowman flying back through the room, knocking a pile of crates over, making one shatter on impact, blue stones rolling out of it. He was just preparing to do the same with the other culprit when the man came charging toward them.

"My turn," Marcus said and walked by him.

"That's somewhat underwhelming," Cedric said and walked toward the bowman, who was just getting up on his feet again. But before he could reach him the guy turned around and ran toward an emergency exit.

"At least we know that we were on the right track." Lucas pointed at the stones on the floor. "They brought enough energy crystals to blow up the plant a hundred times over."

"Yeah. But they don't have any form of reactor. I mean, look around..." Marcus had joined them, his opponent lying unconscious on the ground.

Lucas took a quick look through the hall. Marcus was right. He could see water tanks and turbines, apparently built to harness the heat from the crystal, but in the center of it all was nothing but an empty space.

"There are still lots of crates standing around," Lucas said and pointed at a nearby wall. "Maybe that's what the contraption is in?"

They split up and started looking through the containers, but that proved barely exciting too. They contained pipes, rods, various forms of plates, metal boxes and other similar items, but nothing even remotely resembling technology. Lucas was just opening another one when he heard a cry from the side. Turning around immediately, he could just see Cedric being hurled through the air and straight into a wall, hitting first the concrete and then the ground with a loud thud. He tried to see where the attack was coming from, but whoever had hit Cedric was still hidden from view behind a large turbine. Marcus had also heard the cry and came running over, now standing next to Lucas.

"Are you all right?" Marcus asked Cedric, who barely moved.

"Sorry, he surprised me." He turned to his side, blood dripping from his face.

"Get out of here," Lucas commanded. "Cougar, assist him. I will take care of this until you return."

Marcus was about to reply, but when he saw the strict look on Lucas' face he just nodded and complied. Lucas in the meantime fired up another shield charm and walked toward the area where the attacker most likely would be. When he came closer to the side wall he could see four people in black robes standing there. A large wooden box was placed between them, suggesting that they had just carried it in.

"And who would you be?" one of them asked with a Scottish accent.

"They call me Guardian. And who are you?" Lucas replied coolly.

"I am Crusher," the man answered. "And you will now be crushed."

With that he pushed his clenched fists forward. Lucas could feel a large energy block hitting his shield, but even though the shield had not been built with a whole lot of energy, nothing penetrated. He decided to quickly strengthen his protection though, just to be on the safe side.

"Is that so?" Lucas asked. "Maybe I should crush you instead?"

The four guys started laughing despicably, although Lucas could hear a hint of uneasiness in their voices. He assumed that it was because of the failed attempt to hit him before.

"REPELLUM," he shouted and pushed a medium-sized energy bolt toward the Scotsman.

The opponent tumbled back a few steps, but was otherwise unharmed. Lucas started focusing. A spell with that magnitude of energy would have sent opponents like Cleric flying through the entire room. The negligible effect it had on this guy presumably meant that he was at least at a Magus Major level. He took two steps back, trying to get away from the wall toward a position where he could move more freely. He was just about to cast his next spell when four more people entered the room from behind him.

"You don't want to have all the fun for yourself now, do you?" he heard JJ say.

Peeking to the right he could see him, Dread, Hopper and Marcus line up to assist.

"We cleared the control room. Those guys will not move again anytime soon." JJ grinned. "Unfortunately, one of them hit Angel pretty badly, so she is out for now."

"I think we will make do." Lucas smiled without taking his eyes off the opponents.

And then suddenly all hell started breaking loose. The four black robes had stepped into the open and started throwing spells, flasks and other things at them. Lucas first focused on his initial opponent, but quickly came to the conclusion that at least a second one in the group had very advanced skills. He tossed spells left and right, still trying to conserve his energy as much as possible. JJ had also figured out the two more problematic opponents and started focusing on those now too. The fight raged back and forth for a while, with them gaining some ground, when one of the emergency exits in the side wall suddenly burst open and three more black robes walked in. Lucas spotted the problem first and extended his shield to cover that area too. He then decided to change his focus and starting shooting Ascius charms at the weaker opponents.

"We had that one under control," Marcus protested as one of them got hit frontally by Lucas and fell over, not moving anymore.

"We don't have time to fool around right now," Lucas said. "We need to take some of them out quickly."

The fight continued, Dread shooting spells back and forth with one opponent, Hopper and Marcus engaging in hand-to-hand combat now and JJ still trying to gain the upper hand against the second stronger mage from the first group. Lucas was mainly focusing on the Scotsman, but this time he pushed more energy through his spell.

"REPELLUM," he yelled and sent the mage straight into the wall.

"So much for that," he then said and took a quick look around. Dread and Hopper seemed to be losing ground fast so he again extended his shield, trying to give them the upper hand. Marcus was doing just fine against two opponents now, and JJ and the other Magus Major were also both still standing. Lucas was trying to decide which fight needed his attention the most when the decision was made for him. A lightning bolt from the stronger mage hit JJ, making him tumble back and fall down, shaking violently.

"Hopper, fall back," Lucas yelled. "Bring JJ out."

Hopper nodded and stumbled toward his friend, apparently also having been hit hard in the leg. They had just cleared the room when Dread cried out loudly and stumbled back too. Lucas quickly looked over, spotting a shuriken sticking out of his chest. He leaned against the wall and continued shooting spells at his attacker.

"Dread, get out," Lucas commanded.

Marcus had just finished off both his opponents and was now falling back to cover Dread's retreat. There were still three black mages standing and only Lucas and Marcus left on their side. Before they could do anything else, two more spells had hit Lucas' shields, one penetrating it and hitting him now, making him stumble back a few meters and cutting his robes open slightly, with some blood dripping from the wound.

"Damn it," he said and again pulled his energy together to reinforce the barrier. The hit had bluntly made him aware that he was not dealing with one more Magus Major here, but at least two. He knew that Marcus' magic was no match for them, and that their only chance to stand their ground here was for him to take one of them out quickly. He started channeling his united energy for a decisive blow, while Marcus was already heading out again to take care of one opponent.

"REPELLUM," Lucas yelled again and pointed at the guy that had hit JJ before. He could feel a lot of his energy being absorbed by the black mage's defenses, but it was not nearly enough. He was lifted up almost three meters and tossed back into the far wall of the plant before he came smashing down into the concrete floor.

"Now we are talking again." Lucas grinned and turned toward the other mage that was still standing freely. He blocked a fireball and a flying crate with his Seperatio and was just about to rebound when he heard a familiar, angry-sounding voice cry loudly from the far corner of the room.

"And here comes the big guy." Lucas was getting uneasy.

"Who dares to interfere with me again? Was my last message not clear enough?" Archeveque yelled and came stomping through the hall, flanked by four more black robes.

"Cougar, get back here," Lucas commanded and Marcus reacted almost instantly, pushing his opponent out of the path and then making his way to Lucas' side.

"You made the mistake of attacking me once already, Archeveque. But apparently you haven't gotten the message either," Lucas said

"It's you..." Archeveque laughed despicably. "So I finally have the chance to finish what I started two weeks ago."

"You couldn't finish me back then; you stand no greater chance today," Lucas replied aggressively.

"Look around you, fool. You are almost alone; we are seven over here. And each one of my friends is stronger than you are." Archeveque was again laughing.

"Somehow I doubt that," Lucas replied coolly. "But I guess we will find out."

"Get out, before I eat you for lunch," Archeveque commanded. "Or do you really like the two against seven odds, boy?"

"You have always been terrible at math, Archeveque," a voice suddenly said from the side. "You should be aware by now that this 'boy' is never alone."

"Who are you? Show yourself!" Archeveque was still yelling.

Lucas took a quick look to his side. At first he didn't see anything, but then he saw the sword hovering in mid-air, just a few meters to his side. And without any further warning, with a loud "puff" a man wearing a red robe had appeared.

"The king of the dwarves again. Now I can finish you both at once." Archeveque grinned and bowed. "Good afternoon, Lord Laurin."

"Nice to see you again, milord." Lucas bowed a little without taking his eyes off his opponents.

One of Archeveque's minions was just about to cast a spell when another voice appeared out of nowhere.

"Hey, don't start the fun without me," someone said, the voice apparently coming from the empty space between Lucas and Laurin.

The black mages started getting uneasy, apparently confused by the sudden appearance of people. When a lightning bolt hit the ground right next to Lucas and a man in light blue robes appeared out of thin air, the black mages all took a step back, except for Archeveque.

"The god of thunder and lightning." Archeveque sounded annoyed. "Is this a birthday party now, or what brings you to the grown-up table, Thor?"

"As Lord Laurin said before, this 'boy' is never alone," Thor grinned. "And I actually like our odds pretty well so far."

"We are wasting time here," Archeveque said. "Let's clean this up and get back to work. We are on a tight schedule."

Following that comment his six minions started throwing spells again. Laurin, Thor and Lucas had their hands full countering those at first, leaving Marcus as the only one who had some room to maneuver. He used that immediately to jump forward, taking one of Lucas' opponents on in a fist fight. When the first wave of attacks had cleared, the three Superiors started shooting back. Thor was first to hit an opponent head-on with a lightning bolt. Laurin did not cast but ran into battle with his sword in both hands, which left Lucas to see what he should do next. He decided to toss his now-only opponent back against the wall with another Repellum before taking another look around. Archeveque had just thrown a spell against Thor, who had tumbled back and was just casting another lightning strike against a minion. Laurin was blocking spells with his sword while trying to penetrate the defenses of both his opponents. Marcus was still fighting with another minion, but seemed to be having a hard time. Lucas tried for a moment to help his friend out, but the fight was so fast that he had a hard time doing anything meaningful. So he turned again and spotted Archeveque getting ready to cast against Laurin. He fired up his shield charm to protect him, but the black mage's spell was too powerful once again. It penetrated the shield, as well as Laurin's own defenses, and tossed him back a few steps. Thor now shot a lightning bolt against Archeveque, but it had no impact whatsoever. Lucas took a deep breath and started channeling all available energy into his body.

"REPELLUM," he then yelled and shot as much force as he could toward the black mastermind.

Archeveque's shield absorbed most of the blast; the small remainder just made him stumble one step back. Thor immediately seized the opportunity to fire another lightning bolt, but that one also only barely scratched the surface.

"You are worse than a wart on the nose." Archeveque was outraged, turning toward Lucas. "FULMINICTUS," he yelled, shooting a lightning bolt his way.

"SPECULUS," Lucas countered, again forcing as much power as possible into the spell.

The bolt hit the palm of his hand directly, with Lucas' shield charm reflecting a major portion of it back to the attacker. He could see Archeveque's shield getting penetrated once again, making him stumble back once again. But the spell also took a toll on him, partially burning his hand in the process. He cried out from the pain, but quickly focused again when he saw Marcus flying across the room. Before he could react, another spell from the black mage hit him, cutting his robes open and making blood drip from his left arm. He shifted his focus, fired a quick shot to the side and made short shrift of Marcus' former opponent before he turned back toward Archeveque, the pain still mounting in his body. Laurin had jumped at the black mastermind, hacking at him with his sword time and again. At first the attempts seemed futile, but after a dozen or so hacks, one seemed to penetrate the defenses and left a cut in the black mage's arm. Unfortunately, Laurin was unable to follow up on that success, as another spell hit him and tossed him back through the room. Thor had just taken out the last minion and was now also focusing back on Archeveque. Lucas again started channeling his energy.

"ASCIUS," he shouted, shooting his magical axe at his nemesis.

Again the spell only barely penetrated the defenses, but it did leave a visible cut on his other arm. Thor cast another lightning bolt, but it once again remained without effect.

"FULMINICTUS," Archeveque yelled again toward Lucas.

"SEPERATIO," Lucas countered and to his surprise, the defense held up.

"GAAAAHHHHH," Archeveque yelled and took a few steps forward. "YOU FOOLS!"

Lucas could clearly see the sweat on his forehead.

Thor yet again cast his lightning, but yet again failed to do any damage.

"OCCIDERUS," Archeveque cast in Thor's direction.

Lucas knew the effect that spell had, so he dropped his own defenses instantly to protect his friend in blue.

"GUARDIO," he yelled and pushed as much energy as he could spare into the spell.

The moments that followed that move were painstaking for him. He watched the green smoke hit his shield and push against it hard. But in the end the cocoon he had built around Thor held up and the vapor disintegrated. Lucas quickly looked around to assess the situation. Besides Thor and Archeveque, nobody was standing anymore. Laurin was lying next to the blue stones, Marcus apparently had made it out and Archeveque's minions were spread all over the room. The situation looked OK for them at first, but Thor seemed unable to do real damage and Lucas was also feeling the strain by now. He thought about his options for a moment and decided to go for an all-out attack, focusing whatever energy he had left in him. He started centering his mind, pulling all the energy he possibly could from his surroundings and pushing as many emotions into the spell as he had left.

"INCENDIO," he shouted in a deep, vibrating voice, shooting a stream of flames at Archeveque.

At first it seemed that the black mage's defenses were stronger than his attempt, but after a few seconds it became apparent that his tactics had worked. With Archeveque's shield crumbling, the flames started hitting him head-on, pushing him back into a nearby turbine and setting him ablaze. When Lucas stopped the spell, he sank to his knees, gasping for air. He waited for a retaliatory strike, fully aware that he had no energy left to counter it, but it didn't come. He could hear the black mage scream loudly and when he looked up he could see him, still on fire, stumbling through the room. Hitting some boxes and other contraptions, he finally got caught up in the robes of one of his minions and fell over, hitting the ground with a thud. Lucas was faintly smiling following that stumble but then quickly realized a new problem that had emerged. Without him seeing it at first, Archeveque had fallen right on top of the energy crystals.

"Oh shit..." Lucas mumbled, remembering what had happened last time when the crystals had come into contact with magical energy. "We need to get out of here, NOW!" he yelled toward Laurin and Thor. Laurin only nodded, still lying on the ground, and suddenly disappeared.

"Take my hand," Thor yelled back and extended it toward Lucas, who quickly took it.

Then suddenly everything became blue for a moment, as if he had been trapped inside a lightning bolt. And before he knew what had happened, Lucas found himself kneeling in the grass, next to the barn where his friends had set up camp.

"Thank you," he said and looked up at Thor.

"Anytime," Thor grinned. "But why did we have to leave so quickly?"

Thor hadn't even finished the sentence when a loud bang filled the Sunday silence and moments later a shockwave hit both of them, tossing them to the ground.

"That's why." Lucas laughed in agony, pointing toward the plant that had just exploded. "Do you think Archeveque made it out in time?"

"I don't know," Thor said and stood up again. "But right now I just appreciate your warning; otherwise we wouldn't have."

"Guardian!" Stephanie had come running out of the barn. "Are you OK?"

"I think so, yeah," he said and tried to stand up, but immediately tumbled over and fell down again. "On second thought... Maybe I do need your help once again."

"You are pathetic." She shook her head and took a quick look at him. "Please help me bring him into the barn," she then said to Thor.

On their way in Lucas pulled his cellphone out and dialed Corben's number. Stephanie and Thor had just laid him back down on a blanket when the Inspector answered.

"Mr. Trent, are you all right?" he asked.

"More or less, yes," Lucas said in a voice that was getting weaker with every word. "I believe the scene is all yours now. Or whatever is left of it, anyway."

He then cried out loudly as Stephanie had poured healing potion onto his arm, making him painfully aware of the injuries he had sustained.

"Sorry, I got distracted for a moment," he then said to the Inspector, with a painful laugh. "If it's all right with you, I will sign off now and get in touch later. There should not be any more danger down in the plant, as long as you don't bring a flame thrower."

"We will move in now," Corben replied. "Do you need any help?"

"I am in good hands, thank you." Lucas cried out again as it started hurting even more, once the healing potion kicked into effect. "I'll get back to you later."

He hung up and tried to fight the agonizing pain for a moment longer, before it became so overwhelming that he passed out.

When Lucas woke up again, the pain was still strong. He sat up slowly and looked around. Most of the others had gathered around the gas heater, sipping on what seemed to be warm tea. Pretty much everyone had bandages and splints somewhere, making the carnage once more very apparent. But at first glance it looked as if everyone was accounted for and nobody had gotten majorly injured this time. Dread was the only one still lying, with Stephanie sitting next to him, treating the area where the shuriken had hit him.

"You should lie down." Jasmin had approached him from behind.

"I spent enough time lying around, don't you think?" He laughed and slowly stood up.

"You are pathetic, you know that, right?" She shook her head and took position next to him to catch him if he should tumble over.

"Actually, you are the second person to tell me that in quite a short while, so yes, I do." He nodded and took a few steps. He still felt a little weak, but the pain kept him focused for now.

"Hey, who is the guy in the blue robes who is sitting outside, watching the plant?" she asked.

"That's Thor. If it hadn't been for him and Laurin, that battle would have had a different outcome. We apparently have more friends than we realized," Lucas said. "I better go say my thanks."

He walked out and sat down in the grass next to Thor.

"Greetings, Thor. I haven't had a chance yet to thank you for the assistance" Lucas said and extended his hand. "Thank you."

Thor shook his hand with a grin. "My pleasure. And besides, now that I finally have someone to talk to on an equal footing I could hardly let this goon kill you, right?"

"I think I am still far away from your level, Thor." Lucas laughed.

"You might be right about that." Thor nodded. "You are far superior to me."

"Jesus, Thor, get real." Lucas shook his head. "I only survived because you came to my rescue. And you got us out in the end, remember?"

"Yeah, but I did not make any impact in the battle. The only one who was actually strong enough to get anywhere was you."

"And Laurin..." Lucas added. "He cut him with his sword, remember?"

"I will not get into this discussion with you, Guardian. Accept that you are stronger than anyone else I have ever seen. I am convinced of that,"

Thor said.

"Well, I tend to disagree, but let's leave it at that." Lucas sighed. "And let us hope that we will never have to test that again."

"Amen to that." Thor nodded.

They continued sitting there, watching police, fire department and medics run in and out of what remained of the power plant until the light started to fade. It had been a successful day, but also an exhausting one for both of them.

CHAPTER 19

CERTAINTY

A few weeks later, Lucas was sitting at home, reading through news sites. He normally didn't care too much about them, but now he was following them carefully, looking for signs that there was still something at large in the energy sector. But the longer he looked, the more he was convinced that they had succeeded. There was no significant drop in the stock prices of the energy companies, no apparent other disasters, no hostile takeover attempts, and even the first reports were surfacing that tried to put the former statements of HRC and the other companies in perspective. Everything seemed to have calmed down again. The only thing that was still nagging him was the question if Archeveque was still at large. Corben had promised to give him a call once they had identified the remains from the scene. And today seemed to be the day. He was just about to open another article when his phone rang.

"Good afternoon, Inspector," he said.

"Good afternoon, Mr. Trent," Corben replied. "Would you have some time for me, by any chance?"

"Sure," Lucas said. "Where do you want to meet?"

"Wherever you want."

"All right, let's meet at the Timestop bar in 30 minutes?"

"Sounds good," Corben said. "See you there."

Lucas hung up and cycled to the bar. When he arrived Corben was already there, sitting at a corner table, giving them some privacy. Lucas ordered something to drink and sat down opposite to the Inspector.

"We found DNA matches for six of the bodies either in our own crime database or via Interpol. Do you recognize any of them?" the Inspector said and slid a stack of files over to Lucas.

Lucas looked at them carefully before singling one out.

"That's the one who killed my girlfriend. That's the leader," he said and slid the file back. "I don't know the others."

"Are you sure?" Corben asked.

"Yes, absolutely." Lucas nodded.

"Marius du Vallerie," Corben said. "He lived in South Africa. Had been arrested multiple times there, but nothing ever stuck."

"And you are sure that he is dead?" Lucas asked.

"Very." The Inspector nodded. "He seemed to have been in the center of the explosion."

"Well, I would have preferred seeing him rot in prison, but I guess I can be grateful that he is history," Lucas said.

"So can I," Corben replied and nodded again. "Let's hope we can finally return to a quieter life now."

"I hope so too, Inspector, I hope so too." Lucas nodded and looked down at his glass.

"Well, I will not keep you any longer then. If you need me, you know where to find me. Good afternoon, Mr. Trent," the Inspector said and stood up.

"Godspeed, Inspector, until we meet again," Lucas said and leaned back.

It was finally over, and this time he was absolutely certain that there were no loose ends left.

A few years later...

On an almost-deserted playground in the outskirts of Milton Keynes, England, a 14-year-old boy was sitting at a swing, watching a squirrel run up and down a nearby fence, when a piece from a newspaper got hurled up by the wind and hit him in the face. He grabbed it and had almost tossed it away already when an ad that was printed there caught his attention. "Interested in the occult? Meet others just like you," the ad said, followed by a date and an address. The boy excitedly put the paper into his pocket, jumped up and ran off, waving goodbye to the squirrel as he passed by it.

About hundred meters away, hidden in the shadows, a man wearing grey robes was standing and watching the scene. He had his hood pulled deeply over his face. Almost without a noise another man approached him, looking very similar, just a little bit taller.

"Greetings, Lord Guardian," the arrival said.

"Greetings, Lord Archangel," the other one replied.

"What do you think? Does he have potential?" Archangel asked.

"Do you doubt my decision?" Lucas replied.

"Isn't it prudent to be cautious?" Archangel said.

"Were you cautious when you singled me out ten years ago?" Lucas asked without any emotion.

"Fair point." Archangel nodded.

"The wheels have been set in motion anyway already," Lucas said.

They both stood there, watching 14-year-old Roger McKinnon, who had no idea yet that he was about to embark on an adventure that he had never imagined possible, even in his wildest dreams.

www.ingramcontent.com/pod-product-compliance
Lightning Source LLC
Chambersburg PA
CBHW030353020726
47493CB00003B/799